Also by Sue Fortin

United States of Love
Closing In
The Half Truth
The Girl Who Lied
Sister Sister
The Birthday Girl

Schoolgirl Missing

Sue Fortin

This book is produced from independently certified FSC™ paper
to ensure responsible forest management.

For more information visit: www.harpercollins.co.uk/green

HarperCollins*Publishers*

HarperCollins*Publishers* Ltd
The News Building
1 London Bridge Street
London SE1 9GF

www.harpercollins.co.uk

This paperback edition 2019

1

First published in Great Britain in ebook format by HarperCollins*Publishers* 2019

A catalogue record for this book
is available from the British Library

ISBN: 9780008294489

Typeset in Birka by
Palimpsest Book Production Ltd, Falkirk, Stirlingshire

Printed and bound in Great Britain by
CPI Group (UK) Ltd, Croydon, CR0 4YY

To Mum
With all my love
x

Chapter 1

Neve looked up from the toast she was buttering as her daughter came into the kitchen. Poppy was living up to the floral element of her name, wearing a kaleidoscope of colours; from her pink and yellow spotty top, to her bright red leggings and white socks.

'Good morning, Poppy,' said Neve, smiling fondly at the teenager she'd legally adopted when she had married Kit. 'You look very colourful today.'

'You look very colourful today as well,' said Poppy, mimicking Neve's Welsh accent. She sat down at the breakfast bar, pushing her glasses up the bridge of her nose with her middle finger.

Neve raised her eyebrows slightly, unsure if the middle finger was an intentional gesture on the 14-year-old's behalf or not. Neve passed over the plate of toast. 'Jam OK?'

'You ask me that every day.'

'One day you might surprise me and say you want marmalade.'

'Why would I do that? I don't like marmalade.'

Neve gave a shrug. 'That's why it would be a surprise.'

'Where's Dad?' asked Poppy.

'He'll be down in a minute.' As soon as the words left Neve's mouth, she regretted them. Poppy would now be clock watching and if Kit didn't arrive within the next sixty seconds, she would be chiding Neve for getting it wrong. Neve went for the distraction tactic.

'Do you like my new dress?' she said, stepping out from behind the breakfast bar and performing a theatrical twirl. 'It's not quite as bright as your top, but I thought the pale blue was pretty. A bit like the sky today.'

'I don't like blue.'

'Not even this shade of blue?'

'Dark blue, light blue, green-blue, black-blue. I don't like any blue.' Poppy took a bite of her toast.

Neve pulled a mock disappointed face and turned away before Poppy could see the small smile of amusement that was threatening. Neve knew Poppy well enough by now not to take offence at what she said. Poppy didn't have the same thought filter as others. To Neve, it was just one of Poppy's characteristics, whereas to others, it was disconcerting, borne out through ignorance and/or lack of empathy. It frustrated Neve to think that some people couldn't see past this quirk and dismissed Poppy with words like 'odd' 'weird' and 'strange' or phrases like 'not all there' and 'a bit slow'. She busied herself with opening the back door to let their 2-year-old Labrador in. 'Willow likes my dress, don't you, girl?' said Neve, making a fuss of the dog, sending golden dog hairs floating to the floor. Willow had been an unexpected present from Kit two years ago. A fur-baby, as Neve's friend Lucie had referred to the dog. 'Your child substitute,' she'd said, grinning.

It turned out that Lucie had been spot on with her observation, well, in as much as Kit had intended the gesture to reinforce his message to Neve that he had Poppy and when he'd said he didn't want any more children, he'd meant it. However, Neve hadn't yet given up hope of changing his mind.

'I'm sitting next to Callum at lunch today,' announced Poppy, distracting Neve from her thoughts.

'Are you? That's nice,' said Neve, as Willow placed herself next to the bar stool and stared hopefully up at the toast. Neve poured her daughter a glass of apple juice as she tried to pluck Callum's name from the filing cabinet of her mind.

Ah, yes, Callum.

Poppy had spoken about him a lot recently. He was new to St Joseph's and from what Neve had gleaned from Poppy, he had just come out of mainstream education. Not dissimilar to Poppy's own route to St Joseph's. She'd had a hard time progressing through the education system and her transition into secondary school had been particularly painful. Twelve-year-olds weren't as forgiving or accepting as primary school children; all Poppy's needs were suddenly amplified and her coping mechanisms became inadequate. Her behaviour was sometimes unpredictable and her social skills under-developed, making her prime fodder for relentless teasing. Even though the Special Educational Needs team had tried to help Poppy, Kit and Neve had taken the decision to remove her from secondary school and send her to St Joseph's where they had the resources, the time, the funding and the understanding. Poppy appeared to be thriving at the school so neither of them had regretted it for a moment.

'He's going to share his sandwiches with me,' said Poppy,

3

chomping on her toast. She wiped a splodge of jam from the corner of her mouth with her hand. 'He has cucumber sandwiches.'

'Just cucumber?' Neve glanced at the clock, aware that Kit's sixty seconds to put in an appearance were nearly up. Unfortunately, as she looked back at Poppy, Neve realised the time-check had not been missed.

'Dad will be here in three seconds,' said Poppy. 'Two. One.' She looked expectantly towards the door. 'Dad?'

'He won't be long,' said Neve. 'Drink your apple juice.' She slid the glass closer to Poppy.

'You shouldn't tell lies,' said Poppy.

'Sorry. I didn't mean to. I meant approximately a minute.'

Poppy peered into her glass. 'I don't think blue suits you.'

Poppy's honesty was as charming as it was painful at times. Neve had long since learned to take any negatives on the chin, but every now and again, it did hurt – just a little bit. She looked down at her dress. She'd only bought it last week and had loved it as soon as she had seen it. An unbidden wish to have a daughter who shared her likes and loves flicked through Neve's mind, immediately followed by a rush of guilt. Neve wasn't wishing Poppy was different, it was just sometimes the thought of another child, whose company was easier to navigate, made Neve yearn for that one thing her husband was denying her.

The sound of footsteps coming down the hall cancelled the need to take the conversation further. Kit came through into the kitchen, straightening his tie whilst carrying his jacket in the crook of his arm.

'You're late,' said Poppy, without looking up at her father.

Neve exchanged a look with Kit. 'Late?' he queried and then dropped a kiss on his daughter's head. 'Morning, Poppy.'

'You were supposed to be here about twenty seconds ago,' said Neve, popping a coffee pod into the machine.

'Twenty-five, actually,' corrected Poppy.

'Oops, sorry,' said Kit. He moved around the central island counter and kissed Neve on the cheek. 'What's on the agenda for today?'

'I have some shopping to do, then it's the open afternoon at Poppy's school.' Kit's blank expression told her he'd forgotten. Neve enlightened him. 'Where we get to see the project they've been working on?'

'Town and Country project,' interjected Poppy. 'You said you'd come.'

'Ah, yes,' said Kit, fiddling with his tie. 'I did, didn't I?' He looked at Neve with a 'help me out of this' expression.

Neve was tempted to let him dig his own way out. Kit, of all people, should know that breaking a promise to Poppy wasn't something that could be passed off easily. And why should it? Just because Poppy had a different perspective on life to most other people, why did he think it was OK to let her down? He'd been so distracted with his work lately, he seemed to be putting that above everything, including herself and Poppy. Neve had tried talking to Kit about it on several occasions, but he had been dismissive, saying Neve was over-reacting and he was just distracted while a new contract between the boat builders and marina was being negotiated. There was always some important contract being negotiated lately, Neve had thought wearily.

'It's not nice to break a promise,' said Poppy, her head dipping lower as her gaze remained fixed on the contents of her glass.

'I know, darling ...' Kit began. He held up his hands. 'Sorry, I know I shouldn't break a promise, but I have a really important meeting at work today. I can't miss it.'

'Can't or won't?' Neve couldn't help herself saying out loud, although the thought perhaps should have stayed in her head.

Kit glared at her. 'Sean needs me at a meeting with the marina harbourmaster. They're looking to agree on the development project for the new speedboat. You know that, I told you about it before.' He turned back to his daughter. 'Poppy, I'm really sorry and you're right, breaking promises is not a good thing, but sometimes other things get in the way.'

'You want to see Sean's project but not mine.' Poppy crammed the last piece of toast into her mouth.

Kit turned to Neve again. 'You'll be there, won't you?'

'I will.' Neve kept thoughts of 'aren't I always' and 'why wouldn't I be?' to herself. She didn't want to highlight to Poppy her growing frustration at Kit's increasing lack of commitment to his daughter. She was beginning to feel like a single parent.

'Neve will tell me all about it,' said Kit. 'I'll make it up to you. I'll take you out on the boat at the weekend. How about that?'

It was almost as if he'd read Neve's thoughts, although a one-off boat trip wasn't the same as day-to-day involvement.

Poppy stopped chewing and cast her gaze in Kit's direction, although still avoided eye contact. 'OK.'

Neve watched as Kit heaved a sigh of relief. He grinned

broadly at Poppy. 'Excellent. Now, I have to go. I'll see you tonight.'

'Bye.' Poppy got down from the stool and padded out of the kitchen.

'Brush your teeth!' called Neve after her.

'Thanks for that,' said Kit.

'I didn't do anything,' replied Neve.

'Exactly,' said Kit sarcastically.

'I think you've got away with that very lightly. A trip out on the boat.'

'It's just one of those things. I can't avoid this meeting.' Kit looked over at the shopping list Neve had prepared earlier. He picked up the pen and added to it.

Neve turned the list back round to read the addition. 'Condoms.'

'Yep. We used the last one at the weekend. Remember?' He winked at her and patted her backside.

'How could I forget?' The words came out with a touch more resentment than Neve intended. Kit's insistence to always use a condom was beginning to erode Neve's belief that she would ever change his mind about having a baby. In the hot anticipation of making love, she'd mentioned the thorny subject to Kit and managed to elicit a promise from him that he would think about it again. Now, Neve slipped her arms around Kit's neck. 'I also remember our conversation.'

'About?'

'Don't pretend you've forgotten that too,' said Neve. She cocked her head to one side. 'You know, you were going to think about it again.'

The smile on Kit's face dropped like a stone. He exhaled a long breath and gently removed Neve's hands from his neck. 'We agreed.'

'We didn't. You decided. There's a difference.'

'Neve, I don't want to give you false hope; the answer is still no.'

Neve felt the tears spike her eyes. She blinked hard. She felt desperate. She was finding it increasingly more and more difficult to contemplate a life without a child of her own. She knew there was no middle ground on the issue, no compromise, and this only served to frustrate her even more. One of them had to do a complete U-turn. 'Please don't just say no without thinking about it. I mean, really thinking about it. I'm on the verge of begging you.'

'And we've had this conversation so many times lately. Come on, Neve, it's not like I've suddenly changed my mind about it. I've always been honest with you. You're being unfair. I do wish you could just accept it.'

'And I wish you could accept the risk of something tragic happening again is remote. I'm willing to take the chance.'

'I'm not. I'm not willing to risk losing another wife in childbirth and ...' he glanced over his shoulder, '... and having another child with special needs as a result,' he finished. He fixed Neve with a glare, daring her to challenge him, before striding round to the other side of the island worktop. 'I'm not having this conversation again. Understand?'

Sadly, Neve did understand. She had always thought that she might be able to persuade Kit to change his mind. Never in a million years had she thought that when they first had the conversation about increasing their little family unit from three to four, his reluctance was, in fact, a determination. He was never going to have any more children. He was never going to subject himself to the trauma he went through with his first wife. And he certainly was never going to run the risk of having another child starved of oxygen and suffering brain damage as a result. She understood it wasn't that he didn't love Poppy. He totally loved her, but his time and emotions were stretched enough looking after just one child, so looking after two was a physical and mental impossibility for Kit. Neve's thoughts turned back to her adopted daughter and she followed Kit out to the hall.

'Are you sure there's no way you can cancel Sean and get to Poppy's presentation?'

'No. I can't. I'm sorry,' said Kit. 'You'll be there; that will make her happy.'

'Just as well I cancelled my art class, then,' said Neve. She couldn't help feeling peeved at Kit's lack of concern at missing Poppy's presentation, and in assuming that she'd be there to pick up the pieces. It didn't matter to him that she had to cancel something that was important to her.

Kit gave a laugh. 'It's just an art class. Not like it's a job, or anything.'

'And whose fault is that? You don't want me to have a job!'

'A lot of women would love to be in your shoes and not have to work. I like you here at home, so does Poppy. Why are you getting all worked up about an art class anyway?' asked Kit.

'Because it's not just an art class,' said Neve, resisting the urge to stamp her foot in frustration. 'It's my art therapy class.'

9

'It won't hurt you to miss it just this once,' said Kit.

'You're being so unreasonable,' said Neve. 'Anyway, that's not the point. The point is, I've gone out of my way to make sure I'm there for Poppy. Why can't you?'

Kit gave an exaggerated sigh, as he spun round to face Neve. 'Tell me, is it the fact that you've had to cancel your art class that's pissing you off or the fact that you won't be seeing Picasso this week?'

'What are you talking about?' Neve could feel the colour rising up her neck.

'Jake. You're always going on about him, how he understands art so well, how he uses colours to interpret moods, how the passion shines out from his paintings,' said Kit, mimicking Neve's voice. 'You've even started making your face a work of art in the mornings. More red lipstick, fussing over your hair. Don't think I haven't noticed.'

'What? Are you mad?' asked Neve, hoping her indignation was convincing enough. Really, she felt embarrassed; it was true, she had been fussing over her hair a bit more and as much as she tried to deny it to herself, she knew deep down it was for Jake's benefit. But to be called out on it by her husband was humiliating. She genuinely didn't think Kit had noticed the extra attention she was giving to her appearance and she was annoyed with herself for being so naïve. The last thing she wanted was Kit thinking she was involved with Jake in any way, although, she had to admit to herself that she found Jake attractive and there was no denying it was reciprocated. Not that either of them had said anything to each other, but she could feel it fizzling in the air between them.

'I think the fact that your face has turned bright red and

you have that blotchy rash across your neck is all the proof I need.' Kit took a step closer. 'Is there something you want to tell me, Neve?'

Neve held her nerve, more from pride than innocence. 'There is nothing to tell,' she said. 'Jake is my art tutor, that's all.' She paused, not blinking an eye, daring Kit to say something more. 'Typical of you to jump to conclusions.'

Then, to her surprise, he gave a smile followed by a fleeting kiss on the mouth. 'Good. Let's keep it that way,' he said, before turning and calling to Poppy. 'I'm going now, Poppy. I'll see you later.'

Neve watched as Kit waited for a response from his daughter. She fought hard to hold back the tears that were threatening. Kit didn't know how lucky he was to have a child of his own. He loved Poppy deeply and was even more protective of her because of what had happened and how the events of the past had affected her and, yet, he couldn't understand how not having a child herself tormented Neve. She loved Poppy, there was no question about that, she'd been in Neve's life for the past seven years, the last five as her legally adopted daughter, but Poppy wasn't Neve's. The inner desire and need to have a child of her own had never diminished and, if anything, grew more intense as her now 29-year-old body clock ticked along. And as much as it upset her, it made her cross too. Who the hell was Kit to say what she could and couldn't have?

'Where is she?' said Kit, impatience evident in his voice.

'I sent her up to brush her teeth,' said Neve. She joined Kit at the foot of the stairs and called up. 'Poppy! Your dad's going. He wants to say goodbye.'

No answer.

'Poppy!' Kit had raised his voice to a shout.

They both listened for an answer and when met with silence, they exchanged a look.

'I'll go and get her,' said Neve, not saying what they were both thinking.

Neve knocked at the closed bathroom door. 'Poppy? You OK?' She strained to hear the sound of Poppy brushing her teeth or the water running. Neve tried the handle and the door opened without resistance. The bathroom was empty.

Neve went along the landing to Poppy's bedroom. She repeated the procedure of knocking on the door and waiting for an answer and when she didn't receive a response, she opened the door. Once again, the room was empty. Neve felt her stomach give a little dip. 'Please don't do this,' she whispered as she made a thorough check of all the rooms upstairs.

She leaned over the bannisters. 'See if she's in the car or outside.'

She heard Kit give a groan as he strode out through the door. Neve hurried down the stairs to find her phone. Standing in the kitchen, she dialled Poppy's number, but it went straight to voicemail. She tried a second time, but got the same result.

In the last three or four months, Poppy had taken to running off in a sulk whenever she didn't get her own way. It started when Kit had said no to her having her ears pierced and said she had to wait until she was sixteen. Despite Neve trying to convince him to change his mind, he'd refused, and it had resulted in Poppy running out the door. They'd found her twenty minutes later sitting on the swings at the park. The time after that, they'd argued about whether she could watch something on TV which both Neve and Kit had deemed unsuitable. Poppy had snuck out to her friend's house in a strop, sending Neve and Kit into a ten-minute frenzy trying to locate her, before Libby's mother, Heather, had rung to say Poppy was there. The last time, Poppy had made it all the way into town in an attempt to reach Kit's mother's house but had got hopelessly lost at the bus station and fortunately a concerned passenger had called the police. The repercussions had been embarrassing and unpleasant as the police had involved Poppy's healthcare worker and school, all in the name of safeguarding. It had taken a two-hour meeting to convince the authorities that Poppy was safe and in no danger from her or Kit. No one wanted a repeat performance of that day.

Trying Poppy's number for a third time, Neve hurried down the hall to the front door.

'She's not out there either. I've checked the front and back garden. No sign of her,' said Kit, meeting Neve at the door. 'Are you ringing her now?'

'Yes, but it's going straight to voicemail. She must have switched it off.' Neve cut the call.

'For fuck's sake.'

'We'd better go and look for her.' Neve grabbed her car keys from the table. 'I'll go in my car and look in the village and the playing field. I'll give Heather a call too, just in case she's turned up there.'

'I'll ring Mum.'

'Don't do that yet, she'll only worry. Let's see if we can

find Poppy in the village first. Check down by the river and the meadow.' She looked at Kit as his expression shifted from annoyance to concern. She felt a wave of sympathy for him. 'Don't worry, she can't be far away.'

Chapter 2

It was easy for Neve to say 'don't worry', thought Kit, jumping into his Mercedes; it wasn't her daughter that was missing. He immediately felt like a shit for even thinking that. He knew how much his wife thought of his daughter and he knew it would hurt Neve to know he'd even gone there with his thoughts. All the same, when it was your own flesh and blood, it was different.

He pushed back the fear – it was a useless emotion which clouded judgement. Instead he concentrated on his anger; *that* he could deal with. Poppy knew they would be worried, especially after last time with that bloody social worker, or healthcare visitor, or whatever the hell she was, prying into their lives. Implying that she didn't fully trust him or Neve. Who the fuck was she? The old cow would have a field day now if they didn't find Poppy soon.

Kit drove down the main street of the village past the coffee shop where Neve's friend, Lucie, worked. The place wasn't open yet and there was no sign of Poppy hanging around outside. Kit wasn't even sure if Poppy had any money on her. He should have got Neve to check the money jar on Poppy's windowsill.

The war memorial was at the end of the street and the bus stop was filling up with kids from the local secondary school who were bussed in and out each day. It was also the pick-up point for the St Joseph school bus. Kit scanned the burgundy blazers of the secondary school kids already waiting, hoping to spot Poppy in her home clothes in line with St Joseph's no uniform policy.

For a moment he thought he saw her, but the flowery top belonged to a sixth former. Some of the pupils were turning to stare at the slowing car. Feeling conspicuous and the need to explain he wasn't some weirdo, Kit put the window down and leaned across the centre console.

'Just looking for my daughter, Poppy Masters. She gets the St Joseph's bus normally. Have you seen her?'

The shrugs and blank looks on the kids' faces gave him his answer.

'The St Joseph's bus is just coming now,' said one of the girls nodding down the road.

Kit watched the yellow and white minibus pull up alongside the kerb. Kit jumped out of his car and went over to the driver.

'Hi, I'm Kit Masters,' he began. 'My daughter Poppy usually gets this bus.'

The driver gave Kit an expectant look. 'Where is she? I can't hang about, I get into trouble if I'm more than five minutes late.'

'Yeah, sure. Erm, she's …' Kit stopped himself explaining any further. He didn't want to draw attention to the fact she was missing just yet. 'She's not getting the bus today,' he said. 'Just thought I'd let you know, seeing as she's your only pick-up from the village. Didn't want you hanging around for nothing.'

The driver looked surprised. 'Oh, right. Well, thanks very much for letting me know. I wish other parents were as considerate. Save me a whole load of time that would.' He gave Kit a nod of thanks and the automatic door wheezed shut.

Kit watched the minibus head off towards the bridge. He gave a sigh and hopped back in his car whilst wishing he could give Poppy a bloody good telling off for this one.

Next stop was the river. Neve and Poppy often walked the dog down here and thinking about it logically, it was probably one of the most obvious places to look for her. Parking the Mercedes in the small car park alongside the riverbank, Kit jogged along the path.

Despite it being summer, it was muddy underfoot from the recent rain and every now and then he had to lengthen his stride to clear a puddle. He had his best shoes on today, ready for the meeting later, and despite his athletic efforts to avoid the grey squelchy mud washed down from the surrounding chalk hills, it was easing its way over the stitched welt of his shoes.

There was a bench around the corner, just before the bridge. Perhaps Poppy would be there? He quickened his pace in anticipation, but his heart plummeted at the sight of the empty seat.

His gaze travelled further along the footpath to the arched bridge which stretched across the River Amble. He peered into the shadows of the arch and could just make out two figures leaning on the handrail overlooking the fast-flowing tidal water. He sped up even more.

As he neared the bridge, relief was the first emotion that swept through him as he recognised his daughter. This was rapidly followed by alarm; who the hell was she with? It looked like a man.

'Poppy!' His voice boomed out and he saw his daughter physically jump. The man's reaction was less exaggerated. He simply turned his head to one side, looking towards Kit, and casually moved his body so he was leaning back against the railings, resting on his elbows.

Now Kit was within a few feet of them he could see the man's face. It was hard to say how old he was; the beard gave the initial impression that he was perhaps in his early thirties, a few years younger than Kit. The man had an eyebrow piercing and a lip ring. Kit wouldn't have been at all surprised if the piercings extended to other parts of the man's body too. He wore a scruffy army-green parka with a sweat shirt underneath, loose tracksuit bottoms and trainers.

'It's my dad,' Poppy said as Kit levelled with them.

The man took a drag of his cigarette which Kit thought looked rather too fat to be a regular roll-up. An earthy turpentine smell hung in the air. Kit glared at him. He looked like one of those do-gooder social workers who were attached to The Forum – a half-way home for young adults who, according to the local council, needed extra support when making the transition from being in care to independent living. Personally, Kit considered it to be a half-way home for kids who needed a kick up the backside and a reality check. A bit of hard graft hadn't done him any harm. Kit so easily could have played the victim card when he was sixteen and his dad died, but instead he'd seen it as a wake-up call to grasp life with both hands, to work hard and to make his own luck.

He turned his attention to his daughter. 'Come on, Poppy, you need to go to school.' He held out his arm indicating the way and expecting compliance.

'I don't want to go,' said Poppy.

'You don't have any choice.' Kit fixed his daughter with a firm look.

'Take it easy,' said the man.

Kit turned his stare onto the stranger. 'I don't know who you are but mind your own business.'

'He's my friend,' Poppy announced, folding her arms.

'Since when?' Kit could feel his temper rising.

'Since I got here.' Poppy looked defiantly at her father.

The man smirked, leaned his head back and blew out a plume of smoke.

'I don't care who the hell he is,' said Kit. 'You're coming with me now. You've got school. You're making us all late. Neve is off looking for you.'

'I don't want to go to school.'

'Tough.' Kit was aware he was handling the situation all wrong, but the bloke was pissing him off. Unsettling him. He didn't like the thought of some man sniffing around his daughter. She was vulnerable and unable to read the unspoken social gestures or display the right signs herself. She would get herself into all sorts of trouble if she wasn't careful.

Poppy picked up her bag, scowling at her father, but as she turned to her companion, the scowl was exchanged for a smile. 'See you again,' she said.

'Yeah. I'd like that.'

Pressure rose in Kit's chest. He put a hand on Poppy's arm, shepherding her down the path, before turning and going back to the man. He got right up in the bloke's face. 'No, you fucking won't.' His voice barely much more than a whisper. 'You stay away from my daughter. She's fourteen. I'll have you arrested for grooming a minor.' He paused as he fought to keep his breathing under control. 'Do you understand what I'm saying, or do I need to say it in simpler terms?'

'I know what you're saying but as she told you, we're just friends. There's no law against that.'

'Don't be clever with me. You go anywhere near her again and I'll personally see to it that you're sorry.'

With that Kit marched back down the path, urging Poppy along and ignoring her protests that he was being rude to her friend. Kit sighed inwardly at her simplistic view on the world.

'You can't keep going off like that,' said Kit, as he opened the passenger door for Poppy to get in. 'It's irresponsible.' He gave the door a slam and took a moment to compose himself. Flying off the handle to Poppy right now wouldn't be the best way to tackle the problem. With a remarkable amount of control, Kit got into the car with a much calmer air about him and gave Neve a call.

'Have you found her?' Neve asked immediately on answering the call.

'Yeah. She's here with me now. She's fine.'

'Thank goodness for that,' said Neve. 'I was dreading having to phone the police again after what happened last time.'

20

'She was with some bloke – scruffy looking. Claimed he was her friend.'

'A man? Who?' came Neve's voice.

'I don't know. A friend, apparently. I don't know if he had something to do with The Forum. Looked the type.'

'Which is?'

'Scruffy. Beard. Eyebrow piercing. Lip ring. I know that doesn't narrow it down a lot, but he looked too old to be one of the kids from The Forum.'

'You think he works there?'

'Like I said, I don't know. Sod's law that Poppy should bump into someone like that.' He cast a glance at his daughter sitting beside him, staring out of the window, her back half-turned on him.

'We'll have to speak to her again about going off in a strop,' said Neve.

'Definitely,' said Kit. 'We'll do it tonight. I'm going to drop Poppy off at school now and head straight to the office.' He paused, before speaking, this time ensuring his voice was softer. 'Look, about earlier. I'm sorry we argued. Do you want to call into the marina later and we can grab a coffee?'

'Erm … when were you thinking?'

He didn't miss the hesitation in her voice. 'I don't know. In about an hour?'

'Let's say eleven. I've got a few things to do first.'

Kit wanted to ask what was so important, but he let it go for now to avoid another argument and attempted to ignore the suggestions at the back of his mind as to what Neve was doing. 'That will be great. See you then.' He quit the call and started the engine. 'Right, better get you to school,' he said, with a sigh. It was barely nine o'clock and it had already proved a stressful day. He could really have done without Poppy doing a disappearing act. He felt frustrated with her for going off like that, but more so because she didn't, or rather couldn't, grasp the dangers and the repercussions. He let out another sigh as he reminded himself that it wasn't Poppy's fault and he wasn't frustrated at her – just at the limitations of her cognitive development.

'Neve is wearing her blue dress today,' said Poppy, shifting her position in the seat, so she was looking straight ahead.

Kit was used to his daughter's sudden change in both mood and conversation. 'It's a nice dress,' he answered.

'Neve always wears her blue dress when she wants to look pretty.'

'And pretty she looks,' said Kit. As he spoke, he thought back to Neve that morning. She did indeed look pretty.

'Callum is sharing his cucumber sandwiches with me.'

'That's nice,' replied Kit, attempting to keep up with the conversation. He tried to concentrate on Poppy's detailed and elaborate explanation of the seating arrangement in the school canteen, but his mind kept flitting back to Neve in her blue dress. Although his daughter's observations often appeared random, they were nevertheless spot on. Why was Neve wearing the blue dress? What was she doing this morning that had meant putting off coming to see him? Did it involve Jake?

An unexpected image of Neve rolling around on white linen bed sheets with Jake in a bohemian studio loft room, surrounded by various pieces of art, took Kit by surprise. He gave a shake of his head to rid the thought from his mind.

Surely, Neve wouldn't be involved with a penniless art teacher. What did he have to offer?

Another black thought broke free. Perhaps it wasn't the material things that interested Neve. Perhaps she was looking for something else. Excitement? Attention? Love?

No. His imagination was getting the better of him, he argued. Neve wouldn't do that to him. No, Kit was just over-reacting after a bad morning.

Despite this reasoning, the thought of Neve meeting Jake wouldn't leave him, and Kit found himself becoming more agitated with every thought.

Chapter 3

Neve held her phone to her chest after she had finished the call with Kit and contemplated their conversation. She was relieved Poppy had been found, a little annoyed that her daughter had gone off again and caused all this fuss, and was grateful that the police didn't have to be involved, but the overriding emotion was concern as to who Poppy had been with.

Kit had mentioned The Forum, maybe she had been with one of the kids from there? Although, technically, she shouldn't really describe them as kids, they were young adults, ranging from eighteen to twenty-four. Kit was very disparaging of The Forum and its residents, which niggled Neve. She had met some of the youngsters at Jake's art studio and, on the whole, she had felt a certain amount of empathy with them. Most of them, once you got to know them, were trying to get their lives on track having come through the care system, their backgrounds having little or no positive role models and often horrendous family lives. Neve knew only too well how bad family life could be when you were a young adult.

She wondered who Poppy had met and, as Kit had thought, if they could possibly be from The Forum. She tried to recall the ones she had seen at Jake's studio but no one in particular sprang to mind matching the description that Kit gave.

There was, of course, one person she could ask – Jake. Neve was aware of the little flutter her stomach gave as she thought of contacting Jake and further acknowledged that it only served to back up Kit's observations earlier about how she was making more of an effort with her appearance. It was a good job Kit wasn't aware of her anticipation, it would only upgrade his observation to suspicion, when in actual fact, there wasn't anything to be suspicious about.

She took out her phone and tapped out a message.

Hi, just wondered if you had five minutes to spare this morning?

She received a reply almost straight away.

For you, of course! I have a break between classes in 20 mins.

Great. See you then.

Neve pushed her phone into her pocket and couldn't help smiling to herself at Jake's immediate response and willingness to help. It was flattering and something which Kit hadn't done in a long time.

Rather than take the car, Neve decided to kill two birds with one stone and take Willow for a walk at the same time. Jake's art studio was on the outskirts of the village but less than a ten-minute walk away.

It was the beginning of July and despite promises of better weather, today was definitely not keeping schedule with the forecast. As Neve took her raincoat from the peg, she found herself checking her reflection in the mirror and wondering if her lipstick needed touching up.

She sighed and tutted at herself, Kit's observation had been right, but it irritated her all the same. 'A girl's allowed to wear lipstick,' she said out loud defiantly as she stood up straighter and pushed a stray strand of hair off her face. With that, she shrugged on her jacket and with Willow hooked onto the lead, she set off for the art studio.

As Neve crossed the bridge and turned into Copperthorne Lane, the earlier stomach-fluttering excitement made a return. This was so silly. She was a grown woman. A married woman. Jake Rees was her art tutor. She couldn't let the current harmless mutual attraction develop into anything else. It was one thing thinking these things and having secret fantasies but playing them out in real life was something else.

Jake had converted an old farm building into a working studio about three years ago and lived above the premises. An artist himself, he supplemented his income with traditional art lessons and art therapy. He was involved with the young adults at The Forum – his social conscience, he called it. Those well off enough to pay for lessons and therapy were also funding those less fortunate who needed support in processing their emotions, thus helping them to make a positive future for themselves.

Neve admired his philosophy. Jake did what a lot of people only talked about, or superficially advocated by pointlessly sharing social media memes and believing that was a way to help. Jake acted on his thoughts, he didn't just share and flick through to another status update. And of course, there were those who didn't even do the whole sharing thing. Those like her husband who thought kids today expected everything to be handed to them on a plate and what they really needed was a dose of reality.

Neve sighed. Kit had lost his empathy somewhere along the way. He hadn't been like that when they married, she was sure, but somewhere, somehow, his compassion had leaked away, leaving behind someone she found hard to understand.

Copperthorne Lane wasn't much more than a gravel track and as she rounded the bend, the converted buildings came into view. Neve pushed open the stable door and poked her head into the studio where a group of around six artists were standing in front of their easels in a semi-circle. Neve couldn't see the subject matter but from the boards bearing the half-completed charcoal drawings of a camera, photo albums and some scattered photographs, it looked like they were studying still life.

She caught sight of Jake talking earnestly with one of the women and leaned against the door frame, enjoying watching him without him noticing her. His dark hair, with its relaxed curl, skimmed his eyebrows and equally dark lashes.

'Hey,' said Jake, looking up and smiling. He excused himself from his student and came over, kissing her on the cheek. 'How are you?'

'Hey,' replied Neve, taking in a deep breath of his aftershave, mixed with a more overpowering smell of turps. 'I'm good, thanks.' She nodded at the artists busy working on their canvasses. The woman Jake had been talking to looked up and smiled. Neve had seen her a few times at the studio but didn't know her name. She returned the smile. 'Full house today,' she said to Jake.

'Wednesday specials,' said Jake, lowering his voice and dipping his head so his mouth was near her ear. 'OAP day.'

Neve gave a small giggle. She flinched inwardly. It wasn't even that funny what Jake said. She needed to get a grip of herself. 'I can come back later if you're busy,' she found herself saying.

'Not at all. Come on through. Bring the dog with you as well.' He placed his hand on the small of Neve's back and guided her through the main studio.

Neve smiled at another of Jake's students. This time a gentleman, who Neve estimated to be in his early seventies.

The man stopped what he was doing to make a fuss of Willow. 'Aren't you lovely,' he said, stroking the dog's ears. 'I'd better not stroke you too much, you'll end up with paint all over you, then your mistress won't be pleased.'

'Your picture is looking great, Stan,' said Jake. 'I like what you've done with the greens there. You remembered what we said last week about blending the colours. Good stuff.'

Stan beamed like a schoolboy. 'Thanks. I wasn't sure about this area here. Do you ...?'

Jake moved his hand from Neve's back to Stan's shoulder as if they were mates down the pub, standing at the bar with their pints. 'This is good, but remember, Stan, it's your painting.' He stood back and addressed the rest of the group. 'OK, if you want to take a ten-minute break.'

Jake ushered Neve through to the smaller studio at the

rear of the main room, which, in turn, led through to a small office.

Neve followed him through the open door and as he closed it behind them, she rested against the table in the middle of the room, which suddenly felt small and intimate. She'd worked in here before, it was a room Jake used for one-to-one sessions or with art therapy students who, for one reason or another, weren't happy working in a larger group. Neve liked it in here, she felt she could be freer with her art. When she was alone or if it was just Jake in the room, she was able to express her deepest thoughts, her strongest fears and her darkest emotions on the canvas. There was no one to question her work or ask for an interpretation or, indeed, attempt to interpret it themselves. She hated that. They could just as well have been examining her naked body.

'So, what do I owe this pleasure?' asked Jake, taking the lead from her hand and hooking it under the leg of a stool. He moved to stand in front of her, his arms folded and dipped his head to seek out her eyes.

Neve had been keeping her focus on Willow, it was the safest place to look, she had decided. Sensing his gaze, Neve looked up at him. Her heart was beating faster than necessary, and she took a deep breath to regain some sort of control.

'Well,' she began. 'Erm ... I can't make the class today after all.'

'That's a shame,' said Jake. 'A real shame. It's not the same without you.' His voice had dropped in both volume and tone.

'I'm sorry, but Poppy has a presentation at school which I promised I'd attend and I have to meet Kit soon.'

'Have to?' said Jake. 'You know, Neve, you're a grown woman, you don't have to do anything you don't want to.'

Neve's face was only inches away from Jake's. She could feel his warm breath on her cheek. 'I've already said I would.' She managed to eke out the words, her eyes still magnetised to those gorgeous brown ones of his.

The sound of Neve's phone pinging through a text message broke the moment. Jake stepped back as she fumbled in her handbag for her mobile.

Decided to go the whole hog. I've organised a spot of lunch on the boat for us. See you soon. Xx

Guilt flushed through her. Kit was clearly going out of his way to patch things up and here she was coming dangerously close to Jake in more ways than one.

She moved over to the window, not because she particularly wanted to admire the view, but she wasn't sure she trusted herself being so close to Jake. 'We've just spent the past half-hour looking for Poppy. We had a bit of an argument at home and she went off in a huff.'

'Oh no! Did you find her?'

'Yes. She's at school now,' said Neve, forcing herself to sound composed. 'Kit found her down by the river with a friend.'

'That's a relief. I take it she's all right, then?'

'Yes, she's fine. Just being a grumpy teenager, really.'

'And what about you? Are you all right?' asked Jake, coming to stand beside her. 'It can be a tough job looking out for everyone. You mustn't forget about yourself.'

If Neve moved her right arm just a fraction away from her

body, she knew she would make contact with Jake. A fierce warmth shot through her and she was certain her neck was blotchy.

Neve forced herself to continue looking out at the meadow and the river beyond. Jake's compassion was both immense and tender. How could something so gentle batter her resolve so forcefully?

She tried to gulp down the little cry that erupted in her throat, but without luck.

'Hey, hey, hey,' said Jake, slipping his arm around her shoulder.

She shrugged him away. 'Don't,' she said, muffling another heavy breath with her hand. 'Too much sympathy and I'll be a blubbering wreck.'

Jake held his hands up and took a step back. He gave a smile full of kindness. 'I don't want to be responsible for making you cry,' he said.

'Ignore me, I'm being silly. Just a bit stressed after this morning.'

'You know where I am if ever you want to talk,' he said.

'I do. Thank you, Jake. You're a good friend.'

His smile downgraded to sadness as he acknowledged her comment with a small nod, before picking up some perfectly clean brushes and busying himself with washing them under the tap. He wrapped a towel around them and squeezed the water from the bristles, before popping them into a jam jar on the windowsill. 'So, what did you want me for?' he said, at last. 'You texted.'

'It was about Poppy,' said Neve. 'Kit didn't recognise the friend she was with this morning and thought he might be from The Forum. I just wondered if you might know who it was.'

'A lad? Why do you think he was from The Forum?'

'It was a man, actually. Well, older than Poppy by quite some years, according to Kit. He had a beard and an eyebrow piercing. Lip ring too.' She was uncomfortable at Kit's assumptions and stereotyping but equally aware that she was endorsing this by posing the question to Jake.

'So, you assumed he was from The Forum and must be bad news?' said Jake, an accusing tone creeping into his voice.

'Sorry. It's not me ...' Neve trailed off, feeling both disloyal to Kit and embarrassed.

'They get a bad press round here,' said Jake. 'Some have just had it tough.'

'I know that, honestly,' said Neve. 'I just thought I could put Kit's mind at rest, that's all.'

'Just because a man was talking to Poppy, it doesn't mean he was trying to groom her or something,' carried on Jake. 'He might actually have been trying to find out if she was OK. If she needed help.'

'I get it,' said Neve, feeling a little frustrated. On the one hand she had Kit thinking the worst and on the other, Jake thinking the best. 'I get all that. I'm just checking.'

Jake let out a long sigh. 'I'm sorry,' he said, coming over to Neve again and facing her. He cupped the tops of her arms with his hands. 'I shouldn't take out my frustrations with your husband on you.'

Neve had to concentrate on answering. All she could think of was Jake's hands touching her bare arms. The hot flush reared up again. 'Forget it,' she said.

Jake lowered his head, his chin brushing the side of her hair. She heard him take another deep breath, which he exhaled very slowly. She lifted her face a little, wanting to feel his cheek against her own. Jake moved his face down, his lips drifting over her ear and sweeping her jawline.

Neve closed her eyes and for a second allowed herself the luxury of this contact. She was folding. Caving into a desire she had been trying to ignore for some time now but with each meeting, it had grown stronger. Jake's patience and understanding, his ability to allow her to safely explore her darkest thoughts without judging her, without asking questions, had given her the confidence to move forwards. He demanded nothing. So very different to what she was used to.

Kit.

Her mind churned up an image of Kit. Neve jolted backwards.

'Sorry, sorry,' she muttered.

'Don't be sorry,' said Jake, with a resigned smile. 'There's nothing to be sorry for.'

Neve brushed non-existent creases from her dress, mumbling more apologies. 'I should be going,' she said finally with some clarity.

'You look beautiful in that dress,' said Jake, his voice once again soft and low. 'You look beautiful all the time.'

'Thank you, but I need to go ...'

He stepped between her and the door. 'I know who the man is.'

'You do? Who?'

'I think it's the new guy from the employment agency,

Pillars, they tend to draft in the support workers for the kids at The Forum.' He paused.

Neve nodded. 'Yeah, I know.'

'Did Kit say if he had longish hair, almost dreadlocks but not really?'

'I can't remember if he mentioned that or not,' said Neve.

'I'm pretty sure it's Lee. I forget his surname now, but he came along on Monday and introduced himself briefly. I had a class from The Forum in, he was there with them for a few minutes. And he had a lip ring and eyebrow piercing.'

'It's got to be him, then,' said Neve. 'How old do you think he is?'

'Late twenties, maybe?' said Jake. 'I'm not supposed to, but I can look it up on the system. The Forum sent me an updated register and it always has the staff details on there.'

'Would you mind? Just so I can put Kit's mind at rest.'

'You can't say I showed you, though. Data protection and all that.'

'I won't. I'll just say you remembered him, which is more or less the truth.'

Jake gestured towards the office and Neve followed him through. The office was no more than a box room, with a small window overlooking the back of the building, held shut by several strips of duct tape placed along the bottom of the window frame.

'That looks secure,' said Neve, more for something to say than real concern. If she felt Jake's presence earlier, being in this tiny confined space with him now was almost too much for her.

As if to emphasise the lack of space, Jake leaned round

her and closed the door. 'Just in case someone comes in unexpectedly,' he said. 'I could get into trouble for this.'

'Oh, please, I don't want you getting into trouble if it's confidential information,' said Neve.

'I want to help. Don't worry,' reassured Jake. 'No one need ever know. It can be our little secret.' His hand brushed her arm as he moved to pull out the blue office chair. 'And thanks for the reminder about the window. Must get that fixed. Do you want to sit down?'

'No, I'm fine,' said Neve. She perched on the edge of the desk and waited patiently as Jake opened up the register for The Forum.

'Right, here we go,' he said, scrolling down the names. He tapped the enter key and turned the screen to face Neve. 'Lee Farnham.'

Neve gave a gasp at the name and again when she saw the picture smiling back at her. She looked up at Jake.

'What's up?'

Neve struggled to find words. She couldn't say out loud what was really running around her head. She recognised the face immediately, despite the lapse of time. But she didn't know him as Lee Farnham. She realised Jake was looking quizzically at her. 'I ... erm ... I ...' Shit! Her mind was blank. Quick, think of something. 'I thought ... I mean, he's older than I thought he would be, for some reason. Kit said he was older, but I thought he may be twenty, early twenties, he's ... erm ... well, you know, older.' She was gabbling.

'Yeah, definitely older,' said Jake. He moved the cursor to a box and double-clicked. 'There, twenty-nine.'

Not only could Neve have told Jake his actual age without

him having to look, she could have even recited his date of birth without hesitation. 'Thanks,' was all she said.

A voice from the studio calling out Jake's name, made Neve jump.

'Wait here,' said Jake. He opened the door only enough for him to squeeze through. 'All right, Stan. What's up?' He closed the door behind, leaving Neve alone in the room.

She turned to the screen and gave an involuntary shiver at the face looking back at her. 'What the hell are you doing here?' she whispered.

As she looked at the details again, she noticed a phone number. Realising she had only a few seconds before Jake came back, Neve took out her phone and took a quick photograph of the screen.

Just as she put her phone back in her bag, the door opened, and Jake reappeared.

'Just Stan, wanted to borrow some turps,' he said, shuffling round to the computer screen and logging out of the system. 'And don't worry about Lee. I expect he was just making sure Poppy was all right. That's his job.'

'Yeah, sure. Thanks again,' said Neve, with what she hoped was a convincing smile. 'I'd better go.'

'Neve,' said Jake, turning to face her.

'Yes?'

'Remember, I'm here if you ever need me. Whatever the occasion. You do know that, don't you?'

'I do. And thank you.' His kindness was touching, and Neve appreciated his concern.

'I probably shouldn't say this, and I'll probably kick myself afterwards, but what the hell...' began Jake.

'You don't have to say anything,' said Neve, gently.

'I do, because likewise, if I don't, I'll kick myself for that too.'

'Looks like you're in for a good kicking,' said Neve, trying to make light of the situation, even though the laugh she tagged on was full of nerves.

'You deserve to be happy, Neve,' he said, taking her hand in his and cupping it with the other.

Neve looked down at their hands and placed her free hand on top of his, her thumb brushed the acrylic paint smeared across his knuckles. 'I am happy,' she said. 'On the whole, I am.'

'You deserve to be happier,' said Jake. 'I can—'

Neve made a shushing sound, cutting through the sentence, moving her hand on his cheek. 'I know,' she said, looking him directly in the eye. She resisted the urge to kiss him, instead disengaged herself from him and stepped away. She was dangerously close to giving in to her desire. Pausing in the doorway, she turned to him. 'You're a good man, Jake Rees.'

He gave a rueful look, slipping his hands into the pockets of his jeans. 'I'm not sure if that's a good or a bad thing,' he said and then added sincerely, 'I meant what I said.'

'I know.'

'Go on then, or you'll be late. Reassure that husband of yours that's there's nothing to worry about.'

Neve gave Jake a small smile. 'Nothing to worry about at all.'

Chapter 4

Kit loosened his tie as he sat down at his desk. It had been a stressful morning already and the day wasn't going to get any easier. Thankfully, Poppy was now safely at school, but it was still bothering him that she was hanging around with an older bloke. And then there was Neve.

He could kick himself for giving her false hope at the weekend with his eagerness to make love. He should be more careful about what he was saying as lately she had been pressing him again about having a baby. As much as it pained him to see her so upset about his refusal to agree, the thought, or rather the fear, of having another child was stronger. Besides, Neve knew the score. He'd made it perfectly clear from the word go, but the other night, well, he'd been unfair to her.

She had looked so damn sexy after getting back from her swim. Her hair still damp, and falling in those soft waves, her face clear of make-up which made her green eyes seem larger and more alluring. She'd come in laughing at something Poppy was saying, her T-shirt not quite as damp as her hair, but enough so that he could tell she wasn't wearing a bra. He'd got an immediate erection.

Making sure Poppy was occupied with a packet of crisps, a can of Coke and her favourite tv show, Kit had taken the stairs two at a time and practically burst into the bedroom just in time to catch Neve before she took a shower.

'Well, someone's eager,' Neve had said, raising her eyebrows, as he had pulled her towards him and wriggled her T-shirt off over her head.

'And why wouldn't I be?' Kit had mumbled as he had started to kiss her neck and work his way down to her breasts.

Neve had run her hands through his hair. 'I saw Sophie at the swimming pool,' she said.

'Mmm,' said Kit, distractedly, working her joggers down over her bottom.

'You'll never guess what?' said Neve, as she stepped out of her fit-wear.

'No, you're right, I'll never guess,' said Kit, sweeping her up into his arms and laying her on the bed. 'And I'm not going to. You can tell me later.' He undid his trousers, his eyes lingering over his wife's body.

'She's pregnant,' said Neve.

Kit stopped unzipping his flies. Neve talking about pregnancies and babies was never a good sign.

Neve carried on. 'Twelve weeks. Her and Mark are really happy. She said Mark was over the moon.'

'Stop,' said Kit. 'I don't want to hear about other people's pregnancies. Not exactly a turn on. And before you say anything else, I know where this is going.'

'Please, Kit. I know we've talked about it before but just think about it. I mean, really think about it.'

He wanted to tell Neve that he was never going to change

his mind, but he knew that would mean an argument and (a) he was sick of arguing about it, and (b) he was as horny as hell. If they argued, that would mean no sex.

He felt a twinge in his boxers. 'OK, I'll think about it,' he said, straddling his wife on the bed.

'You will?'

'I will.'

Her face was alight with happiness and any guilt Kit might have felt was brushed away as she opened her legs to him.

And now, of course, he had paid for agreeing to think about a baby in that moment when all he could think about was sex, when he would have agreed to practically anything. Neve wasn't about to let it slide and now he'd upset her. That, together with the stress of Poppy going walkabout, meant he felt sorry for Neve. Being married to Kit probably wasn't turning out quite the way she'd envisaged. Kit knew he had to make amends with his wife. Especially so, with Jake lurking in the background; he didn't want Neve thinking Jake was a more appealing alternative.

Kit didn't want to have to keep tabs on what Neve was up to, but if it came to it, he would. He had far too much to lose to allow himself the indulgence of taking his eye off the ball. It wasn't just that, but Poppy would lose a mother – another mother, and he didn't want that for his daughter. He wasn't sure he'd ever find anyone as understanding as Neve when it came to Poppy. Right from the start, over seven years ago, Neve and Poppy had hit it off. Neve was only in her early twenties then, several years Kit's junior, and had already been through the wringer. He knew she'd gone through a particularly tough time, suffering a miscarriage and then going through a divorce.

Kit appreciated that this was nothing short of harrowing, so much so, that Neve had needed counselling and still did, hence the art therapy. It genuinely made him wonder why the hell she wanted to put herself through all that again. He knew he couldn't face it and he couldn't understand why she was so ... so desperate. So desperate to put herself in that position again, to make herself vulnerable, to open herself up to the possibility of history repeating itself. It was beyond his understanding. And that was where they fundamentally differed.

And now Neve was spending more and more time at her art lessons. Was she desperate enough to do something silly? Did she think Jake Rees was the answer?

Well, Kit wasn't prepared to allow that to happen. He was going to pull out all the stops to make sure it didn't. What was it they said? All's fair in love and war. He nodded to himself. He liked that motto. It suited him. He'd been described by some people as driven, focused and determined. Others, usually those on the opposite side of the negotiating table to him, might chose words like, single-minded, stubborn and belligerent. Kit couldn't deny any of these observations. The strategy he used in the boardroom could easily be transferred into his personal life. Kit was a winner and he certainly wasn't going to lose to anyone, especially to the likes of Jake Rees.

Going into the shower room at the back of his office, Kit had a quick freshen up and splashed his neck with the aftershave Neve had bought him for his birthday that year. He remembered her saying at the time that it was very sexy and her favourite. He looked at the bottle. 'Compulsive'. He hoped it would live up to its name.

He spent the next hour catching up on emails and preparing for the meeting that afternoon with the Harbourmaster. Sean had put together a PowerPoint presentation and forwarded it over to Kit to give it a once over. Kit had tweaked it here and there and added his part to it, before sending it back to his partner.

By the time Neve arrived, at eleven on the dot, Kit was happy everything was in order.

'Hi, sweetheart,' he said, as she came into the office. She was still wearing the pretty blue dress which pleased him, and he noticed she'd applied fresh make up and tied her hair up in a bun with a few loose tendrils around her face, just as he liked it. 'You look gorgeous.' He drew her in and kissed her on the mouth, ignoring her resistance. She was still pissed off with him but the fact that she'd agreed to come over was, he regarded, a good sign.

'You smell nice,' she said.

Kit grinned. 'A birthday present, from an admirer.'

'Is that right? She raised her eyebrows a fraction.

'Neve,' began Kit, taking her hands in his. 'I'm really sorry for upsetting you earlier. About what I said last night and how I haven't been very considerate of your feelings.'

There was a look of mild surprise on her face, but she didn't pull away and didn't launch into a verbal attack. Another good sign.

She gave a sigh. 'I don't really know what else to say. I thought last night you meant it when you said you'd think about it but now I realise it was just to shut me up, so you didn't miss out on a shag.'

'What?!' He stopped himself from feigning indignation, it probably wouldn't go down too well right now. 'I've never shagged you,' he said. 'I've always, *always*, made love to you.'

'You know what I mean.'

'I'm sorry. I can't help it. You're so bloody gorgeous and I'm a hot-blooded male. I apologise, I let my ...'

'Dick rule your head,' said Neve, finishing the sentence for him.

'Guilty as charged,' said Kit. 'Look, let's go out on the boat. I picked up a hamper earlier from that little Italian bistro in town. I don't want to argue anymore and I promise, absolutely promise, cross my heart and hope to die promise, that I'll think more about it.'

'Is there any point?' said Neve. 'In promising, I mean. Will you really think more about it?'

'I will. But if you're asking me to promise I'll change my mind, I can't do that.'

'We're at a stalemate. An impasse.' She looked down at their hands and back up at him. 'I guess it's a game of brink-manship to see who blinks first.'

'I'll think about it as much from your perspective, if you promise me you'll think about it as much from mine,' said Kit. He waited while she gave a resigned sigh.

'I don't really have much choice.'

'It's been a stressful morning. Come on, let's forget about the world and its troubles.'

'Our troubles.'

'You don't seem to be buying into this,' said Kit, unable

to tamp down the feeling of being a little peeved at her lack of enthusiasm. He didn't like to admit it, but Neve's shift in attitude, her more assertive stance, unsettled him. He couldn't help but wonder if she was getting coaching from someone else. OK, coaching might be a little strong, but certainly something, or someone, was influencing her, even if it might only be subconsciously. 'Is there anything else bothering you?'

'No. I'm sorry. Nothing. I think I'm just jaded from it all. You're right, let's check out of the world for an hour.'

He kissed her again. 'Excellent. We'll speak to Poppy this evening, and tomorrow I'm going to pay The Forum a visit and find out who that bloke was with Poppy today.'

'No! Don't do that.'

'What? Why not? Aren't you bothered? You didn't see him, Neve, he had trouble written all over him. I know you think I can be a stick in the mud at times, but he's bad news.' Kit picked up his jacket from the back of his chair. 'Anyway, enough of all that, remember, we're forgetting about the world for an hour.'

'I know but ...'

Kit put his finger to his wife's lips. 'No buts, let's go.'

Chapter 5

Neve hadn't slept well that night, despite the evening's talk to Poppy about the dangers of going off on her own being a marginal success. Poppy appeared to listen and, indeed, agree with Neve and Kit that disappearing wasn't a good idea and talking to strangers was a no-no. Although, Poppy maintained that Lee was her new friend and she liked him, despite Neve pointing out that it was the first time Poppy had met Lee and had then tried to explain to Poppy how it takes time to get to know a person. Neve wasn't really sure Poppy grasped the notion that not everyone she met should be regarded as a friend straight away. None of this had sat well with Kit, but to his credit, he had remained calm and accepted that Poppy hadn't been able to really appreciate the danger she could put herself in.

Neve knew Poppy found it hard to understand the point they were making. She simply didn't have the cognitive development to grasp exactly what they were saying. It had to be broken down into simplistic terms to gain any meaning for Poppy.

The catalyst for Neve's broken sleep however, was Poppy's new friend, Lee. Or, as Neve knew him, Ashley Farnham. A face and a name from Neve's past. One she didn't associate with happy events.

It was bizarre that he had reappeared here in the little village of Ambleton. Surely that was more than a coincidence. Whatever his reasons were for going by the name of Lee, the fact he'd made contact with her daughter troubled Neve. Did he know Neve lived in Ambleton? Did he know of her connection with Poppy?

She had tossed these questions around all night, unable to settle on an answer. Long held but tucked away memories of Ashley Farnham invaded her thoughts. In the end, she had got up and gone downstairs where she'd poured herself a glass of Kit's whiskey in a bid to help her sleep.

It had worked but when she had woken this morning, she instantly knew something was troubling her. It took her a few seconds to remember and her heart dropped when she did. It was no good, she couldn't carry on in this state of uncertainty. She had to find out what he was doing here.

Neve jotted down the phone number from the picture she had taken of Jake's computer screen and added it to her contacts under the name 'Laura', who was one of the mums from school. Neve knew it would be a good cover if she happened to have a text come through and someone, Kit in particular, noticed the alert flash up on the screen.

Neve picked up her phone, tapped out a text message and pressed send. She watched the little blue line race across the top of her screen, followed up by a ping – confirmation her message had been sent. The word 'Delivered' appeared under the message. Satisfied, Neve slipped her phone into her bag and called up the stairs for Poppy to hurry up. 'We don't want to miss the bus!' Neve gave Willow a couple of dog treats and settled her in her basket. 'Stay there. Good girl.'

Poppy clomped her way down the stairs. 'I'm ready.'

'You've got toothpaste in the corner of your mouth,' said Neve, handing Poppy a tissue.

'Can you take me today?' said Poppy as she rubbed the tissue round her mouth and then scrunched it up, leaving it on the hall table.

'In the bin, please,' said Neve, slipping her feet into her shoes. 'And I am taking you. I always do.'

Poppy shuffled off to the kitchen and after disposing of the tissue, came back to put her own shoes on. 'I meant take me to school. Not the bus stop.'

'But I never take you to school.'

'I don't want to go on the bus.' Poppy tugged the Velcro strap across the top of her foot.

'Why?'

Poppy shrugged. 'Just don't.'

'Well, that's not a reason, is it?' said Neve. She knew from past experience, the key with Poppy was consistency. If you let Poppy call the shots too often, then it became a battle for her to be compliant about the smallest of things. Everything became an issue, which ultimately turned into an argument. 'Anyway, your dad's paid for the bus. They'll be expecting you and I can't be driving backwards and forwards into town every day.'

'You've got nothing else to do,' said Poppy, her bottom lip sticking out as she stood up and picked up her bag and hockey stick.

Neve gave a small laugh as she checked her mobile phone.

'Oh, I've got plenty of things to be getting on with. How do you think this ship keeps sailing?'

'It's not a ship. It's a house.'

Neve sighed inwardly. Her mistake. Metaphors didn't figure in Poppy's world. 'Well, what I mean is, if I'm not at home, then who is going to do all the housework, shopping, cleaning, washing and everything else that needs doing? They don't get done on their own.' She placed a hand on Poppy's back and shepherded her out the door.

Neve checked her phone again as she slid into the driver's seat. No reply to her text message yet.

'Why do you keep looking at your phone?' asked Poppy, sitting beside her.

'I don't,' said Neve, although she knew to refute it was pointless.

'Yes, you do. That's twice since I came down.'

'I'm just waiting for a reply to a text message. From my friend, Lucie, you know, who runs the coffee shop. I was waiting to see if she's free to meet up.' Neve mentally crossed her fingers and said a silent apology for the lie as they drove off towards the centre of the village.

Within a few minutes, they rounded the corner, the war memorial in sight where the school bus stopped to collect Poppy.

As usual, Neve pulled up a little further down the road from the bus stop. Poppy liked to walk the last twenty or so metres on her own and Neve was happy for her to do so. It gave Poppy the sense of independence and helped her self-esteem. A small act that some children wouldn't think anything of, but for Poppy, was a big deal.

'I'll wait in the car,' said Poppy, shrinking into the seat.

'What's up?' asked Neve. 'You usually can't wait to get out of the car.' Neve looked over towards the bus stop. There were half a dozen kids there in the local secondary school uniform. Four boys and two girls. She thought she recognised a couple of the lads. It was hard to tell their exact ages, but one of them was definitely Poppy's age. Ben Hewitt. She remembered him from primary school days when Poppy had attended mainstream education. The others, although they were familiar in that she had seen them around the village, she wasn't entirely sure of their names. Neve looked back at Poppy. 'Do you want me to come over with you?'

'No!' Poppy practically shouted. 'No. Don't.'

'OK. That's fine. We can just wait in the car a little longer.' Neve eyed the group of youngsters again. They seemed to have noticed her and Poppy now, looking over towards the car before turning away and laughing amongst themselves. Pretending to check her phone, Neve stole a glance at Poppy who was focused intently on the footwell of the car.

'Can you drive me to school?' asked Poppy without looking up.

Neve grimaced. 'I'm sorry, Pops, I can't today. I've got to meet my friend. Remember?'

'Can't you meet your friend later?'

'They haven't got a phone. I won't be able to let them know.'

'I thought you said you had texted them?'

Neve gulped down her unease. 'That was a different friend.'

'You're lying.'

'Err, excuse me. Who do you think you're talking to?'

'A liar.' Poppy grabbed at the door handle and pushed it open.

'Poppy! Wait.' Neve reached over but Poppy was too quick and was out of the car, slamming the door before Neve could say anything else.

Neve's automatic reaction was to jump out of the car and go after Poppy, but she paused, her hand resting on the door handle. Despite the fact that she hated the thought of parting on bad terms, Neve was painfully aware that when Poppy got into *one of her moods*, no amount of talking would lift her out of it. Poppy needed time to process her anger. Neve was also aware that causing a big scene in front of the other kids probably wouldn't go down well either.

Reluctantly she sat back in her seat and acknowledged this fall-out was her own fault for lying to Poppy in the first place, but what choice did she have? Neve watched Poppy approach the bus stop. The other kids turned and standing on the edge of the kerb, followed Poppy's progress. Poppy kept her head down and huddled into her jacket, tactics Neve knew her daughter used when she felt uncomfortable in certain social situations.

Ben Hewitt seemed to be holding court and whatever he was saying appeared to highly amuse his friends as they all broke out into laughter. Just as Poppy reached the kerb Ben stepped down in front of her. He was tall for his age and his physique was already showing signs of developing into a man. From where Neve was sitting, his face was smiling and in any other circumstance Neve would assume that his approach was welcomed, but there was definitely something about Poppy that told Neve otherwise. Poppy sidestepped

Ben Hewitt who then turned his back on her and returned to his friends.

Neve relaxed again. They didn't seem interested in Poppy now. Perhaps they were just saying hello to her after all. Neve checked her watch.

Shit.

She was going to be late. When she told Poppy she was meeting a friend this morning, she hadn't been lying. Neve took another look at Poppy who had settled herself on the bench, away from the other kids.

Neve switched on the engine ready to go as soon as the St Joseph's bus turned up. Typically, it was late today. Of all days, when she knew being late could be a problem. She took the decision to slowly turn the car around and head off for her meeting. She looked over in Poppy's direction, hoping her daughter would look up so Neve could gauge her level of stress. But Poppy looked firmly at her feet. The group of pupils had swelled in numbers now, none of whom seemed in the least bit interested in either Poppy or Neve.

Neve took one final glance in the rear-view mirror as she steered the car around the corner. Something made her look back a second time. She couldn't swear to it, but she thought she saw one of the kids walking towards Poppy. Too late, Neve was around the corner and the group were out of sight.

Perhaps she was over-reacting. Poppy would be all right. The kids weren't interested in her now their other friends were there. Neve tried to reassure herself as the distance between her and Poppy grew. But no matter how she tried to rationalise it, disturbing thoughts of Ben Hewitt confronting Poppy wouldn't leave her.

'Sod it,' she said out loud and pulled the car over to the side of the road, reversing into the opening of a field and wheel-spinning her way out, back towards the centre of the village.

If she hurried, she would be there before the bus.

As Neve brought her car around the corner, the bus stop came into view and she could see the group of kids standing around the bench that Poppy had been sitting on. She couldn't see Poppy. Perhaps the bus had already been.

But the crowd of youths weren't standing around in a huddle having a cosy chat. There was something about their stance, menace oozing from the collective.

Neve accelerated and sped towards the bus stop, screeching to a halt and charging out of the car. She pushed her way through the group of kids.

'Get out of the way,' she shouted. The burgundy blazers parted like a stage curtain. Only one boy remained oblivious to Neve's presence. He was standing leaning over Poppy who was huddled on the bench, her school bag pulled close to her, hugging it like a comfort blanket, and her hockey stick grasped in one hand. Poppy was looking down at the ground, but Neve could see streaks of tears on the girl's face.

She grabbed the shoulder of Ben Hewitt and spun him round. 'Get the hell away!' she growled through clenched teeth, in a voice she barely recognised. Her vocal chords contorting with rage. He was easily as tall as Neve and his broad shoulders seemed at odds with the schoolboy uniform.

'Hey! Don't touch me,' exclaimed an indignant and cocky Ben Hewitt. 'You're not allowed to do that.'

'I don't give a stuff what you think. You stay away from her.'

Neve shot back at him. She crouched down and looked up at Poppy. 'It's OK now. Come with me.' She eased Poppy to her feet. 'You keep away from my daughter.' She looked Ben Hewitt straight in the eye. 'Don't you dare come anywhere near her again. I don't want you even breathing the same air. Got it?'

'I wasn't doing anything,' said Ben, insolence plastered on his face.

'Don't give me that crap,' said Neve. She looked round at the other faces of the group. 'And that goes for all of you too. You should be ashamed of yourselves. Bullies, the lot of you.'

'We weren't doing anything. We were just asking Poppy about her bag. Weren't we, Poppy?' Ben went to touch Poppy's arm, but Neve was quick and swiped his hand away.

'I told you, stay away from her,' she snarled.

'Or you'll do what? Tell my mum? Ooh, I'm scared.' Ben laughed and looked round at his contemporaries. A few of them sniggered.

'Just keep away, you little shit,' said Neve. Her temper finally unleashing itself from her hold. 'Now, get out of the way.'

'Say please.' Ben folded his arms.

Neve felt the crowd close ranks. She took a steadying look at Ben and when she spoke, her voice was low but full of controlled power.

'Piss. Off.' She pushed Ben with her hand and the lad stumbled back.

'Oi!' he shouted. 'Like I said, you can't do that. That's assault.'

'What are you going to do? Tell tales to your mum?' said Neve, and then mimicking the boy. 'Ooh, I'm scared.'

This elicited another ripple of laughter from the crowd.

Ben's face flushed red. 'Stuck-up bitch with your half-wit daughter,' he said.

Neve stopped in her tracks. She counted to five. Increased the count to ten. God, it was taking all her effort to restrain herself from turning around and smacking that little shit right in the face. She let out a long slow breath. When she spoke, she was amazed at how calm she sounded.

'Come on, Poppy, get in the car.' Neve opened the door and as Poppy climbed in, Neve took the hockey stick from her, before walking slowly back to the group of youths and coming to a halt in front of Ben Hewitt. Their eyes were level and Neve purposefully stood in his personal space. 'You, Ben Hewitt, have been warned.' She lifted the hockey stick and let it fall into the palm of her other hand. 'Stay the fuck away from my daughter. Got it?'

Ben Hewitt swallowed. Neve could see the look of uncertainty and surprise on the boy's face.

'You're a psycho,' said Ben, looking down at the hockey stick and taking a step back.

Neve, sensing she had the upper hand, took a step forward. 'And you are pushing your luck.' She gave the hockey stick the slightest of twitches and was satisfied when Ben Hewitt flinched.

As she walked calmly back to the car, she was aware the other kids were watching her all the way. Hopefully she had made her point.

'You want to watch your back!' Ben Hewitt's voice trailed after her. 'Both of you. Nasty things can happen, even in a quiet little village like this.'

Neve ignored the jibe. The little prick was just trying to regain some credibility from his cronies. The pinging of her mobile phone took her attention away from the scene and pausing before she got into the car, she saw she had a reply to her earlier message.

I wondered when you'd contact me. When and where?

Despite everything and her long-held desire never to have anything to do with Ash again, an undeniable shot of adrenalin raced through her. This must be what it was like for addicts when they weighed up a glass of wine, a line of coke, a betting slip, a cigarette. The rush, even if for just a split second, was always there. Apprehension followed as she sent her reply.

Old boathouse on the other side of the bridge. Today. 1pm.

Chapter 6

Having dropped Poppy at St Joseph's and spoken to the pastoral care teacher about the incident at the bus stop that morning, Neve drove back to Ambleton. She had tried to talk it through with Poppy in the car, but she had clammed up, refusing to enter into any sort of dialogue. Neve had been reduced to talking into the empty space between them, re-inforcing the fact that Poppy could and should speak to an adult she trusted so bullies like Ben Hewitt could be dealt with, with no real gauge of how much Poppy was taking in.

Neve had been a little sketchy recalling her part of the confrontation. It had all happened so fast, at the time she hadn't even considered the consequences of her actions. She had seen the proverbial red rag and proceeded to lose it. Neve was pretty sure she had sworn at Ben Hewitt and, at the time, hadn't even realised she was brandishing a hockey stick. It wasn't until she had got back in the car she registered it in her hand.

Now as Neve tried to recall the incident again, the clarity still wouldn't come. She had a strange sense of feeling removed and watching the argument play out, as if she had been a bystander herself. A feeling she wasn't so unfamiliar with. It

was often a symptom of stressful situations, a coping mech-
anism, a counsellor had once told her. But then what the hell
did that counsellor know?

She wiped each sweaty palm in turn on the fabric of her
dress, as memories of people and places from darker days
filled her mind.

'Megan,' she whispered.

The sudden sound of the blast of a car horn shook her
from her thoughts as she realised she had allowed the car to
drift over the white line in the middle of the road. She yanked
hard on the steering wheel, swerving the car back to the
correct side of the road just in time to avoid a collision with
an oncoming vehicle.

'Concentrate!' she scolded herself. It wasn't until she was
turning into her own driveway that Neve allowed herself to
think of what lay ahead of her that day, specifically, her
meeting with Ash, or Lee as he was calling himself these
days.

Her stomach gave a small roll of anxiety. His reply showed
he was obviously expecting to hear from her at some point.
He must have somehow known she was living here but had
that been before or after he had started work at The Forum?
Had he come here on purpose or had The Forum job been
a pure coincidence? Neve wasn't sure she believed in coinci-
dences.

She let Willow out into the back garden with promises of
a nice walk later and then made herself a cup of tea which
she took out onto the patio with a magazine. Maybe she
could distract herself?

It turned out she couldn't. She read the words but had no

idea what they said, unable to concentrate for more than a few seconds before her mind raced back to Lee, her past, and in turn, to Megan. Usually she did a good job of compartmentalising her life, her thoughts and her past, but today she just couldn't keep those memories under control. And, as always, when she thought of Megan, it hurt in the most brutal way. Whoever said time was a healer was a liar.

Neve leant back in the chair and closed her eyes, allowing the warm July sun to heat her face. Even today, after all this time, Neve still felt the pain as raw as if it were yesterday. She remembered how she'd felt – so utterly devastated. She remembered how everything that happened that August had changed her life for ever. She missed Megan dreadfully but no matter how much she wished she could go back and change history, she knew she couldn't.

The emotional exhaustion of the last twenty-four hours hit Neve without warning. One minute she was resting in the garden chair, the next minute she woke up and realised it was midday and a couple of hours had passed.

She rubbed her eyes and peered at the clock on her phone and then her wristwatch by way of confirmation. Fortunately, clouds had passed over and she had been saved the indignity of a sunburnt face.

Twenty minutes later, she had freshened up, repaired her make-up and changed into a fresh white shirt, which she teamed with her skinny jeans and Converse trainers. She looked at herself in the mirror, vainly wondering what Ash would make of her after all this time. Suddenly, it mattered that she looked good. She didn't want him to think she'd let herself go since moving away. She frowned at her reflection as she tidied up her hair. It annoyed her that she cared. He should be the last person she cared about. The absolute last person in the world.

'Come on, Willow,' called Neve from the hallway as she took the lead off the peg. 'Time for that walk.'

The yellow Labrador skidded across the laminated flooring in anticipation, her whole body wagging with undiluted excitement.

Neve gave a laugh. 'You are a silly dog,' she said, hooking the lead onto the D-ring of the collar. 'Please try to look a bit fierce and menacing when we get to the river. I need you as my bodyguard.'

A small footbridge ran parallel to the old stone bridge which crossed the River Amble, a later addition to the landscape after pedestrians complained of near misses with traffic squeezing between the narrow stonework to cross the river. Effectively, the bridge acted as the village boundary, crossing the tidal River Amble which was prone to breaching its banks every so often and flooding the land beyond. Every cloud had its silver-lining Kit had said. The floodplains would never be built on and as a consequence, Ambleton would avoid a ring of modern housing estates like those that had circled other villages in the county. The greedy amongst them, and Neve had to admit that Kit was one of those, were delighted as it pushed property prices up in the village and kept it relatively exclusive. Of course, there was the local council estate, but that was nothing more than twenty houses in a small cul-de-sac where the majority of homes were privately owned these days anyway. Something else Kit declared a bonus.

Neve reached the other side of the bridge. The old ramshackle boathouse was about fifty metres along the bank to the right and beyond that, around the bend in the river was the small marina where Kit had his office.

Neve cut across the road and down the stone steps to the riverbank. She paused at the foot of the steps, looking towards the boathouse, and took a steadying breath.

From around the corner of the wooden building, stepped the man she had hoped she would never have to see again. Despite seeing his picture on Jake's computer, seeing him in the flesh again was still a shock. She heard herself give a small gasp and she gripped the handrail tighter as a small shot of adrenaline raced through her.

'Hello, Neve,' he said. 'Long time no see.'

His voice was as she remembered, casual, confident, maybe a little deeper, a little huskier. He drew on a cigarette which Neve suspected was the cause of the change. She noticed small creases around his eyes and his mouth, another consequence of smoking. But despite that, he hadn't really changed, only aged. Neve let go of the handrail and unhooked Willow from her lead, moving away from the steps.

'Hello, Ash,' she said. 'Or Lee, as you seem to be going by these days.'

'Busted,' said Lee, with an apathetic look. 'Had to leave Ash behind. He caused me a lot of trouble.'

'And Lee, what's he like?'

'Reformed. Works with young adults. Member of Greenpeace. Loves children and animals. Wants to save the world.'

'Regular Mr Nice Guy,' said Neve.

'Oh, nothing regular about me, Neve.'

They eyed each other for a moment, before Neve spoke first. 'What exactly are you doing here?'

'Working at The Forum. Helping the kids get their lives back on track. Everyone deserves a second chance. Including me.' He held out his arms and smiled almost as widely. 'Come on, Neve, give us a hug. I've missed you.'

Neve held up her hands, to try to push him away but he was too strong, and her hands were squashed against his chest as he pulled her in for a bear hug. He kissed the side of her face, for longer than necessary, his whiskers scratching her skin.

'It's good to see you again,' he said, ignoring her struggles.

'Ash, let me—'

'Lee. It's Lee, not Ash,' he said.

'For God's sake. Lee, let me go!'

He released her from his hold and grinned at her. His trademark grin, Neve and Megan used to call it. He hadn't lost it over the years.

'Sorry,' he said, taking a step back. 'I got carried away. Just suddenly felt all nostalgic.'

'Don't worry about it,' muttered Neve, fiddling with the dog lead.

'Maybe we could go for a drink sometime. You know, for old-time's sake.' He looked at her left hand. 'Ah, married. Will he mind? It's only like catching up with an old friend. Nothing in it.'

'Yes, I am married and no, he wouldn't mind. Not that it's up to him, anyway,' Neve found herself adding onto the end, although blatantly aware that Kit would mind, it suddenly seemed important that she assert herself to him. In truth, she just wanted Ash to disappear back to wherever he'd come from. Her past form with Ash scared her. She didn't want to find herself revisiting those times again.

'So, that's a yes to a drink.'

'No! It's not.' Neve gave a sigh. 'Look, Ash ... I mean, Lee, this isn't an old pals reunion, as well you know.'

'Do I?'

'Yes, you do. When I messaged you, you said you had been expecting me. How? Why? How did you know I lived here?'

'Ahh, well, that will be my powers of telepathy,' said Lee, accompanying his words with a ghost-like noise.

'Stop! Can't you just be serious for one minute? I thought you said you were all grown up now and mature?'

'Spoilsport,' said Lee. 'I see you've really taken growing up to the next level. What happened to Neve Tansley or Neve Howells?'

'Neve Howells grew up and Neve Tansley got divorced. It's Neve Masters now.'

'And a new persona by the sounds of it. Or is it? I'm not sure you can really change.'

'Can we quit with all this beating around the bush? It's boring,' said Neve, her patience finally wearing out. 'How did you know I lived here?'

'It was pure luck,' said Lee. 'I got this job at The Forum and I was on my way over to the art studio with a couple of the residents the other day and I caught a glimpse of you through the windows. You were just leaving and by the time I got there, you were driving out of the car park. This OAP was still packing up and I asked her if she knew you.'

'That was fortunate,' said Neve. She thought back to who it might have been. Probably Edith. She always took ages to set up and pack her stuff away and wasn't averse to a good old chat about anything and anyone. 'Did she say anything else?'

'Oh, I learnt quite a lot about you,' said Lee, grinding his cigarette out with the heel of his boot. 'Married to a local businessman. Stepdaughter.'

'Daughter, actually,' corrected Neve.

'As you wish, daughter,' said Lee, before carrying on. 'You live in the big house down, now where did she say, oh yes, that's right … Long Acre Lane. She's right. It is a big house.'

'What?! You've seen where I live?'

'I just happened to be passing. I saw your car in the drive. No law against that.'

And he was right. There was no law against it, but Neve was now on high alert. She had no idea what Lee was playing at, but she was sure he was messing with her. He'd always liked to tease her, but she knew from past experience, the teasing was just a breath away from danger. Ash liked living on the edge of life and pushing people past their comfort zone. In the past, she had quite liked that element, it had been exciting and frightening all at the same time. Now, though, having experienced the consequences, it just frightened her. 'How long are you here for?' she asked, folding her arms, aware she was glaring but didn't care.

'I've got a month-long contract,' said Lee. 'Which can be extended if I want. Such a shame you don't seem happy to see me. I thought we could relive some of our youth.'

'Get lost,' said Neve. 'I'm not into all that anymore.'

'Does your husband know about it?'

Neve's heart thumped against her chest. 'What does it matter to you?'

'Just curious. You know, I have actually met him. And your daughter. I thought that's probably why you wanted to see me.'

Neve closed the space between them, only just managing to hold onto her rage. She jabbed her index finger hard into Lee's shoulder. 'You stay away from my family. Do you hear?'

The amused look on Lee's face dropped immediately, replaced by a glare equal to Neve's. He snatched at her hand, grabbing hold of her finger and bent her arm over. Neve cried out, twisting her body to relieve the pain.

Lee bent his head down, so his face was once again level with hers. 'It's rude to point.' He pushed Neve away, letting go of her hand and she stumbled backwards. 'That wasn't very nice,' he said. 'Now, you listen to me, Miss-High-and-Mighty. You may think you've come a long way but it's all bullshit. You can't escape who you really are.'

'What exactly do you want from me?' said Neve.

'Nothing. Well, not yet anyway,' said Lee, the casual innocent tone back in his voice. 'I'm just here doing my job. Helping young people. A bit like I helped Poppy the other day.'

'Stay away from her!' Neve found herself practically growling.

'You know what I've found since I've been working with kids? It's often the parents who cause the most problems. Kids like to talk to me. They can relate to me. It's not my job to be friends with the parents. I'm there for the kids. I told Poppy that. I told her I was her friend now. Nice kid. Pretty.'

Neve flew at Lee, her fists clenched as she tried to pummel him. The first two connected with her target, but he was strong and grabbed her wrists. Spinning her around and pinning her up against the boathouse, his body pressed against hers.

'You stay away from her,' repeated Neve. She hoped she sounded convincing because, in truth, he scared her and what he could do to her family scared her even more. 'If you don't, I'll tell them what you're really like. I'll report you for attempting to groom a minor. That won't go down well in your line of work.'

Lee laughed and threw his head back before bringing it down and bumping his forehead against Neve's and then leaning into her. She tried to move, but the pressure of him was too great.

Lee gave a snort and moved his head back, but still kept her arms pinned against the boathouse. 'No, you won't,' he said. 'Because if you do, then I'll have to tell your husband a few home truths about you.'

Neve gulped. 'There's nothing to tell.'

'No smoke without fire. Just planting the doubt would be enough.'

'Likewise. I could plant a few doubts about you with the police. And I'm not just talking about Poppy. I haven't forgotten anything. You've got more to lose than me.'

'Oh, I don't know about that.'

In one swift movement, Lee yanked both Neve's arms above her head and held them with one hand against the planks of wood. He traced his free hand down the side of Neve's face, along the edge of her breast, down her side and gripped the waistband of her jeans between his fingers and thumb.

Neve considered her next move. A swift knee in the balls should do the trick. As if reading her mind, Lee moved his body to one side and then without warning, let go of her.

He laughed out loud. 'Oh, Neve, you should have seen your face. It was a picture. Honestly, I got you there, didn't I?'

'And you reckon you've grown up,' spluttered Neve. 'Hardly.'

'Sorry. I was just messing with you,' said Lee. He held his arms out towards her.

'Piss off,' she snapped, tucking her shirt back into her jeans. 'You may think you're funny, but you're not. You're an idiot. And I meant what I said, you so much as speak to Poppy again and I'll report you. I don't care what you think you have over me, I can repair any damage you think you can do. You, however, won't have the opportunity. You'll be beyond repair. And don't forget, you owe me.'

'Ooh, fighting talk,' said Lee and proceeded to hold his fists up and dance around, shadow boxing.

Neve called to Willow and hooked her onto the lead, before heading up the steps to the bridge. Lee called after her.

'I do love you, Neve! I'm so glad we've found each other again!'

'Go to hell!' she yelled without looking back. If she looked at him now, he'd be sure to see the fear on her face.

Chapter 7

Neve forced herself not to break into a run. She wanted to put as much distance between her and Lee as possible. It had been harder than she imagined seeing him again. And she hadn't been prepared for the mix of emotions it had stirred up.

She could feel the tears sting her eyes as she battled with the memories of what happened that August. The festival had been a watershed moment for her and Megan, as they danced to the music, drank alcohol and took whatever substances Lee had on offer. It should have been the start of her and Megan growing up and experiencing life. They had so much they wanted to do together.

Neve headed across the meadow. She couldn't face going home just yet. She didn't want to bump into anyone in the village in the state she was in. She followed the path along the river bank, cutting across the top of the meadow. From here, she could take the long route around the back of the village and into Long Acre Lane.

The meadow grass tickled Neve's ankles as she circumnavigated the field, following the curve of the boundary round towards the river. Clumps of yellow buttercups, dandelions and patches of red and white clover carpeted the ground like a patchwork quilt. As she walked along, the sun broke free from behind a cloud, making the water look like a sparkly glitter ball.

Willow mooched around, her nose close to the ground, snuffling away at the assortment of smells. Neve stopped to watch a pair of swans glide past, looking serene and elegant. She closed her eyes for a moment, taking in the warmth of the sun, the sound of the river gently rolling its way along and the chirp of a thrush calling from the trees.

It was a gorgeous spot with the stone bridge in one direction and the rolling South Downs National Park opposite. No doubt there was many a picture on social media with the hashtags #Ambleton #gorgeousview #beautiful #perfectspot. Neve couldn't deny the beauty of the little village snuggled in the valley.

'I thought that was you,' came a voice behind her.

Neve jumped and spun round to see Jake coming towards her. She turned away again and wiped the tears from her face with her fingertips. 'Just on my way home,' she said, trying to muster up a light-hearted tone.

'Neve? Are you OK?'

She felt his hand on her shoulder and she turned to face him.

'I'm fine. Really.' Even to her own ears she sounded anything but fine.

'Really, you're not,' said Jake. He pulled her into him and stroked her hair.

The kindness of his touch, just being in his arms, was such a comfort. It took her by surprise and she allowed herself the luxury of his reassurance.

'It's been a bad day,' she said eventually, pulling away from him.

'Want to tell me about it?'

'I won't bore you with the details,' she said. 'There was an incident at the bus stop this morning with Poppy and some of the kids from the local school. I had to intervene.'

'Is she OK?'

'Yeah. She's fine. It's me who has gone to pieces.'

'It's amazing how much emotion children can evoke.'

'You'd make a great dad,' Neve found herself saying.

'I can't wait to have kids. I just need to find the right person to settle down with first. What about you? Do you want more kids?'

'I do. Absolutely do,' said Neve, looking out across the water. 'Kit doesn't, though.'

'Ah, tricky that one.'

'And before you ask, yes, we did talk about this before we got married. I just thought he'd change his mind eventually. I didn't realise it was a for ever decision.'

She felt a tear slide its way down her cheek and she dashed it away. What was wrong with her? Crying like this? It wasn't her style.

Again, Jake put his arms around her, resting his chin on her head. She could hear his heart thudding through his chest – a steady, reassuring beat. Neve lifted her head, her mouth stopping a hair's breadth from Jake's. He moved forward, kissing her. A small flutter of a kiss, as if testing the waters. Neve felt herself respond. He kissed her again, only this time longer and deeper. Neve gave a small whimper as her body curved to his and his broad hand slid down her spine.

'I can make you happy,' said Jake, breaking from kissing her, but still keeping her close. 'We both want the same thing.'

Neve permitted herself to fantasise over his offer. She would be with someone who actually wanted a baby as much as she did. It would be her ultimate dream come true. She'd have to give up Kit and Poppy, of course. Was she prepared to do that?

It was a sobering thought and with it the bubble of desire burst. She pulled back from Jake and out of his arms.

'Oh, Jake, I'm sorry. I shouldn't have done that.' She put her hand to her forehead. 'I didn't mean to. I'm sorry. I wasn't thinking straight.'

He blew out a long breath, a resigned look on his face. 'Don't be sorry,' he said. 'I shouldn't have come on to you like that.'

'Let's just forget that happened,' said Neve, although she knew full well she wouldn't be able to.

'No, let's not,' said Jake.

'What?'

'I don't want to forget that. Forgetting means it meant nothing. And whether or not it's the right time, or if there will ever be a right time, it did mean something to me. It still does.' He went to hold her hands but changed his mind. 'Don't dismiss this as nothing.'

Neve looked into Jake's eyes which flamed with a passion that matched his words. The intensity startled her. He was right, it shouldn't be dismissed as nothing but she also knew she couldn't entertain the idea further. 'I need to get home,' was the only thing Neve could think to say, as she turned and broke into a jog across the meadow and out onto Copperthorne Lane, Willow trotting along beside her.

Neve checked her watch. Bugger! She had arranged with St Joseph's that she would collect Poppy from school that day, so she could have a chat with the teacher about how the day had gone for Poppy, and whether there needed to be any extra support in light of the bus stop incident.

Neve just had time to drop Willow at home and jump in her car to get to the school for three o'clock.

Twenty minutes later, Neve was seated in the head's office, with Poppy's teacher sitting on the opposite seat.

'Thank you for coming in, Mrs Masters,' said Mrs Ogden, smiling at Neve. 'We've kept a close eye on Poppy today and Miss Walker, the classroom assistant, has spoken to me as well.'

'How has she been?' asked Neve. She went to cross her legs and was horrified to notice her once-white Converse were now sporting a sludgy dried tide mark courtesy of the footpath around the meadow. Damn it. Neve tucked her legs under the chair instead.

'On the whole Poppy has been fine,' assured Mrs Ogden. 'She's engaged with the lessons, no particular mood swings or any difficult behaviour. The only thing we did notice was at lunchtime she was particularly upset because one of the other children wouldn't sit next to her.'

'Ah, that will be Callum,' said Neve. 'He was going to share his cucumber sandwiches with her.' She gave what she hoped was a knowing look.

'Oh, I see,' said Mrs Ogden.

'Yes, apparently he had promised her yesterday.'

71

'Right, it seems Callum had a change of heart.'

'How did Poppy take it?'

'Got a little angry. Wouldn't eat her lunch at first. Miss Walker sat with her and persuaded her to eat something. Poppy wouldn't actually say what was wrong and in the end, she stood up, pushed her chair backwards and marched off.'

'Sorry,' said Neve. 'As you know, that's her way of dealing with difficult situations at the moment. To walk off.'

'We spent a lot of time with Poppy this afternoon, talking her reactions through. It was tricky as she wouldn't tell us what was wrong,' said Mrs Ogden. 'However, now we know, we can perhaps make some headway with her tomorrow. If that's all right with you?'

'Of course,' said Neve. 'We have spoken to Poppy about the dangers of walking off but talking to you it's highlighted, to me at least, that she still needs a lot of support in processing her emotions and how she interprets situations.'

They talked some more about Poppy and her behaviour and Neve felt reassured that the school were keeping a close eye on her daughter and constantly striving for ways to provide Poppy with the tools to deal with everyday situations. The school's reputation for their pastoral care was one of the reasons her and Kit had decided to move Poppy there.

'Thank you so much for all your support,' said Neve, as the meeting came to a close and she stood to leave. 'We do appreciate it.'

'Not at all. It's our pleasure,' said Mrs Ogden. 'Now, I think Poppy should be sitting outside the office waiting for you. Miss Walker was going to bring her along.'

Poppy was indeed outside, reading a book, lost in her own

world. She looked so young and vulnerable, thought Neve. Poppy looked up and seeing Neve, closed her book and stood up.

'I'm hungry,' she said.

'Well, we'd better get you home, then,' said Neve, taking Poppy's bag from her. She thanked Mrs Ogden again and headed out to the car.

'Your shoes are muddy,' said Poppy, as she fastened her seat belt.

'I know,' said Neve, trying hard to push away the thought of her and Jake down by the river.

'You've gone red,' said Poppy.

'Have I?' said Neve, aware that her cheeks were burning from a mix of guilt and pleasure. 'It's rather hot in here.' She slipped off her jacket to emphasise her explanation.

'You've got red paint on your face,' continued Poppy, pointing to Neve's right cheek.

Neve's hand flew to her face and she pawed her skin with her fingertips. It must have been from where Jake touched her earlier. Good job Kit hadn't seen it first. 'I must have got paint on my fingers when I moved my art stuff earlier.' Neve said, trying to make her lie sound casual. 'Has it gone?'

'Still a bit there,' said Poppy, watching as Neve rubbed her face again. She gave Neve a long stare. 'It's gone now.'

'Good, now let's get going,' said Neve.

'Callum didn't sit with me today,' said Poppy, as they drove home. 'He sat with Lydia.'

'Oh, that's a shame but never mind,' said Neve.

'Why would I not mind about it? I do mind. He promised he would sit next to me. I don't like him anymore.'

'Maybe he will sit with you tomorrow.'

'I don't want him to.'

'OK, in that case, you don't have to,' said Neve, realising she wasn't going to reason with Poppy at all. Some battles weren't worth the fight.

'That's someone else who has broken a promise,' continued Poppy.

'Sometimes people make promises they can't always keep.'

'I still don't like him.'

They sat in silence for the rest of the journey as Neve navigated their way out of the town and onto the country lane which lead back to Ambleton. They crossed the stone bridge into the village.

Automatically, Neve looked over towards Copperthorne Lane and her thoughts turned to Jake and what he'd said. Had he really been making her a serious offer? She couldn't quite work it out. There was no doubt about the spark between them. She had to admit, she found him nothing short of sexy and when he had kissed her, that was something else. She couldn't remember responding like that to Kit in a long time. And then Jake had said how much he wanted children and how he could make her happy. She'd surprised herself confiding in him, but it had seemed so natural to do so.

Thinking about it now with her detached logical head on, could she really give up everything she had? Could she give up Kit? Could she give up Poppy? All for the promise of what … a baby? Is that what Jake had meant? Surely, she was reading too much into it all. Jake's proposal was quite full-on, it wasn't like they were even involved in a physical relationship yet. She paused. That wasn't true actually. The kiss had upgraded it from an emotional relationship to a physical one and sleeping together was only a matter of time. If she allowed it to happen, that was. Just because they hadn't slept together didn't mean it wasn't physical. Was his offer worth trading in what she had for what she wanted? Did she want Jake, or did she want what he could give her?

Within a couple of minutes, Neve was pulling up outside their house, the wheels of her car crunching on the gravel drive.

'Would you like a drink and a biscuit?' asked Neve, plonking her handbag down on the kitchen chair once inside the house.

'Everyone breaks promises,' said Poppy.

Neve was used to Poppy's abruptness when it came to conversations. It wasn't unusual for minutes, hours or even days to elapse before Poppy responded to a comment. Mostly, Neve and Kit were able to keep up with the disjointed way Poppy held conversations.

Neve took the milk from the fridge. 'I expect we all do but as I said, sometimes it's not on purpose.'

'You broke a promise to Dad.'

'I did?' Neve replaced the lid on the milk bottle and pushed the glass towards her daughter.

'When you got married you said you promised to love him for ever.'

A little flutter rose in Neve's chest. 'That's right.' She returned the milk bottle to the fridge. 'And I will.'

The fourteen-year-old dipped her finger into the glass and then let the drips of milk fall onto the counter.

'Don't do that,' said Neve, tearing off a sheet of kitchen roll and wiping the work top. 'It's dirty.'

'Your shoes are dirty,' said Poppy.

Back to the shoes. 'I know. I'll clean them in a minute.'

'You got them dirty when you were down by the river today,' said Poppy, now stirring her finger around in the milk.

Neve stopped mid-wipe. Her heart fluttered harder this time. 'I went for a walk. It's nice along there,' she said, trying to regain her composure. She dropped the kitchen roll into the bin.

'Did Jake get his shoes dirty?'

Neve, now with her back to Poppy, closed her eyes for a moment. How the hell had Poppy seen her at the river with Jake? She stalled for time. 'I don't know if Jake got dirty shoes today.'

'Why not? You were with him.'

Neve turned to look at Poppy and gave another smile as she went about making herself a cup of tea. Trying to sound casual, she spoke. 'When did you see me at the river?'

'Today.'

Neve swallowed hard. 'I didn't see you.'

'We had swimming lessons.'

Neve filled in the missing information. It was just her luck that the St Joseph's school bus must have gone across the bridge today at the exact same time she was with Jake by the river. The coach always took a short-cut through the village to get to the leisure centre in a different town where there was more specialised equipment and staff for St Joseph's children. That explained it.

'Ah, yes. I forgot you had swimming today.' Neve looked

up to the ceiling. Of all the days! 'I went to pick up some paints from Jake,' she said, grateful that an excuse had sprung to mind from nowhere. A plausible one too. 'For my next painting. I wanted to check it was the right colour before I bought it. We had a little stroll by the river to look at the flowers.'

'And to kiss.'

Neve's heart almost leapt into her throat. Poppy saw them kissing. Shit. Double shit.

'Neve and Jake sitting in a tree. K I S S I N G,' sang Poppy as she swirled her finger around faster in the milk.

'Stop that!' snapped Neve.

Poppy slowly removed her finger from the milk before licking it. Then she continued with the chanting. 'Neve and Jake walking by the river. K I S S I N G.'

'Poppy! That's enough.' Neve slapped her hand on the work top. Sometimes Poppy would be so engrossed in what she was doing, it was hard to get her attention. A sudden noise often brought her back to reality. Neve wasn't having any such luck today. 'Poppy!' She raised her voice above the repetitive verse. 'STOP!' Again, she slammed the counter.

Neve could feel the panic rising in her. Poppy had to stop. Kit would be back anytime now. Before she could consider the consequences of what she was doing, Neve stormed around the island counter and grabbed Poppy by the shoulders, practically pulling her off the bar stool and to her feet. Neve's face was inches from Poppy's. The teenager's warm breath pummelled her skin as she carried on chanting, her voice becoming louder and louder, the words spilling out faster and faster.

Neve could hear her own voice competing with Poppy's, telling her to stop, to be quiet, but Poppy was in no mood for compliance.

Then Neve's hand left Poppy's shoulder and made contact with her face instead. The crack of the slap was like a branch being snapped. Neve gasped and took a step back.

'You hit me,' said Poppy incredulously, as she clasped both her hands to her cheek.

'Oh, Poppy, I'm so sorry,' said Neve, still not quite comprehending what she had done. 'I ... I didn't mean to. It wasn't ... I didn't hit you. It was a slap.' Somehow in her mind a slap sounded better than a hit, but Neve also knew neither were acceptable. What the hell had she done?

Two big globes of tears rolled down Poppy's face, the tear on the right side reaching her chin while the other side, just reached her fingertips. 'You hit me,' repeated Poppy.

'I'm sorry. I really am. I was trying to get you to listen to me. I didn't mean to.' Neve took a step towards Poppy and gently moved her hand from her face. Neve gave a sharp intake of breath. A red slap mark burned on Poppy's cheek. Neve felt sick at the sight of it. 'Come up to the bathroom with me,' she said, taking Poppy by the hand. 'We'll put a cold flannel on it.'

Reluctantly, Poppy allowed Neve to take her upstairs and sit her on the edge of the bath while Neve ran a clean flannel under the cold water. Poppy flinched as the compress was rested against her skin. 'It's cold,' she complained.

'It's meant to be,' said Neve, as she wished with all her heart she hadn't lost control.

'You only had to say please, and I would have stopped,'

said Poppy, her voice sullen. Uncharacteristically, she looked up at Neve from under her thick black eyelashes. Neve had only ever seen one photograph of Poppy's mother, one that Kit had framed and was on Poppy's dressing table, and for the first time Neve could see a likeness between mother and child. It was the angle of the photograph, taken from above, as Poppy's mother looked up at the camera, in just the same way Poppy did now. It was definitely the dark thick lashes that did it. She certainly hadn't inherited her father's fair colouring. Neve wondered, if her and Kit had a child would the baby be fair, like them? A little pang of desire made itself known in her stomach.

'I am sorry, I really am,' she said, taking the flannel away. Fortunately, the pink mark was going down.

'I'm going to tell Dad,' said Poppy, as Neve replaced the flannel on her face.

Neve swallowed hard. 'I didn't mean to,' she said. How would she explain this to Kit? She couldn't even remember having the conscious thought to slap Poppy. If it wasn't for the hand mark, Neve wouldn't have believed it possible.

'I'm going to tell Dad you kissed Jake,' said Poppy. 'Neve and Jake sitting in a tree, K I S S I N G.'

'Don't start that again,' said Neve, with a steel in her voice that surprised her. 'Just stop now.' And then she added in a softer voice. 'Please?'

'OK,' Poppy said and then fell silent.

Neve knelt in front of Poppy. 'Look, I don't think it's a good idea to tell Dad anything. Not about Jake and not about what's just happened.'

'Why?'

'Because he'll get angry. And neither of us like it when he's cross, do we?' She hated herself for manipulating Poppy's thoughts like this, but she had no choice. 'And anyway, I was just saying thank you to Jake for helping me.'

'Dad will be cross with you,' said Poppy.

'And he might be cross with you too,' said Neve. 'For singing a silly song and not listening to me.'

'I did when you said please.'

'I know. Let's just forget about it. We were both in the wrong.'

The sound of the door closing and Kit calling out, made Neve and Poppy look towards the bathroom door in unison.

'Helloooo!' came Kit's voice from the foot of the stairs. 'Anyone home?'

'Up here!' called back Neve. 'Won't be a minute.'

As she went downstairs, Neve could feel the butterflies in her stomach, so she took time to regulate her breathing in a bid to appear unruffled. Maybe Kit wouldn't notice the red mark on Poppy's face. With any luck he'd be preoccupied with work or his lap top or phone, like he often was.

'How's Poppy?' asked Kit as Neve came into the kitchen.

'She's OK. I spoke to her teacher and she said she had quite a good day.'

'Where is she?'

'She's up in her room. Leave her for now.'

'I'll call her down,' said Kit, ignoring Neve. Clearly, any hope that he would be preoccupied was wasted. 'Poppy! Poppy, come down. I want to speak to you.'

Neve took another steadying breath. This was not going to plan at all. She heard Poppy's feet on the staircase.

'Hi Dad.'

Neve picked up on the note of caution in Poppy's greeting

'Hiya, darling. Neve phoned me today and told me what happened at the bus stop. Are you ...' The abrupt stop to the sentence was all Neve needed to know he had spotted the mark on Poppy's face. 'What the hell ...' Kit muttered.

'She's OK,' said Neve, stepping forward and putting an arm around Poppy's shoulders. 'Aren't you, Poppy?'

Poppy nodded obligingly, an uncertain look in her eyes.

'Well, she doesn't look all right to me. Come here, Poppy, let me see. Did that happen this morning?'

'Neve did it,' said Poppy.

'It was an accident,' said Neve quickly. 'I was reaching for something from the cupboard and caught Poppy's face with my elbow.' The lie slipped out before she had time to think about it.

'Wow. I'll say you did,' said Kit, inspecting his daughter's face. 'Poor you, Poppy, you've had a rough day by the sound of it. Now, don't be worrying about what happened this morning, I'm going to speak to that little toerag's mother. He won't be bothering you again, I promise.'

'People break promises,' said Poppy. 'Neve said they did. You do. Neve does.'

'That's enough,' said Neve.

'Yes, that's enough,' echoed Kit. 'Don't be worrying now.'

'Neve's got muddy shoes,' said Poppy.

Kit looked over at Neve. 'I went for a walk by the river. I haven't had time to clean them yet. Right, what do you want for tea?' Neve made an attempt to distract Poppy.

Just at that moment Kit's mobile began to ring. 'Sorry, need to answer this,' said Kit.

81

'Jake's shoes must be muddy too,' said Poppy.

'Hello. Kit Masters.' Kit answered his phone and gave his daughter an odd look. 'Hi, Sean. Yes, it's fine. No, no, don't worry, I can speak now.'

'Jake and Neve sitting—.'

'Poppy! Shhh, your dad's on the phone!' Neve rushed over to close the door as Kit made his way out of the kitchen. He turned and although listening to Sean speaking, he gave Neve a long hard stare.

Chapter 8

Neve woke up early the next morning, her guilt not allowing her the luxury of sleep. She'd put pressure on Poppy to lie to her father, if necessary. But worse, she had taken advantage of Poppy's naivety and of her own ability to manipulate Poppy's thoughts to protect herself. At the time, it seemed justifiable but deep down, she knew it wasn't. The house was still, and Neve padded downstairs to make herself a cup of tea and sit in front of the TV watching reruns of property shows. The latest being a renovation project in Devon.

It seemed even the TV company was conspiring to add to her guilt. Devon immediately took her thoughts back to Megan.

She missed Megan so much.

Neve thought of the glorious holidays she'd shared with her family as a child and the memories made her smile. Mum and Dad always rented a cottage in Devon and they would spend two weeks of the summer there. Neve and Megan loved the big sweeping beaches, the roaring north coast waves and the breeze that came with it. They'd made a pact that one day they would buy their own little cottage in Devon and would live there together with their own children.

A dark cloud raced across Neve's mind, blocking out the happy memories. She picked up the remote control and switched channels. She didn't want to be reminded of what happened. It was too painful to revisit.

'You're up early,' said Kit coming into the room.

Neve looked up and was pleased for the distraction. 'I couldn't sleep,' she replied.

Kit went over and bent to kiss the top of her head. He was already dressed for work and smelt of lemon zest shower gel. 'Have you thought of going to the doctor?'

'No. I don't need to see a doctor. I'm not taking any sleeping pills or anything like that.'

Kit rested his hand on her shoulder. 'OK. It was only a suggestion. It's no big deal taking something to help you sleep. Lots of people do.'

'I said no.' She stood up and brushed past him as she headed down the hall. There was such a lot Kit didn't know about her and taking medication to help with stress and poor sleeping was one of them. The side-effects of walking around in a daze-like state, thinking through a permanent foggy mind and feeling constantly drowsy was awful, and she had no intention of ever going there again.

'What's on the agenda today?' asked Kit, following her into the kitchen.

'Not sure.'

'You're not going to your art therapy class, then?'

Her heart missed a beat. 'Yes, I meant apart from that, I'm not sure,' she replied evenly, although inside she was wary of where the conversation was going. Last night after he had finished his phone call, he hadn't referred to Poppy's comment about Jake's shoes. Neve had been on tenterhooks all evening, waiting for him to remember, but it seemed it hadn't stuck in his mind at all. Thank goodness!

'I've been thinking about your art. I'd really like to see some of your work,' said Kit, taking his freshly made coffee from the machine. 'That's if you don't mind? I thought maybe you'd like to share it with me, rather than just Jake.'

'It's not really art for sharing or displaying,' said Neve, not wanting to meet his gaze. 'It's therapy. It's …' she hesitated, the word 'private' resting on her lips.

'But Jake gets to see it,' continued Kit, clearly not wanting to let the subject drop.

'I'd be embarrassed,' she said, at last. 'I'm not good at art, I just find it an outlet for my emotions.'

'That sounds like a textbook quote,' said Kit. He put his coffee cup down and went over to her, placing his hands on her shoulders, turning her to face him and tipping her chin up to him with his finger. 'I just thought if you showed me your art, I might be able to understand better. You know … what happened. After all this time, you've never really told me about it.'

'You know what it is,' said Neve, attempting to pull away. There was good reason why she'd never spoken about it. It was a parent's worst fear. A nightmare come true. Losing a child was something no parent should have to deal with.

'It's not just that,' said Kit, his voice taking on a firmer line. Neve tried to turn away, but he wouldn't let her. He spoke again. 'If only you'd let me in. Maybe I could help you.'

Neve felt a glimmer of hope. Did he really mean what he said? 'You know how you can help me.'

Immediately his face darkened, and his hands dropped away. 'Don't, Neve. That wasn't what I meant and you know it. We're supposed to be giving each other time to think.' He slipped the knot of his tie up to his collar. 'Piss off to Jake and do your art therapy with him. It's obviously what makes you happy.'

'It's not like that ...' her voice trailed away as Kit left the room. She didn't finish her sentence because, in actual fact, it was like that or at least it could be like that.

'And don't forget we're out to dinner tonight. With the Harrisons,' he called. Neve heard him call out a goodbye to Poppy as he opened the front door, pulling it shut behind him without another word to her.

She let out a sigh. What was it with Kit, lately? He had brought the conversation round to the art course and what had happened to her more than once. In fact, it was becoming a pet topic of conversation for him. Kit was like a dog with a bone. He didn't give up. He always had to win.

She pushed herself away from the worktop. Dinner with the Harrisons. Joy of joys. She couldn't wait. Another evening of small talk with Julia, who would spend most of the time telling Neve how well her children were doing with their studies. Which universities they had applied for or been accepted at. What their interim school reports said. What extra-curricular activity they were doing, which of course, they would excel at. Neve wouldn't have much to offer to the conversation. She couldn't compete with any of that. Oh, she'd tell Julia how proud she was that Poppy could now swim ten metres on her own with the aid of a float and how Poppy had successfully made herself a sandwich the other day. And Julia would nod and smile, but in that sympathetic way she did to hide the obvious relief that her children weren't less than perfect.

And Neve would go along with Kit in the pretence that their marriage was fine, and they didn't have a care in the world, chatting about holidays abroad, boats, wine and fine dining. And this would be totally in Julia's comfort zone. Crikey, if Julia ever got wind that Neve was contemplating an affair then she'd probably arrange for Neve to be put on the ducking stool at the village pond.

The sound of Poppy coming down the stairs brought her from her daydream.

'Why are you looking out of the window?'

Neve turned and smiled at her daughter. 'Morning, Poppy. How are you?' Neve stole a glance at Poppy's cheek. Fortunately, there was no mark to be seen and she breathed a sigh of relief.

'Why were you looking out of the window?' persisted Poppy.

'I was just daydreaming,' said Neve. 'Right, let's get you something to eat. Toast?'

Neve went about preparing the toast and jam. She remembered one of the first times she was around for breakfast and she'd given Poppy a choice of toast, crumpets or cereal. My goodness, that was a long and convoluted conversation. Kit apologised later that day and said he should have warned her not to give Poppy too many choices. Poppy couldn't deal with too many options and she dealt with life better if she had clear and concise instructions. He'd explained that Poppy's reasoning wasn't developed enough to make convoluted choices. Kit had been quite clear about that and Neve hadn't liked to argue, although privately she wondered if Kit was just an over-anxious father trying to care for his daughter. That was then. Now, Neve didn't hail to this conviction.

Keeping to their usual schedule, once they were dressed and ready, Neve drove Poppy down to the bus stop.

'Do you want me to stay with you?' asked Neve, looking over at the small group of kids waiting for the secondary school bus and relieved to see there was no sign of Ben Hewitt.

'No.'

'I'll just wait here in the car, then,' said Neve.

She watched Poppy go over to the bus stop. None of the other kids looked at her and Neve wondered if that was a conscious decision based on the fact that she was standing guard. She didn't care. In fact, she was pleased they seemed a little wary of her now. Within a few minutes the St Joseph's bus pulled up and once Neve had seen Poppy board, she felt happy to leave and head off to her art classes with a clear conscience.

Arriving at the art studio and pushing open the door, Neve was surprised to see the main hall empty. She walked further in and called out. 'Hello! Jake, are you there?'

She could hear voices coming from the studio at the back and assumed Jake must have a visitor. It was unusual that the studio was empty. Her class was a small group but, all the same, there was usually at least three or four of them there at any one time.

The door opened and Jake appeared. Something about the look on his face stopped Neve in her tracks. A movement behind him caught her attention.

Neve's heart thudded against the wall of her chest as Kit walked into the main studio right behind Jake. 'Kit! What are you doing here?'

'Hello, darling,' said Kit, walking over to her and slipping his arm around her waist, pulling her towards him so that her stomach was pushed against his groin. He kissed her on the mouth, lingering for an embarrassing moment too long. 'After our conversation this morning, I thought I'd drop by and see how Jake was.'

Kit released Neve from his clinch but retained a proprietorial arm around her.

'Hi,' said Jake, pushing his hands into his pockets. There was an unease about him and Neve wondered if Kit was picking up on this, or whether she was being hyper-sensitive.

'Jake was just showing me some of your artwork,' said Kit.

Neve's whole body tensed. She looked at Jake. 'You showed him my artwork?'

Jake's expression was somewhere between apologetic and wary. 'I thought you said ...' He looked at Kit and then back to Neve.

Kit spoke first. 'I asked him to. It's not Jake's fault. I asked him to show me.'

'But you know my work here is personal.' She peeled Kit's hand from her body and took a step away, before turning to Jake. 'You shouldn't have shown him.' Neve shook her head in silent disbelief. How could Jake betray her like this? He of all people should know that her therapy artwork was private and personal.

'I'm sorry,' said Jake.

'As I said, I didn't give him a lot of choice,' said Kit.

Neve strode past the two men and into the smaller studio. On the workbench in the middle on the room were several pieces of her work. She went to touch them, to gather them up but stopped. They somehow now felt tainted. Kit had seen her deepest, darkest thoughts.

'They're pretty good,' came Kit's voice as he entered the room and stood next to her. 'I was thinking about getting one framed for you as a surprise for your birthday.'

'They're not for display,' said Neve, looking at the landscape she'd painted from memory. A wide sandy beach, big rolling waves, a wintery sky. Two lone figures standing at the water's edge.

'I particularly like this one,' said Kit, as if watching her gaze. He picked up the painting. 'That's very dramatic. In fact, all your paintings are. I love the use of the blues, blacks and greys. It seems quite a theme.'

'Shut up,' snapped Neve. She couldn't stand listening to him. He wasn't just talking about her paintings, he was talking about her fears, her regrets, her guilt. He was talking about her pain and her shame.

Neve grabbed the painting from Kit's hand and tore the watercolour in half. She heard Jake swear.

'Fuck! Neve, what are you doing?'

Kit tried to grab her arm. 'Hey, hey, hey,' he said. She snatched her arm away and then, spotting the Stanley knife on the side, she swiped it up and slashed at the acrylic painting that lay on the table. Another one of her secrets exposed for Kit to see.

This time Kit was too strong to shrug off as his hand clamped down over her wrist, bending her arm to the side until she was forced to drop the blade. Meanwhile, Jake had rushed over and was pulling the other two paintings away from harm.

'Get off me,' said Neve. 'You're hurting me.'

Kit let go of her wrist. 'Let's get you home,' he said, cupping her elbow in the palm of his hand in an attempt to guide her away.

Neve shrugged him off. 'I'm perfectly capable of getting myself home. I don't want you anywhere near me right now.' She turned to Jake. 'And that goes for you too.'

With that, she darted from the studio, through the larger one and out into the car park, gulping for fresh air.

'Bastards!' she yelled. 'Both of you. Bastards!'

The sound of laughter had her spinning round on her heel tracing the source of the noise.

Leaning against the gatepost was Lee. 'Tut, tut, tut, Neve,' he said. 'That's not very ladylike.'

'What are you doing here?' demanded Neve.

'Thought I'd join the art class. We could buddy up.'

Neve glanced back to the studio and through the full length windows, she could see Kit and Jake talking in the main studio. She took her chance and stomped over to Lee. 'Didn't I make it clear enough yesterday?' she hissed. 'You're not welcome here. Now why don't you just piss off back to where you came from?'

'Next you'll be telling me this town ain't big enough for the both of us and demanding I'm out of here by noon. Now where's the fun in that?' said Lee. 'Besides, I quite like Ambleton. I'm just beginning to settle in and make new friends.'

Neve glared at him. She just wanted him to go away. To leave her alone. She didn't understand why he'd turned up now or what his motive was, but he had the potential to ruin everything. If Kit found out about her past, he'd leave her, she was sure, and then where would she be? She couldn't imagine Jake would want anything to do with her either. No husband, no partner all equalled no child. She needed to get rid of Lee but threatening him and making an enemy of him clearly wasn't going to work. She'd have to get smart.

'Look, Lee, we seem to have got off on the wrong foot. Maybe we should start again?'

'Well, you changed your tune quickly.'

Neve glanced back at the art studio. 'My husband's in there and if he sees you, he's not likely to be very happy. Maybe you should make yourself scarce. I'll text you and we can catch up another day. Properly. Like old friends should.'

Lee cocked his head to one side as if contemplating Neve's little speech. He pushed himself away from the gatepost. 'OK,' he said. 'I'll go. I don't quite know what your game is, Neve, but I'll give you the benefit of the doubt.'

'No game,' said Neve.

'Yeah right. See you soon then.'

'I'll text.'

Neve drummed her fingers on the gatepost as she watched Lee saunter back down Copperthorne Lane. He'd underestimated her. If she was going to turn this situation around, she needed to play him at his own game. What was that saying about keeping your friends close, but your enemies closer? She was about to put that into practice.

Chapter 9

Kit was surprised to find the house empty when he got back. He assumed Neve had stormed off home but her car wasn't on the drive and only Willow greeted him. Not that he was expecting a fanfare from his wife, more like a blazing row, but it was something he could deal with. After all, he had only gone there to try to understand Neve more. All right, it was a bit of male pride too, he had done a bit of strutting and preening to remind Jake that Neve had a husband.

Neve had once called it his silverback gorilla mentality when he had got pissed off with one of Neve's male work colleagues whom she had gone for a drink with one lunch time, apparently to talk over some new assessment system they were implementing at the college where Neve was a learning support worker. Kit had hit the roof and then proceeded to meet Neve for lunch every day for the next week to warn the bloke off. They had moved to Ambleton shortly after that, Kit had made sure the commuting distance was unrealistic and he encouraged Neve to resign. Since then, he'd managed to find a reason for Neve not to apply for any other jobs she'd looked at. So much so, he was inclined to believe she'd given up on the idea – it wasn't like they needed the money, as Kit liked to remind her, and being able to be at home for Poppy had a major influence on Neve's decision not to go back to work.

In all honestly, Kit hated the thought of Neve out working, especially when she didn't have to. He liked providing for his family, it made him feel good about himself. He considered it his job. He knew it was probably an old-fashioned way of thinking these days, but all the time his father was in good health, he'd worked and his mother had stayed at home. Kit had valued this as a child and he wanted his own daughter to have the same security as he'd experienced. This was especially so, given Poppy's extra needs. Besides all that, he knew being at home wasn't any less demanding than going out to work. He didn't want Neve to have to juggle home and work. He didn't only want her at home, he needed her at home. Ultimately, it meant he could work all the hours he needed and Poppy would always have the care she needed.

He sighed at his philosophy, it seemed to be backfiring now. Little did he know that Neve being at home was going to lead to art therapy classes and Jake. She hadn't even thought about going to anything like that until someone mentioned it at a dinner party one night. Suddenly, Neve thought it was a great idea and, how did she put it – oh yeah – a great way to explore her issues.

Kit paced the room, frustration rising like the incoming tide. He wished he could understand his wife more. He originally thought the art therapy classes might help her. If he was honest, he had hoped they would have some sort of epiphany and she'd come home, declaring the need to tell him everything. Instead, she was withdrawing more and, if he was honest, the mere mention of Jake irritated him no end. Jake seemed to know more about his wife than Kit did himself. Kit suspected that Neve had probably told Jake things that she hadn't told him and he couldn't deny it, it made him feel jealous, excluded and angry.

He stood at the patio doors with his hands on his hips, looking out onto the garden. He had to know what the art therapy was all about. He couldn't bear the thought of them having a secret he wasn't party to.

His gaze came to rest on the summer house at the bottom of the garden. The pale green cladded structure that Neve had taken great delight in fitting out with a table, chairs, and a sofa and decorated with bunting – it was almost like she was furnishing a real-life dollhouse. In the summer she liked to sit there to read a book or have a cup of tea. They had used it quite a bit the first summer, but the novelty seemed to have worn off now. The last couple of years, they'd hardly been in it. In fact, it was becoming more of a glorified storage room.

He tapped his lip with his forefinger as he mulled over what Neve had put down there. Some boxes, if he remembered rightly. He had offered to take them down there for her, but she had been adamant that she could manage.

'Hmmm ... I wonder,' Kit vocalised his thoughts. 'What was in the boxes, Neve?'

Going out into the utility room, Kit opened the key safe fixed onto the wall and ran his finger along the key fobs, inspecting the description. Garden gate. Garage. Back door, shed. He got to the final key – summer house.

Standing in the middle of the summer house, Kit looked around. Neve was by nature a tidy and organised person, so he wasn't surprised that nothing appeared to be out of place. He spied two boxes in the corner and was disappointed before he even opened them, as he could see through the clear plastic that one box contained what looked like gardening books and the other some paint and paint brushes from when she had decorated the inside of the summer house.

He gave the box a small kick of annoyance. What did he expect to find down here? It was stupid of him to think Neve would leave anything of importance down here in a plastic box for everyone to see.

He locked the door and made his way back down the garden, still chiding himself for being so fanciful. The squawk of a seagull made him look up to the sky.

'Bloody birds,' he muttered. Mrs Dalton across the road was always feeding them. The gulls were coming ever further inland these days in search of food and well-intentioned bird lovers were encouraging them, at the expense of the garden birds. He hated the way they perched on the roof of his car too, crapping all over it.

He watched as another gull wheeled overhead before landing next to the first on his roof and then padding its way down the tiles and across the small Velux window of the attic room.

Kit stopped in his tracks. The loft. Why hadn't he thought of that before?

With a renewed enthusiasm, Kit hurried inside and took the stairs two at a time. Taking the pole from the spare bedroom, he hooked open the loft hatch and pulled down the extendable loft ladder, before climbing up into the darkened space.

They'd had about two-thirds boarded out when they'd moved in, mostly for Neve's belongings that she'd brought from her old house. Things she insisted she didn't want to part with, which she might need in the future. He hadn't queried it much at the time. Kit wasn't one for hoarding stuff; in his mind, it was either useful or not. If it wasn't current, then declutter. The only box he had was one which he had saved for Poppy for when she was older. It contained some of her mother's possessions, some photos, her wedding veil, her scan photo ... Kit swallowed hard as the feeling of sadness and loss, which he usually had under control, made a bid to resurface. He'd always assumed that by now he would have opened the box and shared the contents with his daughter, but it had never seemed the right time. It was easier keeping the box locked away yet he acknowledged it was at odds with his usual approach to life. He liked to meet things head-on, to resolve problems and issues there and then, which was very different to how Neve dealt with things. She certainly wasn't a believer in the adage of a problem shared was a problem halved.

As he climbed up through the loft hatch and switched on the light, he was sure that Neve didn't just have a metaphorical box where she kept things locked away. Crouching slightly to avoid hitting his head on the slope of the roof, Kit made his way over to the far corner, where several cardboard boxes and two suitcases were stacked. Neve's belongings.

The musty stale air filled his nostrils as he opened the first case, containing nothing more than a clothing tag and a packet of tissues. He checked the inside pocket before moving it to one side to inspect the smaller of the two cases. This one felt heavier as Kit laid it on its side and opened it. Several items of clothing were folded in the case and Kit held up a blue T-shirt with the face of John Lennon on it and a quote about making love not war. Maybe it was one of Neve's from when she was a teenager, it looked quite small and he didn't ever remember Neve raving about the deceased singer, although he shouldn't be surprised, there was a lot about his wife he didn't know.

There was a pair of denim shorts next, two more T-shirts, one with the yellow smiley face symbolic of the late 80s/early 90s acid house days, and another with a cartoon picture of the beach and surf boards.

At the bottom of the case was a Peter Rabbit soft toy and a ragdoll with red hair made of wool, buttons for eyes and an embroidered nose and mouth, wearing a floral dress. Most definitely homemade. A present from an aunty or a grandmother, Kit could only guess. And finally, a white babygro, a handknitted blanket and bonnet. He knew about Neve's miscarriage, so perhaps these had been for the baby, although he didn't think it was usual to buy things until much later in a pregnancy. Maybe they were Neve's from when she was a baby herself? It was a strange collection of things to keep, but they obviously meant something to his wife.

He replaced the items and zipped the case back up. He turned his attention to the cardboard box, which scored a trail through the dusty boarding as he pulled it out into the light. He paused for a moment as a stab of guilt struck him. He was going through Neve's private belongings, things she hadn't felt the desire to share with him, rather like her not wanting to share her artwork with him. A voice at the back of his mind was whispering to his conscience that this wasn't right, that it was somehow seedy.

He thought of Neve and then of Jake. The time she spent in his company. How she could take her art tutor into her confidence, entrust him with her secrets, trust him to heal her, but she could do none of that with her husband.

Anger shuffled places with rejection and any feelings of guilt were tossed into the ether. He pulled out his credit card from his wallet and used the edge to slice through the brittle yellowing tape.

If he thought he was going to find the answer to his probing, he was disappointed. The box contained nothing more than a selection of old books. Children's books mostly. Kit was no expert on this sort of thing but the ones he could see all appeared to be by Enid Blyton, Lucy M. Boston and Louisa May Alcott. Old dog-eared paperback copies which looked to have been well-read and well-loved.

He flipped the lid shut and pushed the box back, frustrated at the lack of answers.

For a moment he stayed kneeling on the floor, looking at Neve's possessions. She had come to him with nothing more than these two cases and a box of books. He had queried it at the time and she had made some flippant remark about a life-laundry when she had separated from her husband and her not being a believer in material things.

Kit opened the suitcase with the clothes in again. Surely he was missing something. Why would Neve keep a few old clothes and a rag doll? The inside zip compartment of the case caught his attention. He hadn't looked in there before. Kit opened the zip and felt inside.

Bingo!

He retrieved a brown envelope. Several photographs fell on top of the clothes as he shook the contents out. They didn't appear to be in any order and looked to span a number of years. Kit instantly recognised Neve as a young child of around ten years old. She was pictured on a wide sandy beach, standing in the waves, the water lapping her ankles, with such a wide grin, Kit didn't think he had ever seen his wife smile with such a lack of self-awareness.

The next photo was of three teenagers grinning at the camera as they stood with their arms draped over each other, a bottle of beer in their hands, taken early evening judging by the fading light. They all looked at ease and were obviously enjoying some sort of beach party, with a small campfire burning in the foreground. He flipped the photograph over and recognised Neve's handwriting – Megan, Scott, Me! Megan's 20th.

Kit pondered the names. He'd never heard Neve talk about a Megan, but he bloody well knew Neve's first husband was called Scott.

He looked through the rest of the photographs. There were a couple more of Neve with the same girl, maybe one or two years apart but definitely in their late teens, possibly early twenties.

Then he came to a photograph of a bride and groom. The bride was definitely Neve, so the groom must be Scott. He flicked back to the beach photo – yep, it was the same guy. Scott Tansley. He'd never seen a picture of Neve's first husband, not that he had really had any particular desire to, but it had always intrigued him as to what he had looked like. Well, now he knew. A tall, slim guy, dark hair, who begrudgingly, Kit admitted was quite good-looking. Kit noted the little shot of jealousy that pinged through him and then chided himself for worrying about a guy his wife had walked out on. Irrevocable differences, Neve had said, although she'd always been vague on the detail. But what was new about that?

There was another wedding photograph, this time of Neve with the same girl again and a group photo of the bride and groom with their respective families either side, together with the best man and bridesmaid. Kit studied the faces on Neve's side. She took after her mother, Kit decided – blonde, slight build with delicate features.

The next picture was of a newborn baby, wrapped in a white shawl with a handknitted bonnet. There was no way of telling if it was a boy or a girl. Maybe a nephew or niece? He had a feeling Neve had once mentioned her brother had a daughter. There was another photograph of a girl about three years old, Kit guessed. Probably the baby when she was a bit older.

The last photograph again was of the beach party. The whole group were laughing and in mid-collapse, looking down at the sand where another person had thrown themselves into the picture, no doubt at the last minute in an effort to beat the timer on the camera. Pre-selfie-stick and mobile phone days. He turned the photograph over and saw the same names listed as before, but this time with the added name of Ash.

Kit looked closely at the lad face-planting at the group's

feet. He was wearing a baseball cap, a T-shirt and swim shorts. His tattooed arm was outstretched, covering his face as he fell.

Kit mulled over the contents of the suitcase, in particular the photographs. He had never considered Neve to be sentimental, she'd always been more of a pragmatic person, who he believed didn't like to dwell on the past, hence her lack of personal possessions. Clearly, these all held some significance to her life.

Kit climbed down from the loft and went downstairs. Neve obviously wasn't coming back any time soon and he really did need to get to work. He'd have to make it up to Neve later. He slipped the envelope with the photographs into his briefcase before heading out to the car. He wasn't quite sure why he'd kept them, but an idea was forming and determination setting in. He was going to find out about Neve's past whether she liked it or not.

Chapter 10

By the time Neve reached home she had three missed calls on her phone, one text message and one voicemail. All from Jake. None from Kit. She thought her husband might at least phone to say he was sorry, but Kit clearly didn't think he had done anything wrong.

She had felt so angry earlier and she hadn't wanted to go home. She needed time to clear her head and calm down. So, she had driven with no particular destination in mind, eventually finding herself in the nearby town of Arundel. She had parked up and spent the next hour walking her temper out by tramping around the lake.

Sitting in her living room now with a cup of coffee, Neve listened to the voicemail. She could hear the desperation in Jake's voice.

'Neve, I know you're really angry with me, and rightly so, but believe me when I say how sorry I am. I should have realised what Kit was doing but he caught me off-guard. Jesus, Neve ... phone me ... please ... let me explain properly. I'm worried about you. Or at least text me. Just so I know you're OK.'

Safeguarding herself from Kit's curiosity, or rather suspicion, she cleared the voicemail and the text messages. She then scrolled through her contacts until she came to Jake and rang his number. He answered immediately.

'Neve. Are you OK?'

'I'm fine.' That was a lie for a start. She was far from fine. 'I'm at home so there's nothing for you to worry about now. You can stop texting and calling.' She sounded sharper than she had planned.

'I'm so sorry,' said Jake. 'Kit called in. It caught me off-guard. I was so busy trying to pretend everything was all right but at the same time, being careful what I said. You know what Kit's like.'

'What did he say to you?'

'Nothing really. Just that he hadn't seen me for a while, that he had been meaning to call in and say how well you had been responding to the art therapy classes. He was interested in what the therapy involved.'

'And you told him what?'

'I just thanked him. Said I was glad the classes were helping you. I'm telling you, Neve, I was very careful what I said to him.'

'How did he get hold of the paintings?' Neve's stomach rolled at the thought. Kit had seen her pictures and that bothered her the most. It wasn't that he had gone to the studio and it wasn't that Jake had fucked up. No, it went deeper than that. Kit had seen her soul. He had seen her past. Kit was clever. He could work it out. He would just need a few pieces of information and he'd be able to join the dots up and what an awful picture those dots would make.

'Kit just sort of let himself into the small studio. He was

asking questions about the place and the people who came to the classes, like he was interested. I got a bit carried away. I think I let it go to my head. I was too busy showing off, I didn't see him over at the rack and the next thing, he'd pulled out one of your pictures.'

'I didn't want him to see the paintings,' said Neve softly, feeling the fight seep away. She'd lost the only piece of her that was hers and hers alone. Sure, Jake had seen the paintings, but he never commented on them in any depth. He might say he liked the colours or the texture or the way a scene had been captured, but he never asked Neve, or any of his students for that matter, what their paintings were about. The only time he talked through the paintings was if someone wanted to and there were several in Neve's group who did have one-to-one sessions with Jake in the smaller studio.

'I know I keep saying sorry, but I truly am,' said Jake.

'It's OK. I do know what Kit's like.'

'Do you think he was genuinely interested or was he fishing?'

'I'm not sure.'

'Look, Neve, I just want to make it crystal clear how I feel,' said Jake. 'I know things aren't good for you at home and I know how sad you are – about lots of things. I'm here for you, you do know that, don't you?'

'Of course, I do.'

'I can be here for you all the time. I want to be here for you,' said Jake. 'In fact, I feel tormented that I can't be, that you won't let me. Please, Neve, seriously consider what I'm saying. Let me take care of you.'

'Jake, please, not now ...'

'Let me finish,' carried on Jake, his tone becoming more insistent. 'I can make you happy. I've thought non-stop about you for days, weeks. You don't need Kit. All he'll ever be is controlling and domineering. I'm not like that. Trust me.'

'Oh, Jake, I don't know what to say.' Neve closed her eyes. It was such a tempting offer but, she couldn't take him up on it, could she? Would things be any different with Jake though once the novelty of being together had worn off? Kit hadn't always been so caught up with work, but any hope he would go back to the considerate and loving man he'd been when they had first met was dwindling by the day.

'Don't say anything. Just think about it,' replied Jake. 'I know we haven't had the usual sort of courtship that comes with a declaration like that, but I mean every single word of it. I love you, Neve. I want you. I need you.'

The line went dead.

The last statement took Neve by surprise. Such a declaration. He had sounded so insistent, so positive, so determined to convince her that he was the answer. Was it possible to know you loved someone when you hadn't even been in a romantic relationship with them? Maybe Jake could see things clearer because he didn't have the fog of a marriage to look through like she did. Neve examined her feelings for Jake, she wasn't convinced she held the same level of conviction. She loved Kit, or she loved the man he used to be more. Whereas with Jake, she cared deeply for him, but she wasn't sure she loved him. Did it matter if she didn't love him as much as Kit? At the end of the day, Jake was willing to give her a baby, which was more than could be said of her husband

Unsettled by the events of the morning, together with the prospect of dinner with the Harrisons that evening, Neve spent the rest of the day cleaning the house to within an inch of its life.

Poppy was going to a friend's house after school that day. It was a rare occurrence as Poppy didn't always excel in social situations, but she had made a firm friendship with Libby, who also attended St Jospeh's, and Neve encouraged the encounters. Libby had Autism, but was high functioning and the two girls had seemed to naturally gravitate towards each other.

Neve had just settled herself in the living room with a cup of coffee, when the sound of tyres on the gravel announced the arrival of Kit. She glanced out of the window to double-check, and sure enough the Mercedes was being manoeuvred into its usual spot under the wisteria covered car port. A short while later, she heard the door open and Kit call out her name. She didn't bother to answer.

'Ah, you're there.' Kit stood in the doorway and from behind his back he produced a bouquet of pink roses. 'For you,' he said needlessly. He stepped further into the room. 'I'm sorry about earlier.'

Neve placed her cup and the remote control on the coffee table and stood up, accepting the bouquet. 'They're beautiful,' she said, cradling them in her arms, rather like she would a child.

Kit took a step closer, his jacket touching the cellophane. 'I was genuinely interested in your paintings. It was a clumsy attempt at me trying to understand. I want to be able to help you, Neve.'

'You don't need to understand,' said Neve.

'I know I don't need to understand, but I want to understand,' said Kit, taking the flowers from her arms and placing them on the coffee table next to her cup. He cradled the top of her arms with his hands and pulled her towards him, lowering his head, his mouth making contact with her own. 'Let me make it up to you,' he said between the kisses.

Neve wanted to pull away. She wasn't used to this level of affection from Kit. It had been a long time since he had done anything more than robotic Sunday morning sex but there was something different about him today. Something different in his touch. Something different in the way he kissed her. An unexpected desire rekindled within her.

'What are you thinking?' asked Kit, his voice soft as his lips made their way around her jawline and the side of her neck.

'That's for me to know and you to find out,' said Neve, with an ease she had forgotten. It was an exchange of comments they had often said to each other in the past. Neve's pulse began to race in her neck as Kit continued to kiss her.

She was taken back to when they were first married and how he could turn her knees to jelly with the merest of touches and kisses. She closed her eyes. How she longed to have the man she married back. If only time hadn't changed him. Or changed her for that matter.

She pushed thoughts of Jake from her mind, allowing

herself the luxury of fantasising that everything was OK with her and Kit again. That the sink-hole in their marriage hadn't yet formed.

As Kit ran his hands down her side and round her thighs, pulling her closer to him, Neve knew that if she didn't stop now, she wouldn't want to stop. Maybe, if she let herself go, then Kit would too and maybe, just maybe, he wouldn't insist on using a condom like he usually did.

It was a calculated tactic. The phrase 'if you can't beat them, join them' popped into her head. Play Kit at his own game. The game where you win at all costs.

Neve found it surprisingly easy to let herself go. She returned her husband's kisses, impatiently pulling his jacket from his shoulders and tossing it to the floor. They fumbled with each other's clothing and in the end, Neve yanked her own jeans off, while Kit took care of his own.

For the first time in a long time, Neve realised that she actually wanted to have sex with Kit. Driven on by her own desire, her own ulterior motive, she realised how passionate she felt.

Now having made it up to the bedroom, they lay naked on the bed together. Neve pushed Kit onto his back and went to climb on top, kissing his neck and then his chest as she made small circular movements with her hips, grinding into his groin.

'Wait,' said Kit, his hand against her hip so she couldn't move. He stretched his free arm over to the bedside table. Neve knew what he was looking for. The condoms.

'Don't,' she said, softly. 'Not yet.'

Kit stopped in mid-reach, turning his head towards her.

Their eyes met and for a moment she thought he might relent this time. 'No dice.' He shook his head.

'Please?'

'Come on, Neve,' he said as he breathed hard and lifted his groin against her. 'Don't spoil it now.'

'Don't you spoil it,' she said, leaning forward and kissing him while at the same time, attempting to move his hand away from the bedside cabinet.

'Not fair,' said Kit, suddenly pulling away and in one movement he managed to flip Neve over onto her back so he was astride her. 'Condom or we don't pass go.' Kit pulled open the drawer and took out a condom. 'Take it or leave it.'

'You arrogant bastard,' said Neve, pushing him to one side and spinning round on the bed. She grabbed her clothes and stomped off to the bathroom. 'Sort yourself out. I'm taking a shower.'

Neve slammed the door on him. She turned on the shower to full blast, before stepping under the pounding water and scrubbing her skin with the soap and loofah.

Take it or leave it! Who did he think he was?

Chapter 11

Despite Neve's parting comment to sort himself out, any desire on Kit's part had well and truly disappeared. He sat on the edge of the bed and picked up his phone. He'd been unusually indecisive about his next move, but after what just happened, he felt justified.

Kit didn't use Facebook for personal stuff, it wasn't his style, but he couldn't run the business Facebook page without a personal profile. As it happened, that personal profile was about to come in handy.

It only took him a few minutes to locate the right Scott Tansley after checking his profile, which Scott had been kind enough to complete with his place of birth, his education and where he was living now. It all tied in with the tiny bits of info he had gleaned from Neve over the years.

Scott was obviously a sharer in life, his privacy settings were probably the most lax possible. Kit was able to navigate his way through all of Scott's photographs and, just out of curiosity, Kit had a quick look at the friends list too. Neve wasn't on there which didn't surprise Kit at all. That would go against the grain of keeping her past in the past.

Kit decided to send Scott a message, even though they weren't friends. He had a vague notion that Scott would still be able to see the message despite the lack of friendship. He hoped it would pique Scott's interest sufficiently to open the message and reply.

Hi, I'm Neve's husband. Wondered if you could spare five minutes. Thanks.

He left it short and sweet. There was no point going into detail if the bloke wasn't interested in talking to him.

Kit left his phone on the side and took a shower. He could do without having to go for dinner with the Harrisons, but it had been in the diary for several weeks now and Gary Harrison had been making noises about investing some cash into a boat. There was the potential to make a decent chunk of profit if Kit was able to persuade him to buy the new Sunseeker. Gary wasn't a sailing or boating enthusiast, he was all about the image, something which Kit was prepared to overlook in the name of profit.

Having showered and dressed, Kit checked his phone and was surprised to see Scott Tansley had already replied.

Hi. What's this about?

Well, that was to the point. Kit tapped out a reply.

Bit delicate. Neve's struggling with things at the moment. Needed a bit of help joining up the dots.

Kit pressed send and kept the message open. He watched as three pulsating dots appeared below. Scott was obviously keen to know what it was all about.

> **What do you want to know exactly?**

> **You and Neve used to hang out with a group of friends. Megan and Ashley? Neve said what happened, just wanted to know your take on it.**

OK, that wasn't exactly the truth, but Kit had to be clever here.

> **All that was another lifetime ago. I wasn't there when it happened. It's no secret that I thought Ash was involved somehow. He's trouble. He's like the proverbial bad penny. I'm sorry to hear Neve is still struggling with it all. Her and Megan were so close.**

Kit studied the string of messages. He really wasn't getting the info he needed. Something had clearly happened which involved the four of them, but other than that, he was none the wiser. Scott wasn't giving anything away. Kit tried a different approach.

> **Any chance we could meet face to face? It's tricky over messenger.**

> **I don't know. Not sure it's a good idea.**

I'd really appreciate it. I want to help Neve. She's really falling apart over it. Please? I wouldn't ask but I'm desperate. I could drive to you.

Several minutes passed without any reply from Scott. Kit wondered if he had over-egged it. Although, to be fair, what he'd said wasn't a million miles from the truth. He dressed and was just splashing some aftershave on, when the message notification pinged on his phone.

Don't want to meet but I'll talk to you on the phone. Ring me on messenger tomorrow morning at ten.

Cheers, mate. Appreciate that.

Kit felt pleased with the outcome of what was a rather speculative message and congratulated himself on his success. Perhaps now he would finally know the secrets Neve held and he could then decide how he was going to use this information to (a) understand her better (b) to satisfy his desire to know everything there was to know about her and (c) to know as much, if not more, than the fucking art tutor. He hated the thought of Jake knowing more about Neve than he did.

Chapter 12

Neve finished showering and reluctantly went back into their bedroom to get ready for dinner. As much as Kit had thoroughly annoyed her, she wasn't about to stand the Harrisons up, not only would it be embarrassing for Kit, but she'd make a fool of herself too. Kit was sitting on the edge of the bed, already dressed, looking at his phone. Despite being angry with him, Neve couldn't help admitting to herself how handsome he looked. Dressed in an open shirt and chinos, he looked casual and sexy in the way only Kit seemed to.

'Heather texted to say Poppy was happy. That her and Libby have eaten tea and are now watching a film,' said Kit, as he walked past her into the en suite to hang up his towel.

'Heather texted you?' asked Neve, surprised that her friend was messaging Kit.

'No, she texted you,' came Kit's voice from the en suite.

'You looked at my phone?' Neve scanned the bedroom and spotted her phone on Kit's bedside table.

'You were in the shower. I heard it go off and knowing Poppy's not here, I wanted to make sure it wasn't urgent.' Kit came back in to the bedroom. 'What's up, anyway? You got something to hide?'

Neve snatched up her phone and read the text message, hoping Kit wouldn't notice her shaking hand. 'Of course I haven't got anything to hide. It's just rude, that's all. You wouldn't like it if I started reading your messages.'

'Wouldn't bother me in the slightest, actually.' Kit took his jacket out of the wardrobe. 'Hurry up and get ready. We've got to be at the restaurant in forty minutes.'

They drove in silence, Kit turning the music up loud in the small TT car. Normally, he would take his Mercedes but when it was just the two of them, he liked to take the little sports car. Poppy was too big now to sit comfortably in the back so they didn't often get the chance.

They pulled up outside the restaurant. 'You could try looking a little happier,' said Kit, as he cut the engine. 'Try smiling.'

Neve turned to him and gave her best sarcastic smile. 'There, is that better?'

'Grow up,' said Kit, rather wearily. He got out of the car and walked around to open the door for her, but Neve still wasn't going to give him the satisfaction of showing off to everyone watching from the restaurant window. She opened the door before he got there and climbed out, ignoring his outstretched hand.

She was rewarded for her small display of petulance by Kit taking her firmly by the elbow.

'You're hurting me,' she complained, trying to move her arm free.

'Sorry, darling,' said Kit, immediately releasing his grip

and instead guided her through the doorway with his hand resting in the dip of her back. A gesture that Neve had always adored, but tonight, she found no comfort from. She knew he was forcing himself not to be angry with her, mainly for the sake of keeping up appearances while they were out. 'There's Gary and Julia over there,' said Kit.

Gary rose as they were shown to the table. 'Kit,' he said, shaking hands with him. 'Ah, Neve, hello. How are you?' Gary kissed her on both cheeks and then openly looked her up and down. 'You look gorgeous as ever. So beautiful.'

Neve gave a small laugh, feeling uncomfortable under Gary's gaze.

'What's the saying about beauty only being skin deep?' said Kit, greeting Julia in a similar fashion as Neve had been greeted by Gary, minus the roving eye.

'Oh, I'm sure Neve's beauty is far more than skin deep,' said Gary, holding the chair for her to sit down.

'Oh, of course,' said Kit. 'I think Neve's perfect, but then I am biased.' He smiled one of his winning smiles at Neve, who made an effort not to return it. She looked over at Julia.

'That's a lovely dress you have on. I love the colour.' It was true, Julia was wearing the most gorgeous turquoise dress. It reminded Neve of Megan and how she had loved to wear bold vibrant colours, unlike Neve, who preferred a more pastel palette.

By the time the meal was over, Neve was more than ready to go home. Sitting next to Gary and listening to him and Kit play one-upmanship and then listening to Julia bleat on about the PTA she was now chair of and how things needed shaking up and that she was the person to do it, Neve had had about as much as she could stomach.

She checked her phone but there were no messages from Heather, which meant that Poppy was perfectly fine. It was one occasion when Neve half wished Poppy was having a moment and wanted to be picked up. Then she scolded herself for thinking such a thought. It was a comfort to know that Poppy was happy where she was. It gave Poppy a sense of normality in her off-kilter world. Heather was an absolute angel and was so patient, Neve couldn't have hoped for a better friend. She considered herself lucky that Poppy and Libby had become such good friends.

'Everything OK?' asked Kit, nodding towards her mobile phone.

'Yep. No news is good news,' said Neve. She turned away from Kit and pretended to listen intently to Julia who was now talking about the flower arranging at the church. Neve wondered if Julia had stepped out of the 1940s. Any minute now she'd be telling Neve how she'd invited the vicar over for high tea.

Finally, it was time to leave and Neve had to stop herself from practically grabbing the keys from Kit's hand and wheel-spinning away like a getaway driver.

'What's up with you?' asked Kit, as he got in the car beside her and switched on the ignition.

'What do you mean?'

'You were out of there like an Olympic athlete. Where's the fucking fire? Bit embarrassing.'

'Sorry. I'm tired and want to get home.'

Kit pulled away and they drove in silence, reaching home

some fifteen minutes later. Once inside, Kit back-heeled the door closed and dropped his keys onto the hall table. 'Come here,' he said.

Immediately, Neve tensed. She could tell from the drop in octave of his voice that he was turned on and wanted sex. She thought of earlier and how nice it had been at the start. Full of such promise. He pushed her up against the wall and kissed her roughly, sliding his hand up her thigh, taking her skirt with his hand as he did so.

Despite her earlier protestations of being tired, Neve once again found her body taking over and the desire blotting out any rational thought that she was still cross with him.

Kit lifted her up and she hooked her legs around him, returning the kisses he was smothering her with.

'Upstairs,' muttered Kit, putting Neve down. Holding her hand, he took her upstairs to the bedroom where only a few hours earlier they had been in the same situation.

Neve peeled off her dress and lay on the bed in her matching lacy underwear. She couldn't help the physical attraction she felt for her husband.

'Do you want me?' said Kit, standing at the end of the bed, as he unbuttoned his shirt.

'What do you think?'

'Say it.' Kit held her gaze with his deep blue eyes.

Neve was sure that if she had been standing, her legs would have given way. 'I want you.' She stretched out her hand to him. She so wanted him. She wanted him back. She wanted 'them' back. Perhaps they weren't too far from reach after all. Perhaps if she really worked, really tried, she could put the unhappiness behind them. Maybe if they got back to the strong stable marriage they once had, then maybe they could talk about children again. Maybe she'd just handled it all wrong in the first place. Neve stared intently back at Kit and couldn't deny the feeling of love and hope that surged through her.

'You really want me?' he asked.

'I really want you,' she replied.

'Well, you know what it's like to want then,' said Kit. His smile downgraded itself to a sneer. Kit rebuttoned his shirt. 'You're not the only one who can take it or leave it.' It was Kit's turn to leave Neve lying on the bed as he walked out of the room.

Neve could hear the door to his study open and close behind him.

She felt the heat of embarrassment flare up in her face. He had totally humiliated her. Just when she thought there was hope of turning their situation around, he had brutally snatched it from her and stomped it into the ground with his heel.

Who did he think he was? Full of his own importance. Treating her like she was some hooker he'd picked up from the street. No. It was worse than that, she reasoned. He would shag the prostitute. His male ego and pride wouldn't let him not.

In exasperation Neve rolled over and pummelled the pillow with her fists. There had to be an answer to all this. There had to be.

Chapter 13

When Kit woke the next morning, it took him a moment to realise he wasn't in his own bed, but on the sofa bed in his study. He groaned as he remembered why he was there.

What a complete and utter idiot he had been last night. He sat up and swung his legs off the bed, planting his feet on the floor. He'd been pissed off with Neve for storming out of the art studio yesterday. It had been embarrassing. Especially so in front of Jake. He'd seen the way Jake had looked at Neve. The bloke definitely had the hots for her.

Last night he had still been smarting from Neve's walk-off stunt in the bedroom and turning the tables on her had seemed justified. He didn't like to use the word revenge, but it was loitering there in the background. In truth, his male ego had taken a battering and he'd wanted to give Neve a taste of her own medicine.

As Kit showered in the main bathroom, he thought back to yesterday at the art studio. There had been an intimacy between his wife and Jake and Kit hadn't missed the look which had passed between them. One look lasting the briefest of moments said so many things. They shared a secret that Kit wasn't party to and they were worried he'd find it out. In Kit's eyes, that could only mean one thing. Neve was having an affair.

Kit turned the shower onto pulsate, enjoying the pummelling of the water on the back of his neck and across his shoulders. He was tense. Had been for a while now. Too much work and he'd taken his eye off things at home.

He knew carrying on in this macho, bullish way wasn't going to win Neve over. He had to try a different approach. Once he'd spoken to Scott later that morning, he would hopefully have a better idea of what was going on in his wife's head.

By the time Neve joined him downstairs, he was cooking a full English breakfast; the bacon was sizzling away in the pan and the sausages under the grill.

'Good morning,' he said, smiling at her. 'Just in time for the house special.' He gave a little laugh and winked at her. A private innuendo they had long shared about one of them being the tasty dish of the day. A joke which would normally elicit a giggle or at the very least a knowing smile from his wife. This morning though, Neve didn't appear amused.

'Morning,' she said, sitting down on the other side of the centre island.

Kit went over and slipped his arms around her and dropped a kiss on the top of her head. 'Shall we forget about last night? I'm sorry for arguing.'

Neve took a moment to respond. 'Is that an apology for what you did or just for arguing?'

Kit reined in a sigh. He was going to have to work at this.

He nuzzled her neck. 'Sorry for both,' he said. 'I was a complete dickhead.'

Her shoulders relaxed. 'I suppose I was too, earlier on. Sorry.'

'I guess I've been a bit wound up and leaving you like that, well, I know it was a stupid and immature thing to do. Tit for tat. Bloody stupid. I feel a bit of an idiot this morning. Am I forgiven?'

Neve promoted her earlier begrudging response to one of more sincerity. 'Sure, let's have a better day.'

Kit kissed her again. 'Good stuff. Now, what time are we picking Poppy up? I want to get out on the boat today.'

'I said I'd get her mid-morning. I've got to pop to the shop as well to get a couple of things. Shouldn't take too long at all.'

'Perfect,' said Kit, thinking how it couldn't be working out better. If he got a shift on with breakfast, Neve would be out doing whatever it was she had to do while he phoned Scott. He gave Neve a smile. 'Right, breakfast, here we go.'

Neve finally headed off at five to ten, with Kit watching from the door to make sure she went. At ten on the dot, Kit opened the Facebook messenger app and called Scott.

'Hel-lo. Scott here.'

The voice sounded older and thinner than Kit expected. It also sounded wary. Kit needed to put Scott at his ease if he was going to find out anything useful.

'Hi, Scott, it's Kit Masters here. Thanks very much for taking my call.'

'I haven't got long,' said Scott. 'I'm supposed to be taking my daughter swimming soon.'

'Sure. I'll get straight to the point,' said Kit. 'As I said in my message, Neve's not too good at the moment, mentally, I mean. She's become very anxious and it all relates back to when she was younger. She's been having therapy, but it doesn't seem to be helping at all. She's always been sketchy about what happened and I'm just trying to get some clarity so I can help her in some way.'

'Neve and therapy were never a good combination,' replied Scott.

'How do you mean?'

'She went a couple of times when we were married, after losing the baby. And, I suppose, she never really dealt with what had happened to Megan. Anyway, I thought it was a good idea and actually believed that's where she was going every week. One night, I thought I'd surprise her and meet her, take her for dinner and all that. What a mug I was. Saw her coming out of the pub with some guy. Turned out it was Ash of all people. She hadn't been going to therapy for weeks after him randomly turning up out of the blue one day.'

Kit could hear the indignation in Scott's voice, even though this must have been getting on for ten years ago.

'Was she having an affair with Ash?' asked Kit. Christ, if she'd done it once before, then who was to say she wasn't doing it again, this time with Jake?

'God, no! It was more like an unhealthy friendship. Bad influence on her, he was.'

'You mentioned before that you thought he was involved with what happened. How?'

'I swear he was there that day, but Neve point-blank

refused to say, even when she was questioned by the police. Covering for him through some misguided loyalty, you know, not grassing on your mates, omertà, that sort of thing.'

Kit phrased his next question carefully. 'What do you think happened that day?'

'On the beach? With Megan? Well, I'd have thought it was pretty obvious ...' Scott paused and when he spoke there was an air of suspicion in his voice. 'She has told you about Ash, hasn't she?'

'Yeah, well, not much if I'm honest. I just assumed he was an old friend.'

'He's a user, in every sense of the word.'

'A user?'

Scott gave a small laugh. 'You really don't know anything about him, do you?'

'I know he's trouble, like you say. You've just confirmed that to me. What about Megan?' Kit replied, trying to sound casual.

'What about her?'

'What sort of friend was she? Neve's never really said much about her either.'

'You're asking me what sort of friend Megan was?' said Scott. He paused and let out a sigh before speaking again. 'I tell you what, I'm going to end this conversation now. I suggest you talk to your wife. Ask her what happened, not just on the beach that day with Megan, but with everything after that, with Jasmine, with Ash.'

'Look, I'll level with you,' said Kit. He might as well; he had nothing to lose. 'I don't know what happened on the beach or after that. Neve won't talk about it and I'm trying to find out so I can help her.'

There was a long silence and Kit wasn't sure if Scott was still there. Finally, he answered. 'It's not for me to tell,' he said. 'All I'll say is, Neve's been through a lot and hasn't always made the right choices. I'm not surprised to hear she's a bit unstable. I hope she does open up and talk to you and I hope you can help her, because I tried, I really did, but it wasn't anywhere near enough.'

The line went dead.

Kit looked at the phone accusingly. That didn't end the way he had hoped. And who was Jasmine? He took the photographs out from his case and flicked through them again, inspecting the reverse of each one, but other than the ones of Megan's twentieth birthday on the beach, none of them had anything written on the back. He looked again at the photograph of the new-born baby and the toddler. Was this Jasmine?

He mulled over his conversation with Scott. The man clearly regretted not being able to help Neve, and Kit had to admit that he could empathise with that feeling. Kit wanted to help Neve but didn't know how because she wouldn't confide in him. Thinking about it in that way, rather than from the jealous husband point of view, it saddened him to think she was struggling and with more than one problem by the sound of it.

Neve needed fixing. Kit was a fixer. That's what he did. He fixed things. He didn't like anything being out of his control and that included Neve's issues. If he was honest, they were probably his issues too. He hated the fact that he was discovering an ever-increasing number of people knew more about his wife than he did. He couldn't deny the roll of jealousy in his gut, coupled with a sense of unease. It seemed to be more than just a miscarriage that was at the root of her problems. He didn't just want to know, or even need to know – he had a right to know and he was as sure as hell going to find out.

The marina never failed to give Kit a sense of happiness. Kit liked the simplicity of Ambleton's marina; with its one hundred berths, it was small and intimate and gave Kit a sense of nostalgia for his childhood.

He had loved the water since he was a kid and would spend his weekends taking his little sailing dinghy out whenever the weather allowed. There was something majestic about the open water, the way the waves rolled lazily about one moment and on the turn of the tide or the whim of the wind, they could morph into angry angular waves, chopping their way inshore. Today, however, was a beautiful day, the water was calm, the sky was blue, the sun warm and a gentle on-shore breeze made it a perfect day for taking his launch out. *Blue Horizon* was his live-aboard 1930s boat and had been inherited from his father. One of the original Little Ships which had sailed across the Channel to Dunkirk during the war. Kit's father had begun restoring it and after his death, Kit had taken up the challenge. It had taken many, many hours but Kit was immensely proud of the finished result. The only disappointment was that his father hadn't lived to see *Blue Horizon* restored to its majestic former glory.

Kit glanced across to Neve as they pulled up at the marina. The sun was catching the golden highlights in her hair. She took her sunglasses from her bag and popped them on before turning her head to him and smiling.

The smile warmed his heart like the sun warming his skin. She had such a delicate, almost frail, look at times. Her wispy blonde hair, today tied in a ponytail, accentuated her pale skin. Sometimes he looked at her and thought a strong gust of wind would blow her over, but he knew that despite the outer vulnerability, inside she was strong. She was resilient. She was a survivor. She was also a liar, a voice piped up in the back of his mind. She'd always let him believe her miscarriage was at the heart of her problems – she'd deceived him and he'd been a fool not to question her. There was something else lurking in the shadows and it was threatening their marriage, driving a wedge between them.

'Shall we, then?' said Neve, pausing, her hand on the door handle, waiting for his cue.

'Yes. Hurry up,' said Poppy from behind his chair.

'Absolutely,' said Kit. He turned in his seat and smiled back at Poppy. Her face alight with excitement melted his heart. His daughter had inherited his love of the water. It was the one place that Poppy seemed truly at home. It had the power to take away all her stresses and worries, even as a small child, her mood always peaked whenever they had gone out on the boat.

'Let's make this a good day,' he said.

'Sure,' Neve said as she gave him one of her enigmatic smiles. One that, even after all this time, he couldn't quite read.

Then, before he could question it any further, Poppy was pushing the car door open.

'Come on, Dad! Let's go,' she said. 'I want to see the water.'

In a few minutes they had taken their dry bags from the car and were clomping down the wooden jetty that sloped from the shoreline to the harboured boats, with Willow trotting alongside Poppy on the lead. Being on a tidal river, and a little inland, it wasn't too popular with the yachting fraternity and their river and seagoing cruisers. It was rather more industrial, with fishing boats that went in and out every day, and hardened boating enthusiasts.

'Go steady!' called Kit as Poppy skipped along the floating pontoon, towards their boat.

'She makes me nervous,' said Kit. 'She's not looking where she's going half the time. Head in the clouds.'

'She's fine,' said Neve. 'Just excited.'

'Thanks for coming today,' said Kit, cutting his stride so Neve could walk alongside him. 'I'm glad you came. I am really sorry about last night. I was a bit of a wanker.' Kit stopped mid-sentence, realising his faux pas. 'Sorry, I didn't mean that literally.'

Neve laughed. 'Let's forget about last night once and for all,' she said graciously and slipped her arm through his.

'Just one more thing ... I'm also sorry about what happened at the studio. I didn't mean to upset you like that.' Kit felt this apology was slightly more forced.

'Like I said, let's forget about it,' said Neve. 'I don't want to ruin the day by talking about it all. Let's just enjoy the moment.'

'Hurry up, Dad! Hurry up, Neve!' called Poppy, now

hopping from one foot to the other, making the pontoon bounce up and down on the water.

'Someone's eager,' said Neve.

The rigging tingled against the masts of the boats in the gentle breeze. Perfect weather for being out on the water. 'Remember when I first brought you here?' said Kit, as they came alongside *Blue Horizon*.

'How could I forget?'

'We moored up a little way down river,' said Kit. 'And I cooked us a meal.'

'I seem to remember it was beans on toast.'

'It was still a meal.' He gave a mock indignant look and was rewarded by a small laugh from Neve.

Kit had been pleased, if not a little surprised, when Neve had agreed to come out on the boat. It wasn't her most favourite pastime. She didn't have the love of water that he and Poppy shared so today, he felt, was a significant gesture on her part. He planned to take the boat along the river so she would feel more comfortable about the whole trip. The river she said she could deal with, but the open sea frightened her.

And how appropriate that the openness should frighten her. It wasn't just the physical open space, but being open with her heart too.

He had always known from the start that she'd had a troubled background. There was something about herself that she hadn't quite given him. She'd given him her heart but not entirely. Many a time he'd tried to dig deeper into what was troubling her. Once he thought she might actually tell him, but she had stopped short at the last minute, made a lame joke about there not being enough hours to explain and then had flatly refused to talk about it anymore.

Kit had always hoped she would eventually open up and tell him. He had to admit, it hurt that she didn't feel she could talk to him about everything. He knew for a fact that there wasn't anything about his life he hadn't told her. She knew it all; the good and the bad. But it had never been a fair exchange. Neve knew his soul, but he didn't know hers and the more he dwelled on this, the more it pissed him off.

'All aboard,' he declared in his best sea dog voice, extending a hand to help Poppy breach the gap between the pontoon and the edge of the boat. Fortunately, the tide was at a good place and the pontoon was just the right level for boarding, neither too high nor too low.

'Permission to come aboard?' said Neve, good humouredly.

Kit smiled. She hadn't said that for a long time. He held out his hand to help her step onto the gunwale of the boat and hook her leg over the side rail. 'Permission granted.'

Neve gave a mock salute. 'Aye, aye, Captain.'

'Right, life jackets on,' said Kit, opening up the cubby hole and pulling out the vests. Neve attended to hers and Poppy's, while Kit did his own and performed some of the checks. 'OK, let's go.'

'Yay!' cried Poppy, as Kit slipped the boat from its moorings. 'Anchor's away, Captain!'

The 1930s launch glided away from the pontoon and Kit turned the wheel with expert ease, navigating the craft out on to the open river. Willow settled herself on the deck next to Kit's feet. He glanced back at his passengers. Poppy was sitting on the foam cushioned seat, peering over the side at the wake left by the boat. Neve was sitting opposite, smiling fondly at his daughter. Kit couldn't help being thankful that Neve had taken Poppy on, as if she were their daughter.

And then the pang of something akin to guilt struck him. He looked away, as if not looking at Neve would make the feeling go away, He didn't often feel guilty but today he did. Maybe it was part of the remorse from last night. He knew how much Neve wanted a child of her own and yet he knew with even more certainty that he could never give her that child.

How could he put himself through that torturous hell he'd gone through with his first wife, Ella? He couldn't bear the thought of it. No, his fear was greater than Neve's need. He was certain of that. Selfishly so, but he had always hoped that Poppy would be enough to plug that gap in Neve's life. Maybe he'd got it wrong. Maybe Neve needed to need Poppy more. If that was the case, then perhaps the need for a child of her own would dissipate and eventually vanish altogether. He mulled over this thought as he steered the boat along the river.

'Oh, look over there,' said Neve, above the engine noise. She pointed to the bank of bulrushes on the other side. 'A heron. Can you see that, Poppy?'

Kit watched as Neve went over to sit next to Poppy and patiently got her to focus on the location of the bird.

On a beautiful day like today with Poppy so happy and Neve seemingly content, Kit couldn't think of anything nicer. He wanted it to stay this way for ever. Just the three of them. They made a good team and he was frightened of upsetting the equilibrium they had. Or rather, they'd once had. He sensed a turning of the tide with Neve and it scared him, although he'd never admit that to anyone. It was all he could do to admit it to himself. He didn't want Neve to turn with the tide. He had to do something to ensure she swam against it and made her way back to him.

Chapter 14

Neve woke to the early morning dawn chorus of the birds in the trees. She laid there enjoying the peace and tranquillity. There was no traffic in the background, no one mowing their grass or the general sounds of Long Acre Lane coming to life on a Sunday morning.

Yesterday they had moored up a few miles down the river, just outside the village of Little Bury. The three of them had sat out on the deck, Neve and Kit drinking wine and Poppy a fizzy drink. Wrapped under blankets for warmth, they had watched the night sky appear, star gazed and made wishes. Even Poppy had seemed to enjoy the time they spent together, purely being. No pressures of life or computer screens or mobile phones.

Later on, Neve had cooked them a meal. Nothing too fancy, after all there was only a two-ring burner and a small microwave come cooker. There wasn't much room for anything else in the galley.

Kit stirred beside her in their cabin – a small room at the bow of the boat where the seats turned into a bed, not dissimilar to a caravan. A compact space where more often than not, everything had a dual purpose.

'Morning,' said Kit, with a groan. 'Jesus, my head is killing me.' He went to sit up and flopped back down on the bed.

'It's what's known as a hangover,' said Neve. 'Must admit, I don't feel too great either. How much wine did we drink, for God's sake?'

'No idea,' said Kit, holding his hand over his eyes. 'I can't remember much after the first bottle.'

'Me neither,' said Neve. 'I'm not sure if I'm even sober now.'

'I need the loo, but I don't know if I can even get out of bed,' groaned Kit. He moved onto his side. 'I'll just lay here a bit longer.'

'Don't be sick. There's no way I can be dealing with that this morning,' said Neve, pulling the cover up to her chin.

'Have you seen Poppy this morning?' asked Kit. The words sounded heavy and a little slurred.

'No. Haven't got up yet,' admitted Neve. 'Head's a bit too delicate.' She reached over the side of the bed and padded her hand around until she found the bottle of water she'd brought to bed with her last night. She opened the lid and took several long gulps. 'Want some?' she dangled the bottle over Kit's shoulder.

'Thanks.' Kit took several large mouthfuls. 'I could murder a cup of coffee. I might just have to get up. Besides I really do need the loo.' He clambered over Neve, stopping to give her a kiss as he straddled her body, still fully clothed from where he'd passed out on the bed the night before. He ran his fingertip down Neve's breastbone. 'Such a waste, as well,' he muttered.

Neve pulled a sad face. 'You'll have to make it up to me later.'

'A lot later,' said Kit, groaning with every movement he made. 'I feel like I've been run over!'

'Stop being a wimp,' said Neve, giving Kit a playful shove. 'Go on, put the kettle on while you're up. And let Willow out too!'

She listened as Kit staggered out of the cabin, trying to be quiet but with little or no success. The door to the toilet rattled as he struggled with the handle and then clattered as he shut it behind him.

Sharing a small space on a boat, meant there was little privacy, so Neve heard Kit relieve himself.

'Noisy pisser!' she called out. Another of their shared jokes, another they hadn't visited for so long.

The flush of the toilet and more clattering of the door signalled Kit had finished. 'Come on, Willow, want to go out?'

Kit crashed around some more as he let Willow up onto the deck, waiting for the dog to jump onto the riverbank. A few minutes later, hound and master were back below deck.

'Morning, Poppy,' she heard him say. 'Hmmm? Poppy?'

Neve laid very still and listened to Kit walking across the saloon of the boat to the aft cabin, where Poppy slept. She heard Kit knock on the door. 'Morning, sleepy head. Fancy a hot chocolate?'

She listened as Kit filled the kettle with water and flicked it on to boil, before taking out the cups from the cupboard. 'Looks like we managed to polish off two bottles of wine,' he called back to Neve.

'That explains a lot,' replied Neve.

'Poppy, you OK?' Kit's voice filled the boat. He knocked

on the door and Neve heard the little creak of protest the old boat gave as the door opened. 'Poppy?'

The concerned tone in Kit's voice instantly alerted Neve. She slipped out of bed, grabbing her hoody and pulling it over her head. She saw Kit disappearing up the steps to the cockpit, calling Poppy's name.

'Is she there?' Neve asked, leaning on the handrail and looking up through the cabin door.

'No! Fuck. Where is she?' Kit clattered across the deck. 'Poppy! Poppy!'

Neve jammed her feet into her wellington boots and clambered up to the deck. By now, Kit had disembarked and was on the riverbank, still calling Poppy's name. He turned back to Neve. 'She's gone!'

Chapter 15

'Wait, wait. Keep calm,' said Neve. 'Just have another look around. I'll double-check the boat.'

Neve dived downstairs and although she knew it was pointless – hiding on a small boat like this was near impossible – she went through the motions of double-checking. She grabbed her mobile and went up on deck just as Kit was jogging back down the riverbank to the mooring.

Neve climbed over the edge of the boat and onto the grassy riverbank. 'Definitely not on the boat,' she said to Kit.

'I can't see her anywhere round here,' said Kit, rubbing his temples and screwing up his eyes.

'I'll try her phone,' said Neve, opening up her mobile. She called up Poppy's number and waited for the call to connect. The sound of Poppy's phone ringing sounded out from below deck. Neve darted down the steps and located the mobile on the table. 'She hasn't got her phone,' she called across to Kit.

'Shit.' Kit climbed back on the boat and took the phone from Neve. 'What's her passcode. I need to check her messages.'

'2602. Her date of birth,' said Neve. She peered over Kit's shoulder as he looked through the phone. There wasn't much to look at. Poppy used her phone mostly for photographs and games, her contacts list running to a handful of people, Kit, Neve, her grandmother, Libby and her teacher. 'Anything?'

'Nothing.' Kit pushed the phone into his pocket.

'Shall I call the police?' asked Neve.

'No! Not yet. All we need is the police and social services getting involved again.'

'I know, but it's different this time,' insisted Neve, as she moved further up the bank to get a better signal. 'She's not gone off after an argument or anything. Everything was fine last night. She's disappeared, and we have no idea when she went. She could be in danger.' Neve didn't need to elaborate. She could see the unspoken fear written all over Kit's face.

'Shit. Call them,' said Kit. 'I'm going to have a look further down the road. Maybe she's in the village?' He looked at his watch. 'It's only eight-fifteen. Nowhere will be open on a Sunday at this time. Oh God, Neve.'

Neve's pyjama trousers were soaking wet from the morning dew on the riverbank. In her hurry to put on her boots, she hadn't bothered to tuck the fly away trouser leg in the top. She held the phone to her ear waiting for the emergency service to answer.

'My daughter is missing,' she said urgently. 'Police. I need the police.'

In what seemed like a surreal few minutes, Neve relayed details of Poppy and her last known whereabouts to the police officer on the other end of the phone.

'She's a vulnerable teenager,' said Neve. 'She has learning difficulties. She doesn't read social situations well and comes across as quite young for her age.'

'We'll get someone out to you right away,' said the officer. 'Stay where you are.'

The line went dead. Neve did a 360 degree turn, looking once again for any sign of her daughter. She hadn't bothered to explain the technicality of her relationship with Poppy to the police officer. She just needed to get them out here as quickly as possible. She needed them to search for Poppy. There wasn't time to waste.

With Willow tagging along, Neve walked up the bank and onto the road which lead down to the village. She held her hand to her eyes to shield the early morning sun. She couldn't see Kit. He must have practically run down the road. Neve wondered if it had been wise to let him go off on his own. Perhaps she should have gone with him? But then there would be no one here to greet the police or to search the immediate area.

Neve thought back to last night, trying to recall the chain of events. Her mind was racing through the timeline, but her memory was jumbled and she couldn't quite get everything to fit together. She could feel panic setting in and every time she thought of Poppy, the image of another child kept pushing to the fore. Jasmine. Her brother's daughter. She was three years old, standing on the beach, holding Neve's hand as they jumped the waves.

'One, two, three ... jump!' Neve could hear herself saying as she watched the delight on Jasmine's face. Jasmine's chubby little hand pushed her hair from her face as her long curls were lifted by the sea breeze.

They squealed in delight at both their success and their failure. The water splashing their legs and clothing. It had been an impromptu trip to the seaside, a decision Neve had made on the spur of the moment. It had all been with the best intentions. Neve would have never knowingly put her niece at risk.

Her empty stomach lurched and for a moment she thought she was going to be sick, as she was propelled back to the present. She needed to concentrate. It was Poppy who mattered now. She just hoped that the police wouldn't automatically blame her for Poppy's disappearance.

Neve dialled Kit's number and within a couple of rings, his panting voice answered. 'Have you found her?'

'No. I haven't,' said Neve. She could hear the panic mixed with anger in Kit's voice. Poppy disappearing was outside his control. Not something Kit would like.

'I'm at a shop now. It's open,' said Kit. More panting. Neve could hear Kit ask in the shop if they had seen Poppy.

'She's five foot four,' he was saying. 'With long dark hair. It's tied back in a ponytail.' He went on to describe the jacket she had with her. 'Have you seen her? Has she been in the shop? Walked past? Has someone, anyone, mentioned her?' He was rattling the questions off in quick succession. 'If you do see her or anyone says they have seen her, please call the police. Or my number. Here's my business card. Please.'

'Any luck?' she asked needlessly.

'No. Nothing. I'm going to try the pub now,' said Kit, his breathing coming hard down the phone. 'Maybe not. It's shut.'

'I've looked all around the mooring site and there's no sign of her,' said Neve. 'The police are sending someone out.'

'Did you tell them about Poppy? How she's not like a normal fourteen-year-old?'

'Yes. They didn't seem too bothered at first. Thought she might have just done a normal teenage thing and wandered off. You know, bored of being on the boat but once I explained, they were more interested.'

'They better be,' snapped Kit. 'Oh, Jesus, Neve, where the hell is she?'

'Keep calm. She can't have gone far, surely.'

'You say that, but we've no idea when she disappeared. My head is killing me. I can't seem to remember much about last night at all,' said Kit, blowing hard now. 'Look, I'm just going to check around the village. Bus shelter. Church. Playing field. Ring me when the police get there.'

'Someone will have seen her,' said Neve, trying to offer words of comfort. 'She'll turn up. I'm sure.'

'Don't say something you can't possibly know is true,' said Kit. 'We've no idea what's happened to her. For all we know she could have gone off with someone.'

After ending the call, Neve took a long deep breath. She needed to stay calm. The police were on their way and once they were here, it was up to her to convince them to take Poppy's disappearance seriously.

Less than five minutes later, the blue flashing lights of a police car came around the corner, bumping over the loose gravel track which ran down to the river bank.

'Mrs Masters?' said the female officer as she climbed out of the car.

'That's right,' said Neve, stroking Willow's ears, more for something to do with her fidgety hands than anything else. 'I made the call about my daughter going missing.' She took out her phone from her pocket. 'My husband is in the village looking for her. I'm just going to ring him to let him know you're here.'

The next few hours seemed to both drag and speed by. The police wanted to ask what seemed like endless questions about Poppy. What was she wearing, when was she last seen, when did they realise Poppy was missing, did she have her passport, any money or need any medication? Kit had become frustrated at times and once had even raised his voice to the police officer when she had inferred that Poppy would probably turn up, like she had before.

'How can you say that?' Kit had demanded, jumping to his feet. 'You have no idea if she's safe or not. You certainly can't assume just because she was OK last time that she will be this time.'

PC Crossley had back-tracked rapidly, assuring Kit they were treating Poppy's disappearance seriously. 'I assure you, Mr Masters, finding your daughter is our highest priority. We have officers on the ground looking for her already and they've just brought the police helicopter in.'

'Why is it all taking so long?' demanded Kit.

'We're doing everything we can. Unfortunately, the helicopter was already tied up with something else in Hampshire. But it's free now so we've got it. We've also got officers knocking on doors of anyone local that is known to us.'

'Paedophiles, you mean,' said Kit. 'It's all right, you don't have to dress it up. I know exactly what that means.'

Crossley moved the conversation on. 'Do you have Poppy's hairbrush or toothbrush we could have, please?'

Neve could see Kit wince as if taking a physical blow. 'Her hairbrush ...' he began.

'Or toothbrush,' said Crossley.

'For DNA to identify her,' said Kit, becoming agitated. 'That's what you want it for, isn't it?'

Crossley looked at Kit and then at Neve. 'It's routine,' she said. 'I'm sorry.'

'I'll get you her hairbrush,' said Neve, standing up and going through to Poppy's cabin and reappearing with the purple paddle style brush. 'It was on the floor, she always brushes her hair before she goes to sleep.'

'Fifty times,' said Kit, his voice cracking as he spoke. 'She always brushes it fifty times. Once in the morning and once in the evening.'

Neve passed the brush to Crossley and resumed her position next to Kit. She squeezed his hand while addressing the police officer. 'Is there anything we can do? Help with the search, maybe?'

'No, we'd rather you let us do the searching. If needs be, we'll be going door-to-door with a picture. Once you're home, we'll ask for an up to date photograph of Poppy.' Crossley wrote a few more notes in her pocketbook before looking back up. 'One of my colleagues has spoken to the publican in the village and he's open now and said you're more than welcome to wait in there. He'll give you a hot drink and something to eat. He said there's a private room at the back you can use.'

'That's very kind of him,' said Neve.

'I don't think I can stomach anything,' said Kit. 'I need to be out there looking for her. I can't just sit happily in a pub while my daughter is missing.'

'No one is expecting you to, sir,' said Crossley. 'And I know you feel you should be helping with the search, but it's better for us if you stay here, just in case she turns up.'

Neve thought that Crossley probably meant in case something horrible had happened to Poppy and either of them found her. She shuddered involuntarily at the thought, dismissing the disturbing image from her mind.

'The police officer is right,' she said, gently. 'Let's go down to the pub.'

'The boat. I'm not leaving the boat,' he said.

Neve was aware that Kit was starting to sound a little irrational, and who could blame him really? Everything was totally out of his control now. Even down to looking for his daughter, which he was being told he couldn't do. Kit didn't like taking orders from anyone. However, Neve noticed a vulnerability about him now, something she had never seen in him before. Even when he had spoken about his first wife dying, he had been strong and resilient. But now, there were cracks showing in his tough exterior that Neve didn't even know existed.

'Just for a little while,' she said, coaxing him rather like she would Poppy. It felt strange having Kit lean on her, not just for moral support but for physical support too.

He nodded. 'OK, but just for an hour.'

'We're going to check over the boat again,' said Crossley. 'Can I just go back over a couple of points first?'

'Of course,' said Neve, aware of Kit's impatient sigh.

'It won't take a minute,' said Crossley, nodding towards Kit. 'Now, Mrs Masters, you say you were the last one to bed.'

'That's right,' replied Neve.

'And you're certain you locked the cabin door from the inside?'

Neve hesitated. 'I think I did. I can't honestly remember but I'm pretty certain.'

'And, Mr Masters, you're certain it was unlocked when you got up this morning?'

'Yes.'

'There's no sign of a forced entry, in fact, no damage whatsoever to the lock or door, so we must assume that it was opened from the inside,' said Crossley. 'Or it wasn't locked at all.' She looked again at Neve.

'I'm really sorry, I can't say for certain,' said Neve. She glanced over at Kit to seek reassurance that she shouldn't feel guilty, that he didn't blame her for Poppy being missing.

'You were the sober one, you must remember locking it,' said Kit, flinging his hands in the air.

'I'm sorry,' was all Neve could think of to say.

'OK. If you do remember, it's important you let us know,' said Crossley. 'Now, do you have that list of friends and family?'

Neve passed over a sheet of paper. It only had Cheryl, Kit's mother, the school and Heather and Libby's names. 'She doesn't have many friends outside of school,' said Neve.

'I don't want you calling my mother out of the blue,' said Kit.

'No, of course not. Why don't you phone her from the pub?' said Crossley. 'Just one thing before you go. Has Poppy got a mobile phone or a laptop?'

'She does have a phone,' said Kit. He pulled it from his pocket. 'It was on the table where she left it last night.'

'Do you mind if we have a look through it?' asked Crossley. 'Just in case.'

'I've already done that,' said Kit but nevertheless he passed the mobile over. 'She hasn't really got anyone to text. You won't find anything of any use.'

Crossley took the phone. 'Laptop?'

'Not here. Back at home,' said Neve. 'It's in her bedroom.'

'OK. We will want to have a look at that too when we take you home,' said Crossley.

'Come on, Kit,' said Neve. 'Let's go down to the pub. Just for an hour and then …' She looked at Crossley.

'And then, once we've done another thorough check of the boat and immediate area, we can arrange for you to be taken home,' she said.

'Just for an hour,' said Neve reassuringly.

Kit grunted his reluctant consent. Neve couldn't help noting how the balance of power had shifted. How she was the one in charge and making the decisions. It was an empowering thought and she could feel herself stand taller.

'Wait!' said Kit, stopping in his tracks. He turned to the police officer. 'The other day, when Poppy went off, I found her talking to some bloke.'

Crossley took out her pocketbook. 'Do you know who he was?'

'No. I hadn't seen him before, but he was a scruffy looking sort of bloke.' Kit went on to describe the man.

'And neither of you know who this could be?'

'Not at all,' said Kit. 'But you need to ask at The Forum. There's all kinds there. I wouldn't be surprised if this bloke is something to do with it.'

'OK, I'll get this description circulated and ask around, see if we can find out who he is.' Crossley looked up at Neve. 'And you don't know who he is either?'

'No. No idea whatsoever.' Neve was surprised at how easily the words came out, but when she thought about it, it wasn't the first time she'd lied to the police where Ashley Farnham was concerned.

Chapter 16

Kit allowed Neve to take him back into the village where he had been just a couple of hours earlier. He was sure everyone was looking at him, judging him. Wondering what sort of father allowed his own daughter to disappear in the still of the night.

'I think this is a bad idea,' he said, as Neve pushed open the door to The Fox & Hounds.

'Don't start all that again,' interrupted Neve. The command in her voice startled him, but at the same time comforted him. He wasn't used to this feeling of total and utter helplessness. He was used to making decisions and getting things done. He was a man of action. Doing nothing did not come naturally to him.

'Let the police do things their way. They know what's best,' she was saying.

'Hello. Kit and Neve, is it?' said the barman. 'Brian Johnson. Guvnor here.' He extended a hand to which Kit found himself automatically shaking. He gave a nod and Brian continued. 'I'm sorry to hear about your daughter. I'm sure the police will find her soon.'

'Thanks,' said Kit. He really didn't want to get into a

discussion with the pub landlord about the police search. It wasn't like they were discussing the latest football results or the weather. Conversations that could be picked up and put down in any pub in any part of the country. No, this was his daughter, they were talking about. Far too precious for flippant, banal platitudes.

Kit glanced around the pub and couldn't help but notice that the other customers were looking at him and Neve, together with the police officer who insisted on coming with them. It was like having a fucking shadow. One he didn't need. Kit wanted to be able to speak to Neve in private. He didn't want the whole bloody village and local bobby listening in on their conversations. 'I don't know if I can do this,' he muttered in Neve's ear.

'Do you want to come through to the back room?' said Brian. He indicated towards a door at the side of the bar. 'Take the dog in as well. I'll bring you both in a hot drink, unless you fancy something stronger?'

Kit momentarily considered the idea of a whiskey but changed his mind and opted for a coffee.

The back room was about the size of an average classroom, with six tables and several plastic chairs pushed together in the middle of the room. More chairs and tables were stacked in the corner. The curtains were drawn and the police officer went to open them.

'No. Can we keep them closed?' said Kit. 'The car park is just there. I don't want to be a freak show.'

'OK. Right, well I've just got to nip outside to make a call to my boss,' said the police officer. 'Shout if you need me.'

'Thanks,' said Kit, relieved she wouldn't be joining them.

Once the officer was outside, Kit turned to Neve. 'I suppose that's a good thing.'

'What's a good thing?' asked Neve.

'The police officer waiting outside. They obviously don't think we've got anything to do with Poppy's disappearance otherwise they'd be sitting with us, waiting for us to say something.'

'Christ's sake, Kit, the way your mind works,' said Neve, shaking her head. 'Honestly, I didn't for one moment think we were under suspicion.'

'Don't underestimate the police, and the way their minds work,' said Kit. 'Family members are usually the ones at the top of the suspect list. Especially the male relatives.'

'Why would they suspect us?'

Kit let out a long sigh and ran his hand through his hair. 'I don't know. Ignore me. I'm talking bollocks,' he said. 'The stress is getting to me. I'm not good at this sitting around and waiting business.'

'I know you're not,' said Neve, 'but you just have to, for now.'

'She could have been gone for anything up to eight or nine hours. Maybe more! The longer she's missing the more I think something awful has happened,' said Kit.

Neve put her arm around his shoulders. 'Don't think like that. You mustn't go down that road.'

Kit looked at his wife. Her sincere green eyes looked back at him. He admired how calm and in control she was and at first he was surprised. However, as he pondered her control he realised that he shouldn't be surprised at all. Neve had been composed ever since he'd known her. Never really letting her guard down. Her years of experience, keeping her shit together and not giving anything away was paying off. Now, in potentially their darkest hour, she was the one in control.

Neve inclined her head towards Kit and he returned the gesture – their foreheads resting against each other's. 'Tell me this isn't really happening,' whispered Kit.

'Sorry to interrupt.' It was Brian, with a tray bearing two coffees and a selection of sandwiches. 'I thought you might like something to eat too. You've probably not got the appetite, I know, but you should try to eat something. There's some water for the dog as well.'

'Thank you,' said Neve. 'That's very kind of you.'

As Neve added milk and sugar to his coffee, Kit was distracted by his phone ringing. 'Shit. It's Mum,' he said, looking at the screen. 'I should have phoned her.'

'You'd better answer it. She might know already but if she doesn't you should be the one to tell her,' said Neve.

Kit swiped at the screen. 'Hello, Mum?'

'Kit. Is everything all right? Is Poppy OK? Only one of the women from my sewing club has phoned because someone in the shop was talking about a missing girl from Ambleton. She wanted to know if it was Poppy. She said something about her going missing from a boat!'

'Mum. Mum, listen to me. Stop talking,' said Kit. He could hear the hysteria rising in his mother's voice. He had a sudden wish that his father was still alive so that his mother didn't have to deal with this on her own. He went to speak, but the emotion got the better of him and his voice came out in some sort of frog-like croak. He cleared his throat and tried

153

again. 'Mum, it is Poppy that's missing.' He paused as she let out a cry of alarm.

'Oh, my goodness! How? I mean when? Why didn't you tell me?'

'It's all been a bit of a blur. I was about to call you,' said Kit. 'The police are going to speak to you. I should have told you before. Sorry.'

'Just tell me what's happened?'

'We went out on the boat yesterday afternoon. Ended up staying on it overnight. When we woke up this morning, she was gone. Vanished. Disappeared.' Kit took a breath. 'The police are out there looking for her now.'

'Oh, dear lord,' said his mother. He imagined her sitting down in her armchair by the window, the air knocked from her lungs in the same way as it had been knocked from his. 'Where are you now? Shall I come over?'

'We're in Little Bury, we moored up just outside the village. Stay at home, just in case Poppy somehow manages to find her way to you. The police are putting an officer at ours, so don't be alarmed if someone says they've seen the police parked up outside. We're going home as soon as the police have finished checking the boat and the village.'

'Yes. Yes, of course. Oh, this is just awful. You have told them about Poppy's problems, haven't you?'

Kit hated the way his mother described Poppy as having problems. It gave a negative feel to his daughter. Poppy wasn't a problem. It never failed to irritate him the way his mother always associated that word with Poppy – Poppy's problems – like it was a double-barrelled name. He felt Neve gently rub her hand up and down his back. She had leaned in to listen and had no doubt heard the conversation. 'Yes, the police know all about Poppy. Look, as soon as I hear anything, I'll ring you.'

'Promise?'

'Promise. You'll be the first to know.'

'I'll light some candles and say a prayer,' said his mother.

'That will be great,' said Kit, although privately he couldn't help thinking it would do no fucking good at all. He didn't believe in God. In fact, he didn't believe in anything that wasn't tangible, concrete, there to be seen and touched. Faith had no place in Kit's life but if it kept his mother happy, then so be it. He reassured his mother once again and ended the call, before turning to Neve. 'She's lighting some candles.'

'She means well,' said Neve. 'It doesn't do any harm.'

'Doesn't do any good either.'

Chapter 17

'A press conference?' said Neve. 'This seems really soon.' She looked at the Detective Chief Inspector sitting in front of them. It was twenty-four hours since Poppy had gone missing. Kit's business partner, Sean, had arrived at the pub yesterday with his wife, who had driven Kit and Neve home, while Sean sailed *Blue Horizon* back to Ambleton marina.

Kit had been reluctant to leave Little Bury in the end, just in case Poppy turned up. He'd spent another hour walking around the village several times in the faint hope she was just sitting somewhere waiting to be found or had fallen over and hurt herself and couldn't get up. The police officer hadn't wanted him to, but he'd been insistent. It had taken all Sean and Neve's powers of persuasion to convince Kit he was better at home.

It had been a bleak night where the search had been called off until first light, a night that had stretched far too long and one where they had tortured themselves with scenarios of what had happened to Poppy, their imagination taking them to the darkest corners of their mind. In the end Kit had got up and with Neve following him downstairs, he had fired up his laptop and set about creating a Facebook post with a photograph of Poppy and the words MISSING typed in capitals across the top and then a paragraph urging people to look out for Poppy and to share the post. He'd done the same thing on Twitter, using the hashtags #schoolgirlmissing #findPoppy.

'We've got to try everything,' he'd said as he had refreshed the page time and time again, checking for comments and shares.

Now this morning, after little sleep, Kit and Neve were sitting opposite DCI Pearson listening to his action plan.

A Family Liaison Officer had been assigned to them to stay with them at the house during the day. Sally Ames was an experienced police officer who, Neve estimated, was in her late thirties. She had been outside when the DCI had arrived, to have a cigarette, Neve had guessed. There was a hint of nicotine about her which she had been marginally successful at disguising with a sickly sweet smelling body spray and an extra strong mint which rattled against her teeth every so often.

It reminded Neve of her brother and how he used to have a crafty smoke in the back garden, behind the shed, thinking their mum never spotted him. In fact, Mum knew full well what he was up to. From the kitchen window they would often see a small trail of smoke drifting around the corner of the brick-built outhouse. When he came back in the house, Mum would remark that he would lose his teeth if he kept crunching on all those polo mints. She never said anything directly about the smoking. It was like they were all pretending, all part of the same game when really, they all knew the truth. That was when things were better at home. When they functioned pretty much like every other family.

She had another flash of a memory skate to her conscious thoughts. A different time, a different mother and father sitting in front of a different police officer. Neve could see herself laying in a hospital bed, watching her parents through a gap in the curtain, standing in the corridor. She couldn't remember what happened next. It was all fragmented, cut up into chunks and put back together but with bits missing. The next image was of two police officers at her bedside, asking her the same questions over and over again. She distinctly remembered the fleeting glance the two officers exchanged when she said it was just her and Megan on the beach.

'So, Neve, a press conference later today would really help with raising Poppy's profile,' the detective was saying. Neve blinked herself back to focus on what he was explaining.

'Yes, it's a good idea but do I have to be in it? I mean, wouldn't it be more appealing coming from Kit, he is her father,' said Neve.

'In our experience, having both parents there is more effective,' replied DCI Pearson.

'But I'm not her mother.'

Kit made a huffing noise. 'For fuck's sake, Neve, you're as good as. Poppy thinks of you as her mother. You are the only mother she's known. What is wrong with you?' He rose and paced to the window with hands on hips. 'We need to do everything we can to get her back.'

Neve felt herself shrink into the seat. He was right of course, but the thought of having to face the cameras, to be on television and in the newspapers was freaking her out.

'Will it be aired locally or nationally?' she asked.

'Nationally,' said Pearson. 'Poppy is a high-risk category.

She's a vulnerable teenager and we want to pile all our resources into finding her. And quickly.'

'Of course,' said Neve. Her stomach gave a flutter of nerves. Someone was bound to recognise her but what could she do? There was no way out of this.

'We strongly feel you should both attend the press conference.' Pearson paused, as if weighing up his words before speaking. 'Is there any particular reason why you don't want to do the press conference?'

'I'm just a bit nervous, that's all. I'm not sure I could speak in front of all those cameras and press.'

'It's not about you!' snapped Kit. 'It's about Poppy.'

Neve clasped her hands together. 'I know. I'm sorry but the thought makes me feel sick.'

'There's really nothing to worry about,' reassured Pearson. 'I'll be heading up the press conference, we can help Kit prepare an appeal and he can speak. If you can say anything too, that would be great, but if not, we still really need you there.'

'What the detective is trying to say,' interjected Kit, 'is that it will look bloody odd to the press if you don't put in an appearance. Like you don't care, or you've got something to hide and then the press will be all over that and not focus on what they are supposed to be, i.e. finding Poppy. You going AWOL won't help at all.'

The detective didn't correct Kit and Neve realised that to dig her heels in now would be a mistake. Of course, finding Poppy must be the priority and if her absence at the press conference only sparked more interest in Neve, then her determination to stay out of the limelight would only be counterproductive.

'I'm sorry. I'm being silly. Of course, I'll attend. Anything to help find Poppy.'

'Thank you,' said Kit. He went over and pulled her in for a hug. Neve thought it was more for his benefit than for hers. She returned the hug and hoped she generated the same warmth that she was receiving.

'Any news on the bloke from The Forum?' asked Kit.

'We're still making enquiries,' said Pearson.

Neve felt her body stiffen at the evasive answer. She wanted to ask exactly what that meant, but Kit beat her to it.

'But you've found out who it is? You've spoken to him?'

'We've still got a couple more support workers to speak to. We've left messages for them to contact us,' said Pearson.

'That all sounds rather casual,' said Kit, his arms slipping from Neve.

She reached out and held his hand. 'Just let the police do their job,' she said. 'We need to concentrate on what we can do to help.'

'Neve is right,' said Pearson. 'Focus on the press conference. Sally will help you prepare a statement.' He stood up. 'I'll see you at the station later.'

Kit wasn't entirely happy with the DCI's response and spent most of the day grumbling about it. Neve gave up trying to reason with him, especially as she became increasingly more preoccupied with the press conference.

Neve looked through her wardrobe for something suitable to wear. Pearson had advised that they shouldn't wear anything too formal, that he wanted them to appeal to as wide an audience as possible. He didn't want them to come across as middle class and unmoved.

She took out a black dress from the wardrobe and held it up. 'Too formal?'

'It's not a bloody funeral,' said Kit.

She heard the words catch in his throat and could see the pain etched into every line on his face. Lines that she hadn't noticed before. Had they always been there or had the stress of the last twenty-four hours dug deep into him, showing itself by ravaging his usual good looks?

'I'll just wear this blouse and jeans,' said Neve, slotting the dress back into the wardrobe and removing a white blouse with a pale blue dragonfly print. Smart but casual. 'What are you going to wear?'

'Casual shirt and jeans too,' said Kit. He sat heavily on the edge of the bed. 'Jesus, it's like we're going out for a drink with friends or something. Never did I think I'd be deciding what to wear for a press conference because my daughter was missing. How did we let this happen? How did we let her disappear? Or ... be taken?' He held his hands to his face and slumped forwards.

Neve sat next to him, putting her arm around his shoulders. She didn't know what to say. How could she comfort him?

As if reminding her that life goes on for everyone else, her mobile pinged a message alert. With her arm still round Kit, she reached with her other hand for her phone. It was from Jake. Kit hadn't even bothered to look up. She swiped the screen and the message disappeared. She would read it later.

Neve rested her head on Kit's shoulder. It was true what they said, that a life changing event, something serious, and of course a child's disappearance was one of the most serious things, made you reflect on your life and realise what was

161

Sue Fortin

important. Family was important. Loving was important and being loved was important. Neve wondered if this would change things between herself and Kit. Would it make Kit see things differently? Could they pull through this and become a better couple than the one they started out as yesterday morning? Would this make things right?

Of course, she couldn't answer these questions, but she promised herself that when they came through this, in whatever shape or form, that she would plough all her efforts into her marriage. Jake wasn't the answer. She wasn't going to run off into the sunset with her art tutor on the promise of happiness and a baby. What she wanted, what she'd always wanted, was a baby with Kit. It was up to her to make that happen.

In the meantime, she had other things to worry about. Like this press conference. 'Come on, Kit, we need to get ready,' Neve said. She kissed the top of his head, a gesture that he had often done to her in the past. She felt his grip tighten for a moment.

'Thank you,' he said, looking at her, his lapis blue eyes full of sincerity. 'I don't know what I'd do without you.'

They dressed in silence, each lost in their own thoughts. Neve stole a glance at Kit. His shoulders were hunched, and his six foot frame was stooped in defeat. The pain had spread from his face to his body. She didn't think she had ever seen him look so dejected and downtrodden. Neve wondered if he was like this when his first wife had died. He had come back from that. She hoped he could come back from this too.

She picked up her dark sunglasses and put them on, turning to look at herself in the mirror, contemplating

162

whether she could justify wearing them to the press conference.

'No,' said Kit, shaking his head. 'You look more like some celebrity recovering from a hangover.'

Neve took them off and turned to look at him. He was standing tall now, adjusting his jacket on his shoulders. He was back in control of himself. 'Yeah, you're right,' she said.

'You rocking up like you've just been to an all-night party isn't going to help win the public's support. We want everyone out there sympathising with us, wanting to help us.'

'I know. I get it,' said Neve. There was no hiding anywhere now. She was going to be in full sight of the press and her face plastered all over the country. It was like a nightmare, but she knew she couldn't get out of it.

The press conference was every bit as horrendous as Neve had thought it would be. They were briefed by the DCI what would happen. He would introduce them and give the press details of Poppy. Neve and Kit had been asked to provide a recent photograph of Poppy which the police had used on the posters. There was going to be a call for volunteers to help search the surrounding areas and they were going to dredge the river. Something that caused Kit to close his eyes and lift his head up to the ceiling, whilst swallowing hard. Neve held his hand, sending what she hoped was both moral and physical support.

Pearson told them it would then be their turn to read out the statement the FLO, Sally, had helped prepare.

'We would really like you to say something too,' said Pearson and reluctantly Neve had agreed.

Now entering the room, facing a bank of photographers

with their cameras, microphones and voice recorders, Neve could feel her whole body begin to shake. This time it was Kit who held her hand and offered strength through a gentle squeeze. They took their seats and a hush descended upon the room.

'Good afternoon,' began the detective. 'Thank you for coming. We are currently searching for fourteen-year-old Poppy Masters, who was last seen …'

Neve found herself tuning out to his words as she kept her head bowed and her grip on Kit's hand. The cameras clicked as the detective spoke. The noise got louder and louder. The click-click, click-click of the shutters filled the room and Neve could no longer hear what Pearson was saying. She slid her free hand up to her ear, and under the cover of her hair, she pushed against the ear, trying to block the deafening click-click sound.

She didn't know how long she sat like that for but suddenly she was aware of Kit speaking. Neve raised her eyes just enough to see his left hand shaking ever so slightly as he held the paper with his pre-prepared words.

'We are appealing to anyone who has seen Poppy to get in contact with the police. Poppy is a vulnerable young teen, who we desperately want home safe and well as soon as possible …' His voice cracked, and Neve heard him gulp before carrying on. 'If anyone has seen her or even *thinks* they have seen her, please, please get in touch with the police. It doesn't matter how insignificant or how unsure, just let the local police know. We desperately want Poppy back. Thank you.'

He stopped talking and offered Neve the piece of paper. She had only two lines to say but felt herself freeze up. She couldn't take the paper. Kit gave it a little shake. This time Neve looked fully up at Kit and could see so much angst in his eyes, she knew she couldn't let him down. With trepidation, she took the piece of paper from her husband and began to read out loud.

'Poppy, darling, if you're watching this, know how much we love you and we are doing everything we can to find you. We love you very much.' Neve couldn't say any more, she gave one glance up to the press which sent the click-clack of the shutters into overdrive as they took what sounded like hundreds of photographs. Kit put an arm around her and they leaned into each other, their heads resting together. Another flurry of shutters opening and closing rapidly filled the room before DCI Pearson was thanking the press and a colleague was handing out flyers with Poppy's face smiling out at them and the word MISSING in bold red capital letters emblazoned across the top.

As Neve gazed at the stack of flyers on the edge of the table, the picture of Poppy seemed to come alive, but it distorted and morphed into another face. Another girl. A younger girl. She was only three. Everyone was looking for her. The flyer no longer said Poppy. Instead the name Jasmine stood out.

Neve felt her head roll and as she tried to refocus, all she could see was a long dark tunnel ahead. There was a circular light at the end, but it was getting smaller and smaller. The tunnel sides grew and grew, drawing her into darkness until the light disappeared and she was swallowed up whole.

Chapter 18

Neve heard the voices first and felt the cold compress on her head. Her eyes flickered open and she saw snatches of faces, fading in and out. She could hear Kit's voice. Soft and then louder.

'Neve? Neve, you OK?'

She could feel her hand being held and knew, without having to look, that it was Kit. The smooth texture of his skin and the long-boned piano playing fingers. She opened her eyes again and this time, they stayed open. Gradually, Kit's concerned face came into focus.

There was a smell of strong coffee and Neve turned her head to the side, where a plastic cup was sitting on a low rectangular table. The smell turned her stomach.

'What happened?' she asked, shuffling herself into a sitting position. She was on a black leather-look sofa in a small room which was trying hard to imitate a comfortable sitting room, but the water filter machine and fire regulation notice gave it away. She was in the family room of the police station where she and Kit had sat earlier waiting to go into the press conference.

'You fainted,' said Kit. 'Out there at the end of the press

conference. I managed to catch you and take you out before the press really knew what was going on.'

'I'm sorry,' said Neve, bringing her hand to cover her face.

'Hey, it's OK,' said Kit. 'It's you I'm worried about. The duty doctor is coming to check on you.'

'I'm fine,' Neve said quickly, alarmed at the fuss she was causing. She sat up further and swung her feet round to the floor to demonstrate her recovery. 'I promise. It was just a bit hot in there.'

'Just humour us,' said DCI Pearson. 'I wouldn't be doing my job properly if I let you walk out of here without the doc looking at you.'

'It doesn't look like I have much choice,' said Neve.

'You've never fainted before,' said Kit.

'I've never been in a press conference before,' said Neve and then seeing the hurt look on Kit's face, she changed her approach. 'Sorry. I just feel a bit embarrassed, that's all. I hope the press don't make a big deal out of it, they need to concentrate on helping us find Poppy.'

The doctor arrived and after checking Neve's pulse and listening to her heart, she convinced him that she was OK and promised to see her GP if anything like that happened again.

Once again, there was an unmarked police car waiting to whisk them away from a few journalists who were waiting outside.

'I'm afraid there are rather a lot of press camped outside your house,' said Sally, their FLO. 'It's best not to say anything though. They'll be asking you all sorts of questions, just ignore them. Let us deal with it.'

'I don't want to go home if that's the case,' said Neve.

'Don't worry. Just go straight indoors.'

Twenty minutes later, they were pulling into Long Acre Lane and Neve was even more dismayed when she saw the press lining the road. The gate to the driveway was closed and a uniformed police officer was standing outside. He exchanged a nod with the driver and then opened the gate.

As they stepped out of the car, Kit hurried around the back and put a protective arm across Neve's shoulders as they both scurried indoors. Immediately, Neve went into the living room and closed the wooden blinds to the window which overlooked the front garden.

'Why are they waiting out here? Why aren't they doing something else?' she said, slumping in to the sofa.

'These days they can do the report from anywhere they are. It's all sent electronically. They're just camped outside now, waiting for a development,' explained Sally.

'Can't you tell them to clear off?' said Kit. 'In fact, I've got a good mind to go out there myself.'

'No. Don't do that,' said Sally. 'That really won't help. They're on our side, remember? We want them to keep Poppy in the headlines and we can do that all the time they're on our side. We can feed them titbits of info. Keep them sweet. We need them as much as they need us.'

'I don't know if I can cope with all this,' said Kit.

'We have to,' said Neve. 'We don't have any choice. I'll make us a coffee.' She turned to Sally. 'When will the news conference go out?'

'Local radio is covering it and so is the local TV. It's going on the national six o'clock news too.'

'Any developments on the search?' asked Kit, taking his jacket off and slinging it onto the armchair.

'Nothing yet. They're searching further along the riverbank today and in the neighbouring fields.'

'I should be out there,' said Kit.

'You're best here,' said Sally. 'In case Poppy turns up here somehow. It's not a good idea for parents to be involved in the search. Look, I'll check in with my sergeant and see if there's any news, but I'm sure we would have heard if there was.'

Neve wondered if Sally was just placating Kit for now. As she went out to the kitchen, her mobile vibrated in her pocket. She had muted it earlier because of the press conference. Neve looked at the screen and wasn't surprised to see Jake's name flash up. She pushed the kitchen door closed and opened the messages, the first being from earlier, asking if she was OK and now a second one.

Any news? Thinking of you. Xx

Neve tapped a quick reply.

No news. I'm fine.

Jake must have been sitting waiting for her to answer as he replied straight away.

I'm here if you need me. xx

Neve sighed. Dear sweet Jake. He was a good man. If things had been different, if she wasn't in the middle of this right now, she would probably have taken him up on his offer. But in the midst of all this angst and upset, Kit seemed to be changing. He was being stripped bare in front of her. His emotions exposed. He was vulnerable. He needed her, and she couldn't abandon him now. Not now. Things had changed. There had been a shift. The fault line that was once running through their marriage had stopped expanding, maybe even closed a little. She hoped she could get Kit back, and once this was all over, they could be the family she so desired.

'How's that tea coming on?'

Sally's sudden appearance in the kitchen made Neve jump and she dropped her phone. It hit the tiled floor. 'Shit!' Neve bent down to pick it up.

'Sorry. It's not broken is it?'

Neve inspected the phone and fortunately, the protective case had done its job. 'No, it's fine,' she said, slipping it back into her pocket. She busied herself with filling the kettle and putting it on to boil, before preparing the cups. Sally being there made her feel uneasy and Neve wished there was a radio she could put on to fill the awkward atmosphere.

'Everything OK?' asked Sally, as if sensing Neve's unease.

Neve stopped what she was doing. 'OK aside from my daughter being missing? Bit of a stupid question.' She couldn't help herself snapping at the FLO. She wished Sally would just clear off.

Sally nodded towards Neve's pocket. 'I meant your text message. You seem jumpy.'

Neve snatched the phone from her pocket and held it out to Sally. 'Want to read? It's my art tutor. He knows about Poppy and was checking to see if there was any news. As for being jumpy, it's hardly surprising with you creeping up on me and quizzing me about text messages.'

'I don't need to read it, Neve. I was just asking.'

They both looked at the phone for a moment and Neve was silently grateful for Sally's response. The words of the text were innocent enough, but the two kisses Jake had put at the end might be a little harder to explain. Neve put the phone into her pocket once again. 'This whole thing is making me jumpy,' she said in a more conciliatory tone. 'I can't help thinking it's another night and we still don't seem to be any closer to finding Poppy. I mean, what the hell is going on? Where is she?'

'I know how frustrating and upsetting it can be but, I promise you, we are doing everything we can to find her.'

'Are you? Look, you can tell me, I won't say anything to Kit, I promise, but what really is happening?'

'Honestly, Neve, there is nothing to tell. I don't know any more than you do,' said Sally, walking over to the now boiled kettle and pouring the water into the cups.

'Are you staying here tonight?' asked Neve.

'Only if you want me to, but I'd need to OK the overtime with my boss and sort out a babysitter.'

Neve looked at Sally, who shifted awkwardly. 'It's OK,' said Neve. 'You can mention children.'

'Sorry, I didn't think,' said Sally.

'How many have you got?' Neve was genuinely interested. Up until this point, Sally had just been a police officer but behind the uniform there was another person. A woman. A mother.

'Two boys. Twins. They're seven.'

'Ah, lovely. Who's looking after them?'

'My mum. My husband's in the force too. We try to work it that our shifts don't clash but it's not always the way.' Sally put the kettle down and fished out her phone from the side-zip on her jacket. She scrolled through the pictures and then turned it to Neve. 'That's Kai and that's Aiden.'

'Gorgeous. You're so lucky to have twins.'

Sally gave a laugh. 'You wouldn't say that when it's Christmas and birthdays. Or when they're fighting with each other.'

'But the rewards outweigh all that, surely?'

This time Sally smiled, and Neve could see the love she had for her boys.

'Absolutely,' confirmed Sally. 'You and Kit didn't have children, then?'

'No. We agreed not to have any. Not with Poppy needing so much care.'

'Really? I thought she was quite high functioning. That's what Kit said.'

'She is but only to the ability of a ten-year-old. She still needs a lot of looking after,' Neve explained, dropping two sweeteners into her husband's coffee. 'It was Kit's idea really. He didn't want another child. Not after what happened. His first wife died in childbirth and Poppy suffered from a lack of oxygen to the brain.'

'That must be hard on you? I'm not sure I could take on someone else's child, at the expense of having one of my own. That doesn't bother you, no?'

Sally was fishing, Neve decided. She was still in police officer mode, despite the dampener of showing Neve the photo of her kids. Neve wondered if they were even Sally's

172

children. She might just be using a random picture to lure Neve into a false sense of security. To make it feel they had something in common so she would confide in Sally. Female solidarity and all that. Well, Neve wasn't going to drop her guard, she was wise to it.

'No, I don't mind,' she lied. 'We talked about it before we got married. I totally understand and support Kit's reasons.'

'You're a better woman than I am,' replied Sally.

It took enormous effort on Neve's part to continue the conversation in a civil tone. She didn't trust Sally. Neve was sure she had an ulterior motive to spy on them, to try to trip them up in case either of them were involved in Poppy's disappearance.

It was another thirty minutes before Sally left and, much to Neve's relief, the press appeared to have given up for the day and decamped from outside. Neve watched Sally pull out of the driveway and the police officer standing on duty outside closed the gate behind her.

'Thank goodness for that,' said Neve, going into the living room where Kit was sitting near the window.

'She was only doing her job,' says Kit.

'I know, but I didn't like her in the house. I felt like she was spying on us. Judging us.'

'How do you mean?'

'She started showing me pictures of her kids and then managed to get the conversation round to why we didn't have any together.'

Kit raised his eyebrows. 'You don't think she was genuinely interested?'

Neve shook her head. 'Don't think so.'

'I knew this would happen!' Kit paced back and forth across the window. 'Next thing we'll have social services round here again. In fact, I'm surprised they haven't been here already, going on past history.'

He let out a cry, almost a growl, of frustration and kicked the side of the armchair, before falling to his knees. Neve rushed over to him, crouching beside him, her arm across his hunched shoulders.

'Oh, Kit,' she whispered, rubbing her hand up and down his back in an attempt to both comfort and soothe him.

'I don't know if I can cope with all this.' His shoulders heaved, and he gave a muffled sob.

Neve didn't say anything this time. What could she say? All she could do was to be there for him. It was another minute or so before Kit calmed himself down.

'I'm so sorry,' he said, straightening up. He fished out a handkerchief from his pocket, blew his nose and wiped his eyes. 'I think I'm losing it.'

'I do understand your pain,' said Neve. 'I know this may sound a bit odd, but I understand how it feels to want something that is out of your reach. You want Poppy back, we both do, but there's nothing we can do to influence that. We've got to sit tight, stick together and try to come through this.'

'I'd do anything, absolutely anything, to have Poppy back safe and unharmed,' said Kit. 'I'd literally give my life if it came to it.'

'I know. I do understand.'

'Do you? Can you really understand what it's like? You're not a ...'

His voice trailed off. Maybe because he could see the anger and hurt flash across Neve's face. 'I'm not a what?' she demanded, standing up, hands on her hips. 'Go on, say it. I'm not a mother so I can't possibly understand what you're going through.'

'I didn't mean it like that,' he protested.

'Don't lie! Of course, you did. That's exactly what you meant.'

Kit gave a shake of his head. 'I didn't mean to hurt you.'

Neve was hurt. More than he could imagine. 'Whose fault is it, that I'm not a parent?' Neve shouted at him. 'Certainly not my fault. You're the one who doesn't want any more children. You're the one who refuses to let me have a baby of my own.'

'And for good reason!' He shouted back at Neve. Kit hardly ever shouted. It was not in his nature to lose control so much.

In a strange way, it made Neve feel powerful. She had the ability to evoke that much emotion from him. It was a new sensation for her and she had to admit, in some perverse way, she quite liked it.

Kit slumped onto the sofa, his head in his hands, his elbows propped on his knees. He was muttering sorry again. Over and over. 'Neve, I'm sorry. That was uncalled for. I'm so sorry. I don't mean it. I love you. I need you.'

'Don't push me away,' she said softly, coming over to sit beside him.

'I just want Poppy home.'

'So do I,' said Neve. It was true, she did want Poppy home, but she felt a shifting of control between them and she didn't want to compromise that just yet.

Later that night, when they were in bed, side by side, their hands entwined in each other's, Neve tried to find some order in her jumble of thoughts. It was hard to keep up with Kit's mood-swings. She knew he was suffering, deeply suffering. She was trying to comfort him, but it was almost as if by giving into his raw emotions, he then had to make up for the exposure and over-compensate by going the other way.

Kit's breathing changed as he slipped into sleep. Neve looked over at him in the light of the bedside lamp. At least he was resting and for a moment the strain had lifted from his face. A small vibration on the bedside table took her attention away from Kit. Neve looked at her phone.

Am thinking of you. Xx

Neve smiled at the message, acknowledging the flicker of warmth that rose in her heart but also the drop that followed. She deleted the message without replying.

Chapter 19

Day three of Poppy being missing and Neve awoke to an empty bed. Unsurprisingly, neither one of them was sleeping, simply getting by on an hour here and an hour there. Neve reached for her phone and checked Twitter for any news of Poppy. Prior to this she didn't have any form of social media and had set up a Twitter account under a fake name. The original post now had over four hundred retweets. Neve scrolled down the replies.

Julie Kay @JulesK68
We are praying for Poppy's safe return.
#schoolgirlmissing

Bev Markham @Bevvers
Have shared. Hope you find her safe and well #findPoppy
#schoolgirlmissing

FelixChelseaBlood @ChelseaBloodBoy
Every parent's worst nightmare. #schoolgirlmissing
#missing

Jimmy Logan @LogansRun
Is this the kid from the special school. Parents should look after her better

Julie Kay @JulesK68
Replying to @LogansRun
She is 14. You can't keep a teenager under lock and key.

Jimmy Logan @LogansRun
Replying to @JulesK68
But the kids got special needs. I stand by what I said. Parents fault.

Julie Kay @JulesK68
Replying to @LogansRun
I hope this never happens to you or anyone you care about.

Sara James @Saraaaaaaaa-no-h
Replying to @LogansRun @JulesK8
Jumping in here. Kids with special needs still have rights like any other teenager. #equalrights #schoolgirlmissing

Terry Hadwell @Tel_1955
Replying to @LogansRun @JulesK8 @Saraaaaaaaa-no-h
It's just the dad who is the parent. His wife is stepmum. She collapsed at the press conference. Bit over the top if you ask me.

Sara James @Saraaaaaaaa-no-h
Replying to @Tel_1955 @LogansRun @JulesK8
She adopted Poppy so is her mother. You don't have to
be birth mother to be a proper mother. #schoolgirlmissing

Jimmy Logan @LogansRun
Replying to @Tel_1955 @JulesK8 @Saraaaaaaaa-no-h
Crocodile tears? Dad seemed very calm. Shifty looking.

Terry Hadwell @Tel_1955
Replying to @LogansRun @JulesK8 @Saraaaaaaaa-no-h
Wouldn't be the first time. More likely to be someone the
victim knows than a stranger.

Julie Kay @JulesK68
Replying to @LogansRun Terry Hadwell @Tel_1955 @Saraaaaaaaa-no-h
Stop speculating. You're diverting attention from finding
Poppy. #schoolgirlmissing #findPoppy

Neve closed the app. She'd read enough. She didn't need people
like LogansRun spouting righteous tweets when they knew
nothing about what was really going on.

Neve went downstairs where Kit was already in the living
room occupying his usual spot by the front window, with a
coffee cup in one hand and his mobile in the other with
Facebook open.

'Any news?' asked Neve, nodding towards the phone.

'No. Lots of shares and good wishes,' said Kit. 'But nothing.

No one has seen her. It's like she's disappeared off the face of the earth.' His face crumpled and he looked away out of the window. 'Do you think today will be the day?'

'I hope so. All we can do is hope.'

'I'll never take anything for granted again,' said Kit. 'All this has made me realise how precious you and Poppy are to me,' he continued. 'I've been a shit husband of late and a crap father. I've been bogged down with work, fixated on making and breaking deals. I lost sight of what's important to me.'

'We're all guilty of that,' Neve said.

He turned to her. 'No. You're not. It's me. I have been an inconsiderate and selfish man and if nothing else comes of this God-awful situation, I promise you, I will be a changed man.' He looked at her intently. 'From now on, I will always put yours and Poppy's needs ahead of mine. Whatever they are.'

For a moment Neve wanted to believe him. He looked so sincere and his words were so full of passion – of hope and despair, all at the same time. And perhaps, in that moment, Kit really believed it too. Neve wasn't so sure that would be the case when Poppy was found. Would he still want to make her happy, to put her needs first? It would be a big turnaround for Kit and she wasn't sure if he could see it through. She wanted to believe him, she truly did, but there was an element of doubt.

'I mean it,' Kit spoke as if reading her mind. 'I'd give anything to have Poppy back. Anything. I'll do whatever it takes when she's home, I'll do whatever it takes to make us happy again.'

'Anything?' Neve ventured. She looked into his eyes. He must know what she was asking. She didn't push the point. It wasn't the time and she lowered her gaze. Maybe deep down in her heart she knew he was not quite ready to commit to another child. Nearly, but not quite. She couldn't help wondering what would have to happen to make him change his mind.

'Oh, shit,' said Kit, looking out of the window. 'It's Sally. I wish she didn't have to come and sit round here all day with us. I feel I'm being watched all the time. Like I'm being scrutinised.'

'I know what you mean, but she's just doing her job,' said Neve, going across the hallway. 'Maybe she'll have news.'

'Oh, and look who else is here. DCI Pearson.'

'Good morning,' said Neve, opening the door wide and stepping aside. 'Come in.'

Greetings over with, DCI Pearson stood in the living room, flanked by Sally. 'I'm afraid I haven't got any news on Poppy's whereabouts. We've had a couple of sightings that we're following up.'

'Sightings?' said Kit. 'Where? By who?'

'In Little Bury, where you moored up, a taxi driver thought he saw two teenage girls walking along the road to Lower Bury. One matching Poppy's description.'

'Two girls?' said Neve. 'You think Poppy went off with someone?'

'We're looking into all possibilities. Did she know anyone in the village? Anyone from school maybe?'

Neve exchanged a blank look with Kit. 'Not as far as we

are aware,' she said. 'Not from Lower Bury. She goes to school at St Joseph's.'

'We're checking with the school anyway and I have two officers going door-to-door in the village. It could be a case of mistaken identity.'

'You said there were two sightings?' said Kit.

'Yes, the other was in town in the suburbs. Hostead area. Again, two people, one of them a teenager, walking along Meridian Street.'

'The same girls?' asked Neve.

'Again, we're not sure.'

'For fuck's sake,' said Kit. 'Have you got officers down there looking for her?'

'We have, Mr Masters. As we speak, they're also going door-to-door and handing out leaflets in the area of Meridian Street. It's mostly residential down there but one or two of the small shops have CCTV, so we're checking that too.'

'It's just taking so long. I don't know how she can manage out there on her own,' said Kit. 'Is everything, and I mean absolutely everything, being done to find her? If it's money, we can pay. We have savings. I'll get a loan, remortgage the house, anything ...'

'Mr Masters, Kit, please be assured we are piling every resource into finding your daughter. I promise you. Every lead is being followed up and then followed up again.' Pearson gave Neve a sympathetic smile which she thought was meant to be reassuring.

'Have you found anything on her laptop?' Neve asked. 'Anything that might say where she's gone or what she's doing?'

Pearson shook his head. 'No. I'm sorry, nothing there.'

'We kept a close eye on her when she was on her laptop,' said Kit. 'She is too vulnerable to be allowed on social media.'

'There's nothing there. You don't have to worry about that,' said the DCI. 'There is something else. We've tracked down the man you saw with your daughter earlier in the week. It's Lee Farnham. He's a support worker at The Forum.'

Neve's heart gave an extra thump at this piece of news. She wondered how far into the past the DCI would dig. The police wouldn't necessarily be looking for the connection but there was always the chance they'd find it. She flicked a glance at Kit.

'Bloody knew it! Had to be someone from The Forum. Have you spoken to him?' Kit asked.

'When there's something to report back, we'll let you know.'

Kit shook his head in frustration. 'Why is everything taking so long!'

Neve got the feeling that Pearson was here for another reason as, basically, other than identifying Lee Farnham, he had nothing to tell them. No solid leads or information, just a couple of possible sightings.

'Would you like a coffee or a tea?' Neve asked, as a way of testing whether he wanted to hang around or whether this was merely a PR exercise.

'That would be nice. Thank you,' said Pearson. 'Coffee. White. Two sugars. I'll give you a hand actually.'

'Won't be a minute,' said Neve, leaving the room with Pearson following.

'Actually, there is something I wanted to quickly ask you

while you're on your own,' said Pearson, perching on the bar stool. 'It's about Jake Rees.'

'My art therapy teacher?' Neve maintained eye contact but felt herself blink several times as she tried to push aside her feelings of guilt.

'Yes. That's right.'

'What do you want to know?'

Pearson glanced back towards the door. 'I'll get straight to the point and please don't be offended, but I have to ask these questions for the purpose of my enquiry.'

Neve continued to prepare the coffee. 'Go ahead.'

'Can you tell me about your relationship with Jake?'

Neve balked at the question. She'd been expecting the DCI to say he'd made the connection between her and Lee. As for Jake, it was a friendship, that's all, just a close friendship. Thinking of having an affair with someone, wasn't the same as actually doing it.

'Jake? There's nothing to tell. He's my art tutor, that's all. Why?'

'We're just trying to build up a picture of all the people who know Poppy and how they relate to Poppy and Poppy's family. When I spoke to Mr Rees earlier, call it intuition from doing this job far too long, but I got the distinct feeling Mr Rees thinks a lot of you. I don't mean to be rude, but I have to ask these things.'

'Jake and I are very good friends,' said Neve, resting against the worktop. 'He's helped me a lot.'

'With art therapy?'

'Yes.'

'And what, may I ask, is the therapy in relation to?'

'Well, I'd sooner you didn't ask actually but, if you must know, it's to do with the estranged relationship I have with my family. It's complicated.'

'Estranged from your family?'

He said it in a tone that was asking Neve to elaborate. She had absolutely no intention of obliging. Instead, she settled for something far less dramatic than the truth. 'My parents divorced, and I didn't see my father for a long time. And then it was just the once before my mother died. I have issues over abandonment.'

Pearson nodded and for the time being seemed content to leave it there. Outwardly, Neve tried to maintain a composed front, but inwardly, she could feel her stomach squirming as if it was a pot full of eels.

'The coffee's ready. Do you want to take yours through?' said Neve, passing Pearson his cup.

Neve watched him cross the hall and go into the living room before following with a coffee for Kit. As she crossed the hall, the letterbox gave a small rattle and three envelopes fell onto the mat. Neve put the cup on the hall table and picked up the letters, flicking through them as she did so. Two looked like household bills but the other was hand-written with a stamp in the corner, addressed to Kit. She peered at the postmark and as she made out the words, her heart almost leapt out of her throat. She didn't have time to think it through properly, but quickly folded the white envelope in half and shoved it into her back pocket. Trying to remain calm, Neve retrieved the cup of coffee from the table and with the other letters in her other hand, joined Kit and the police officers in the living room.

'Anything exciting?' asked Sally, nodding towards the brown envelopes in Neve's hand.

'No. Just bills.'

Neve could hear Kit questioning Pearson again on what the next phase of the search would be. He seemed determined to join in the search party, telling Pearson that he was not sitting around doing nothing. Neve sighed inwardly – poor Kit. It was becoming something of a mantra.

She listened as the DCI patiently went over the plan of action again and made a very persuasive argument for Kit not being involved in the search for Poppy. Finally, Kit agreed.

'I'm sorry,' he said. 'It's the not knowing. It's killing me.'

'Perfectly understandable,' said Pearson. 'But as I say, you're best off at home, in case you're needed for anything. That way, we can get hold of you quickly.'

After seeing Pearson out, Neve left Kit and Sally in the living room and went upstairs, shutting the bedroom door behind her.

Taking the letter from her pocket, she examined the seal, wondering if there was a way she could open it secretly. Maybe steaming it open? It worked in the movies. The sound of the door opening and Kit walking in, made Neve jump. She tried to stuff the letter back in her pocket.

'Don't bother,' said Kit, nodding towards Neve's hand. 'Want to share with me?'

'What?'

'Oh, come on, Neve. I saw you through the crack of the door, picking those letters up and slipping one into your pocket.'

Neve felt herself go red. She held out the letter to her husband.

Kit inspected the front of the envelope and then sliding his finger under the flap, opened the letter. He extracted a single sheet of paper and read it.

'What the ...?'

Chapter 20

'What is it?' asked Neve, although something told her she wasn't going to like the answer.

Kit thrust the letter to her. 'You'd better read it.'

In bold black letters, printed from a computer, she read the message.

Saw you and your wife on TV.
   Your daughter is missing, huh?
   Maybe you should look a bit closer to home.
   They say history has a habit of repeating itself.

'What does that mean?'

'I've no idea.' Kit took the letter back. 'Look a bit closer to home. History repeating itself. It's obviously to do with Poppy. It's like someone knows what's happened to her.'

'Why would someone do that?' said Neve, noticing the tremor in her own voice. 'Is this some sort of sick joke?'

'I don't know,' said Kit. 'We need to show this to Sally.'

'Do you think that's a good idea?'

'Of course it is, why wouldn't it be?'

'I'm just thinking what if it's some nutter who saw us on the TV?' Neve placed a hand on her husband's arm. 'That's why I didn't want to do the press conference. I read somewhere that it causes more problems than it solves. That it attracts psychos.'

'You think this is from some lunatic?'

'I don't know but what if the police do look closer to home? The police might think we're involved with Poppy's disappearance.' Neve could hardly disguise the desperation in her voice. *History repeating itself. Look closer to home.* Those words were definitely aimed at her.

'No, wait. You're looking at it all wrong. Why the hell would the police think we're involved?'

'Because, like you said, they always suspect those closest to the missing person. I looked it up online afterwards. The police are advised to think of a missing person as an indicator that something isn't right at home,' said Neve, in hushed tones. 'Why do you think Sally has been here with us most of the time? It's not to relay any information, she knows nothing and if there was something to tell, the DCI would tell us. No, she's here to spy on us.'

'I don't know what to think anymore,' said Kit. 'I know I said the same thing before, but now, I'm sure if they thought we were involved, we'd already know. All that talk, it's paranoia.'

'I'm not being paranoid, I'm just being careful.'

'Look, Neve,' Kit's voice was even, but firm at the same time. 'I'm going to put this down to you being as stressed about Poppy going missing as I am but you're not thinking straight. We have nothing to do with it. We shouldn't have to try to protect ourselves. The police don't suspect us. This could be vital in finding Poppy and if we don't tell the police, then who knows what they will think when eventually it comes out that we've received a note?' He waved the piece of paper in his hand. 'Poppy being found is far more important than us not being suspected.'

Neve allowed her arm to drop. 'I'm sorry. You're right – I'm not thinking straight at all. Of course, we must tell the police.'

She followed Kit out of the bedroom and down the stairs.

'You should look at this,' said Kit, going into the kitchen where Sally was now pouring herself a drink. He put the piece of paper down on the worktop. 'It came through the door just now.'

Neve stood in the doorway as Sally read the note and reread it. 'It came just now?' she asked.

'Yes. Neve picked it up.'

'Have you got the envelope?'

'It came with the other post,' explained Neve.

Kit passed the envelope over to the FLO, who checked the postmark.

'Newport?'

'Do either of you have any idea what it means or who could have sent it?' asked Sally.

'None,' said Kit.

Sally looked at Neve. 'You're from Wales. Could it be from someone you know?'

Neve shrugged. 'It's possible but I've no idea who. Or even if it would be someone I used to know. It could be anyone, a complete stranger, who just happens to live in Newport.' It was more than possible, in fact, it was highly likely but Neve wasn't going to give Sally any hint of fears.

'Bit of a coincidence,' said Sally, looking at the letter again. 'OK, I'll let the DCI know. We'll take this down to the station and have a closer look at it.' Sally took the note and went outside.

Neve turned to Kit. 'See what I mean? She's made the call away from us. She doesn't want us to hear what she's saying. Why would she do that if she was being completely open and honest with us?'

'You're letting your imagination run away with you,' said Kit, resuming what was becoming his usual post by the living room window. He tipped the blinds with his fingers. 'Poppy ... where are you?' he whispered. He looked haggard. In the light of the window, his eyes looked blacker underneath the puffy bags which had appeared in the last few days. His face looked thinner, as if someone had taken an ice cream scoop to his cheeks.

Neve stood beside her husband and slipped her arm into his. She didn't know what to say. Words seemed inadequate. She thought of the note. To Kit and the police, the meaning was unclear. To Neve, it was perfectly clear. As to the sender, well, it could be one of several. If it hadn't been postmarked Newport, she might have blamed Lee for it.

She sifted through the possibilities. Scott, her ex-husband, Lisa, her sister-in-law and an outside bet, her brother, Gareth. It hurt her to think that one of them would stoop that low, would want to upset her by implying she was involved with

Poppy's disappearance. If they wanted to exact some sort of revenge for what had happened, why wait until now? Why hadn't they told Kit before? It had to be an opportunistic moment, surely.

Whatever the reasons, Neve knew that if Kit was to find out, he wouldn't understand. It would be the end of her marriage, and no marriage meant no baby.

The morning limped by and Kit became increasingly agitated having to wait around while the police carried out yet another search of the area. When Sean called by soon after ten o'clock, Neve was relieved to see him. The tension in the house was becoming unbearable. Every room felt claustrophobic. Neve hadn't been able to settle and she roamed around the house, desperate for some relief.

'Hello, Sean,' said Kit.

'Kit. Neve.' Sean shook hands with Kit and gave Neve a fleeting peck on the cheek. 'Neve said it was driving you nuts sitting around the house.' He thrust a wad of A5 flyers towards Kit. 'I got these printed out. I thought you might be able to put some up in the town and other villages. Thought it might give you something to do.'

'Ah, cheers, mate,' said Kit. 'I appreciate that.'

Sean gave one of the flyers to Neve to look at. It tugged at her heart. Poppy's smiling face, taken at a garden party the firm had thrown last month. She looked happy, just the way Neve thought of her.

'These are better than the police ones,' she said. 'Poppy looks more natural.'

'Yeah, that's what I was thinking,' said Kit. He stifled the sob in his throat that followed.

'Thanks, Sean,' said Neve.

'It's the least I can do,' said Sean.

'I wanted to join in the search, but they won't let me,' said Kit.

'It's for the best, mate,' said Sean. 'Look, I've got the morning free, I can drive you around, if you like? We could get some of these flyers pinned up.'

'That would be great,' said Kit. 'I can't tell you how sitting around the house all day is getting to me. I think I'm going to go fucking crazy. I need to be doing something.'

'I could hand some out in the town,' said Neve.

'On your own? Perhaps Mum could go with you,' said Kit. 'I'll give her a call. At least that way she'll feel like she's helping.'

Neve managed to stop herself from protesting. An afternoon with Cheryl wasn't something she would look forward to but if it kept the peace ... Some things weren't worth arguing about, not at a time like this anyway.

'I'll give Lucie a ring,' replied Neve, opting for reinforcements. 'She texted me yesterday and offered to help in any way she could.'

Kit gave a shrug. 'Up to you.'

'No Family Liaison Officer today, then?' asked Sean.

'She's gone back to the station to follow up on a few things and got the afternoon off apparently,' said Kit. 'I don't think overtime can stretch to sending someone else in her place.'

When Neve picked Lucie up later that morning, she was thankful she didn't have Sally tagging along.

'Hi, hun,' said Lucie, getting in the car. 'How is everything?'

'Hiya. Pretty grim,' said Neve, resting her head back in the seat. 'I didn't think we'd be at this point. I genuinely thought she'd be home by now.'

'It must be awful for you,' said Lucie. 'Everyone in the village is hoping she's found soon. Everyone's thinking of you and Kit.'

'It's the waiting and doing nothing that's the worst thing,' admitted Neve. 'Thank goodness Sean showed up today with these flyers.'

'At least it's something positive and I know it probably won't make you feel any better, but no news is good news.'

'Let's hope so,' said Neve. She put the car into gear and headed out of the village. As they passed the memorial where the St Joseph's bus stopped, Neve was reminded of last week's incident with Ben Hewitt. If only last week's troubles were all they had to worry about this week.

Cheryl was waiting in the car park in town as arranged. Neve spotted her mother-in-law's distinctive soft-top sports car immediately.

'There she is,' said Neve. She held up her hand so Cheryl knew she'd seen her.

'Hello, Neve,' she said, as her daughter-in-law neared her. She offered her cheek which Neve duly air-kissed.

'Thanks for coming, Cheryl,' she said, although not entirely feeling it. She handed Cheryl a wodge of flyers. 'Sean made these. I thought maybe we could stand at the pedestrian crossroad and take a street each. This is Lucie, by the way, she's a friend from the village. She's going to help too.'

Cheryl inspected the flyers and gave a small sob.

Neve took a tissue from her bag and passed it to her. 'You don't have to do this,' she said, gently.

Cheryl accepted the tissue and dabbed at her eyes. 'Oh, I do. I most definitely do,' she said, resolutely. She stood straighter and adjusted her white blazer. 'It's just these posters, they add another dose of reality to what is such a surreal thing. I keep thinking I'm going to wake up and this is a horrid nightmare.'

'I know exactly how you feel,' sympathised Neve, giving her mother-in-law a hug. 'It's hard to believe we're even doing this.'

They made their way to the centre of the pedestrian streets. 'I'll catch the people coming up South Street,' said Lucie. 'Neve, why don't you take East Street and, Cheryl, you take North Street.'

It was a busy day; the market was in town and this always increased the footfall. Neve had only just started handing out the flyers when her phone rang.

From the ring tone, she knew it was Kit and snatched the mobile from her pocket.

'Hello. Any news?'

'No,' said Kit, his voice held the now usual flat and dejected tone. 'Just letting you know that we've blitzed Lower Bury. It felt awful being there, knowing we were so close to where Poppy last was and yet so far from knowing where she actually is now.'

'I can imagine,' said Neve.

'How's it going there? Is Mum with you?'

'We've only just got here,' said Neve. She looked across the square where Cheryl was launching herself in the pathway

195

of everyone and anyone coming within a few feet of her. 'Your mum's not letting anyone get past her without taking a leaflet.'

'Let's hope we can jog someone's memory,' said Kit.

'Don't give up hope, Kit. You've got to keep believing she's coming home.'

It took a moment for Kit to reply and when he did, his voice had a steely determination to it. 'I'm not giving up. All the time she's not found, it gives me hope that she's still alive somewhere.'

'That's right,' said Neve, through tears that had taken her by surprise. 'We don't ever give up.'

'See you at home later,' said Kit.

Neve felt overwhelmed with emotion and compassion for Kit, as she slid the phone back into her pocket. Taking a deep breath, she focused on handing out the flyers.

'My daughter is missing,' she said, as people hurried along. 'Please if you've seen her, contact this number.'

Mostly out of kindness or too embarrassed to say no, Neve found people taking a leaflet from her hand. Some stopped and spoke to her, offering words of support, saying they had seen the press conference and all wishing her well. Neve was quite overwhelmed by the support of shoppers.

As she stopped to take a sip of water from a bottle she'd brought with her, Neve saw the unmistakable sight of Linda Hewitt with her bright pink hair, long on one side and shaved on the other, walking towards her with her son, Ben. She spotted Neve a few seconds later and almost stopped in her tracks. Neve hoped she was going to divert away, but Linda clearly had other ideas. She strode up to Neve and snatched a leaflet from her hand.

'Still missing, then?' she said needlessly, with an air of disdain.

'If you see her, could you call that number, please,' said Neve, amazed at how controlled she sounded even to herself.

'Maybe she doesn't want to be found,' said Linda. 'Can't say I'd blame her for wanting to run away.'

Neve was taken aback but fought to recover quickly. 'I don't want any trouble, Linda,' she said. 'I'm just trying to find my daughter.'

'Your daughter? That's a joke,' said Linda. 'Stepdaughter. You don't have any kids, do you?'

Neve sucked in the verbal body-blow and remained composed. 'Daughter. I adopted her. That makes her my daughter.' She wasn't letting this cow of a woman rile her. 'Look, I'm busy. If you can just help spread the word, I'd be grateful.'

'I've had the police round my house, thanks to you,' snapped Linda. 'Asking me all sorts of questions about Ben and that little madam. First about the alleged bullying and second about her being missing. I don't need crap like that.'

'The police are only doing their job,' said Neve, her own anger spilling over. 'If your son wasn't a little thug, the first visit could have been avoided.'

'That's rich coming from you,' snarled Linda. 'I've told the police about you. Threatening my son with a hockey stick.'

'What are you talking about?' demanded Neve. 'I did no such thing. That's a downright lie.'

'Oh, is it? Well, Ben has witnesses.'

'Mum, leave the snooty cow alone,' said Ben, tugging at his mum's sleeve.

197

Neve ignored the remark, she was rapidly replaying the confrontation with Ben in her mind. Did she threaten him with the hockey stick? To be honest, she couldn't say for certain whether she did or not. Everything was a little bit hazy, she wasn't entirely sure what exactly happened. It was almost like she had been watching someone else. She looked back up at Linda, whose face was twisted with hate.

'I don't care whether she's missing or not. She's a trouble-maker and whilst I don't wish the kid any harm, you and your snob of a husband deserve what's coming to you.'

'You are one evil woman,' retorted Neve. 'Now piss off and leave me alone.' She stood almost toe-to-toe with Linda Hewitt, her anger held back by the merest of threads.

Linda Hewitt gave a laugh and stepped back. 'Don't worry, love, I'm going,' she said.

Neve stood motionless for several seconds, until Linda was lost from sight in the throng of shoppers. How could another person, another woman, another mother, be so cruel? It was beyond belief. Neve could barely believe the exchange of words that had just occurred.

'You all right?' It was Lucie. 'I saw you and Linda Hewitt at loggerheads. What was going on there?'

'She's screwed in the head,' said Neve. 'I'm fine. Don't worry. Look, I'm just nipping to the loo. I'll be back in a minute.'

'Sure,' said Lucie, appraising Neve with a concerned look.

'I'm fine. Honest,' said Neve. She gave her friend a smile. 'Won't be long.'

Neve hurried off towards the Marks & Spencer store where there was a coffee shop and toilets.

In the safety of one of the cubicles, Neve closed the toilet lid and sat down, resting her head in her hands. Linda Hewitt's outburst had disturbed her, not just because the woman was clearly heartless, but she'd accused Neve of threatening Ben with the hockey stick. Neve tried to remember exactly what happened at the bus stop, but her mind's filing system seemed not only to be muddled, but also guilty of totally misfiling events.

Neve knew from past experience, it wouldn't be the first time she'd made a mistake. She thought all that was behind her now.

Neve sat up straight and took several deep breaths, breathing slowly in and out. 'Keep it together, Neve,' she whispered to herself. 'Everything is going to be OK.'

Opening her bag, she took out a small black mobile phone from the zip compartment. It was an old phone Poppy used to have until Cheryl had bought her a new smartphone last Christmas. The old one had been shoved in the back of her drawer and forgotten about, until now. Neve checked her text messages. A number one was displayed by an icon of an envelope. Neve opened the message.

Need to see you.

'Shit.' Neve shoved the phone back into the zip compartment. What did he want? It must be important otherwise he wouldn't have texted.

Neve hurried back to the town centre where Cheryl and Lucie were still handing out leaflets. Neve beckoned the two women over.

'I'm sorry, but I'm really not feeling well,' she said. 'I need to go home.'

'Oh, but we've still got leaflets to hand out,' protested Cheryl.

'You stay and carry on, if you want,' said Neve. 'But I need to go.'

Lucie put a comforting hand on Neve's arm. 'It's OK,' she said. 'It probably hasn't helped that bloody Linda Hewitt starting on you. I'll come back with you.'

Cheryl made a huffing sound, which Neve chose to ignore. Everyone was under pressure at the moment, Neve may never have been able to completely fill the shoes of Cheryl's first daughter-in-law, but she liked to think they had got past that point these days and that Cheryl knew how much Neve loved Kit and Poppy. However, every now and again, Neve couldn't help feeling she was being compared to her predecessor. Now, being one of those times. The huff from Cheryl was heavily laden with unspoken words that Kit's first wife would not have abandoned her position so readily.

'I'll phone you later,' said Neve before Cheryl decided to pass a comment which Neve knew she wouldn't be able to ignore.

'Now, are you sure you're going to be OK?' said Lucie, as Neve pulled up at the rear of the coffee shop. 'I can stay with you if you like.'

'I'll be fine,' said Neve. 'I just need to get some rest.'

'Let me know if you need me, then,' said Lucie. 'I'll call you later.'

Neve watched as Lucie trotted up the steps to her flat

above the coffee shop. She waved and then pulled away back onto the main road. But instead of turning left at the junction for Long Acre Lane, Neve turned right and took the back road out of the village, accelerating hard. She didn't have much time.

Chapter 21

Having dealt with Linda already that afternoon, Neve now had another problem to sort out. She turned her car into Cornflower Close and drove steadily along the tree-lined road. Number 32 her destination. She had been here once before. When she had dropped Scott home. It was the last time she had seen him. Almost eight years ago now. After all this time, she wasn't quite sure how she was going to react to seeing him again. But she had the upper hand and she had rehearsed in her mind several times what she was going to say. He wasn't expecting her and even if the thought had crossed his mind, he would have dismissed it, thinking she wasn't brave enough to do anything like this.

Her shock had turned to anger at the thought that Scott would write the note. She never in her darkest nightmares thought he would betray her. She knew what she had done was wrong. What her and Megan had done, but she thought that when she'd left him it would all be over. That she could put it all in the past.

Neve pulled up outside number 32. There was one car on the drive. A four-wheel drive Discovery, the sort that she could imagine Scott driving. He had always liked his cars. It looked like he had got the Range Rover he had always admired. The number plate caught her eye and confirmed what she thought. Three digits followed by his initials 659 ST.

As Neve got out of the car, she hoped she was right in her assumption that no one else was at home. She didn't know what Scott's marital status was these days, although when she had looked at his timeline, there was a picture of a family get together and in amongst it was Scott standing next to a woman who was holding a toddler in her arms. Neve had felt a small pang of jealousy as she had looked at it and even now, she couldn't deny that feeling was still there.

She had prepared what to say if the woman opened the door – she was going to pretend to be carrying out an opinion poll. Neve had even printed off a fake pass, which she would waft in front of the wife, only briefly, not long enough for her to read it. Neve had also planned an escape route if the woman did decide to go ahead with the survey. Neve would fake a phone call and tell the woman she would come back another day.

Neve stood in front of the door, a clipboard clutched to her chest as part of her cover story. There was still time to change her mind. She could turn around and walk away now if she wanted to. She considered this idea and dismissed it all at the same time. She had to find out what Scott was playing at.

She pressed the doorbell and rattled the knocker for good measure.

The sound of footsteps approaching the door could be heard. Neve's heart gave a little flutter and she drew a deep breath as the door opened.

Standing in front of her was Scott Tansley, her ex-husband.

He still looked just the same. His dark hair cut short, maybe thinning a little at the sides and flecked with a touch of grey. His green eyes looked at her appraisingly. He appeared neither warm nor cold and certainly not surprised.

'Hello, Scott,' she said evenly, trying to keep her pulse rate to an acceptable level. This wasn't as easy as she had imagined.

'I wondered when you would turn up,' he said.

'You're not surprised I'm here then?' she said, slightly thrown by his laconic reaction to her presence on his doorstep.

He shook his head. 'Not really. It occurred to me that after the phone call I had the other day, sooner or later you'd turn up. Only, I had rather hoped it would be later.'

'Phone call? What phone call? From the police?'

Scott ignored her as he squeezed his eyes closed and pinched the bridge of his nose between his finger and thumb, a gesture Neve had seen him do so many times before. One where he couldn't quite fathom out what to say. It was his time stalling gesture.

'Can I come in?' Neve looked past his shoulder. So far no one else had come to the door to see who the unexpected caller was. She guessed he was probably alone.

'I'd rather you didn't. Amy will be home soon,' said Scott, moving his hand to the door, ready to slam it shut.

Neve gave a shrug. 'We can always have the conversation on the doorstep.' She leaned back slightly and looked from one neighbouring house to the other. 'I don't expect anyone will hear us.'

'Look, as I told your husband, he really needs to speak to

you. I know it's not your strong point, but you should talk to him.'

'My husband? Kit phoned you?' Had she heard him right?

'I believe that's what he said his name was, unless of course you've got another husband somewhere. I mean, who knows with you.'

'Fuck off, Scott.'

'With pleasure.' He went to shut the door, but Neve rammed her foot across the threshold. She rested her hand on the doorframe. 'Look, I'm sorry. Can I come in? I need to talk to you.'

'For a moment there, I thought you said sorry.'

'For God's sake, Scott, just let me in.'

'Shouldn't you be back in West Sussex looking for your daughter?'

Neve had to stop herself from swearing at him again. Instead, she spoke in what she hoped was a non-confrontational voice.

'You've seen the appeal?'

'Of course. Everyone has.'

'Did you send the note?'

She studied his face closely, looking for any flicker of guilt or knowledge, but could detect nothing.

'I've no idea what you're talking about.'

'Someone sent me a note after the appeal went out on TV. Someone who knows about ... about Jasmine.'

'It wasn't me. I can't actually believe you thought it was.'

'You're lying,' said Neve, her voice rising again, despite her attempts to remain calm.

'For God's sake,' muttered Scott. He pulled the door open and stepped aside. 'Come in. But just for five minutes. That's all you've got. You're not even supposed to be here. I could call the police.'

Neve didn't argue with him. She didn't want him to change his mind.

It felt strange walking into his house. She looked at the black-framed photographs of a woman and a toddler that were lining the hall. 'I take it you're alone,' she said.

'Just get to the point,' said Scott, now standing in the middle of the comfortably furnished living room. It reminded Neve of their first home together. The wood flooring, the clean lines that Scott liked, no fuss and no frills, almost geometric. In fact, she recognised the oak table at the side of the armchair from their days together. Scott had bought it from a local Scandinavian furniture maker. It had cost a fortune, but Scott had said it was worth it. On the table was another photograph of the child, which looked like it had been taken in a nursery setting.

She nodded to the picture. 'Your daughter?'

Scott glowered at her. 'Yes. If you must know.'

'She's gorgeous. She has your eyes.'

Scott's shoulders dropped slightly. 'Thanks. She's two next month.'

'What's her name?'

Scott hesitated some more. 'Olivia,' he said carefully, eyeing Neve as he spoke.

Neve swayed a little. Her head felt light. 'Olivia,' she said in a whisper. 'That was always your favourite name for a girl.' An unexpected lump rose to her throat. She swallowed it down hard.

'What do you want?' Scott said, this time his own voice was softer.

'My daughter is missing,' said Neve.

'I know. Like I said, I saw the appeal on the television. I'm sorry. I hope you find her.'

'I received an anonymous note, or rather my husband did.' It seemed strange talking about her husband to Scott who had once carried the same title.

'And ...?'

'I thought you must have sent it.'

Scott gave a snort. 'We're going around in circles. Why would I send you a note?'

'Have you heard from Ashley at all?' asked Neve, purposely throwing the conversation off course.

Scott blinked in surprise. 'Ashley? As in Ash Farnham?'

'Unless you know another one.'

'I've not heard from that scumbag since ... since what happened.'

'He turned up in the village where I live,' carried on Neve.

Scott looked to consider Neve's disclosure for a moment before replying. 'Don't suppose you're too happy about that,' he said finally. 'What did he want?'

'He claims it was a coincidence. He's working as some sort of support worker for young adults.'

Scott burst out laughing. 'You're not serious, are you? A support worker? I've heard it all now.'

'I'm deadly serious.'

'I'm surprised they let him anywhere near vulnerable young people. Not with his track record.'

'They're adults so it doesn't count, apparently. I looked it up,' confessed Neve. 'I take it you don't know why he's turned up?'

'No idea, but if Ash is about, you'd better watch yourself. I don't suppose for one minute the leopard has changed its spots,' said Scott. 'Present company excepted.'

Neve shot him a look. 'Uncalled for.'

'Yes, it probably was. Tell me, did your husband ask you about Megan and Jasmine?'

Neve's breath caught in her throat, if Kit started asking about them, she wasn't sure how much longer she could keep her secret for. 'No. And he doesn't need to know either,' said Neve.

'I'm sure you've considered this,' said Scott. 'But don't you think it's a coincidence that Ash turns up and your daughter goes missing.'

'Ash may be many unsavoury things, but kidnapping is not his style.'

'Really? It doesn't have to be kidnap. He's very persuasive, as you well know. It would be more like coercion.'

'He's not involved,' insisted Neve.

'What about the note – not him either, I suppose?'

'Postmarked Newport, so unless he can teleport, then no, it's not him.'

'Still protecting him,' said Scott.

'Not that it's any of your business,' snapped Neve.

'To this day, I still don't know why you protected him.'

Neve shifted on her feet, anxious not to get bogged down in unfinished arguments from years ago. 'Did you send the note?' She looked Scott directly in the eye, looking for any sign he might attempt to lie to her.

'No. I didn't! For fuck's sake. And if it's postmarked Newport, that would be a bit of drive out for me.' Scott let out an exasperated sigh.

Neve's hand was tapping involuntarily against her leg. She felt hot and stifled. She ran her finger around the collar of her blouse. She saw the picture of Olivia again. More pain surged through her. She looked back at Scott.

'You didn't send it to get back at me?'

'For what? For what you did to your family? For making me move away from Newport with you? For getting yourself into so much trouble that you were arrested? For making me remortgage so I could pay a defence lawyer, so you didn't end up in prison? For then, after all that, after standing by you, you divorcing me?' He waved his hand in the air in exasperation. 'You're asking me if I sent the note for revenge? Well, I could have and who would have blamed me?' He crossed the room in two strides, standing in front of her, his face creased in anger. 'But the truth is, I didn't. In fact, if I'm honest, you leaving turned out to be the best thing that ever happened to me. I've got a wife who I love and who loves me. I've got a daughter I adore. I've got the life I always wanted. I've got a life with the right person now.'

The words hit their target. Neve grappled for the arm of the chair. 'Bastard!' she snapped, perching on the edge.

'I think you need to leave for your own good,' said Scott. 'Now.'

'Is that some sort of threat?' Neve pushed herself to her feet. Anger giving her the strength to stand her ground.

'You can read into it what you like. Just leave now, will you?'

'Don't threaten me.'

'Or you'll do what? Call the police?' Scott gave a dismissive snort. 'I think we both know whose side they'll be on.'

209

Neve brushed past Scott and out of the living room. She snatched open the front door, not bothering to close it behind her.

'All this that's happening to you, it's called karma,' shouted Scott from the doorstep.

Neve didn't want to hear what he was saying. It was bringing everything back into much closer focus. She slammed the car door and holding onto the steering wheel, rested her head on her hands.

'It wasn't my fault. I didn't do anything,' she heard herself say between sobs of anger and frustration. 'It wasn't me. It was Megan.'

Chapter 22

The following morning, Neve was up first. Cheryl had given her some over-the-counter tablets designed to help with sleep but Neve had decided against taking any. It was not a road she intended to go down again, having relied on various forms of uppers and downers in the past. She had, however, managed to persuade Kit to take one. The past few days had taken a dramatic toll on him. He was looking totally ragged and rundown, which had taken her by surprise. Worry was an understatement of how Kit was feeling. She searched for a stronger word but could only come up with pain. Kit was in pain.

Wrapping her dressing gown around her, Neve padded downstairs. The letters on the doormat ground her to a halt, sending her stomach somersaulting. The same white envelope as before was face up, staring at her. Kit's name was written in the same black pen as before. Neve assumed whoever had sent it, didn't have the knowledge or ability to print the envelopes, only the note inside.

She hurried down the stairs and swiped the letters up, placing them on the kitchen counter, but taking the one for

Kit with her through to the downstairs toilet. Locking the door, she ripped open the envelope, disregarding Sally's caution not to open any more letters and to give them straight to her.

Neve's body shook involuntarily and she leaned over the toilet and threw up. Her empty stomach relieving itself of bile which burnt her windpipe as it was forced out.

She spluttered and spat into the toilet bowl. Running the tap in the hand basin, she took a glug of water, swilled her mouth out and spat into the toilet.

Her carefully constructed new life was being damaged by her carefully concealed old one. She had always taken precautions not to let the two cross over but now it seemed someone had other ideas.

As she sat there, Neve realised she couldn't be a bystander in all this. She had to put things right.

Neve looked at the note again. She closed her eyes and said a silent prayer that what she was about to do would work. This was her chance to get Poppy back. Kit would be ecstatic. Neve would be the heroine. He would do anything she asked. Even agree to them having a baby together. She was sure of that.

She thought of Poppy and her heart lifted and fell almost in one action. She hoped Poppy was OK. That she wouldn't be too scared by what had happened, and she prayed that Poppy hadn't been harmed in any way. Neve wasn't sure how she would cope if something had happened to Poppy but somewhere in her heart of hearts she knew that her daughter was safe. She had to believe it otherwise what was the point of all this?

Taking care not to disturb Kit, Neve quickly dressed and unhooked her coat from the peg in the hall, before hooking Willow up on the dog lead and creeping out to the car.

As Neve pulled out of the drive and down the road, she let out a sigh of relief that she'd successfully managed to get out of the house.

Taking care not to break the speed limit, she headed into town for the local bank. She ignored the look the cashier gave her when she handed over the cheque to withdraw ten thousand pounds cash from her savings account.

'It would be much safer if you could complete the transaction by bank transfer,' said the cashier as she put the wad of notes into a money bag.

'It's fine as it is. I'll be careful.' She gave the cashier a reassuring smile, before making her way back to Ambleton.

It wasn't long before she was pulling up in the car park by the river. 'Come on, Willow,' she said, opening the boot to let the dog out.

She checked her watch. He should be coming along here any time now.

Five minutes later the lone figure of Jake appeared ahead of her. Willow bounded up to him, her tail wagging a sincere greeting.

'Hello, Willow,' Neve heard Jake say as he bent down to stroke the dog. 'There's a good girl.' Jake looked up. 'Hey. How are you?'

'Hey, yourself,' said Neve, offering a small smile. 'How are you?'

Jake shrugged. 'You know.' He paused before speaking again. 'Any news on Poppy?'

Neve stopped herself from answering. She looked out across the river into the middle distance. She could feel the nerves jingle all through her body. She wanted to cry. She didn't know if she could go through with this. Jake took a step closer, his arm outstretched to embrace her.

'Don't. Too much sympathy and I'll start crying.' She looked down at the ground as she shuffled a step away. 'I don't know what to do,' she said at last.

'About what?'

She hesitated for a moment before pulling the now scrunched up note from her pocket. 'I'm being blackmailed.'

'Blackmailed?' Jake took the note she offered and opening it out, read the message. 'What the hell? Have you shown this to the police?'

'No! It says not to,' said Neve, snatching the letter back from him.

'But you must. They need to know.'

'Why? Why do they? Didn't you read it? If I tell the police then there will be no chance of getting Poppy back. They'll take her away. I don't know what they'll do. Traffic her or something. Or worse ...' The words caught in her throat. 'Then it will be my fault.'

'You seriously can't be going along with this?' said Jake. 'Neve, it's a ridiculous idea. And ten thousand pounds! Have you got that sort of cash?

'I've just been to the bank,' she said, gripping her bag to her.

'And then what?'

Neve shrugged. "I'm going to get Poppy back.'

'Whoa! Wait a minute. You're not doing this on your own.

It's dangerous. You don't know who you're dealing with. What if something happens to you too?'

'Don't worry. I have it covered. I've made a note on my computer. A letter for Kit, if you like. Telling him what I'm doing. If anything happens to me then the police will check my laptop and they'll see the message. I've said where I'm going, that way they'll have half a chance of rescuing both Poppy and myself, or at least Poppy.'

'This is a crazy idea.'

'I don't care. It's what I'm doing,' said Neve.

'Wait, you can't go on your own. Let me come with you.'

'No. I couldn't do that.'

'Why not?' Jake looked intently at Neve. 'In fact, I insist on coming with you if you're going to do this crazy thing.'

Neve couldn't deny the feeling of relief that kicked the nerves down. She would never have asked Jake outright to come with her. 'OK,' she said. 'Thank you, Jake.'

She called Willow and as they made their way back to the car, in what seemed a spontaneous action, Jake slipped his arm across her shoulders and gave her a brief hug.

'Just thought you needed one,' he said.

Neve smiled. 'You thought right. Thank you.' She would like to have stayed in his embrace a little longer, but she knew she didn't have time and hurried over to the car, with Jake at one side and Willow the other. Within a few minutes they were heading out of the village and towards the South Downs.

'Are you sure about this?' asked Jake. 'You really don't want to involve the police?'

'Positive,' she said, not taking her eyes from the road. She had to stay calm. She couldn't waiver now. This was her chance, her last chance to make things right with Kit.

After driving for ten minutes, Neve pulled over into a small layby. Looking out of the window ahead of them up on the hill was the iconic landmark, visible from miles across the countryside, Halnaker Windmill. The eighteenth-century brick-built structure, with its four white sails, looked majestic on the crown of the hill.

Neve re-read the instructions. 'OK, it says after parking here, there will be another note under a stone to the right of gate post.'

'It must mean over there, at the stile,' remarked Jake.

'I'll leave Willow in the car,' said Neve, making sure the rear windows were both open an inch and the dog's water bowl was filled with fresh water. She gave Willow her chewy toy, which was stuffed with treats. 'Won't be long. Good girl.'

'It's pretty deserted up here,' said Jake, as they left the car. 'Apart from those houses.'

Two farm cottages flanked the foot of the hill, marking the start of the old Roman road which passed adjacent to the windmill.

'Never mind that,' said Neve, walking over to the stile. She looked on the ground and had she not been looking for it, wouldn't have noticed the stone, sticking out from under a clump of stinging nettles. She pushed the stingers back with her foot and keeping them squashed to the ground, lifted up the stone to reveal a white piece of paper, folded in half.

Jake looked over her shoulder as she read the note.

'The windmill,' said Neve aloud. 'It just says the windmill.' She looked up the tree lined path which ran from north to south. About a quarter of a mile along, a track branched off and a footpath led up to Halnaker Windmill. 'Poppy is in the mill?' she said, more to herself than to Jake.

'I still think ...'

'No! Don't even say it,' interrupted Neve, already climbing over the stile. She jumped down, landing on two feet and immediately set off at a run up the stony track.

Jake ran to catch her up. 'Let's just be cautious. We don't know if that's where Poppy is. It might just be another note.'

'I don't think so,' said Neve, puffing slightly now. 'Something is telling me she's there. The mill has been closed for repairs for the last three months. It's the ideal place to keep her.'

'You think she's been there all this time?'

'I don't know. Maybe she's been held somewhere else and they've brought her here now.'

Neve stumbled her way as quickly as possible over the uneven Roman road, climbed the second stile and set off to the left. The last climb up the hill along the edge of a field before they reached the old mill.

'I can't see anyone about,' said Jake as they approached the gate which lead to the mill at the top of the hill.

'Poppy!' called out Neve. 'Poppy! Are you here?'

Even though her legs felt as if they had been encased in concrete after the fast and undignified scramble up to the hill, Neve managed to find some energy to break into a run. Fuelled by adrenalin, she ran towards the eight foot high metal fencing that surrounded the mill.

Neve shook the fencing. It was too heavy to move. She hurried round so she could see the opening to the mill. And then from the blackness beyond emerged the huddled figure of Poppy.

The child's tear-streaked face, with tousled hair, looked up at her. She was clutching a blanket around her shoulders.

'Oh, dear God,' cried Neve. 'Poppy, darling. It's OK. I'm here. Jake! Help me with this fencing.' She turned to see what was taking Jake so long but the sight that met her paralysed her.

Jake was being held by two policemen in uniform and hi-vis jackets. His face the picture of confusion and fear. Three men, who Neve assumed were police officers, dressed in black riot type gear, pointing guns at her, rushed towards her.

'Armed Police! Stop where you are. Put your hands in the air.'

Voices shouted these commands at her. People rushed towards her. Suddenly someone had their hand on her shoulder and was pushing her to the ground. Too much was happening all at once for Neve to take in.

'Poppy!' she cried out, her only thought of how alarmed and frightened her daughter would be.

A plain-clothed police officer appeared to be in charge and was shouting orders at his team. 'Someone get the bolt cutters.'

Lying on the cold damp grass, Neve felt her hands being pulled behind her back and the cold metal handcuffs being fixed in place. 'What are you doing?' she yelled. 'Why are you handcuffing me? Stop it!'

'Please, Mrs Masters, don't fight against the cuffs,' said the one in charge. 'OK, stand her up.'

Neve was hauled to her feet and one of the officers began to search her pockets. She pulled out the two notes. 'Sir. You might want to look at these,' said the female officer. She then checked Neve's other coat pocket, pulling out a key on a red tag. 'What's this key for?' she asked Neve.

Neve looked at the key and then up at the officer. She shook her head. 'I don't know. I've never seen it before.'

'You're saying it's not your key?'

'No. It's not.' Neve looked beyond the senior officer's shoulder at Poppy standing in the doorway. Looking up under her fringe, Poppy's eyes wildly searched the scene in front of her. She looked bewildered and frightened. Neve called out to her. 'It's OK, darling. We'll soon have you out. Don't worry. It's all over now.'

The senior officer inspected the key and then walking over to the fencing, tried it in the padlock. The lock pinged open and the chain fell against the metal fencing with a clatter. He looked back at Neve and raised his eyebrows. 'Never seen it before, eh?'

A medical crew appeared from somewhere behind Neve and together with another female officer, rushed through the now open fence, swooping Poppy up, with reassuring words that she was safe, while another team of armed police swept the building, declaring it clear within a matter of seconds.

'That key is not mine. I promise,' said Neve, struggling to be let free. All she wanted to do was to get to Poppy and cuddle her and hold her. 'Please, let me go. I need to see my daughter.'

The senior officer shook his head. 'Neve Masters, I'm arresting you for the kidnap of Poppy Masters, anything you say ...'

The rest of the words were lost as Neve screamed out to Poppy and Poppy screamed back to Neve, calling each other's names over and over again before Poppy was led away by the paramedics.

Chapter 23

Neve rubbed her wrists where the handcuffs had been. It seemed a totally unnecessary thing to do. She was hardly going to run off anywhere. All she was grateful for was that Poppy had been rescued and, she prayed to God, that she hadn't been harmed in any way. She took a sip from the glass of water on the desk in front of her and looked around the interview room.

A tape recorder was on the side of the desk and she assumed they were going to record her interview as she was under caution. So far, Neve had declined to answer any questions until she saw her solicitor and had been allowed to phone Kit to say where she was. It had been quite a surreal telephone conversation.

'DCI Pearson has just told me,' said Kit. 'Look, Neve, I have no idea what the fuck is going on. Right now I'm on my way to the hospital to see Poppy. I've already called Edward and he'll be with you anytime now. He said do not say anything until he has spoken to you.'

Neve breathed a sigh of relief. Edward, their solicitor, was an old-school, take-no-prisoners type of solicitor. She'd want him defending her any day. 'Thank you,' she managed to eke out.

'Neve,' said Kit, his voice turning solemn. 'DCI Pearson said you were ...' The words faded away.

'Involved? I know, but it's not true, Kit. You have to believe me.'

'But what the hell were you doing there? Why didn't you tell me?'

She imagined Kit running his hand through his hair, rubbing his forehead with his fingertips, an agitated look on his face. 'I can't speak here,' said Neve. 'But believe me, I did not have anything to do with it.'

'They said Jake was with you,' said Kit and she could hear the tension in his voice.

'Please. I really can't speak now,' she paused, before continuing. 'Just remember that I love you. I know things have been shit lately but, Kit, I love you and I love Poppy. This will all get sorted. I promise.'

Kit had hung up, leaving Neve listening to the continuous drone of the dial tone. She replaced the receiver and the police officer had taken her back to the interview room.

It was another twenty minutes before Edward arrived.

'Hello, Neve,' he said, walking round and giving her a kiss on the cheek. 'How are you bearing up? Do you need anything?'

'Hi, Edward. I'm fine. Well, you know. Not fine being here but fine otherwise and no, I don't need anything, thanks. Do you know how Poppy is?'

'She's in safe hands at the hospital. As far as I know, she's unharmed but obviously shaken by the ordeal,' said Edward.

'Much the same as you, I expect. Now, have you said anything at all to the police? Made any comment whatsoever? Even something like, I didn't do it. I'm innocent.'

Neve thought back. 'Err, I'm not sure. If I said anything it would only to have been to protest my innocence. I might have said something like, I had nothing to do with this.'

Edward opened his notebook. 'Right, that's good. Now, you've been arrested on suspicion of abduction. The other charges they are potentially looking at will be things like, holding a person against their will, perverting the course of justice, interfering with a police inquiry and withholding evidence and the like.'

'That's quite a list for an innocent person,' said Neve.

Edward nodded and grunted in acknowledgement. 'Before we go any further, Neve,' he said, looking up and leaning back in his chair. 'Is there anything I need to know?'

'About what?'

'Anything that might help me or prepare me in defending you here?'

Neve shook her head, whilst acknowledging that if ever there was a time to come clean about what she had done, then it was now. But self-preservation was a strange beast. She imagined it was like when a person was fighting for their life, they'd do or say anything to stall for time, to keep them alive for just a minute more. And that was what she was doing now. Living from one minute to the next, all the time keeping just a little bit ahead.

'Are you sure?' pressed Edward.

Did he know? Was he testing her honesty? There was no way of telling. For now she'd brazen it out. 'Positive,' she replied.

Sue Fortin

Edward looked at her for what seemed like a long moment, before appearing to come to a decision. He sat forward. 'OK, that's good. I don't like surprises.' He smiled at her. 'Do you want to tell me from the beginning what happened?'

'Where from?'

'From this morning.'

'I was the first one up and I found a note on the doormat,' began Neve. 'We had received one before and I assumed it was from the same person.'

'What did the previous note say?' asked Edward, as he made notes in his Moleskine notebook, aided by his no doubt highly expensive, fountain pen. The blue ink gracing the paper in wave-like motions.

'It was implicating me in having something to do with Poppy's disappearance. I can't remember the exact words, but the police have it. I showed it to the family liaison officer, Sally. Kit said it was probably some nutcase. You know how the media attention brings out the weirdos. The note came after the press conference,' said Neve.

'And the second note? Tell me about that.'

I came downstairs this morning and there was this other note on the doormat. I was fully expecting it to be one from the previous nutter. But it wasn't. It said if I wanted to see Poppy again I was to follow the instructions below.'

'Which were?'

'Not to tell anyone. To take ten thousand from the bank and go to Halnaker Windmill.'

'That's not a great deal of money for a ransom,' said Edward.

'I did think that. But I did what it said and took the money from the bank.'

'And you didn't tell the police about the note?'

'No. It said not to involve the police.' Neve dropped her gaze. 'I thought – I thought I could be the hero of the hour. It was silly of me. Foolish. Vain.' She stopped talking and looked up at Edward. 'I don't know if Kit has said anything to you, but we've been going through a bit of a rough patch.'

'Not in so many words, but I got the impression the last couple of times I've spoken to him.'

'I thought if I could rescue Poppy, it would make everything right between us. That he would love me again, like he used to. This sounds so bloody stupid when I say it out loud, but I wasn't thinking straight. I couldn't have been. I should have told the police there and then, but I didn't.'

A tear leaked its way from Neve's eye and streaked down her face. Edward fished out a packet of tissues from his briefcase and passed them over.

'Ever the Boy Scout,' he said.

'Thank you.' Neve took a few moments to compose herself again. 'I let my vanity and stupid idea get the better of me and decided I'd go along with it. I took Willow for a walk along the river path. Just to clear my head and to pluck up courage really. I bumped into Jake.'

'Jake ...' Edwards consulted his notes. 'Jake Rees, the man who was arrested with you.'

'He's my art therapy tutor.'

'Art therapy? May I ask why?'

'I'm estranged from my family. It was to get over that really. You know, issues and all that.' She left Edward to fill in the gaps.

225

'So, you bumped into Jake. How did he come to go along with you?'

'I told him about the note and he didn't want me to go on my own. He said I should go to the police but when he realised I wasn't going to, he said he'd come with me.'

'What made you confide in Jake? You didn't say anything to Kit, but you seemed quite happy to tell your art teacher.'

'Jake has turned out to be a very good friend of mine. He saw I was upset. It seemed easier telling someone who wasn't directly involved. Besides, he was my therapist, it seemed easier to talk to him.'

'A good friend, you say. Just a good friend?'

Neve looked Edward in the eye. 'Just a good friend.'

Edward made more notes in his pad. 'So, what happened next?'

Neve proceeded to tell Edward how they had gone up to Stane Street and found the second note, before running up to the mill and finding the fencing locked. 'And the next thing I knew, the police were there arresting me. Honestly, Edward, this is like some sort of nightmare.'

'Now the police are saying they followed you up there after a tip-off,' said Edward. 'I don't suppose you know who that could be?'

'A tip-off? Someone knew what I was doing?'

'Maybe watching you. It wouldn't have been Jake, would it? If he was the only person you told.'

'I've no idea. Maybe someone from the bank?' said Neve. 'The bank clerk did look at me a bit odd when I said I wanted to withdraw ten thousand pounds.'

'Well, we won't dwell on that just yet,' said Edward. 'From

what you've told me, none of this indicates your involvement in the kidnapping of Poppy. However, bringing into play the fact that the police found a key to the padlock on you, puts a whole different spin on things. How did it end up in your pocket?'

'Oh, Edward. I have no idea,' said Neve, aware that a sob was rising in her throat. 'I honestly don't. I mean, why would I be shouting to Poppy and rattling the fencing if I had a key? Surely, I would have just got it out of my pocket. It's ludicrous to suggest I was involved and how could I be?'

'It still doesn't rationally explain the key in your pocket and that is what the police are hinging this on.'

'Someone must have put it there,' said Neve, wiping at her face again with the tissue. 'I can't think of any other explanation.'

'Someone planted the key to put you in the frame?'

'Yes! They must have done.'

'Right, before we get carried away with this idea, we must look at how they planted the key. Why? – we'll keep that for later,' said Edward, tapping the notepad with the end of his pen. 'It was found in your pocket. Who had access to your coat?'

'It was hanging up at home. So, Sally and Kit.'

'Anyone else? A cleaner? Kit's mum? When did you last wear the coat?'

'Yesterday, when I was handing out missing posters in town.'

'And you didn't find the key in your pocket then?'

'No. I would have said something.'

'Did you go alone yesterday?'

'No. Cheryl, Kit's mum, and my friend Lucie came.'

'You all went in the same car?'

'No. Lucie came with me, but Cheryl met us there.'

Edward wrote something down. 'Have you left your coat anywhere in the last four days since Poppy's been missing?'

'No. I've either been wearing it, or it's been at home.'

'Now, you met Jake on the canal path. Could he have put the key in your pocket? Did he get close enough? Perhaps when you were in the car? Which pocket did the police find the key?'

'Err, my right pocket.'

'Hmm, so probably not when you were in the car. Are you left or right handed, by the way?'

'Right.'

'So, if you were putting something in your pocket, it would be more than likely you'd put it in your right pocket.'

'But I didn't!'

'I'm just thinking how the police would,' reassured Edward. 'Back to Jake. Could he have put it in your pocket when you were by the river or walking back to the car?'

Neve thought back. 'Maybe when we were walking back to the car, but I honestly don't remember feeling him slip anything in my pocket. And why would he?'

'A motive is always helpful,' said Edward. 'Is there any reason why Jake would want to set you up? Why he would have any involvement in Poppy's kidnapping? Think, Neve, this is extremely important. Had you and Jake fallen out about anything?'

Neve looked down at her hands as she rubbed the edge of the desk with her thumbs. She knew this moment would come sooner or later and that she couldn't put off the inevitable. More tears dropped from her eyes, splodging onto her jeans.

Without looking up, for she couldn't face looking Edward in the eye, she spoke. 'It's a bit awkward, but Jake and I, we've become very close lately. We're not having an affair, but he has said things, sort of offered, if you like, a way out of my marriage.' Too embarrassed and ashamed to look at Edward, Neve continued studying the edge of the table.

'And what was your response to that suggestion?'

'I said no. I didn't want to have an affair and I didn't want to leave Kit.'

'How did Jake take the rejection? Was he angry? Upset?'

This time Neve did meet his eye. 'He was very dignified and gentlemanly about it.'

'So, he accepted this and didn't try to change your mind?'

'Yes, as I said, he accepted my decision,' said Neve. 'He is a very kind and compassionate man. I probably leant on him a bit too much when things between me and Kit were going wrong.'

'Neve, please, you don't have to explain to me,' said Edward, this time there was a gentleness to his voice. 'I'm not here to judge you or to speculate on your marriage. I'm here to get you released and off the charge as quickly as possible.'

Neve gave Edward a small smile. 'Thank you.'

'Save all that for Kit. He'll be the one who needs to know. Me, I just need to know the bare facts. What I'm trying to establish is if anyone else had a motive for kidnapping Poppy and trying to blame you.'

'Oh, Jake wouldn't do that, I'm sure,' said Neve, massaging her temples. 'I mean, why would he?'

'Strictly speaking that's up to the police to decide but before that, we'd have to suggest to them that Jake planted the key in your pocket. Technically, I'm here to prove your innocence, not someone else's guilt but if it helps your case, then I'll run with it,' said Edward patiently. 'Do you understand what I'm saying?'

Neve nodded slowly as Edward's words sank in. 'Yes. I do,' she said.

'Right, now moving on,' said Edward. 'Is there anyone else, anyone at all, who you've crossed swords with recently?'

'Linda Hewitt. Her son was bullying Poppy one day and I confronted him about it. His mother took exception. She had a go at me in the street when I was handing out missing posters of Poppy.' She watched as Edward made a note in his book.

'Sounds a charming family,' commented Edward. 'Apart from Linda Hewitt, is there anyone you're concerned about? Kit mentioned to me about a man he found talking to Poppy. He's told the police about him, I believe. Do you know anything yourself?'

Neve gulped a lump down from her throat. 'Erm … yes. I made some enquiries, you know, asked around and it turns out he works at The Forum.'

'Do you have a name?'

'Lee Farnham.'

Edward noted the name in his book underneath Linda's name. 'OK, I'll speak to the police and see what's happening there. Now, is there anything else you can think of that I should know?'

Neve looked down at her hands, as if the answer lay there.

Should she tell Edward about her connection with Lee? Would the police dig that far back into her past and make the connection themselves? 'I ...' she began but hesitated. Yes or no?

'Neve,' said Edward, leaning forwards and speaking softly. 'Whatever you say to me, you can say in total confidence. I won't repeat anything to anyone, unless it's to save your skin. And, even then, it will only be to the police. Kit may be my friend, but client confidentiality comes first. Of course, I can't speak for the police, but anything you tell me, I will treat with the utmost respect.'

Chapter 24

After much wrangling and a long interview with Pearson, it was finally agreed that Neve would be released without charge, but she was still under caution. As they left the station, a few journalists who had got wind of Neve's visit were waiting outside. Neve gulped at the prospect of having to face them.

'Don't be tempted to reply to any questions. Keep your head down and leave them to me. My car is just over there,' said Edward, before hustling Neve outside, a protective arm across her shoulders. 'No comment. No comment,' said Edward, as he navigated Neve safely to his car, before speeding away.

'Thank you,' said Neve, putting her head back and closing her eyes for a moment.

A short time later they swung into Neve's driveway. Her car was parked in its usual spot and she assumed Kit had been up to collect it at some point, possibly with Sean or his mother. Willow had been taken out of the car at the time of her arrest and reunited with Kit, according to Edward. Neve was relieved to see the press hadn't taken up position outside the house.

'They were here earlier when Kit came home,' said Edward, looking across at Neve, as if reading her mind.

'Funny how the tables turn,' said Neve. 'One day they're your best friend, your ally, the next, they're your enemy and spies. Speaking of spies ...'

Neve looked across the road where Mrs Dalton was in her front garden. She appeared to be sweeping the drive, but Neve guessed she was really waiting to see what was going on. Neve turned away. She didn't have the time or patience for Mrs Dalton right now.

'Do you want me to come in with you and speak to Kit?' asked Edward.

'No, it's OK. I've texted him already,' said Neve.

'Looks like he's expecting you,' said Edward, nodding in the direction of the front door.

Neve followed his gaze and saw Kit standing on the doorstep, looking casual with his hands resting loosely in the front pocket of his jeans and wearing a white T-shirt. He looked so young. The weight of Poppy's disappearance lifted from every line and contour of his face and body. The relief was evident and yet it was his eyes which told the true story. They spoke volumes. He was seriously pissed off with her.

'Thank you,' she said to Edward, getting out of the car. She watched the solicitor drive away, taking a few moments to calm her nerves. She had got through several hours of interrogation by Pearson, who finally seemed to believe her, now she had to repeat the process with her husband. She wondered how much Pearson had told him.

She turned and walked towards Kit, coming to a halt a

few paces from him. 'Hi.' Such a casual greeting seemed so insufficient.

'I don't want you in the house,' said Kit.

Neve was taken aback. She hadn't been expecting to be barred from her own home. 'We need to talk,' she said, gently. 'I need to explain.'

'There's not much to explain,' said Kit. He reached behind him and closed the front door. 'You shagged your art therapy tutor. You decided to take him with you to rescue MY daughter. You had the key to the padlock. It all seems pretty self-explanatory to me.'

'I didn't shag my art tutor, as you so politely put it,' said Neve, prickling at his tone.

'You were going to. You wanted to. It's as good as.'

'No! No, it's not. Please, Kit, let's talk about this.'

'So, you're denying everything DCI Pearson told me? He's just made all that up, has he?'

'Do you really think for one moment I had something to do with Poppy's disappearance? How could I? Why would I?' Neve kept her voice level, she didn't want to match the sarcasm in Kit's. 'Someone put that key in my pocket. I've been through this with Edward and I know he's spoken to you and I've been through it with Pearson. I've been released. Doesn't that tell you something?'

'It tells me that they don't have the evidence.'

Neve took a step closer, her hand reaching out to touch Kit's forearm. 'Please, let's go inside and talk.' She glanced back over her shoulder at Mrs Dalton who was now leaning on her broom handle gawping over, making no attempt at a covert surveillance. Neve turned her back on the woman and looked pleadingly at Kit. 'It's still my home,' she said softly. 'You and Poppy are still my family.'

'I'll be the judge of that last statement,' said Kit. 'Look, Poppy's sleeping and my mum is in there. It's probably not the best place to talk. I'll grab my keys and we'll go for a ride in the car.'

The atmosphere in the car was suffocating. The tension sucked up the oxygen and at one point, Neve thought she was going to have to ask Kit to stop the car so that she could be sick. Instead, she let the window down and drank in the fresh air, not dissimilar to the way Willow liked to poke her nose out. Neve's journey, however, wasn't for a pleasant walk along the river path. Hers was more like a journey to the gallows.

Kit drove out of the village and up to the top of the Trundle, pulling up in the car park which overlooked the West Sussex coastal plain, taking in the city of Chichester and the English Channel beyond. It was one of their favourite spots and Neve took this as a good sign. 'We should have brought Willow with us,' she said.

'This isn't a jolly,' retorted Kit, causing Neve to instantly regret her light-hearted remark.

'Sorry,' she said.

Kit got out of the car and zipping up his jacket, waited for Neve to follow suit. She pulled her collar up on her coat and looking down at her boots, saw they were still muddy from her walk along the river path that morning. Was it really the same day? It seemed a lifetime ago. Now it was nearing five o'clock. She felt exhausted, as if she'd just gone ten rounds in the boxing ring with no gloves, gum shield or head guard.

But that was nothing to what she had to face now. A new opponent and a different fight.

'Right, first of all, what's this about that bloke who was hanging around Poppy last week? Pearson said you knew who he was?'

Neve noted the wording. Knew who he was, technically, was different to being accused of knowing Lee. 'I found out who he was,' she admitted. 'He works at The Forum, he's a support worker.'

'And you never thought to share that information with me?'

'I didn't want you to do anything, like confront him.'

'So, why, when I told Pearson about him, didn't you mention it then?'

'I was going to tell him but later. I thought you'd be mad at me. I didn't—'

'Too right I'd be mad at you!' Kit almost shouted. 'Poppy goes missing and all you can think about is yourself.'

'I'm sorry. I was upset. I wasn't making rational decisions.'

'You can say that again,' snapped Kit. 'And what about Jake? What the fuck is going on there? I got the distinct impression from Pearson that you are more than just friends. I'm really hoping you're going to tell me what a complete load of bullshit that is.'

Kit walked over to the edge of the car park, stopping in front of the wire fencing. The valley below was bathed in a stripe of sunlight that had escaped from the cloud-filled sky.

Neve positioned herself next to him, relieved that he'd dropped the subject of Lee, but it was definitely a case of out of the frying pan and into the fire. 'Please listen to what I'm going to say, listen to it all,' she said. She took his silence as agreement. 'I haven't had an affair with Jake. I promise you.' She took a deep breath. 'We have become good friends, though. What started off as a tutor/student relationship, quickly turned to friendship. I felt happy with him. Safe.' She noticed Kit bristle at her comment, his shoulders tensed, and his breathing deepened. 'Not as in safe from you, but safe from the crisis of our marriage.'

'I'd never hurt you, Neve,' he said, maintaining his stare into the distance.

'I know that,' replied Neve. 'I don't mean the physical fear, I mean the mental fear. That we were going so desperately wrong and that we seemed to be at a stalemate. I didn't know what to do. I didn't know how to make you change your mind about a baby.'

'And you thought having an affair would do the trick? Jesus, Neve! What fucking planet are you on?'

'I didn't have an affair!' Neve fought hard to keep her frustration under control. She grabbed at his arm, preventing him from turning away from her. 'I was safe at art therapy from everything that hurt me, everything that frightened me, everything that I couldn't control. I could express my fears in a safe place, through a safe medium. No one, not even Jake, would know what any of those pieces of art meant. No one would be able to interpret them. It was a release. It was doing its job.' She paused, letting the words sink in, feeling a sense of realisation. She had never been able to put what she felt into words before. She had never taken the time to internalise her thoughts and emotions. She had never been asked

237

and had never had to, but now explaining to Kit, was almost a light bulb moment.

'As things became worse between us, I gravitated more and more to art therapy and Jake. It wasn't a conscious decision. It just kind of happened.'

'You can spare me the details,' said Kit, with the bitterness of sour apples.

'I didn't mean it to develop into anything. I was at a particularly low point, but I somehow got caught up in it. It was like an escapism. I could pretend everything was all right in my world. A place where I didn't have responsibilities. I didn't have to be hiding from shit because there was no shit there.'

'In other words, hedonism. A fantasy world. Honestly, Neve, aren't you a bit old for all that crap?' Kit shrugged off her hand. 'I know things have been crap. Don't you think they've been like that for me too? But I didn't run off and fuck the first female that showed me a bit of affection.'

Neve blanched at his words. He made it sound so crude and despite everything, there had been nothing crude about her and Jake. 'It wasn't like that,' she said. 'I promise you, Kit, I didn't sleep with Jake.'

'Then what was it like? Do you want to shag him? Did you want to?'

'No, I don't. I was in love with the escapism. With the romantic notion that I could have a happy ever after. That I could have a world without all the responsibilities,' she paused. 'A world where I could have what I wanted.'

As soon as the words came out, she regretted them. They were far too honest for this conversation.

'What you wanted. Eh? A baby? You thought Jake could give you a baby because I wouldn't? Is that what this was all about?' He grabbed the top of her arms and for a second Neve thought he was going to shake an answer from her.

'No. Yes. I mean, I don't know. Maybe part of me thought that. In some far-fetched corner of my mind, maybe I thought that.'

He released his hold on her, his hands dropping to his side. He took a step back and looked at her, his head slowly shaking from side to side. 'I don't know you at all, do I? I have absolutely no idea who I'm married to.'

'You do, Kit,' said Neve, rushing forward. 'You do. What happened with Jake, or rather what didn't happen, was a knee-jerk reaction. It was a stupid, stupid notion. I would never do that to you. It's because I love you that I didn't.'

His eyes shone with tears. Neve couldn't remember the last time she had seen him cry prior to Poppy going missing.

'I don't know you,' he repeated. 'I know nothing about your past. What happened to make you estranged from your family. I knew something had happened and I always thought that one day you would tell me, but you never did. Even after we married, you kept that part of your life secret from me.' He took another step backwards. 'That's what you do best, Neve. You keep secrets.'

Neve wanted to deny it. To tell him he was wrong, but the words stuck in her throat. He was right, of course, she could keep a secret like no one she knew.

'I'm sorry but it's too painful,' she said.

'But I'm your husband. I'm here, or at least was here, to

stop you from hurting but you've never trusted me enough to let me try.' A single tear trickled down his face.

Neve could feel her own tears rising. 'I didn't want to contaminate you. Us.' She looked out over the hills, blinking hard. If she didn't keep control of her emotions, she would crumble right there on the spot. 'What we had was so beautiful and so precious. I couldn't believe that you loved me like you did. That despite what you had gone through, you still wanted to love again. I was honoured when you asked me to marry you. I truly was.' She gulped, maintaining her composure. 'I didn't want anything to spoil that. I didn't want my problems tainting us.'

'Christ, I can almost believe you,' said Kit, giving a small laugh. 'I want to believe you, but I just can't. You've deceived me. Not to mention Poppy. Where was she in your thoughts when all this was going on? Never mind what you were doing to me, what did you think you were doing to Poppy?'

'I love that child, like she's my own,' said Neve, the passion in her voice surprising her.

'But you don't,' said Kit. 'That's just it, you don't love her like she's your own because if you did, then you wouldn't have kept saying to me that you wanted a child of your own.'

'No, that's not true. You don't understand. Just because a woman has one child, it doesn't quell her desire to have another. And that's exactly how it was ... it is ... for me.'

Kit walked over to the bench and sat down. He rested his forearms on his knees, his hands clasped together, and his head bowed.

Sensing the fire had, for now, abated, Neve sat herself beside him. 'I'm sorry,' she said.

'Don't keep saying sorry,' said Kit. He lifted his head slightly to look at her. 'I just need to know the truth about everything. If I don't know that, then I can't even think about what's going to happen to us.'

Neve felt her stomach drop. 'I can't just spill it all out here,' she said, her mind treading water.

'I don't expect you to,' said Kit. 'To be honest, I'm totally rinsed. Exhausted. I don't think I can deal with much more today. But we need to have the conversation.'

'I know,' she whispered. He was throwing her a lifeline, one where there still might be hope for them as a couple.

'I don't think it would be a good idea to stay at the house right now. Mum's there. It won't be good for Poppy.'

Neve went to protest but changed her mind. She wasn't in a position to argue. 'I could stay at Lucie's,' she said.

'Yeah. That's what I thought. At least that way you'll still be close by.' Kit stood up. 'I need to get back to Poppy.'

'Can I just see her?' asked Neve. 'I just want to see her safe at home.'

Kit grunted an approving sound and they climbed silently back into the car, before heading home. On the way, Neve messaged Lucie asking if she could stay over for a few days. Lucie replied almost straight away, saying of course Neve could and she would put a bottle of wine in the fridge right that minute. Neve thanked the stars that she had such a good friend.

'Does Lucie know about … about your friendship with Jake?' said Kit, breaking the silence between them.

'No. There was nothing to tell,' said Neve. She couldn't see from the look on Kit's face whether he thought this was a good or a bad thing but decided not to push for an opinion.

Ten minutes later, Kit swung his Mercedes onto the drive and led the way into the house. From the living room Cheryl appeared.

'Hello, Neve,' she said, folding her arms as she stood at the foot of the stairs. 'I'm surprised to see you here.'

'Hello, Cheryl. Nice to see you too and, by the way, it is my home.' Neve looked at Kit.

'Home is where the heart is,' said Cheryl. 'And from where I'm standing, your heart isn't here.'

'Mum,' admonished Kit. 'Leave it.'

'I'm only saying what I think,' said Cheryl. 'Honesty is the best policy.' She looked pointedly at Neve.

'Just go and sit back down, Mum,' said Kit.

'In other words, don't get involved,' Neve found herself saying. After seven years of marriage, Neve was an expert at biting her tongue, but today she was in no mood for offering Cheryl any leeway.

She ignored Cheryl's protests to Kit that Neve shouldn't speak to her like that and headed for the staircase. At the half-landing, she glanced over the banisters to see Kit closing the door on his mother, rather like you would a toddler or a puppy you didn't want escaping.

Kit looked up at her. 'Thanks for that.'

'She started it,' said Neve, acknowledging she sounded rather childish; a thought reinforced by the eye-roll Kit gave.

Neve nimbly made it to the top of the landing and, stopping outside Poppy's bedroom door, she gently turned the handle. The spring gave a small squeak of displeasure before releasing and allowing Neve entry. She poked her head round the door.

The curtains were drawn but they were thin enough to allow a soft haze of daylight through for Neve to see Poppy's sleeping figure on the bed. Dressed in her pjs and cuddling the bear that Neve and Poppy had brought from the bear workshop place in Brighton. Neve padded across the deep carpeted floor.

Poppy's hair had been washed and was still a bit damp at her scalp. Cheryl had probably washed it for her and a small pang of jealousy shot through Neve. It was her job to wash Poppy's hair. It was their twice-weekly ritual, something they spent time together doing. A gesture that often reminded Neve of the monkeys and gorillas in the zoo and how they groomed each other in a display of affection.

Neve knelt down at the bedside and tucked a strand of hair behind Poppy's ear. Then very carefully, she picked up the patchwork quilt she had made Poppy several years ago and draped it over her daughter's shoulders.

As she stood up, she noticed Kit standing in the doorway. She couldn't quite read the look on his face. Was it sadness, love, warmth or was it pity? She wasn't sure she wanted pity. What was he feeling pitiful about? Her? Them? Poppy?

He jerked his head towards the landing and Neve followed him out of the room, pausing to take one last look at Poppy. She was home and really, at the end of the day, that was all that mattered. With an overwhelming realisation, Neve acknowledged that wanting anything else from this situation had been totally selfish.

It shouldn't take something like this to repair her broken

marriage. Her and Kit should try to work it out themselves, although she wondered now if she had left it too late. That she had made an error of judgement and got this whole thing totally wrong.

Chapter 25

'There she is,' said Kit, slipping his arm around Poppy's shoulder and giving her a hug. '*Blue Horizon*. And the sun has even come out for us.'

Poppy gave an indifferent shrug. 'The sun comes out every day, so it's not true to say that it has come out for us.'

'True,' said Kit, with a smile. It seemed that whatever had happened to Poppy, it hadn't affected her. Not that he had noticed yet anyway. The psychologist had said it may be some time before the effects were fully understood but Kit hoped with all his heart that wouldn't be the case. Still, they'd deal with it if and when it happened. He wasn't sure if bringing Poppy back to the boat so soon was a good idea or not. He gave his daughter a sideways look as he tapped in the entry code for the moorings' gate and opened it for her to walk through. She did so without hesitation. He took this as a good sign.

'Is my bag still on board?' she asked as they approached the boat.

'Everything is,' said Kit. 'I had Sean bring her back after ...' His voice trailed off, not knowing how to describe her disappearance.

Sue Fortin

'After I went missing,' supplied Poppy, in her matter of fact way.

Kit inwardly sighed at his daughter's bluntness. A child psychologist had counselled Poppy a couple of times now, but had been unsuccessful in gleaning any information out of Poppy, who it appeared remembered very little and certainly nothing of note. Her memory appeared to be either blank or locked out of reach. It was difficult to say what, if any, the long-term effects might be.

'Yes, after you went missing,' said Kit. He could feel a lump in his throat the texture of ballast. He felt weak compared to his daughter. Even the thought of what happened was bringing him to the edge of sanity.

As the pontoon bounced gently under their step, one of the other boat owners was climbing down from his launch. As he looked up, Kit watched the man startle at the sight of Poppy and Kit walking along. He then quickly schooled his face into a smile and gave a nod of his head.

'Morning,' he said, making eye contact with Kit.

'Morning,' replied Kit, looking away. He had never exchanged more than a few words with the guy, perhaps accompanied by some inane comments about the weather, and he certainly didn't want to start now. Kit felt self-conscious. Not a feeling he experienced often. And there was another emotion tucked away there, one he didn't like and could barely admit to himself. Shame. He felt ashamed of himself. Everyone in the marina would know what had happened to Poppy and, no doubt, they all had their own opinions about who was to blame. Kit could forgive them for blaming him. They had every right to. He had failed as a father to keep his daughter safe. He hadn't been able to protect her when she needed him. He wasn't sure he could ever forgive himself for that one.

Now alongside *Blue Horizon*, Kit pulled himself up and over the side ropes. As he did so, he felt a moment of light-headedness. He closed his eyes, waiting for the sensation to pass. He'd been feeling like this since Poppy had disappeared off the boat. The whole incident had put a tremendous amount of stress on him and he was finding it hard to even think straight at times. The moment passed, and he placed the small step ladder against the side of the boat, so Poppy could climb up.

'I can do it,' said Poppy, refusing the hand her father held out to her. She climbed over, her foot catching on the rope but still insisting she didn't need help.

Kit wondered how she had managed to get off the boat so easily on her own the night she went missing. She would have either had to lower the ladder herself and slide it back onto the deck which would have made a noise. Or someone helped her. He still couldn't make sense of her exit that night. He wished he could remember at least some sort of detail.

He unlocked the cabin door and descended the three wooden steps, ducking his head as he did so. The crime scene team had been in and searched the place. All their belongings lay around, as if they had been freeze-framed. Poppy's sleeping bag, pillow and rucksack were spread out across the aft cabin. Another blanket that Kit vaguely remembered being over Neve's legs at some point, was on the floor. From the two washed up wine glasses sitting on the draining board, it was obvious he and Neve had been drinking. An empty bottle of

Shiraz was on the small worktop next to the sink and another empty one was in the bin. Had they really drunk two whole bottles between them?

A sudden image of himself and Neve sitting on the sofa, wine glasses in hand and Neve throwing her head back, laughing, came to mind but disappeared the next second. So fleeting was the image, Kit hadn't been able to pin down the time or the occasion. Was it last week, last month, last year? He tried hard to think, to visualise them on the boat a few days ago, but he couldn't. He could get as far as mooring up and even that was hazy, but beyond that his memory was just empty.

He closed his eyes and tried to recall the snapshot of memory he had just experienced. If he could just hit the refresh key in his brain, then maybe it would trigger a whole host of other memories.

'I need my bag.' Poppy's voice broke his thoughts as she made her way into the saloon and then brushed past him to her cabin. Her blue and white daisy patterned rucksack was on the bed, the contents strewn across the sleeping bag where the police had searched for clues.

Kit stared around the small living space. What the hell had happened that night? As his gaze brushed the door to the cabin at the forepeak where he and Neve had slept, he experienced another flashback. Neve propping him up with her shoulder lodged under his arm, as he draped himself over her. Just as before, the mental image was gone as quickly as it had arrived. But that brief snippet of information was enough to convince Kit that he had been very much more drunk than he had assumed.

Where was Poppy when all this was going on? Again, he had no recollection to call upon. He could only suppose that she was sleeping in her cabin. Reluctant to ask her, in case it pre-empted a funny turn or traumatic memory, Kit was none the wiser. If only Poppy could remember or at least open up with what she did recall, then the police might stand half a chance of catching the bastard who did this.

'Your shoelace is undone,' said Poppy, coming into the saloon and plonking herself down on the bench seat. Picking up her rucksack, Kit watched her fish around for her purse and taking the coins from it, she began counting them out, stacking them on the seat cushion. 'Your shoelace is undone,' she repeated without looking up at him.

He crouched to tie up the errant lace. As he went to stand, he rested his hand on the seat to push himself up. The cushion sank and sent the pile of coins tumbling across the floor of the boat.

'Dad!' cried Poppy, diving onto the deck to gather up the coins.

'Oh, sorry. Here, let me help.'

'There's a two-pound coin missing,' said Poppy, after they had collected all the coins. 'It's a special one. It has St Paul's Cathedral on the back.'

Kit looked around but couldn't see it anywhere. 'Are you sure?'

'Positive.' Poppy was frantically searching through the coins.

'Here, I might have one in my pocket,' said Kit.

'No. It has to be the St Paul's Cathedral one.'

Knowing his daughter wouldn't accept anything less than

finding the exact coin, Kit dropped to his knees once more and swept his hand slowly back and forth across the floor in the hope of locating the coin. He had no luck.

'Maybe it rolled away,' he said, still on his hands and knees. He crouched even lower and peered under the freestanding kitchen units. Taking his phone from his pocket and switching on the light, he illuminated the two-inch gap. 'Aha! There it is.' Kit slid his hand underneath and patted around on the wooden boards. Something brushed his fingertips. Not the coin, but something else. He pulled out the item and inspected his find. It was a small glass vial with a cork stopper in the top. It reminded him of something from his chemistry set when he was a lad.

'That's not my coin,' said Poppy.

'Oh, yes. Sorry.' Kit slid his hand in for the second time and retrieved his daughter's treasure. 'There you go.'

As Poppy put her money back in her purse, Kit stood up and took a closer look at the vial. He tipped it at an angle, and a minuscule drop of liquid slid down the tube. Strange, Kit couldn't for the life of him think what it was or where it had come from, but he had an uneasy sense of déjà-vu. He forced himself to focus on that feeling, trying to pull a conscious memory from the subconscious thought. The vial felt important, but he had no idea why. He took the stopper out and gingerly sniffed the tube but there was no aroma. Again, he tried to harness some connection to the tube as he gazed at the worktop but all he could picture was a hazy memory of Neve looking over her shoulder at him and smiling.

'Will we be long?' came Poppy's voice.

Kit turned to his daughter. 'What? Oh, no, not too long.' He adjusted his estimation for Poppy's peace of mind. 'Twenty minutes and we'll be done.' He watched his daughter pull a face of displeasure. 'Poppy,' said Kit, sitting down beside her. 'Are you OK being here after what happened?' He didn't want to upset her, but it felt a good time to ask. He wished he knew what had happened to Poppy. Not knowing was the worst possible thing. He'd hated not knowing where she had been during those missing days and he'd thought that once she was back, he wouldn't care. At the time, just having his daughter home was the most important thing. Now, though, the not knowing was another kind of torture to endure.

Kit had at one point or another suspected practically everyone of taking Poppy or being involved with her disappearance, but he'd come to the same conclusion every time, the only conclusion that made any sense – Jake must have been involved. He either wanted Poppy out of the way, so Neve wouldn't have any qualms about leaving Kit or, and this one seemed more likely, he wanted to play hero to Neve by finding Poppy.

Kit looked at his daughter as she considered his question. 'You know you can talk to me, don't you?' he said.

'Yeah. I'm just bored. Can we take the boat out?' Her eyes lit up with excitement.

'Not today. But we will another day. Soon. I promise.' Kit took a reassuring breath before he spoke again. 'Being back here, has it reminded you of anything that happened that night?' He ventured.

'I won at Monopoly,' said Poppy.

'Apart from that?'

251

'You were drunk.'

'What?' Kit gave a laugh.

'You were!' replied Poppy, clearly amused at what she was saying. 'I saw you.'

'I had a glass of wine,' said Kit, glancing back at the two washed up glasses on the drainer. He attempted and failed to dredge up the elusive memory of that night.

'Neve had to help you to bed,' said Poppy gleefully. She stood up and, swaying from side to side, staggered to the bedroom, holding onto the doorframe as she did so. Then collapsed back down beside Kit in a fit of giggles.

Kit ruffled his daughter's hair. 'I was that bad, huh?' It was good to see Poppy laughing, she had such a beautiful smile, just like her mother's. Kit felt a small tug at his heart. It didn't happen often, but now and again the memory of his first wife caught him off-guard. Although, he acknowledged that these days it wasn't so much a small pain, but a deep sadness. He pulled Poppy in for a hug, reminding himself of the fact that he had his daughter back. And somewhere at the back of his mind, a distant nagging voice grew a little louder, prodding his conscience that he was denying Neve the very same privilege he cherished so dearly.

He had so many mixed emotions where Neve was concerned. The revelation that she had been on the brink of an affair with Jake hadn't been as much of a surprise as Kit thought it should have been. He acknowledged that somewhere, deep down inside him, somewhere he had avoided visiting, he knew, or at least suspected, that Neve and Jake were closer than was normal for a student and tutor. Now, he supposed, he had been in denial because it would have meant challenging his own behaviour and how he had treated Neve, what he had done to cause his wife to seek comfort and love from someone else. It cut him deep. He felt betrayed and yet guilty, at the same time. Ultimately, he could have stopped the situation from snowballing any further, by speaking to Neve in the first place. Speaking to her when things first started to go wrong for them, but he had been too bloody stubborn and full of injustice to himself. He wasn't sure where or when he'd crossed the line into being bloody-minded and passing the buck to Neve, but that's what he'd done. He realised that now. He'd made a huge mistake and his heart was paying dearly.

He was embarrassed to admit that it had taken Poppy's disappearance to bring it all into sharp focus. Now, it was startlingly obvious he had neglected his wife and he was partly responsible for driving her into Jake's arms. Again, the darkest of thoughts teased him from the shadows of his mind. Had he been so neglectful of Neve that she had been driven to drastic measures to find the happiness she craved? He had learnt a lot about his wife in the last week or so, but there were still many unanswered questions. He was a pragmatic man and he knew wishing and regretting wouldn't change anything. If he wanted things to change then he needed to make sure he was at the helm of those changes. It was no good leaving it to someone else and then to complain after-wards when he didn't like the course his marriage was steering.

The next fifteen minutes were spent hurriedly cleaning and tidying the debris from their night on the boat. Kit was aware that Poppy was now clock-watching and his promised twenty minutes until departure was imminent.

'Are you sure you've got everything?' asked Kit, taking one last glance into the sleeping quarters and then around the saloon.

Poppy tapped her rucksack which she had balanced on her knees. 'Everything,' she said. She looked at her watch. 'Time to go.'

'Aye, aye, Captain,' said Kit, giving a mock salute. 'All present and correct.' He picked up the overnight bag that contained his and Neve's clothes and was just about to follow Poppy up the ladder when he spotted the glass vial he'd left on the worktop.

He scooped it up and went to drop it into the bin, but something stopped him and instead he slid it into his jacket pocket. He couldn't put his finger on what was troubling him about the vial, apart from the fact he'd no recollection of seeing it before and he knew every inch of this boat. Yet, at the same time it felt familiar. The sensation was tantalizingly close to forming a tangible memory and it felt important. It felt hugely important that he should remember.

Chapter 26

'Thanks so much for letting me stay, I really appreciate it,' said Neve to Lucie, wiping down the kitchen worktop after their evening meal. She had been at the flat for a few days now, barely venturing out, not wanting to see anybody. She was desperate to see Poppy, but so far, Kit had been reluctant to agree to anything, stating that Poppy needed time to recover.

She sat down on the sofa as Lucie opened a bottle of wine and poured two glasses, passing one over to Neve. 'Do you think you'll be able to sort things out with Kit?'

'I hope so,' said Neve. 'Don't get me wrong, there's nothing I'd love more than to be at home with Kit and Poppy but we need time. And the fact that the police think I'm involved with Poppy's disappearance isn't helping.'

'I still can't believe they even think that,' declared Lucie. 'They must be looking at other suspects. They can't think it's you.'

'I had the key in my pocket,' said Neve. 'I can't explain how it got there. I just hope they are doing what Edward said they should be and interviewing everyone else.'

'Who do you think it was?'

'I have not got a clue. Every possibility keeps going around and around in my head in a loop – it's never ending.'

Lucie shifted position and ran her finger around the rim of her glass. 'There's something I should tell you,' she said, not meeting Neve's eye. 'About what people are saying.'

'Spit it out,' sighed Neve.

'I don't believe it, of course,' said Lucie quickly.

'Just say it. I've broad shoulders,' reassured Neve.

'Well ... I hear things in the café, they're saying you and Jake are having an affair.' She pulled an apologetic face.

Neve sighed. 'Me and Jake are friends, good friends but we are not having an affair.'

'It's just talk. I don't believe them for a start,' said Lucie. She took a sip of her wine. 'Mind you, I wouldn't mind an affair with him. He can wine and dine me anytime. He's bloody gorgeous, if you ask me, all dark and brooding and arty but, then again so is Kit but not the dark bit.'

Neve looked up at the ceiling in a mixture of despair and amusement. 'You're such a romantic,' she said.

'I try. One day, I'll have some Prince Charming wanting to ride off into the sunset with me.' Lucie smiled fondly at Neve. 'Seriously, though, haven't you even been tempted?'

'He's a lovely man,' conceded Neve. 'But I have too much at stake. I might have considered it, but I couldn't do that to Poppy. I couldn't leave her. I couldn't do it to Kit either, just in case you're wondering. Look, I'll be honest, and this must go no further ...'

Lucie crossed her heart. 'I promise.'

'I *did* consider it. Jake knew how sad I was and said he could make me happy.'

'Wow, that's romantic, if not a little confident.'

'He's a nice guy. Really nice but (a) I couldn't leave Kit or Poppy, and (b) even if there was the slightest chance I could take Poppy, Jake wouldn't have wanted to take on another man's child. No, it was just fanciful, head in the clouds, talk.'

'Kit wouldn't ever let you take Poppy,' said Lucie.

'Exactly. Although, technically, I am her mother. I adopted her when Kit and I got married, so in the eyes of the law, I am equally entitled to custody.'

'Why doesn't she call you Mum? If you don't mind me asking?'

'It's hard to get Poppy to see things differently once she's made up her mind. I was introduced to her as Neve and, in her eyes, that's that. I would always and will always be Neve.'

'Oh, right. Didn't think of that. So, despite you adopting her, Kit is her biological father and that has to count for more, surely?'

'We had all this explained when the adoption was going through. It's all about parental responsibility. I'm Poppy's adoptive mother, I have the same parental responsibilities as Kit does.'

'I'm no expert but wouldn't the courts take into account Poppy's wishes,' said Lucie. 'Or does that not apply because of her learning difficulties?'

'She's under fourteen so no. It would be up to the judge.'

'All seems a bit complicated,' said Lucie.

'It is and it's all hypothetical anyway. I'm not running off with Jake. I'm going to try to salvage my marriage,' said Neve. 'If I'm honest, I got swept away in the excitement of having someone giving me attention. Someone who was interested in me as a person. Kit's forgotten all that. Or at least he had.' Neve tutted at herself. 'I sound so bloody needy and selfish when I say it out loud.'

Lucie gave her a sympathetic glance, which only further convinced Neve that her self-appraisal was correct.

'I don't think I ever wanted to leave Kit. Not really. I think I was testing both myself and him.' Neve shuffled position on the sofa, so she was facing Lucie. 'What I really want is to have a baby with Kit, but as you know, that's been a major sticking point. It's such a bloody mess.'

'You're telling me,' said Lucie. 'Maybe Kit will come round, if you give him some time. He's been through a monumentally traumatic event, you both have. Maybe when things have settled down, you two will be able to patch things up.'

'We have lots of things to patch up before we go any further,' said Neve, with a sadness at the realisation of the things that were still between them. 'I might have gone too far.'

Lucie gave Neve a curious look but before she could form any kind of question, there was a long and insistent ring on the doorbell to the flat.

Lucie put her glass on the table and went over to the window, peering out onto the metal staircase at the rear of the café.

'Shit!' She ducked back from the glass and turned to Neve. 'It's Jake.'

'Shit,' echoed Neve. 'What the hell is he doing here?'

'Sorry, telepathy isn't working right now,' said Lucie. 'I'm guessing it's you he wants to speak to, not me.'

'Tell him I'm not here,' whispered Neve, jumping up and darting through the door into the bedroom.

With her ear to the door, she listened to the conversation that ensued.

'Jake! Hi, you OK?'

'I need to speak to Neve.'

'Oh, hello Lucie. I'm fine, thanks. How are you? Oh, that's good. Look, sorry to bother you, but you haven't seen Neve by any chance have you?'

Neve allowed herself a small smile. Good old Lucie.

'Oh. Sorry. Yeah.' She could hear Jake stumbling over his words, clearly taken aback by Lucie's sarcasm. 'I'm trying to find Neve. She's not answering her phone and it's really important I speak to her.'

'She's not here. I can try to get a message to her.'

'Is that why her car is parked downstairs, there's two wine glasses over there by the sofa and I'm pretty sure that's Neve's bag.'

Damn it. In her haste Neve hadn't thought to clear any evidence.

'Actually, it's my bag,' Lucie was saying now. 'And, err, I poured two glasses by accident ...'

Neve sighed and opening the door, stepped out in the living room and into Jake's line of sight. 'It's OK, Lucie,' she said.

Lucie pulled a sorry face at Neve. 'Look, I've got to nip downstairs to the café and take a couple of things out of the freezer. You've got ten minutes.' She looked from Neve and then to Jake. 'I'll be honest, I'm not totally in love with the idea of a clandestine meeting taking place in my flat.'

'My car is outside if you prefer,' offered Jake.

'OK.' Neve picked up her handbag and followed Jake out

of the flat, pausing along the way to give Lucie a peck on the cheek. 'Won't be long.'

The old Saab that Jake drove was still warm inside, and Neve settled herself into the seat. 'Maybe drive out of the village, away from prying eyes,' she suggested.

'My thoughts exactly,' said Jake, as he pulled away.

He drove out to the edge of the village and down Wharf Hill to a small car park overlooking the harbour.

'I take it things are pretty shit at home or you wouldn't be staying with Lucie,' said Jake, breaking the silence.

'How did you know?'

'I had the pleasure of bumping into your mother-in-law outside the post office this afternoon. She soon put me in my place and updated me on your situation.'

'Sorry,' said Neve.

'Least of your problems right now, I'd say.'

'Thanks. You really know how to cheer a girl up.' Neve looked across the harbour at the little boats moored on the chain. The tide was on its way out and some of them were leaning to one side as the water seeped away from under their hulls. Rather like her own predicament. Kit and Poppy were the tide, and Neve both the boat and the slipping sand.

'The police released you, then?' she said, turning her attention back to Jake.

'Yep. Without charge. Neve, I swear to you I didn't have anything to do with Poppy going missing,' said Jake, turning in his seat, his jacket rustling against the leather interior of the car. 'The police kept asking me if I'd put that key in your pocket. Insisting that I must have done. Asking me where I got the key from. They even asked me if I was involved with Poppy being kidnapped!'

'What did you say?'

'That I didn't, of course! Jesus, don't tell me you think I was too.'

'No. I don't,' said Neve. 'But I also can't explain what the key was doing in my pocket or how it got there.' She dipped her head and picked at her nails before speaking again. 'They think you have the motive.'

'I fucking know it!' Jake practically cried out. 'They think I was getting rid of Poppy so you would leave Kit. I've no idea where they got that notion from. I told them they were barking up the wrong tree. If I'd done that, why the hell was I keeping her alive.'

Neve winced at his words. 'Don't say that.'

'Sorry, I didn't mean to upset you, but you can see what I'm up against,' said Jake. 'They're grasping at straws. None of it makes sense.'

'It doesn't make sense, I agree but it's the key, Jake. No pun intended but that is key,' said Neve, now looking at him. 'They think you put the key in my pocket when I met you at the canal path.'

'It's bollocks. My solicitor said it won't stand up in court.'

'They're implying that you sent the ransom note,' added Neve. 'It was hand delivered so they think it's someone local.'

'I never sent a bloody ransom note.' Jake's voice pitched higher than normal. 'Someone is setting me up.'

'That's exactly what I said.'

'I wouldn't be surprised if it's Kit himself,' said Jake. 'He engineered all this to get his revenge on me. On both of us.

I can't think who else would do that. He's one sick bastard anyway.'

'I can't see it, but then people do some strange things,' said Neve, thinking through the scenario. 'There are other people too, who may be involved.'

'Who do you mean?' said Jake. 'Tell me. I need to give my solicitor every possible bit of information I can.'

'Well, that Ben Hewitt I told you about. The kid who was bullying Poppy. And his mother and father.'

'Really? A fifteen-year-old? I don't buy that. And the Hewitts, I know they're a bit rough, but kidnapping ...'

'A bit rough. The mother is a bloody psycho,' said Neve, recalling her altercation with Linda.

'The police asked me about Lee,' said Jake. 'Did you know he's disappeared?'

'No,' said Neve. 'Is he still missing?'

'As far as I know and, like I said, that Pearson was quizzing me about him today, so I'm assuming so. Has Poppy said anything about it all?'

'No. She's not talking about it yet. She just keeps saying she doesn't know to every question she's asked. From how she got off the boat, to who took her away, where they took her, or how she got to the mill. All they do know is that she was looked after and that no one touched her or harmed her in any physical way.'

'And all for ten grand. It doesn't add up.'

In the fading light, Neve could see the tide had now receded, leaving the boats stranded on the mud. Again, she couldn't help likening it to her own situation. She was stranded. Nowhere to go. She had to sit tight until the tide changed. Sit tight. Hold her nerve. There was no room for error or she'd sink like a shipwrecked boat.

'Did you know Lee before he came here?' asked Jake.

The question took Neve by surprise. 'Lee? Erm ... no. What makes you ask that?'

'Just something he said,' replied Jake, pursing his lips.

'Like what?' Neve tried to keep the anxiety from her voice.

'I saw you and him talking outside the studio that day that Kit was there looking at your artwork. When I say talking, I actually mean arguing.'

Neve shrugged. 'And?'

'He came in muttering about Neve Tansley being a stuck up ... well ... he didn't say anything particularly flattering,' said Jake. 'But the point I'm making is that he said Tansley. I corrected him and said your name was Masters and he was, like, oh yeah, that's right, I got it wrong.'

'So, he got my name wrong,' said Neve. Sweat pricked her brow and she wiped it away with her fingertips.

'He wouldn't say what you were arguing about but, to me, it didn't look like two strangers arguing.'

'What exactly are you trying to imply?' demanded Neve.

'That you know Lee. That's why you were keen to find out about him when you came to me. I was gullible enough to show you his profile on the database. You know Lee Farnham from before, don't you?'

'It's irrelevant and none of your business,' said Neve.

'Others might not think so.'

'What do you mean?'

'Look, Neve, I'm not trying to drop you in it or anything, but I'm trying to save my own backside here. You and Lee have got a history. I don't know what it is, but if he's gone missing the same time as Poppy has, it's no wonder the police are interested.'

'And you've told the police all this, I take it?' said Neve. More sweat, this time under her arms and down her spine. Her leg jiggled involuntarily.

'No. Not yet,' said Jake. He moved his hand across to Neve's leg, holding it still. 'I wanted to make sure that you were absolutely certain about us. Or not us, as it turns out.' He leant over and went to kiss her.

'What are you doing?' cried Neve, pushing him away. 'Jake! Stop!'

Jake slumped back in his seat. 'I'm sorry. Sorry, that was really stupid of me.'

'Yes, it was! We're both under suspicion for kidnapping and you're trying it on with me. I told you, I love Kit. I'm not leaving him. I was never going to leave Kit for you.' Shock had taken over and her words were clumsy. It was a moment or two before Neve calmed down and realised she had been less than tactful. She could see the hurt on Jake's face. 'I didn't mean it to come out like that.'

The hurt morphed into anger. 'You're actually quite a cold-hearted bitch.' Jake almost spat the words out. 'All this, woe is me, I'm fragile, I've got issues – it's just an act. I was a fool to be taken in by it.'

'You don't know what you're talking about,' said Neve.

'I know exactly what I'm talking about. As for you and Lee, there's definitely something of interest there for the police. I don't know what it is, but I can sense it.'

'You know what, Jake, you're talking out of your arse,' said

Neve. She grappled with the door handle. 'You do what you like but I don't ever want anything to do with you. Got it?'

She yanked open the door and jumped out. Before closing it, she leaned down, peering into the car and Jake's face, mostly now cast in shadow. 'You're the one who the police should be interested in. You wanted to meet me at the foot-path the other morning. You're the one who put the key in my pocket.'

With that, she slammed the car door shut and marched back up the hill away from the harbour. She glanced back over her shoulder at the sound of Jake's voice.

'You're a liar!' he shouted across the roof of the car. 'I'm not taking the blame. This is my life we're talking about. This isn't some stupid game.'

Neve carried on walking up the lane, wishing there was more than the single street lamp at the bottom of the hill. The sound of a car approaching broke through the still of the night. Instinctively, she stepped back into the shadows of the tree, waiting for it to pass. She didn't want to be seen with Jake.

The walk back to Lucie's didn't take long at all and Neve was grateful she had her flat boots on. Lucie was sprawled out across the sofa when Neve let herself into the flat.

'Ah, you're back,' said Lucie, sitting up. 'Everything OK?'

'Yeah. Fine. I need a drink. Any of that wine left?'

Lucie bent down and picking up the wine bottle by the neck, waved it in the air. 'Just enough for another glass each, I'd say. Fear not, though, I have some more downstairs if we need it.'

Neve plonked herself down next to Lucie. 'That was

awkward. Jake still thought there might be a chance of us getting together.'

'You're joking?'

'Nope. I had to put him straight.'

'How did he take it?'

'Wasn't too happy but he'll get over it. I probably wasn't as tactful as I could have been, but to be honest, Jake is not a priority, right now.' Neve took a gulp of her wine. She suddenly felt weary and tired of thinking about her situation and everything that was going on. 'Let's talk about something nice for a change.'

They chatted in the relaxed way that good friends do, and Neve was grateful for the distraction. She was even amenable to Lucie putting on an old film and found herself enjoying the gentleness of a Doris Day movie. At some point, she must have nodded off because she was woken by the thundering of fists on the door of the flat.

'What the hell is that?' cried Lucie, jumping to her feet.

Neve was a second slower in propelling herself from her sleep and joining Lucie at the door. Lucie switched on the outside light and looked through the window. Neve peered over her shoulder.

'It's DCI Pearson,' said Neve. 'You'd better open the door.'

'Sorry to bother you. DCI Pearson, this is my colleague PC Radcliffe,' said Pearson to Lucie, before looking beyond her at Neve. 'I need to speak to you, Mrs Masters.'

Lucie opened the door to allow the detective and his colleague in.

'Neve,' began Pearson. 'Can you tell me when you last had any contact with Jake Rees?'

Neve quickly ran through the list of dos and don'ts Edward had given her and was pretty certain that speaking to Jake hadn't featured on there. Despite this, she had felt wary about confessing to seeing him earlier. She contemplated telling a lie but opted for a reply worthy of a politician fielding an awkward question.'

'Why? Is everything all right?'

DCI Pearson gave a small rise of his eyebrows. 'What makes you ask that?'

'Well, I'm guessing you wouldn't be banging on the door at ...' she checked her watch, '... eleven thirty at night unless it was an emergency.'

'Very well,' said Pearson. 'Jake Rees was found by the harbour this evening, with a serious head injury. He's currently in intensive care at the local hospital. His condition is critical. He was slipping in and out of consciousness and the paramedic who attended the scene said he kept repeating the same thing over and over. Neve. He said your name several times.'

Chapter 27

Neve spent the evening once again at the police station in the presence of her solicitor.

'I'm so sorry you've been dragged out at this time of night,' she said, as Edward took his place beside her.

'All part of the job,' said Edward. He opened his case and took out his notebook. Right, do you want to run me through what happened?'

'I was at Lucie's flat last night. I got there at about eight. We had a drink and then at about nine o'clock, Jake came to the flat.'

'Unannounced?'

'Yes. I wasn't expecting him at all. He wanted to speak to me, so we went out to his car.'

Edward scribbled some notes down. 'And then?'

'We drove down to the harbour. Jake wanted to talk. Not so much about Poppy, as about us. I told him that I didn't want to see him anymore. I left him at the harbour and walked back to Lucie's flat. We watched a film. We fell asleep and the next thing I knew, the police were banging on the door.'

'You make it sound very simple.'

'It is,' said Neve. She dipped her head into her hands. This was so difficult. She couldn't get her head round the fact that Jake had been attacked. Edward added to his notes and asked Neve for some more detail before telling Pearson they were ready for the interview.

Pearson and another officer came into the interview and set up the recording device.

'All set?'

'Yes, thank you,' said Edward.

Pearson cleared his throat. 'I just need to remind you, Neve that you are still under caution.'

He went over the early part of the evening with Neve. No difficult questions but Neve was careful to consider her answers first, just as Edward had instructed.

'So, Jake called round and you went off with him – where did you go?' asked Pearson.

'We drove out to the harbour,' said Neve. 'It was Jake who suggested we go there.'

Edward placed a hand on Neve's arm. 'Remember, just answer the questions. If the DCI wants any more information, he'll ask for it.'

Pearson gave Edward a glare but carried on. 'And what happened when you got to the harbour?'

'We talked.'

'About what?'

'About what happened at the mill,' said Neve. She caught the irritated look on Pearson's face as she followed Edward's instructions to the letter.

'Please expand. Tell me in more detail what was said.'

'We tried to guess who was behind it all.'

'You didn't argue?'

'No.'

'How did you get home?' asked Pearson.

'I walked.'

'What time was that?'

Neve considered the question. She couldn't really remember what time she left. 'About ten-fifteen. I'm not entirely sure.'

'Why didn't Jake drop you back?'

'I wanted some fresh air. A chance to clear my head.'

'And when you left Jake, he was perfectly OK?'

'Yes.'

'You didn't see anyone else while you were there?'

'No.'

'And you got back to the flat when?'

'About ten-thirty, maybe ten-forty. As I said, I can't really be sure of the times.'

'Did you go anywhere else?'

Again, Neve took a few moments to think about the questions before answering. She couldn't really remember walking home. She must have been on autopilot. She remembered getting out of the car and walking up the hill and seeing another car, but after that it was a bit of a blank. Still, she decided not to share that information with Pearson. 'No. I went straight there.'

'When you left Jake, did he mention about seeing anyone else, was he planning on meeting up with anyone?'

'Not that I remember. I assumed he was going back to his studio,' said Neve.

'He didn't mention anyone he might have fallen out with recently?' said Pearson, and then with a smile added, 'Barring your husband, of course.'

Neve shot the detective a look, unsure what he was getting at. She felt like she was being lead into a trap blindfolded. It was like one of those stupid corporate trust games and team building exercises. Except she had no intention of trusting the police officer in front of her.

'Jake never mentioned anything to me about anyone,' she said.

Edward sat up straight. 'I think my client has answered all your questions now. She's been very co-operative and helpful. Unless you have any further questions or evidence linking her to the crime, then we're done here.' Edward closed his notebook and rose from the chair. 'Come on, Neve.'

Pearson gave another of his glowers, but Neve knew he couldn't keep her there any longer than necessary. 'Don't go very far,' he said. 'You're still under caution.'

Neve bit down the urge to tell him he sounded like a broken record and she was well aware of the fact.

'I'll drop you at home or wherever you want to go,' said Edward, as they left the police station.

'That's kind of you,' said Neve. 'I'll go to my friend's flat. I'll direct you.'

'Sure, no problem.'

Soon after, Neve climbed the steps to Lucie's flat.

'Neve! Thank goodness. I was getting worried about you. Are you OK?'

'I'm fine. Just tired. Are you? Did the police need to speak to you?'

'They just wanted to confirm what time you got here last night, when you went out and when you got back. I didn't have to go down to the station or anything. I still can't believe it about Jake. You must be feeling awful.'

'It's all just so surreal,' said Neve. As she spoke, her legs gave way and she grabbed the handrail to steady herself.

'You need to get inside,' said Lucie, supporting Neve under the arm and helping her into the flat. She guided her to the living room. 'Sit there, I'll make you a strong sweet cup of tea.'

Neve did as she was told, allowing her body to relax into the sofa, where she finally let the tears fall. Silent tears, turning into sobs and then into a rolling ball of pain from the pit of her stomach.

Lucie was by her side, holding her, comforting her, soothing her. 'That's it, let it all out. It's the shock,' she said softly. 'It's just hitting you now.'

Neve wasn't sure how long she cried for, but exhaustion finally got the better of her and she was vaguely aware of Lucie putting a cushion under her head, lifting her feet onto the sofa and covering her with a blanket.

When Neve awoke some time later, it took her a moment to get her bearings, to remember where she was and then why she was there.

She could hardly believe what had happened in the last twelve hours. A night that had felt like it would never end. How the hell did it get to this point? Taking a shower, Neve scrubbed at her body as if the action would somehow get rid of the past week. If only it were that simple to cleanse her soul and mind as it was her body. The despair and grief clung to her.

'Where are you going?' asked Lucie, as Neve came into

the café having now dressed and made herself somewhat presentable.

'I'm going to see Poppy,' said Neve. 'I haven't phoned Kit, in case he makes some sort of excuse for me not to go round, but I need to see her. Just so she knows I'm still here and I still love her. I'm fed up waiting for Kit to say when's a good time. It's probably because his mum's there. Who knows what Cheryl's been saying.'

'Do you think it's a good idea?'

'I don't know,' admitted Neve. 'But it's what I'm doing. See you later.'

It only took five minutes to walk over to the house. Neve was relieved to see Kit's car on the drive. At least that way she wouldn't have to battle with Cheryl who, left alone to defend the family, would no doubt have put up a fight to let Neve in. At least with Kit she could have a reasoned debate.

The door opened before she had even rung the bell. It was Kit.

'I didn't know you were coming,' he said, stepping out onto the porch.

'I didn't know I had to make an appointment to come to my own home,' said Neve. 'Can we not have a repeat of last time. You know, a stand-off on the doorstep, where you make your point, I make mine but ultimately, I end up coming in. I could do without giving Mrs Dalton a matinee performance, albeit in the morning.'

She saw the corner of Kit's mouth twitch slightly before he gave a small flick of his head towards the house and lead the way inside. 'Poppy! Someone is here to see you,' he called up the stairs and then turned to Neve. 'I'm assuming it's Poppy you want to see.'

'It is but I'd like to talk to you as well. Afterwards.'

'Sure.'

'Oh, it's you,' came Cheryl's voice, as she appeared from the kitchen.

'Hello, Cheryl,' said Neve, smiling in what she hoped was a sincere manner.

'Dreadful news about Jake,' said Cheryl.

'Yes, it is,' replied Neve, evenly. What she really wanted to do was to shout at her mother-in-law and tell her not to cause trouble by mentioning Jake.

As Kit called up the stairs again to Poppy, Neve noticed his hand on the newel post. 'What have you done?' she asked, genuinely concerned at the bruised and swollen knuckles. The skin on the middle knuckle was actually cut. Like she imagined it would look if he had been in some sort of fight. The thought made her catch her breath. Jake? No, surely that was the most ridiculous idea. Kit wouldn't do anything like that. He was a lot of things, but he wasn't a violent man. She dismissed the notion and took his hand in hers. 'That looks sore.'

Kit went to move his hand away and then changed his mind, allowing it to rest in her palm. 'I scraped it in the garage, against the wall,' he said. 'I put my keys on top of the chest freezer and then lifted up the lid. The keys slid straight down the back. I could only just reach them. Those concrete blocks aren't very forgiving.'

'Ouch,' said Neve. She wasn't sure if it was her heightened emotional state or whether it was just wishful thinking, but she felt something shift between her and Kit.

'Neve! You're back!' Poppy's voice came from the landing above. She galloped down the stairs and bundled into Neve's arms. 'I've missed you.'

'Oh, sweetheart, I've missed you too,' said Neve, overcome with emotion at Poppy's willingness to hug her. Physical contact from her daughter was a rare occurrence. She pulled away slightly to look at Poppy, running her hand down the girl's hair and face. 'Are you OK? I mean, really OK?'

Poppy, with her gaze fixed to the ground, nodded as two fat dollops of tears dripped from her eyes. 'Oh, come here,' said Neve, pulling the child to her again. She kissed the top of her head and stroked her hair. 'I'm so sorry. So sorry for what happened. I'm never going to let anything like that happen to you again. I promise. I'm always going to keep you safe.'

Over the top of Poppy's head, Neve looked at Kit, realising she had no idea if she could keep such a reckless oath. If Kit wasn't prepared to give their marriage a chance, then she would be going back on her word almost as soon as it was given.

Kit stepped closer to them, he placed his hand on Poppy's head. 'We will all look after you, Poppy,' he said. 'Me and Neve have to sort some things out, but we will always be here for you.'

Neve closed her eyes as Kit's words sank in. He was going to give her another chance and by default, that meant she hadn't lost her chance for a baby. Neve felt the small flame of hope inside her heart, grow a little stronger.

Chapter 28

Despite the way they had parted, Neve hadn't been able to stop thinking about Jake, whilst at the same time, she felt disloyal to both Kit and Poppy for not giving them her full attention.

She had spent the evening with Poppy and Kit, Cheryl having made herself scarce. Kit hadn't said anything direct, and maybe Neve was reading too much into it, analysing his every word and every gesture to the nth degree that evening, but she couldn't help wondering if, in some way, Kit held her responsible for Poppy's disappearance. After all, as Kit had said, she was the sober one that night, she was the one who should have checked in on Poppy, she was the one who supposedly locked the cabin that night. No one could prove anything one way or the other, not even the police but there was an element of doubt which Neve wasn't convinced Kit had entirely dismissed.

And then there was Jake. Neve knew that she couldn't just ignore Jake, not while he was critically ill in hospital but she knew Kit wouldn't be happy to know she was worrying about him. She hoped she had managed to hide her concern from Kit. She had stayed at Lucie's again the night before and now, while Kit was taking Poppy and Cheryl out to do some shopping, she knew she had to visit the hospital.

Neve left the flat, calling in on Lucie downstairs at the café.

'Do you think they'll let you in?' asked Lucie.

'I don't know. I'll soon find out,' replied Neve, undeterred.

Half an hour later, Neve was being directed up to the ward Jake was in. She squirted her hands with antibacterial gel from outside the ward corridor and then made her way down to the nurse's station.

'Hi, I've come to see Jake Rees,' she said, hoping the nurse wouldn't ask for any detail like who she was and whether she was supposed to be here. Neve wasn't sure what the protocol was when someone had been attacked and the police were investigating.

'Are you related?' asked the nurse.

'I'm ...' Neve hesitated for a moment, deciding a small white lie wouldn't do any harm in this instance. 'I'm his sister. I've been out of the country. Only just got back.' One lie followed another, but it had to be done.

'He's in and out of consciousness, so you can't stay very long, I'm afraid. He's just down there. Second door on the right,' said the nurse, indicating with a nod of her head. 'Ten minutes.'

'That's fine,' said Neve. 'I just want to see him.'

She walked towards the room before the nurse could continue the conversation or change her mind. She pushed open the door, which squeaked ever so slightly, and went into the room. There were four beds in the small ward. Two unoccupied. One immediately on the left had its disposable purple curtain drawn. Neve stepped further into the ward, enabling her to see the patient in the cubicle beyond.

She took in an involuntarily sharp breath and had to do a double-take. If it wasn't for the familiar mop of black curls, Neve couldn't believe the person in front of her could be Jake.

Both his eyes were swollen with deep dark bruising, the colours, ranging from purple and black through to yellow, spread across the bridge of his nose. His right cheek was grazed, his top lip split and his head was bandaged.

'Beautiful, eh?' mumbled Jake through his swollen lips.

Neve startled. 'Sorry, I thought you were asleep.' She took a few steps closer to the bed, not sure of the reception she would receive. She felt unsure of herself. Maybe she shouldn't have come here after all. 'I can't believe what's happened,' she said, now at the edge of the bed. 'I suppose it's a stupid question to ask how you are?'

Jake gave a small grunt.

'I'm so sorry,' said Neve, she could feel the tears rising in her eyes.

'What for?' Jake managed to form a sentence, albeit only two words.

Neve wrapped her fingers around his, while with her other hand she fumbled for a tissue in her coat pocket. 'I shouldn't have marched off,' she sniffed. 'If I had been with you …'

'Don't.' Jake gave her hand a little tug. 'Glad you weren't.' He paused while he coughed and then groaned at the pain.

'Have you any idea what happened?'

'No,' said Jake, eventually.

The door opening and a nurse poking her head around

the corner brought a halt to the conversation. 'I'm sorry but Mr Rees really needs his rest.'

'I won't be a moment,' said Neve. She waited for the nurse to leave. 'Is there anything I can get you? Anything I can do to help?'

'Probably a bit late,' said Jake. 'My parents ... travelling here with my brother today.' It clearly pained him to even speak.

'That's good.' Neve gave Jake a small smile. 'Probably best if I don't come again.'

'Probably not,' agreed Jake. His fingers found her hand again. 'Will miss you.'

She went to say she'd miss him too, but the words faded before they reached her lips. 'Take care of yourself, Jake,' she said instead. She gave his hand a squeeze, before leaving the room.

Once in the car, Neve let her emotions run riot. Small sniffles at first, quickly followed by free-flowing tears. She wasn't sure what she was crying for. Who she was crying for. The relief that Jake was going to be ok despite his awful assault? Or were the tears for the end of their friendship – sad tears or tears of relief? Or was it because she had made her peace with Jake? She wasn't sure. Maybe it was all of those things. Whatever the reasons, she allowed herself the luxury of a self-indulgent release of emotion.

Finally, she'd cried all the tears she had and with a clarity she realised she had a lot to thank Jake for. He had shown her kindness when she was in a dark place, lighting the path back to her heart. And ultimately, he had made her realise that her marriage was worth fighting for. She wasn't sure if he'd feel the same sense of gratitude, she wasn't sure what she'd given him, other than heartache, but he was a kind man and Neve was sure he'd find happiness with someone he deserved.

Neve started her engine and drove out of the car park, briefly looking up towards the building.

'Goodbye, dear-heart,' she whispered. 'Thank you.'

As Neve was leaving the hospital, a text came through on her phone. It was Kit.

Fancy a spot of lunch? Meet me at The Anchor in half an hour? Xx

Neve smiled. The Anchor was a lovely old pub, situated on the edge of the harbour where her and Kit had stopped for a drink after viewing their home for the first time. It was from there Kit had phoned the estate agent and put an offer in on the house. An offer which was accepted half an hour later and Neve and Kit had celebrated with a glass of champagne, toasting their future together in Ambleton.

Neve was touched by Kit's gesture. He knew she'd remember the significance of the meeting place, one where they had looked forward to the future together, and one where they would do so again.

She texted back a reply saying she'd love to before setting off, not worrying that she'd be early as there was no point going all the way home now.

'Hey, you beat me,' said Kit, as he walked over to the table in the corner of the pub. He dipped his head and kissed Neve. 'And you got the drinks in already.'

'Never let it be said I don't believe in equality,' said Neve, shuffling up on the bench so Kit could sit beside her. 'How did the shopping trip go?'

'It was a success, although my wallet is a bit jaded.'

'Your mum and Poppy OK?'

'Fine, they're baking cakes. I think Poppy wanted to surprise you.'

'That's sweet. As long as your mum doesn't put arsenic in my slice.'

Kit gave a small laugh. 'Give her time, she'll be back on form soon. All this has knocked her for six. She does think a lot of you.'

'Just not very good at showing it.'

'Let's not worry about Mum. If it helps, I'll be your professional food taster,' said Kit, he gave Neve a small nudge with his shoulder and then his face took on a more serious expression. 'There's far more important things to worry about anyway ... like us.'

Neve returned her husband's gaze and a feeling of love, not without its fair share of desire, rose up in her. She did love him. She absolutely did.

'I love you,' she said. 'You do know that, don't you?'

He brushed her cheek with his fingertips. 'I know you do. And I love you too.'

'But what? I feel there's a but coming.' She curled her fingers around his hand.

'We need to be totally honest with each other if we're going to get through this together,' said Kit. 'I don't want any more secrets between us.'

'Me neither,' said Neve. She wanted to cry at her words.

More lies. If she told him the truth, she would lose him and not only him, she'd lose the chance of having a baby. Nothing was worth that price. Nothing. Not even the truth.

Chapter 29

The next day, Cheryl announced that as she wasn't needed any more because Kit was still off work, she would go back home but he was to call her the moment he needed her or if anything changed.

Despite the less than subtle note of disapproval from Cheryl, Neve resolved to carry on as if she was unaware of this. She gave her mother-in-law a hug goodbye, thanking her for everything she had done. Neve figured if she carried on outwardly playing the dutiful daughter-in-law and gave Cheryl absolutely no reason to say anything against her, all Cheryl's griping would come back to bite her. It would be Cheryl who looked like the bitter spiteful woman, not Neve. Privately, Neve had very different thoughts which she shared with Lucie when she went back to collect her bag.

'Honestly, you should have seen the look on Cheryl's face when I turned up,' she said, hooking her bag on to her shoulder. 'She could have curdled milk at a glance.'

Lucie giggled. 'Oh dear. Although, to be fair, she's bound to be biased towards Kit and her granddaughter.'

'Ah, bless you. Always the voice of reason,' said Neve, smiling at her friend. 'Yes, I do realise that. I just wish Cheryl wouldn't make her dislike for me so obvious. If she really does have Kit's best interests at heart, then she should be happy that we are going to try to make a go of things.'

'I'm really pleased for you,' said Lucie. 'You make such a great couple.'

'We're not out of the woods yet,' admitted Neve. 'We talked about things yesterday when we managed to snatch an hour at lunch together. It's been hard to talk at the house with Cheryl there and Poppy following me around like a second shadow. Which is great, but it hasn't given us much breathing space.'

'If you need more time or space, you know where I am,' said Lucie.

'Thank you. I do appreciate that, but we decided that we would never be able to make a go of things if I didn't move back in.'

'That's good,' said Lucie. 'What's happening with the police? You know Poppy's kidnap and Jake's attack?'

'As far as I know, from what Edward said this morning when he phoned, they are treating it as two separate incidents at the moment but someone at the station who Edward knows said that on the QT they are looking to see if they can make a connection between Jake's attack and Poppy's kidnapping.'

'Really? Jake was involved in it?'

'Who knows what they think.'

Lucie gave a huff. 'Have they really not got any idea?'

'I'm still officially under caution so I guess they haven't ruled me out,' said Neve. 'Poppy just says she can't remember anything. I think she's frightened she's done something wrong.

She is opening up little by little. Tomorrow she's going to see a trained counsellor to see if they can get her to talk. I'm a bit doubtful myself, but you never know.'

'So, she hasn't said anything at all?'

'Not really. Just that she doesn't remember leaving the boat and she doesn't remember how she got to the windmill. Any questions about what happened in the missing days, she just goes silent. The only thing she's managed to convey is that she wasn't harmed. To all intents and purposes, she seems to have been looked after.'

'Thank heavens on both counts,' said Lucie.

'My thoughts exactly.' Neve pushed herself away from the counter. 'They're trying to find Lee. They think he might have something to do with it.'

'They can only do that if they've got evidence, surely,' said Lucie.

'I don't know, the police aren't keen on sharing their info.' She gave an exasperated look to the ceiling. 'I really must get on. I'll catch you later.'

Pulling up outside the converted outbuildings of what was once a busy boat builders, Neve got out of the car and paused to take in the beautiful coastline. The marina had undergone a regeneration in recent years. The old workshops had been converted into offices, Kit and Sean's build and design service being one of the first to move in. This was swiftly followed by a clothing shop, specialising in sailing gear and then a chandlers, supplying all the boating and sailing equipment. The coffee shop and restaurant being the most recent addition. It was now a busy, thriving boating community.

She crunched over the gravel parking area, towards the building and pushing open the marine office door, was immediately greeted by Veronica, the office receptionist.

'Neve! How nice to see you. How are you? We're all so relieved to hear that Poppy was found.'

'Thank you,' said Neve. 'It's been a difficult time, that's for sure. But Poppy is OK and that's the important thing.'

The door to the right opened and Sean appeared. He immediately enveloped Neve in a big bear hug. 'Thank goodness it's turned out all right,' he said. 'Kit was keeping me up to date with everything. Or rather, I was badgering him. I was going to come around, but Kit put me off.' He shepherded her into his office, closing the door behind him. 'Is everything OK with you and Kit?'

Neve sat down in the chair. 'It's been tough on us, no doubt about it.' She felt slightly embarrassed talking about her marriage to Kit's business partner. 'But we'll get through. It's just going to take some time.'

'Of course. Of course,' said Sean. 'With the best will in the world, it would put even the strongest of marriages under strain.' There was an awkward pause and they both went to speak at the same time. 'No, you first,' said Sean.

Neve rummaged in her bag. 'I've got some post. It came to the house by mistake. It looks like some promo stuff.' She handed the bundle over.

'Thanks. I'll get Veronica to look at that. Is there anything I can get you? Tea? Coffee?'

'No, I'm fine, thanks. I was only calling in,' said Neve. 'I'm just going to pop into Kit's office. I have a new photo frame for his desk. It's a surprise.'

'Sure, you go ahead. I'm glad you called by. Let me know if I can do anything to help.' The phone on the desk began to ring.

'I won't keep you,' said Neve, nodding towards the phone.

Sean picked up the phone, but held it to his shoulder, before calling to her as she opened the door. 'You tell Kit to take as much time as he needs. He's not to rush back to work.'

Neve smiled and gave a wave as Sean attended to his phone call.

She crossed the reception area to the other side and let herself into Kit's office which overlooked the marina. Neve had printed off a photograph Poppy had taken on her phone last night. It was a selfie of the three of them sitting on the sofa together. Kit had remarked how much he loved it. So, this morning, Neve had commandeered Lucie's printer.

She picked up the brushed steel photo frame he had on his desk, which currently housed a picture of Kit, Neve and Poppy taken on holiday two years ago, sitting by the pool of the Spanish villa they had rented. Neve unfastened the clips at the back and slipped last night's picture behind the glass, replacing it on Kit's desk.

She checked her watch, she ought to head off otherwise she would be late for the meeting she had planned. She was about to leave, when she had a sudden thought. She smiled to herself and looked around Kit's desk for a notepad or sticky note. In Kit's usual fashion, everything was tidy and neat. She opened the top drawer of his desk and picked up a biro languishing in the bottom and the pad of sticky notes by its side.

Surprise!
Love you!
xxx

She scribbled the note and then placed it in the drawer. Her and Kit used to leave notes for each other all the time when they were first married. Neve wasn't quite sure when they had stopped doing so, but maybe this would spark a little feeling of nostalgia in Kit, help him to remember the people they were before things went wrong.

On impulse, Neve wrote out another note.

Gotcha again!
Still loving you.
xxx

She looked around for somewhere less obvious to hide it. Ah, Kit had a small shower room off his office. In fact, both he and Sean did. It was always useful if they had to attend a function after work or if one of them ended up getting wet whilst out on the boats with clients or test driving.

She opened the door to the wet room and looked round. There wasn't really anywhere to put it other than in the vanity unit. She didn't want the cleaners coming in and finding it stuck to the mirror or sink.

She bent down and opened the doors. There were a few bottles of shower gel and shampoo. Neve stuck the note on top of the deodorant can. Kit would spy it immediately. It was then she noticed a carrier bag shoved to the back of the cupboard with a sleeve poking out.

She reached in and retrieved the bag. Kit must have left some clothing in there by mistake, forgetting to bring it home to be washed. She stood up and peered in the bag. It was a checked overshirt he usually kept in the car. She was just about to close the bag when something caught her eye. Her heart did a funny sort of double beat against her breast bone and her stomach pitched. Slowly, she pulled out the shirt and held it up.

Splattered across the front was a stream of red. Dried and crusted. But there was no mistaking it for what it was. Blood spatter.

Visions of Kit's bruised and swollen knuckles jumped before her. She tried to rationalise the thought lurking just behind the image. Kit had injured his hand trying to retrieve his keys. He could have wiped his hands on his shirt.

But then that would be smears not splatters.

Why was his shirt here? Stuffed in a bag at the back of his vanity unit?

Why wouldn't he have taken the shirt off at home and washed it?

She knew she was just stalling, trying to avoid the inevitable answer.

New images of Jake swamped her. His smiling face. The way his eyes crinkled when he laughed. His sensuous full lips, the fall of his dark hair across his brow. She clasped the blood-stained shirt to her chest, as she sank to a crouch. Her mouth opened in a silent cry and she rocked back and forth.

There was a knock on the door. Neve wasn't sure if it was the first knock or second or even third.

'Mrs Masters,' came Veronica's voice. 'Are you in there?'

Neve nearly tumbled over in shock.

'Just using the bathroom,' she called back.

'Oh, OK,' said Veronica and Neve heard her close the office door again.

Neve stood up. Thoughts swirling in her mind. She had to get a grip of herself. Work out what to do. She stuffed the shirt back into the carrier bag, which she then managed to push into her own handbag, grateful for its generous proportions.

Checking her appearance in the mirror, Neve closed the vanity unit doors and left the office.

'I didn't mean to disturb you,' said Veronica.

'No, it's fine. I was just desperate for the loo,' said Neve, with a liberal amount of cheer. 'See you soon, Veronica. Bye.'

She hurried out of the office. Her hands trembled as she unlocked the car and got in. Placing the bag on the passenger seat, she paused.

The logical thing to do with a blooded shirt would be to confront her husband. To ask Kit how it had happened and why he was hiding it at the back of the vanity unit in his office. The other logical thing would be to take it to the police, pointing out that Kit had bruised and bloodied knuckles and that he may well have had a motive for attacking Jake.

Neve did neither of these things. She didn't want her husband arrested for manslaughter, or even murder. What if they found him guilty? He'd go to prison. Their marriage would be in tatters. No father for Poppy. No baby for Neve. She'd fought tooth and nail to avoid that, there was no way she was allowing herself to be put in such a position. Besides, Kit wouldn't harm anyone physically. Sure, he got angry. He was possessive. He didn't like being made a fool of, but he

290

wouldn't attack anyone, would he? She had to believe that. The alternative wasn't an option.

She went home and relieved to see Kit was still out, she went into the double garage and hid the plastic bag in a trunk at the back. She had to move a few things to get to it, like the surf board Kit had bought five years ago when he decided he wanted to take up a new hobby, but which only lasted one summer. She also had to move the punch bag. Another one of Kit's new hobbies, this one lasted only a few weeks, if she remembered rightly. There was also a box of old books that for some reason hadn't made it to the charity shop. Once the shirt was stowed away inside the trunk, along with spare life jackets and water-proofs, Neve replaced everything and returned to the house.

She went into the kitchen and made herself a cup of tea. Leaning back against the breakfast bar, Neve looked out onto the garden and tried to rationalise her thoughts and actions some more.

If she confronted Kit, she might not like the answer. If it was the answer she feared, then what was she to do with the infor-mation? Her automatic response would be to go to the police, but the knock-on ripple effects could be huge. Was she ready to deal with those? And if he told her and she didn't like the answer, but did nothing, could she really live with herself and Kit for that matter? What sort of justice would that be for Jake?

For now, she reasoned, she had done the right thing. This was a case of self-preservation. She wanted to continue to repair the cracks in her marriage, to continue to grow and to find what they had lost. If she confronted him about the shirt, then it would force her to act. She wasn't ready to do that. Not yet.

As she stood there contemplating her predicament, her

mobile phone pinged. She took it from her bag and looked at the message thinking it might be Kit.

She almost dropped the phone in surprise when she saw it was Lee.

It is true about Jake?

Neve tapped in a message.

Yes. It is. Where are you? Police are looking for you.

I need money. Meet me now at boathouse.

Too dangerous.

Just be there.

One hour.

Neve cursed Lee under her breath. He was the last person she wanted to hear from, let alone see but she knew she had unfinished business with him.

Lost in thought, she jumped when she heard Kit and Poppy's voices from behind her. She swung round, dropping her cup, which smashed against the tiled flooring.

'Oh! You two scared the life out of me,' she gasped, shoving the mobile into her bag and crouching down to pick up the broken pieces of china.

'You've broken your favourite cup,' said Poppy. 'Dad gave you that.'

'Don't worry, it's only a cup,' said Kit, taking off his jacket and hanging it over the stool.

'Keep Willow out of the kitchen,' she said, gently pushing the dog away from the shattered china.

'I'll put her in the garden,' said Kit, taking hold of Willow's collar. 'Come on, girl. Out you go. Don't want you cutting your paw and getting blood everywhere.'

Neve stopped at the mention of blood. Images of the shirt invaded her mind's eye. 'Ouch!' She looked down and realised her thumb was bleeding.

'Neve's bleeding!' cried Poppy. 'Dad! Neve's hand is cut.'

'It's just a small cut,' said Neve, standing up, but wincing at the stinging sensation.

'Let me look,' said Kit, coming over. 'Run it under the tap. Here, let me see. I want to make sure there's nothing in it.'

He examined her hand with care, smiling at her but Neve found it hard to stop her gaze from resting on his bruised knuckles. How could the same hands, so loving and tender towards her, possibly be so violent and brutal at the same time? It wasn't possible, was it?

'I think you'll survive,' he said. 'Might need a plaster on it, though.'

Neve slipped her hand away. She wasn't sure she could cope with his touch. 'I think there are some in the cupboard here,' she said, turning and rummaging in the cupboard below the sink until she found the small first aid kit she was looking for.

Kit cleared up the broken cup and wiped the floor clean of the remaining coffee dregs that Neve hadn't finished. 'Let me have a look at your thumb again,' he said and once again

293

took Neve's hand in his and his finger gently stroked the back of her hand and he inspected the plaster.

'It's fine, honest,' said Neve, aware of the intimacy in the gesture. He looked so bloody sexy this morning in his black T-shirt and jeans. The stress-lines from the past week were nowhere to be seen, making him look younger. He reminded Neve of when she'd first met him.

He returned the look with the same longing in his own eyes. 'Why don't you have a lie down?' he suggested, softly. 'I'll come up and make sure you're comfortable.' He gave Neve a small kiss on the mouth.

'Err, gross,' came Poppy's voice. She held up her hands as a physical barrier between them. 'I'm going on the PlayStation,' she said, turning and heading down the hall to the living room.

Neve couldn't help letting out a small embarrassed giggle. 'Awkward,' she said.

Kit pulled her towards him, their bodies touching. He slipped a hand down to her buttocks and pulled her a bit closer. Kissing her on the mouth, his tongue playing with the edges of her lips. He gave a small groan. 'She'll be busy for ages now. And I still think you need bed rest.'

Neve pulled away and gave a rise of her eyebrows. 'Bed rest?'

'Well, not so much rest, but definitely bed.'

Neve hesitated just for a second, but in that moment, a maelstrom of thoughts rampaged through her mind.

Was this a good time to go upstairs to make love? Was she ready to be intimate with her husband again? But the thought that careered to the fore, pushing all others aside was that maybe this was the time that Kit would say yes to what she wanted more than anything.

She took his hand and lead him upstairs, looking in through the open doorway of the living room to see Poppy sprawled out on the sofa, with her controller in her hand. Another glance to the front door. Kit took the initiative and slid the dead bolt, taking the key with him so Poppy couldn't leave the house if the notion suddenly took her.

They almost skipped up the stairs, the deep beige carpet deadening their tread. Inside the bedroom, Kit locked the door. Poppy had never mastered the art of respecting the privacy of a closed bedroom door, never mind knocking or waiting for an answer. She had caught Kit and Neve out the first time Neve had stayed over, when Poppy was just seven years old. Neve had pulled the sheet hastily over her, but later that morning when they were all sitting down for breakfast, Poppy had proceeded to ask Neve why she didn't have a vest on in bed. That very day, Kit had gone out and bought a lock for the bedroom door.

Kit drew Neve towards him, his mouth tentatively at first touching hers with feather-like kisses. She responded the same, but more urgently after a few moments, deepening their kiss. It sent a tingling sensation right through her body. She hadn't remembered feeling like this about Kit in a long time. She actually wanted to make love to him. She paused in her mind to churn the expression over – to make love. Yes, that's what they were going to do now. She had been foolish to think their love had died, it had just been buried under a mountain of stress and strain from everyday life. Guilt gave a brief appearance. She should never have doubted the strength of their marriage, she just needed to be patient and wait for the right time. She was sure that after everything that had happened, Kit would be ready to agree to what she wanted most of all. Hadn't he said when Poppy was missing that he would give anything to have Poppy back, and now Neve had made that happen Kit wasn't going to renege on his word, was he?

She moved her hands to the back of his neck, running her fingers up his nape and through his blond hair, pulling him harder to her. He responded, his body firm against her. She could feel from his bulging crotch how much he wanted her. She wanted him to want her more than anything else, so that nothing would come between them, not even a thin layer of latex.

Neve pulled up Kit's T-shirt, yanking it over his head. In seconds they were both naked.

'Oh, Neve, I've missed you so much,' said Kit, running his hands down her sides, dipping his head and trailing a path down her cleavage with his tongue. His hands stopped at her hips and his mouth moved on down.

'I've missed you too,' murmured Neve, her breathing deepening and growing faster. She pulled him to his feet and totally in tune with her need, Kit put his hands under her buttocks and lifted her up. Neve hooked her feet around his back and in two steps, Kit had carried her across the room and onto the bed.

This was the moment Neve had been waiting for.

Kit kissed her and manoeuvred himself so he was astride her. From the corner of her eye, Neve saw Kit reach out his hand to the bedside table where the condoms were. She gave a small moan, looked him straight in the eye and reached out her own hand, running her fingers down his arm and gently tugging his hand back to her.

Kit paused.

The acid test.

Neve didn't say anything. She didn't need to. The unspoken question lingered in her eyes.

Kit moved his hand back and kissed her harder.

'I love you,' he said. 'I came so close to losing you. I don't ever want to get to that point again.'

'I love you too,' she said. 'We mustn't let anything get between us again.'

'I won't let it, I promise.'

As Kit pushed into her, Neve put all thoughts of the blooded shirt away. She was good at pretending things had never happened. She'd spent many years compartmentalising her life. She could do it again. She knew that.

She focused on what was happening now. To feel Kit inside her was all she wanted. She knew she was in control of the situation. He was lost to the rhythm of their love making, he was beyond the point of no return. She urged him on, the excitement of how their lives could change just as fierce as the excitement she was experiencing from sex. She forced Kit to slow down, she didn't want it to be over too soon. Kit gasped for breath, and allowing Neve to be in charge, he slowed his thrusting. Neve liked the new-found power she had over Kit and how she could make him feel like this.

Afterwards, Kit didn't move for a long time. Lying on top of her, sweat dripped from his forehead, mingling with her own and trickling into her hair. And when he finally rolled onto the mattress next to her, he held her in his arms, dropping small kisses on her head, telling her how much he loved her and how things would be better now.

Neve snuggled into him and smiled to herself. Things had changed. She was in control now, the power-balance of their marriage had shifted and Neve liked it. She would call the shots now, she would have her baby.

Chapter 30

Neve couldn't remember a time when she had felt so happy after making love to Kit. Well, not for many years anyway. Not since the thorny subject of having a baby had become an issue. Although they hadn't actually spoken about it before, the fact that Kit hadn't protested about not wearing a condom was, in Neve's eyes, as good as agreeing they should have a baby.

She snuggled up to him and dropped a small kiss on his lips. 'We'd better get up before Poppy comes pounding at the door.'

Kit gave something between a groan and a sigh. 'We need a weekend away,' he said. 'Once things have settled down, maybe my mum will look after Poppy.'

'That would be lovely.' She smiled at her husband as she began to get dressed. 'I've got to pop out for half an hour,' she said, glancing at her watch and ensuring her tone was casual.

'Really? Why's that?'

'I told Lucie I'd drop in and see her,' said Neve, not meeting Kit's eye. 'Just to let her know that everything's all right. I'll take Willow with me and give her a run too.'

'Can't you do that over a text?'

'She has something she wants to give me apparently. And as far as I know, there isn't an app to walk your dog; that's something we still have to do manually.'

'Right, OK. Don't be long though,' said Kit, pulling her back onto the bed. 'I thought maybe we could all go out for some tea. Me, you and Poppy.'

'That would be lovely,' said Neve, wriggling free from his arms. 'I'll be as quick as I can.'

Looking in on Poppy as she went, Neve hurried out to the car. It would be quicker to drive as she had to take a detour and go via the post office. As she pulled out onto the road, she saw Heather coming along with her daughter Libby. Neve slowed down and undid the window.

'Hi, Heather,' she called.

'Oh, hi, Neve! We were just passing and thought we'd call in to see Poppy. Libby has made her a card.'

'Oh, that's sweet. She'll be really pleased to see you. Kit's at home. I've just got to run an errand, but I won't be long.'

'I don't want to get in the way, but Libby was insistent.' She gave a small grimace.

'Honestly. It's fine,' said Neve. She liked Heather and Libby; it was easy being in their company. They didn't query Poppy's behaviour or social graces, they were in the same boat and appreciated social norms weren't always observed.

Neve headed off to meet Lee, stopping at the cash point outside the post office to withdraw her daily limit of five hundred pounds. Then she drove on towards the river, grateful that Willow was with her. It certainly acted as good cover for her regular trips down here or across the fields.

Before that though, she pulled up outside the cafe and

leaving the window down a fraction so Willow could poke his nose out, Neve nipped into the shop.

'Hi, Lucie,' she said, pleased to see the shop was relatively quiet.

'Hiya! Wasn't expecting to see you,' said Lucie, the surprised expression giving way to one of concern.

Neve approached the counter and lowered her voice. 'I think Kit and I are going to be able to work things out.'

'That's great news. I'm really pleased for you.' She reached over and squeezed Neve's hand.

Neve couldn't prevent an excited little smile settling on her face. 'It's like all that's happened over the past week or so has made us both realise what we could lose. It's put everything into perspective.'

'Any news of Jake?'

'No. I went to see him yesterday,' said Neve. 'He looked bloody awful.'

'He's lucky he's not dead,' said Lucie matter of factly. 'One of his students was in here yesterday saying how touch and go it had been.'

'It doesn't bear thinking about,' said Neve, resisting the urge to put images of Jake's blooded face and Kit's shirt in her mind. 'He doesn't remember a thing about it, apparently.'

'I hope they catch who did it. I hate the thought of someone running around capable of doing something like that,' said Lucie.

'It's awful. He had his wallet stolen. They didn't take the card or his phone, just the cash.'

'Seems a bit odd, I mean, no one really keeps large amounts of cash on them these days.'

Subconsciously, Neve found herself stroking the strap of her handbag. 'Look, I just called in to let you know everything was OK,' she said, refocussing. She scanned the glass counter. 'Can I have that sponge cake at the back, please?'

'One slice?'

'No. The whole thing.'

'Wow, someone isn't calorie counting,' said Lucie. She boxed up the cake and passed it over.

Having paid Lucie for the cake, Neve went back to her car and drove down towards the river. She let Willow out and then hurried along the muddy path towards the bridge.

'Willow! Come on, Willow!' called Neve. Willow gave a small bark and was on the verge of running back along the path. 'Oh, no you don't.' Neve caught hold of the collar and hooked on the lead. She stopped and gazed back to see what Willow was barking at. A sudden notion that someone might be watching her came to mind. She shook her head. She was overreacting. She looked back at Willow. 'There's nothing there, you silly old doggy,' she said out loud, possibly to reassure herself more than anything else. She stood perfectly still, her eyes scanning the surrounding bushes. A squirrel scrambled up the tree and Neve let out a sigh of relief. 'Ah, squirrels. Is that what you were after? No time for chasing them today. Come on, good girl.'

Lee was leaning against the boathouse, just as he had been when she'd seen him before. Smoking what looked like a joint, he smiled as she approached.

'Finally, thought you weren't coming. Did you bring the money?'

Neve pulled the wad of notes from her handbag and

passed it over. 'Oh, and just in case you're interested, Poppy is fine.'

Lee grabbed the money and fanned it out between his fingers. 'I know. I saw her watching the television.'

'You've been spying on us?' Neve shivered at the thought.

'Just checking up on my interests,' said Lee. He looked up at her. 'How much is here?'

'Five hundred.' She thought for a minute he was going to complain. 'It's all I can get out at one time. Besides, I hardly have any money left.'

'Business is tough,' said Lee. He separated some twenty-pound notes and folding them in half, slipped them into the front pocket of his jeans. The rest of the money he separated again, this time into four equal parts, putting them in various places of his rucksack. One pile into a side pocket. One pile into an inside pocket and the other two piles into a sock and the bottom of a pair of trainers. 'Less chance of it all getting stolen at the same time.' He stood up and hooked his bag onto his shoulder.

'Where are you going?' asked Neve.

'Brighton, I think.'

'I went to see Jake yesterday.'

'And?'

'He's in a bad way.'

'Serious, then. Shame, I liked the guy.'

'We're quits now,' she said. 'I've never told a soul you were there that day on the beach with me and Megan. That you were the one who supplied the drugs. I did you a favour then, you've done me a favour now. One that I've paid you for, I think it's fair to call it quits.'

303

Lee looked at her for a long moment. 'Yeah, we're quits.'

Neve stood under the bridge for a long time, watching Lee trudge along the riverbank and eventually disappear out of sight. He hadn't looked back once. Lee was so much like her. Always moving forwards. Never going back. And she had to do the same.

Chapter 31

Later that day, Poppy's teacher, Mrs Ogden, came to the house to discuss Poppy's return to school. They had decided that it was best if Poppy returned to her normal routine sooner rather than later. Poppy was all about routines so Neve and Kit had agreed that the following day would hail her return to school.

Poppy seemed to be taking the return to school in her stride. Kit had left for work that morning, saying goodbye as if nothing had happened the previous week. Neve knew it had been hard for him to do so. She had seen it in his eyes. His face may have fooled Poppy, but his eyes didn't fool Neve.

'She'll be fine,' said Neve. 'Like Mrs Ogden said, the sooner she's back in her normal routine, the better.'

'I know,' admitted Kit. 'I'm just ... well, if I'm honest, I'm scared.'

Neve nodded and standing in front of him, adjusted his tie and then on tiptoes, gave him a brief, but reassuring kiss. 'You're bound to be, but stay calm. The school said they'd phone during the course of the day. I think they are more worried about reassuring us than they are about Poppy.'

Kit let out a small sigh. 'I know you're right.' He took her hand in his. 'Thank you.'

Neve gave a small laugh. 'What for?'

'For being here. For me and Poppy. I don't know what we'd do without you.' He stroked the side of her face. 'I thought for a while I'd lost you and I didn't know how to change it. I thought if I let you get it out of your system, you'd come back. I was foolish, arrogant and naive.'

'Hey, you don't need to say all that,' said Neve. 'We've both been careless with our marriage, with each other but that's stopped now. We both know we've got to cherish what we have. Move forwards, make us better, make our family better. In every way. And that means changes. Knowing what's important to fight for and what's not.'

'I suppose you ever telling me about what took you to those art therapy classes in the first place is off limits?'

'It's not worth dragging up pain from the past that has no place in our future,' she said carefully. She didn't want to add the shame it would bring either. She had brought shame onto her family once before, she wasn't going to do it again, not when everything was so fragile. She couldn't risk losing everything she had just to satisfy Kit's desire to know. She couldn't change the past, as much as she wanted to, but she had control on how her future would play out and that was the most important thing. 'I just want to focus on us. Our family. Remember how desperate we felt when Poppy was missing? Remember what we said, that we'd do anything to put things right?'

'Of course, I do,' said Kit. 'And I meant it. I know what it will take to make you happy and, I must admit, these last few days have made me realise what a stubborn idiot I've been. How my own selfishness has been denying you the one thing you want. I know how precious Poppy is to me, how much she means, and there I was denying you that very thing. I was stopping you from having a child of your own to love so fiercely. I get that now.'

Neve felt tears spring to her eyes. 'Oh, Kit, you don't understand how much that means to me.' She thought she was going to cry but she managed to rein in the tears. She didn't want them to distract from this moment. Kit was openly saying that they could try for a baby together. However, when she looked at him through clear eyes, she could sense a hesitancy on his face.

'What?'

'I don't know if I can go forwards without knowing things behind us are clear. I don't want us to make the same mistakes again. It's give and take, Neve. It has to work both ways.'

Neve could feel the disappointment drag in her stomach. Kit wanted a trade-off. How much would it cost her though if he did find out the truth? He may still love her, but he wouldn't love what she had done, past or present. She wasn't sure Kit would be able to get around that. He wouldn't be able to stay with her and without him she had nothing. She didn't want to start her life yet again. She fashioned a conciliatory smile onto her face. 'Let's talk tonight,' she said.

Kit had headed off to work leaving Neve pondering her next move. She had to give Kit something, but she couldn't give him everything. Everything was too dear a price. Giving Kit everything would ultimately leave her with nothing. He'd walk away, she was certain he would.

'It's eight fifteen,' said Poppy.

Neve smiled at her daughter, relieved that she seemed to be slipping back into her old routine as if there had never been a break from it. 'Excellent. Shall we go?' she suggested, putting the return to routine theory to the test.

'No. We have three minutes,' said Poppy. She stood by the clock in the hall watching the hands move.

'Ah, yes, of course we do,' said Neve. Yes, Poppy was on perfect form.

Three minutes later they were walking out the front door and climbing into the car

'Do you want dropping at the bus stop?' asked Neve.

'Yes.'

Neve hid her feelings of surprise. She really didn't think Poppy would want to get the bus anymore. In fact, Neve and Kit had talked at length about this, in the end deciding to let Poppy have autonomy here. Neither were comfortable with the idea of Ben Hewitt starting up again, but Neve had reassured Kit she would stay in the car, watching from across the road until Poppy was safely on the bus.

'Right, let's go,' said Neve, injecting a cheer into her voice.

Poppy gave her a sideways look but said nothing.

As Neve stopped at the end of the road to let traffic pass by, she noticed Linda Hewitt's little red Mini, with its distinctive white viper stripes, charging along. Neve tracked the car as it approached. Inside she could see Linda's face staring straight ahead and in the passenger seat was Ben. Neve's heart gave a wallop of relief against her chest wall. She had just glimpsed his blazer and tie. The little shit was being given a lift to school. Hopefully this was going to be the normal mode of transport for Ben from now on. Maybe Linda wasn't so confident in her son's innocence after all.

'Did you see that?' asked Neve, as she pulled out and joined the traffic, travelling in the opposite direction to the Hewitts.

'What?'

'Ben Hewitt in the car with his mother.'

'Yeah. He gets a lift to school now.'

'How do you know?'

'Nan told me.'

'Oh. And how does she know?'

'She's friends with his nan,' said Poppy, as if it was already a tiresome conversation.

'I see,' said Neve and left it there.

Once Neve had seen Poppy board the St Joseph's school bus, she gave a sigh of relief. Mission accomplished. Well, that particular mission. She still had one more to do.

She needed to lay the ghosts of her past to rest. She needed closure and she needed to make sure whoever was behind those notes wouldn't torment her, damage her or even destroy what she had now. She'd worked too hard for this life to allow that to happen.

She turned the car around and headed out of the village towards the motorway. She could get to Newport in three hours if she put her foot down, three and a half allowing for traffic. All she needed was an hour there and then she could be home again in time for tea. Poppy had an after-school club hockey session today and Kit was picking her up and taking her to tea at his mum's.

Neve had already primed Kit with an excuse of why she

wouldn't be there. She'd give him a call in half an hour or so and advise him of her emergency dental appointment. She had made sure this morning she had commented on her non-existent toothache.

Neve neared her destination just on the edge of Newport city – the small Welsh town she'd grown up in. As she drew off the motorway, her stomach churned, curdling her insides. She felt physically sick. Maybe she should have got a sandwich at the last service station.

Old memories came flooding back of her days growing up in the long-forgotten town. The glory days of a high street packed full of shops had disappeared, now replaced by charity shops and boarded up windows. She remembered coming here with Megan. How they used to rush into town on a Saturday to spend their pocket money and when Megan was older and had cooler friends than those of Neve's, she would let Neve tag along. Neve always thought it was very grown-up to hang out with her older sister's friends. They accepted her. They didn't speak to her much, but they weren't bothered she was there. Neve especially liked it when some of the girls from her year would see her hanging out with Megan's crew.

It gave Neve the courage to throw a cocky look. One which she wouldn't dare do without the safety of Megan's friends and one which instantly made the girls from her year turn their heads and look the other way.

Neve blinked hard. She missed Megan. If only Megan were here now. She'd be at Neve's side in an instant. She wouldn't have let Neve face this homecoming alone. But Megan wasn't here and much as Neve wanted to reach out to her sister, she knew she mustn't.

And here she was now, at the turning to Cygnet Walk – home to her brother Gareth. It suddenly occurred to her that she hadn't taken into account that Gareth may no longer work from home. What if he wasn't here? She couldn't leave without seeing him. She had to find out the truth. There was no way she could move on with her life if she didn't. Despite what she had said to Kit, she still needed closure.

Her tummy felt like it was trying to pole vault itself out of her. Being here in Cygnet Walk brought back so many emotions and memories. Many she hadn't wanted to revisit, hoping she had managed to lock them firmly away for ever. Neve was beginning to realise that there was no such thing as for ever.

She checked her watch. She didn't have time to dither. She pulled up alongside the curb, not wanting to park on the drive. Somehow that felt too familiar. It was something you did when you knew someone well. She didn't know her brother well anymore.

Her feet carried her to the front door, even though her heart was dragging behind. It was a solid oak door, with three square glass panels running vertically down the side. The detached house was clad in pale grey boarding on the top half and the lower half rendered and painted a soft cream. As she waited for the bell to be answered, Neve reminded herself of all the reasons why she needed to do this – Kit, Poppy, her marriage, her sanity and, most importantly, her much longed-for child.

Through the glass she could see a figure walking towards

the door. She couldn't make out if it was male or female. 'Please let it be Gareth,' she whispered, casting a skyward glance.

The door opened.

Neve stared at the person ahead of her. Her mouth dried, and her words stuck in her throat. Her armpits suddenly felt damp.

'As I live and breathe,' said her brother eventually. He stared back at Neve as they both took in the person before them.

Gareth, now aged forty-two, still mostly looked the same but he was wearing glasses, black-rimmed which seemed to stand out against his pale complexion. His eyes were still the same grey they had always been, but fine lines now fanned the corners. His hair, once fair like Neve's, was now scattered with grey. And, although still slim, he had clearly started to gain a little middle-aged spread, as his V-neck sweater stretched across a slight paunch.

'Hello, Gareth,' Neve said, finally managing to eke the words out.

'Neve. What the hell are you doing here?'

Neve could see in his eyes that he was totally bewildered by her presence. Then there was a shift as the surprise turned to alarm. He stepped forward, one hand on the door acting as a blockade should Neve try to cross the threshold. He glanced over her shoulder. 'You can't just turn up on my doorstep unannounced.'

'I need to speak to you,' said Neve. 'It's important. I don't want to cause any trouble, but I need to talk to you about something.'

'I don't think this is a good idea.'

'Please, Gareth. It's important.'

'We did all our talking years ago, Neve. I don't have anything to say to you.'

'Just five minutes, that's all I ask and then I'll go away, and I promise you won't ever hear from me again.' Neve felt the words choking her as before. She hated saying out loud to Gareth's face that she was prepared never to contact him again, but if that's what it took to stop anyone from damaging her future, then she'd do it.

Gareth's shoulders dropped a fraction and Neve could see the features in his face loosen. He stepped onto the doorstep, pulling the door behind him but leaving a slipper to stop the door from closing.

'I don't know if you saw on the television about my daughter Poppy going missing?' Neve asked.

'Yes, I saw that,' confirmed Gareth. 'I'm glad she was found safely. I take it she's OK?'

'She's fine, thanks,' said Neve. 'The reason I've come is because while she was missing, my husband received two notes, referring to what happened here.'

'Right,' said Gareth, folding his arms and looking down at her. 'What's that got to do with me?'

'They must have come from here. They were postmarked Newport. No one else knows about what happened.'

'When you say here, you mean here in this house, don't you?' said Gareth, a touch of sarcasm entering his voice. 'What you really mean is, me or Lisa.'

Neve kept her nerve and returned her brother's challenging look. 'Yes. I do, as it happens.' She pushed her lips together while she steadied herself. 'It can only be one of you. I've already spoken to Scott.'

'Scott! My my, you are doing the rounds of yesteryear.' He gave a sigh. 'Sorry, that was uncalled for.'

'So, are you saying you didn't send those notes?' pressed Neve.

'No. I bloody didn't. Why would I? For Christ's sake, Neve, I know we haven't spoken to each other in years, but I wouldn't do that to you. You're still my sister.'

Neve wanted to fall into his arms and hug him for saying that, but she knew she didn't have time and if she did, she would dissolve in a complete mess of tears. 'Thank you,' she said softly, pausing for a moment. 'So, it must have been Lisa.'

'No. It wasn't. She wouldn't do anything like that.'

'She hates me. That would be enough.'

'I don't believe it,' said Gareth. 'What would she gain from it?'

'Revenge. Satisfaction. I don't know.'

'Shit!' Gareth looked towards the drive.

Neve turned and saw a grey Ford Focus pull up. 'Shit,' she echoed, as the driver's door was flung open and Lisa stormed across the grass towards her. Neve took a step back as Gareth hurried towards his wife, stopping her from reaching Neve.

'What the hell is she doing here?' screamed Lisa, pointing a finger in Neve's direction. 'Get that bitch out of here!'

'Lisa! Keep calm. Don't be shouting now,' he said, trying to placate his wife.

'I'll shout all I want. I don't care who hears.' She stopped in her stride as Gareth put his arms around her.

Neve could see the anger and loathing on her sister-in-law's face. Gareth may have softened over time, but Lisa hadn't.

And she probably had every right to still be as angry as she was. In that moment, Neve knew she had the answer she'd come for.

She looked at Gareth. 'I think I know the answer.'

'Answer? What answer?' shouted Lisa. 'Oh, wait a minute.' She gave a laugh. 'I know why you're here. Obviously arrived safely then?'

'Lisa!' exclaimed Gareth 'Why?'

'Because she's a danger to children and her husband obviously didn't know. He had the right to know.'

'How did you get my address?' asked Neve.

Lisa gave an exaggerated eye-roll. 'That was easy. I just had to Google your name, pay a small fee to one of those on-line companies and they gave me the details.'

Neve's mind swirled. She felt dizzy. A black tunnel was closing in around her. She gasped, trying to inhale a lungful of air as she dropped to her knees. The grass was cold and soggy, the dampness seeped through her jeans. She dipped her head and breathed in through her nose and out through her mouth. The light-headedness passed and she raised her head.

Her breath was taken away for a second time as she saw the passenger door of the car opening and the occupant stepping out. Her brown hair, now laced with low-lights, still long and still wavy, caught by the wind, rose and drifted back onto her shoulders. She looked at Neve with concern and confusion all over her face.

It seemed to be happening in slow motion as the thirteen-year-old broke into a run towards her mother.

'Jasmine,' whispered Neve.

'You stay away from my daughter!' screamed Lisa, pushing Gareth away.

'Jasmine, go inside!' shouted Gareth, grappling with his wife.

It seemed so dreamlike, Neve could hear their voices fading out as she watched her niece look anxiously from one adult to another. A tear dropped from Neve's eye, followed by another one on the other side but she was too focussed on the young teenager before her. She was so beautiful, her face had slimmed and her features sharpened, but she still looked exactly as she did before. She was a daughter to be proud of. Neve's heart lurched as the young girl ran inside, pausing in the doorway to take one last look at Neve.

Neve gazed at the closed oak door for a long moment, vaguely aware that someone was shouting her name. She turned her head and through teary eyes, she could see Gareth dragging his wife towards the house and yet beyond them she could see a figure standing on the driveway. She tried to blink away the tears but still her vision was blurred.

Neve rose to her feet.

It couldn't be. Not after all this time.

The figure came into focus.

This time she whispered a different name from her past. 'Megan?'

Chapter 32

'Good morning,' said Kit to Veronica.

'Hello, Kit. So nice to see you back. How are things?' she asked, looking up from the computer screen.

'Taking our time, but all OK,' said Kit. 'Poppy has gone into school today. Fortunately, it's a no-go area for the media, so I'm hoping it will all go smoothly.'

'I thought they would lose interest by now,' said Veronica.

'Most have, but one or two seemed determined to make a story out of everything. It didn't help that the police interviewed Neve.'

"Yes, I heard that. How awful. I hope she's OK.'

'Thanks.' He smiled at his receptionist. 'I suppose you heard about the attack on Jake Rees too?'

Veronica pulled a sympathetic face. 'Awful, isn't it? The papers haven't exactly said it's connected but they've been hinting at it.'

'They're just trying to sell copies, I suppose,' said Kit, with a sigh. 'I do wish they'd leave us all alone now.'

'Oi! Oi! Is that the man himself I can hear?' Sean's voice boomed from his office. The man's six foot muscular frame filled the doorway. It was no wonder he had been a prop in his rugby playing days. The size of the man never failed to impress Kit.

'Hiya, buddy,' said Kit, going over and shaking his partner's hand.

'Wasn't expecting you back today,' said Sean, giving Kit a pat on the back, his huge hand covering Kit's shoulder blade.

'Always expect the unexpected,' said Kit. 'Thought I'd better come in and make sure you were coping.' He gave Veronica a wink, who grinned at her bosses.

'Didn't even know you weren't here, to be honest,' retorted Sean. 'We've been fine haven't we, Veronica?'

'I really couldn't comment,' she said diplomatically.

'Want a coffee in my office?' asked Sean.

'I'll pop in later,' said Kit. 'I need to check my emails to make sure I haven't missed anything important.' He had made a conscious decision not to access his emails while he'd been at home. In truth, he'd felt no inclination to do so. His priorities had changed. Once work would have come first, but the nightmare he had just endured had served to show him that his family was, by far, the most important thing in his life. Everything else could wait in line.

'I did have a look myself the other day,' admitted Sean. 'I wasn't sure when you'd be back. The only urgent thing was that guy, err, George Hanks, wanted to come in and take the new Sunseeker out.'

Kit gave a small groan. 'He's such a time waster.'

'Yeah, found that out a bit too late,' said Sean. 'I took him out Friday. He brought some young woman with him, said it was his business partner, but I think he was just wanting to show off to her. I reckon she's tagged to be more than his business partner.'

'He's a dick. Glad I missed him,' said Kit and then added, 'Sorry.'

'Yeah, right,' said Sean, with a grin. 'I'll catch up with you later. We could wander round to the cafe for a bit of lunch if you're free.'

'Sounds good to me.'

Kit crossed the reception area into his office and closed the door behind him. He took a moment to survey the room. It all looked how he had left it. Placing his case on the desk, he flicked on the coffee machine, sat down and opened his diary. It was of course empty for today. He opened the drawer to find a pen and as he did, spotted a yellow sticky note.

He smiled as he read Neve's message. Surprise indeed.

She must have come into the office at some point without telling him. The notion sat uncomfortably alongside the happier thought that she had left him a note. It was the sort of thing she used to do when they were first married. It warmed his heart, she was making just as much an effort as he was.

It was then he noticed the photo. He had been expecting to see the image of himself, Neve and Poppy on holiday a couple of years ago in Spain, but instead it was the selfie Poppy had taken the other day. He reached forwards and picked up the frame. The three of them looked so happy to be together. He hoped it would stay that way.

Never in his life had he felt so helpless, so emasculated, so insignificant as when Poppy was missing. The despair had taken him to dark places in his mind and it had frightened him. He had coped with losing Poppy's mum only by having Poppy to focus on. That week, without her, life had seemed pointless. Even Neve couldn't give him anything to live for. He knew in his heart of hearts that if Poppy hadn't been found safe and well, he wouldn't be here either. As it was, both he and Poppy were here and he was so much more than grateful that Neve had been there with him every step of the way.

Now he hoped that Neve would have what she had always wanted and their little family of three could become four. Hopefully it was enough to keep Neve from ever thinking about leaving him or looking for love elsewhere. He had been so careless. He would climb mountains, swim oceans and walk barefoot over hot coals to stop that happening again.

Leaving the photo frame on the desk, he pushed himself up and went into the shower room, locking the door behind him. He crouched down and opened the doors to the vanity unit.

Another note from Neve.

Shit.

She'd been in here? He dipped his head to look in the back of the cabinet but couldn't see anything. He reached in and fumbled around in the emptiness. The carrier bag with his blood-stained overshirt was gone.

He stood up and drummed his fingers on the side of the sink. Had Neve taken the shirt? Surely it was the only explanation, but why hadn't she said anything? Maybe she was going to wash it and return it. He didn't think Veronica would have done anything with it, she had no reason to come into the shower room. And even if she had, she would have told him.

But what if Neve had other ideas about the shirt? What if she suspected he was responsible for the attack on Jake? He rested his forehead against the cool glass mirror. Neve might be playing him – she might be pretending everything was fine between them, that she wanted to make a go of their marriage, so she could lure him into a false sense of security. Behind his back, she might go to the police with the shirt.

He stood up straight and shook his head. That wouldn't make sense. If she went to the police and he was arrested, their marriage would be over and Neve wouldn't be able to have the baby she was so desperate for. It wasn't like she could run off with Jake now.

Returning to his desk, he buzzed through to his receptionist.

'Veronica, has anyone been in here while I've been away?'

'Err, no. Just me and Sean. Oh, and Neve. She popped in to bring some post the other day and I believe put a new photograph on your desk. I think it was supposed to be a surprise. It's a lovely photo but I can always change it if you don't like it.'

'No, no. I do like it. I just can't find a file, that's all. So, no one else,' he tried to make his tone casual. 'I don't suppose the police have been here, have they?'

'No, they haven't. I can come and search for the file if you want me to, just give me the name ...'

'No. I'll have another look. What with everything that's gone on, I'm not really sure what I've done with a few things.'

He replaced the receiver and steepling his fingers together, rested back in his leather chair. The more he thought about what Neve would do with the shirt, the more he was certain she wouldn't go to the police. However, there was still an element of doubt, one he didn't like. He needed to shorten the odds in his favour.

The sound of wheels crunching on the gravel outside, drew Kit's attention to the window.

'For fuck's sake,' he muttered. 'Speak of the devil and he shall appear.' He watched through the tinted two-way glass, which afforded him the luxury of being able to monitor who was arriving without them seeing him.

DCI Pearson and Sally, their FLO, got out of the car and headed into the building.

Kit poured himself a coffee, opening a document on his laptop and waited for Veronica to buzz his phone.

'Send them in,' said Kit, not waiting for them to be announced.

He rose and shook the DCI's hand and nodded a hello to Sally. 'Wasn't expecting to see you two so soon. Any news?'

Pearson motioned to the seat and sat down, Sally taking the opposite chair. 'No. We're still following up leads,' said the DCI. 'We've been doing some background checks, routine stuff, to make sure we haven't missed anything when we came across something about your wife.'

'Neve?' Kit took a sip of his coffee. 'This sounds serious.'

'It's a bit delicate,' said Pearson.

'More delicate than telling me you've arrested my wife for kidnapping my daughter? And then not actually having any evidence,' said Kit, fixing Pearson with a look. He still hadn't quite forgiven the detective for that one.

Pearson, shuffled in his seat and had the grace to look slightly embarrassed, which pleased Kit. 'I know Neve said she was estranged from her family. Has she ever told you why?'

Kit looked from the DCI to the FLO. He had the distinct feeling they had the upper hand here. They clearly knew what it was Neve was hiding. He felt a mix of excitement that he would finally know what Neve had been keeping from him, and concern that he was being told by a police officer and not Neve herself. He wondered if Neve knew they were about to spill the beans. 'Does my wife know you're here?'

'No. We thought we would speak to you first. We've tried to call her but she's not answering her phone.'

'Really?' Kit checked the time on his watch. 'She has a dental appointment today. She's had toothache all weekend, maybe she's in bed.'

Pearson nodded and Sally made a note in her pocketbook.

'When Neve was married to her first husband, were you aware that she had a stillbirth?' asked Pearson.

Kit tried to hide his surprise at the terminology. Neve had told him she'd had a miscarriage, not a stillbirth. There was a difference. 'She has spoken to me about it,' he opted as a response.

'The baby was delivered at eight months,' put in Sally, which earned a glance from the DCI.

'What has this got to do with anything?' asked Kit, baulking inside. *Eight months? Eight months!*

'I'm getting to that. Just bear with me,' said Pearson. 'Did Neve ever speak about how this affected her?'

'Look, I really don't want to discuss my wife's emotions about a stillbirth,' said Kit. 'It's something very personal and private.'

323

He didn't add that it was so private, she'd never bloody told him. How on earth had she carried that secret on her own? No wonder she'd never wanted to speak about it. What a horrendous thing for her to endure.

'Did Neve say that she had mental health problems as a result?' asked Pearson, seemingly ignoring Kit's request.

'Well, that's hardly surprising, is it?' snapped Kit.

'Quite severe mental health issues,' added Sally.

Kit gave an exasperated shrug to convey his *what do you expect* answer.

'Neve said she doesn't speak to her brother or father anymore,' said Pearson. 'That they are estranged.'

'That's right. And her mother passed away a few years ago.'

'And her sister.' Pearson looked at Kit.

'Her sister? What sister?'

'Megan Howells. She drowned in a swimming accident. She was twenty-one at the time. Neve was eighteen.'

'What? I ... I had no idea.' Kit slumped back in his seat. Neve had a sister who died? Jesus Christ, she'd never told him. 'I'm sorry, I'm finding this hard to take in. Neve has never mentioned a sister to me. Not least one who died.'

'Apparently, Neve had gone down to the beach with her sister and the tide was high. The girls went swimming, despite it being a blustery day and the warning flags were out on the beach. Neve went in too deep and got caught in a riptide. Megan went in after her. Neve was somehow pushed out of the current and managed to swim to the safety of some rocks, but Megan wasn't so lucky.'

'Jesus Christ,' muttered Kit. He remembered the photos he'd found in the loft, of Neve and her friends on the beach.

On the reverse it said Megan's 20th, so Megan wasn't Neve's friend as Kit had assumed, Megan was her sister. Another revelation to knock him sideways. First the stillbirth and now a dead sister and Neve had never been able to tell him. He couldn't help feeling angry that she had kept this from him but, putting his own feelings aside, he could only imagine how awful Neve felt. His heart went out to her.

'Her sister's body was found three days later, washed up further along the coast,' put in Sally. 'The post-mortem and toxicology reports found cocaine in her bloodstream.'

Kit snapped his attention back to what Sally was saying. 'Cocaine?'

'That's right,' said Sally. 'Neve always maintained she didn't know her sister had taken drugs. Claimed she hadn't taken any herself and she had no idea where or how Megan had come by the stuff.'

'The local police in Devon have confirmed they always suspected someone else to be there at the time,' said Pearson. 'Neve consistently denied this.'

Kit was perplexed, he looked at both police officers sitting in front of him. 'And you're telling me this because ...?'

'Because, Devon police believed the supplier to be one Ashley Farnham. Or, as he is known around here, Lee Farnham.'

'It seems Lee Farnham has quite a history for being involved with the drug scene, although unfortunately, a lot of it can't be proven,' said Sally. She looked at her pocketbook and flicked through a couple of pages before reading out loud. 'Supplying cocaine at a youth group – complaint from a parent but never proven. Tampering with a girl's drink, possibly a date rape drug. Questioned after the girl reported to the police but, again no evidence as it was several days after the event – complaint dropped. He did actually serve six months of a nine-month sentence for setting up his own mini hydroponics farm in the loft of the house he was renting.' She flipped her notebook shut.

Kit was aware he was staring at Pearson as he tried to process the information. It didn't surprise him in the least that Farnham was involved with drugs, but the fact that Neve knew Farnham and she never said? A wave of anger surged again. Surely, she must have put two and two together with the names. He didn't think she'd met him, or at least not that he was aware of, but then again, what exactly did he know about his wife?

Somewhere at the back of his mind, Kit was aware of a connection being made. A small piece of the puzzle was falling into place. He couldn't quite reach that thought just yet, but it was there.

'I take it she never said that she knew Farnham?' said Sally.

Kit gave a shrug, hoping to seem indifferent.

'And the stillbirth. It's a pretty momentous event,' said Pearson. He paused, weighing Kit up with an observant eye, 'I'm guessing from your expression she never told you about that either. Why do you think that was?'

Kit clearly wasn't fooling the DCI. He cast his gaze around the room, as if he was going to find some magical answer somewhere. 'I've no idea. Perhaps she found it too difficult to talk about.' He closed his eyes and took a deep breath, before opening them again. 'Look, this is all heavy stuff for me to take in right now. I need time to think and speak to my wife.'

Right now, Kit had conflicting feelings about Neve. On the one hand, he wanted to demand some sort of explanation about why she never let on about her connection with Farnham, and on the other, all he wanted to do was to go home and wrap Neve in his arms, cradle her and let her pour her soul out to him about the death of her sister and the loss of the baby. No wonder she had always had this burden behind her eyes, always something that she had kept from him. Perhaps she thought he couldn't deal with knowing about the stillbirth after what he had been through himself. That would be it. She wouldn't have wanted to bring up his past, it was all too close to home. Too much pain for them both. She must have been protecting him by sacrificing her own needs to talk and share her horrific experience.

Kit stood up. 'I need to be at home with my wife,' he said.

Pearson waved his hand in a downward motion. 'Please, Kit, sit down. There's more.'

Chapter 33

Neve was aware of a pair of hands scooping her up from under her armpits. She was lifted to her feet and then drawn into her brother who had an arm around her shoulder and the other hand holding her arm.

'Come on, Neve,' he said. 'Come inside.'

Neve's feet responded, and she allowed herself to be taken indoors as she sobbed quietly into Gareth's chest.

He sat her down on the sofa and pulled a throw from the armchair to put around her shoulders. He uttered comforting words that Neve couldn't make out, but his tone was soft, if a little nervous.

'Pitiful,' came a voice from the doorway. It was Lisa. 'You're a pitiful sight, Neve Howells or whatever your name is now.'

Neve could feel the weight of her sister-in-law's stare, but she remained looking down at her hands. They were shaking so much, it was sending shockwaves up her arms.

'There's no need for that now,' said Gareth to his wife. 'I'll make her a cup of tea.'

Neve could hear their voices in the kitchen.

'I don't want her in the house,' said Lisa.

'I can't leave her outside. Not in the state she's in,' replied her brother. 'Didn't you see her? Hear her? She thinks she saw Megan out there.'

'What?'

'She's hallucinating or something. I don't know. Maybe she's having another breakdown.'

The rumble of the boiling kettle made it more difficult for Neve to hear the rest of the conversation. She pulled the throw tighter around her body.

Was she having a nervous breakdown? She tried to think back to what she had been like after she had lost her own child. Did she feel the same now as she did then? She didn't think so. But then there was Megan. Did sane people really think they could see dead people? It sounded ridiculous, even to her own mind but she also acknowledged she had seen Megan on the path outside. Was it her mind satisfying her deep desire to see her sister again?

Tears rushed to Neve's eyes. How many times had she wished for just one more moment with Megan? The rational part of her brain told her that it wasn't possible and that hurt so very much. Her heart was being physically battered like a boxer's exercise ball. The irrational part of her brain told her something different, that Megan was with her still. There to look after her. To see her through the tough times.

At one of the few therapy sessions she'd attended, Neve was told she shouldn't fantasise about Megan again. That Neve had to accept her sister was dead. It had been hard. So very hard.

'Here, drink this,' said Gareth coming back into the room. 'A nice sweet cup of tea will help you get over the shock.'

'Shock?'

329

'Of seeing us again. Seeing Jasmine and Lisa,' he paused, as he arranged the next words. 'And of thinking you saw Megan.'

'She seemed so real,' said Neve softly.

'Has this happened before?'

Neve stalled for time, taking a sip of her overly sweet tea. 'Yes,' she finally admitted.

'I told you she was crazy,' said Lisa who had appeared in the living room.

'Lisa,' admonished Gareth, 'that's not helping.'

'No, I'll tell you what will help though – you call the men in white coats to come and take her away.'

'Why don't you go and see if Jasmine is OK?' said Gareth, sitting on the footstool in front of Neve and facing her.

'Jasmine is absolutely fine,' said Lisa. 'She's staying in her room until it's safe to come out.'

Gareth shook his head despairingly but turned his attention back to Neve. 'Does anyone know you're here? Did you tell your husband you were coming here?'

Neve shook her head. 'He doesn't know.'

'Does he know what happened? What you did?' asked Gareth.

'I hadn't told him.' She turned to Lisa. 'And it wasn't your place to tell him.'

'He had a right to know,' said Lisa, a defensive yet belligerent tone to her voice. 'His own daughter was missing. He had a right to know what sort of psycho he was married to. I don't regret sending them for one moment. I'm just glad the child was found. I know what it's like when your child goes missing.'

'You weren't the only one who suffered that weekend,' snapped Gareth.

'Then you should be on my side, not defending your sister,' retorted Lisa.

'It's not a case of taking sides,' said Gareth. 'Neve is clearly not well.'

'In the head!' Lisa stabbed her finger at her temple to underline her meaning. 'She's not well in the head!'

'If you can't say anything constructive, go and find something else to do,' snapped Gareth. He turned his attention back to his sister. 'Neve, have you got your husband's number. I should call him. He'll be worried about you.'

'Please don't. I don't want him to know.'

Gareth reached across and held his sister's hands. 'I think it's time to tell him.'

'I can't face him,' said Neve. 'I've totally messed everything up. My whole life has been a mess.'

'You can say that again,' muttered Lisa, still standing her ground.

'You haven't, Neve. You just need help coping sometimes. It's nothing to be ashamed of,' said Gareth. 'You need to speak to your husband.' He hesitated as if wrestling with what he wanted to say. 'You need to let Megan rest in peace.'

A huge sob from deep in the pit of Neve's stomach propelled itself up through her chest. It took several minutes before she could calm down enough to speak again. 'But I don't want to leave Megan. I need her.'

'You don't, Neve. Not after what happened with Jasmine. You let Megan get in your head and she nearly destroyed you. Don't let it happen again. Please.'

331

Neve knew what her brother was saying was right, but at the same time it sounded impossible for her to do. She couldn't just leave Megan. Couldn't just abandon her sister after all this time.

Neve looked towards the doorway, sensing somebody there, as Jasmine walked into the room.

'Oh, no you don't,' began Lisa.

Gareth rose to his feet and put a steadying arm on his wife's. 'Leave her be.'

Neve looked at her beautiful niece standing in front of her. Her big brown apprehensive eyes returned her gaze. 'Hello, Jasmine,' she said, taking a tissue from her pocket and wiping her face, as she stood up. 'Do you know who I am?'

Jasmine flicked a glance to her parents before saying to Neve, 'Yes. You're my dad's sister. My aunty Neve.'

Neve smiled. 'That's right. You look exactly as I remember you,' she said. 'Just older.'

'I've always wondered if you'd come here,' said Jasmine. 'I know what happened. Mum and Dad have told me. I don't remember it hardly though.'

'You were only young,' said Neve.

'I always had this vague picture in my mind of what you looked like,' said Jasmine, fiddling with the hem of her school blazer. 'I remember your blonde hair and I can remember you laughing as we built sandcastles.'

Neve smiled at the memory. 'It was a lovely day. Breezy but the sun was shining. You were crouched down and the wind was lifting your hair …'

'Enough!' said Lisa. 'I don't want to hear this.'

'Mum!'

'I said *enough*,' insisted Lisa. She turned to Neve. 'Don't you have a husband and child to go home to?'

As Neve stood there looking at Jasmine, she could feel herself drifting away, back to that day on the beach. Lisa's voice was becoming more and more distant, gradually blocked out by the sound of the waves, the rush of the water as it broke and scrambled up the shore line, the squawk of the seagulls overhead, the bluster of the wind as it buffeted in off the tide and the taste of the briny sea air on her mouth.

And then the scene changed.

Dark clouds swamped the sky, the wind upgraded from blustery to fierce. The water was cold, rushing around her ankles and then her knees. A big wave knocked her off balance, sending her sprawling into the wake. She could feel the sand and stones beneath her being torn back out as the sea regrouped. She was buoyant and pulled out with it. Her hands scoring drag marks in the sand. She tried to stand but the water was too deep. She could feel the slime of the seaweed as it wrapped itself around her legs. The waves crashed over her head and she took in a mouthful of the cold salty water.

Megan was screaming her name now. Neve looked back. The shore seemed so far away and she was being dragged further and further out. It was all she could do to keep afloat. Another wave pounded her and then she was over the crashing waves and moving fast out to sea. She couldn't see Megan anymore.

She remembered Gareth once telling them you could swim out of a riptide if you swam parallel to the shore. Neve was a strong swimmer, she'd competed at junior level when she was younger. She moved to the side of the channel and although it took all the strength and stamina she had, she finally felt herself slip from the current. There was a small spit of rocks protruding out into the water. It was going to be painful trying to hold onto the jagged and scored surface, but it was her only chance.

Neve hauled herself out of the water and onto the rocks, gasping for breath, coughing and spluttering as her lungs cleared themselves of the sea water.

As she looked back into the water, Neve couldn't see Megan. There wasn't any sign of her anywhere and no matter how much she shouted her sister's name, she never saw Megan again.

Neve felt herself wobble as she relived the moment. Her head felt light on the inside but at the same time too heavy to hold up. She felt herself sway.

'Megan ...' she heard her voice, her eighteen-year-old self, calling her sister's name over and over again, but it was so faint, so distant.

The next thing she was vaguely aware of was her knees giving way, someone catching her and what sounded like her brother's voice calling for an ambulance.

Chapter 34

'Thank you for phoning. I'm just sorry we couldn't have spoken under better circumstances.' Kit ended the call and slipped his mobile back into his pocket.

'Neve?' Pearson looked questioningly at Kit.

Kit hesitated for a second, wondering whether he could conjure up an alternative answer to the truth but ultimately decided there was no point trying to blag it. 'It was Neve's brother, Gareth,' he said. 'Apparently, Neve turned up at his house this lunchtime. She's had some sort of funny turn. I'm not sure of the details, but she's in Newport hospital.'

He hooked his jacket off from the back of his chair.

'Serious?' asked Sally.

'Like I said, I don't know the details,' said Kit, shrugging on his jacket. 'But the fact she's in hospital, kind of says it all.' He didn't have time for the police officers now. He needed to get to Newport. What the hell she was doing over there, he had no idea. Gareth hadn't elaborated, and it hadn't been the time to ask. Not with these two here anyway.

'Did you know she was going to see her brother?' pried the DCI. 'I thought she didn't speak to him.'

'Turns out she does,' said Kit, not bothering to hide the sarcasm from his voice. 'I'm sorry, but I need to go.' He picked up his briefcase and walked over to the door, holding it open for his visitors to exit.

'Yes, of course,' said Sally, following her boss's lead and walking across the office. 'Do keep us up to date.'

Kit managed a cordial nod and said his goodbyes as the DCI and FLO left the building. He was still trying to take in what they had just told him, but it was as if there wasn't quite enough room. There were so many thoughts jostling for attention. He'd have to push the latest revelation to the back of the queue for now.

'Cancel all my meetings today and tomorrow, please,' said Kit to Veronica. 'I've got a family emergency.' And then, seeing the look of concern on his employee's face, elaborated, 'Neve's been taken ill at her brother's in Wales.'

The door on the other side of the reception area opened and Sean came out. 'Trouble?' he said and then taking a look at Kit, asked, 'Are you OK, mate?'

'Yeah. Sort of. The police were just asking some background questions. Formalities, that sort of stuff.'

'Neve's been taken ill, though,' said Veronica. 'Kit's just heading off.'

'Neve? What's happened?' asked Sean, frowning.

Kit gave a brief summary of what little he knew. 'I'm going there now. Probably won't be back tonight.' He was just about to turn and leave when he suddenly thought of Poppy. 'Oh, shit. I was supposed to be taking Poppy to my mother's tonight. I'll have to call her.'

'I can do that for you,' said Sean.

'No, I'll do it. She'll only try to phone me anyway. Thanks all the same.'

'No worries. Mind how you go. Give Neve my love.'

'Cheers mate.'

As Kit drove off towards the motorway, he hoped that Poppy wouldn't freak out too much about his mother picking her up. She didn't do well with surprises. His fingers drummed the steering wheel. He'd go to the school first and tell her in person. It would only take another fifteen minutes or so, and it would ease his conscience at having to leave her just when he was hoping things would settle back down into a routine.

As he drove, he couldn't ignore the latest information Pearson had given him, and his wife's connection with Farnham played on his mind the most. Especially as the bloke had disappeared and the police were still keen to talk to him. She'd known Farnham since she was a teenager and yet he had never once heard her mention him.

And the whole drugs thing! What was that all about? Was that what Scott Tansley was hinting at? Kit assumed that Farnham was the other lad in the photograph, the one who had tried to beat the timer on the camera, whose face was covered by his arm as he dived into the shot. It would make sense.

Had Megan died because they'd taken drugs? He found it hard to believe that Neve would be so reckless, it was like she was some stranger to him.

Kit called his mother on the hands-free device in his car. 'Hi, Mum. Look, I'm afraid there's been a change of plan for tonight,' he said and continued quickly, ignoring the little 'oh' of indignation from his mother. 'I don't have time to explain in detail but Neve's in Wales and been taken ill so I'm heading up there now to see her. Can you collect Poppy from her after-school club and take her back to yours for tea. I'll give you a ring later when I know what's going on. You might need to take Poppy home tonight, depending if we come back tonight or not.'

'What? Neve? Ill? In Wales?'

Kit gave a roll of his eyes. 'Yes, Mum. I'm driving so I can't speak now but can you get Poppy, please?'

'Well, I don't know if it's a good idea leaving Poppy after all that's happened ...'

Kit cut in before his mother could say any more. 'Mum, it's not ideal, I know, but it's happening. Can you get Poppy or not? Please?'

'Yes, of course I will. Has she got a key?'

'No. I'll leave one with her teacher though. You can collect if from the school office.'

'It would be so much easier if I had a key,' his mother was saying.

'Sorry, Mum. Driving. Bad line. I'll phone you later.' He cut the call before his mother could say anything else.

Luckily, Poppy's school were very accommodating to irregular and unusual student needs and ushered Kit into the chill-out room, as it was signposted on the door in big colourful letters, while someone went to fetch Poppy. The room was painted in a pastel primrose and the pictures on the walls, painted by the children gave it a homely feel. There were two brightly coloured beanbags next to a small book case with a selection of books and other educational resources. One corner had been dedicated to a small water feature and the trickling sound of the water tumbling over the pebbles and into a little pool was very soothing.

Kit checked his watch and hoped the teacher wouldn't take too long fetching Poppy. When Mrs Ogden returned with Poppy, Kit gave his daughter a reassuring smile. 'Hi, sweetheart,' he said. 'Look, your nan is going to pick you up tonight. I've got to go to Wales.'

'Wales?' said Poppy. 'Where's that?'

'A few hours away,' said Kit, and then clarified for his daughter's sake. 'Three hours away by car. Neve is there and not feeling very well, so I'm going to see her and bring her home if I can.'

'OK,' said Poppy with a shrug.

Kit was relieved that Poppy seemed to be taking his explanation at face value and not asking for any further clarification. He wasn't sure what reassurances he would be able to offer her, after all, he couldn't even offer himself any. He didn't have any control on the situation and he was aware of unwelcome anxiety stirring in the pit of his stomach.

Ten minutes later, Kit was in the car and speeding to the petrol station. Perspiration dotted his forehead and he wiped it away with a tissue from the box Neve liked to keep in the car. He still needed to dive home and grab an overnight bag for himself and some fresh clothes for Neve.

Why hadn't she told him what she was doing? What about her dentist appointment? Maybe that's why she was ill. Perhaps she had a severe infection or something. Sepsis even! Shit. People could die from that.

Then he shook his head. No. That didn't make sense. She said she had an appointment this afternoon. She'd rung him just a little while ago to tell him she wouldn't be at his mother's.

'For fuck's sake, Neve!' he cursed out loud. 'What the hell were you playing at?'

Despite what Pearson had told Kit just an hour ago about his wife, Kit knew he couldn't abandon her now. He had to process the new information. It put everything into a whole new light. He wasn't sure how it changed things, but it was a significant revelation. In fact, it was pretty damn huge.

Kit now knew things about Neve that shocked and saddened him at the same time. And he began to understand how much his wife had to carry on her shoulders.

By the time Kit pulled up in the car park of the Royal Gwent Hospital, his eyes were aching from the concentration. He rubbed them with his fingertips before exiting the vehicle and heading off to find Neve.

The sterile smell of the ward hit him and made him feel queasy as he entered. He'd never liked hospitals. Not since Poppy was born. For him they were a place where bad things happened. Bad memories hung in the air like cobwebs.

'I've come to see Neve Masters,' said Kit to the nurse.

Checking on the white board, she directed Kit to the ward further down the corridor.

Neve was in the bed immediately to the right. Kit could see her pale face, almost the same colour as the white pillow case on which her head rested. Her eyes were closed but Kit had the sensation she wasn't sleeping. A man who Kit estimated to be in his fifties was sitting in the chair next to the bed. His grey head was dipped as he read a newspaper. The man looked up as Kit approached the bed.

'Kit?'

'Gareth?'

'That's right.' A Welsh lilt accompanied the man's voice and he extended his hand to Kit. 'We meet at last.'

Kit gave a nod. 'How is she?'

Gareth grimaced. 'Very upset.' He motioned towards the corridor.

Kit took the hint and the two men walked outside.

'She turned up at my house totally out of the blue,' said Gareth. 'I opened the door and there she was. Took me by surprise, I can tell you.'

'I'm sure,' said Kit.

Gareth looked uncomfortable as he shuffled from one foot to another. 'The thing is,' he began, rubbing his chin. 'The thing is, my wife ... oh God, this is so awkward.'

Kit waited patiently while the other man collected himself.

'OK. We saw on the television about your daughter going missing – and I'm sorry about that, but I'm glad she's home safe now.'

'Thank you,' said Kit.

'Well, of course, we recognised Neve straight away. It upset my wife. You see, we all had a falling out ...'

Kit put his hand on the other man's shoulder. 'I know what happened with Jasmine.'

Gareth looked up at him in surprise. 'You do?'

Kit dropped his hand. 'I found out earlier today. The police told me.'

'Oh,' said Gareth, raising his eyes and extending the word. 'I see. And I take it you know about the notes.'

'Yes.'

'Right. But you don't know who sent them, I'm assuming?'

'I have a pretty good idea,' said Kit, tamping down the sigh that was threatening. He wished Gareth would just get to the point.' 'Am I right in assuming it was your wife?'

'She can't really forgive Neve for what happened. For what Neve put her through.'

'I can appreciate that,' said Kit, successfully managing to maintain an even tone.

'Did the police also tell you what happened to our sister, Megan?' asked Gareth.

'I understand she drowned,' said Kit. 'I'm sorry.'

'Terrible accident. One that Neve has never been able to come to terms with. She had to have psychiatric help. She went through a phase of blaming things that happened on Megan.' Gareth shuffled his feet some more. 'She used to have conversations with Megan. I heard her once in her bedroom. I was just passing on the landing and wondered who was in her room. I stopped and listened and realised she was talking to herself. When I tackled her about it, she denied it; got quite angry. Told me in no uncertain terms where to go.'

'Really? I didn't know that,' conceded Kit. He thought back to the first few months after his first wife's death, he had found himself talking to her on more than one occasion. It had made him feel Ella was still with him, partly because he hadn't been ready to let her go, even though everyone else was moving on in life. 'Maybe it was a comfort to her.'

'Oh, I dare say it was, but she's never stopped doing it. In fact, earlier today outside my house when she collapsed, she was a bit delirious and thought she saw Megan and then when she properly collapsed the second time indoors, she was just calling Megan's name over and over again. Reaching her hand out as if Megan was really there.'

'What has the doctor said?' asked Kit, his concern ramping up a gear. This sounded more than just the funny turn Gareth had implied on the phone. Far worse than he imagined. 'Has she had some sort of breakdown, do you think?'

'I wouldn't be surprised,' replied Gareth. 'The doctor wants to refer her to the mental health team when she leaves. He said it's a disassociation thing. I don't think when Neve was younger it was ever given a name, you know, where she almost imagined it was Megan doing stuff, when really it was her. I just thought I'd better give you the heads up about it all.'

'Thanks, Gareth. I appreciate that,' said Kit, retaining a calmness in his voice he didn't feel. If he was honest, he was unnerved by the revelation. His wife hadn't just spoken to her dead sister, she'd actually imagined Megan doing things. He needed some time alone with Neve to talk to her properly. 'Why don't you get yourself a coffee. You look done in. I'll sit with Neve and see if I can speak to a doctor.'

'If you're sure?'

'Of course.'

Gareth frowned, he went to walk away but hesitated, turning to Kit, his forefinger tapping his lip as if he was trying to come to a decision.

'Everything OK?' asked Kit.

'You seem to really care about her,' said Gareth.

'I do, very much so,' said Kit.

'That's good. There's a lot to understand with my sister.' He looked pointedly at Kit. 'And a lot to forgive.'

Kit watched Gareth head off down the corridor, an air of tiredness, possibly sadness, hung over his drooped shoulders.

Kit stood there until Gareth disappeared through the swing doors, before returning to the ward. He leaned down and kissed Neve on the forehead, taking her hand in his. 'Hey, Neve, it's me, Kit.'

Her eyelids gave a little flutter.

'I know you're not asleep. Come on, I've driven all this way, you could at least talk to me.'

Neve opened her eyes and looked up at him. 'I'm surprised you came.'

'Why wouldn't I? My wife has been taken ill and is in hospital.' He sat down on the edge of the bed. 'What's going on Neve?'

'What do you mean? I know Gareth's told you why I went to his house. He told me he explained on the phone.'

'I want to hear it from you,' said Kit and when it looked like she wasn't going to speak, he added. 'The thing is, Neve, I'm not really sure I do know everything. I've been told various things by various people but nothing from you.'

It was a few moments before she answered. 'You know they all think I'm mad and I've had some sort of mental breakdown.'

'Is that what you think?'

He watched as tears rushed to fill her eyes before she looked away, blinking hard.

'I know I'm extremely sad,' she said. 'That coming here has made me sad.'

'Why's that?'

She turned her head to look at him again. 'Megan,' she

said. 'I miss her so much. And being here has made it so much worse. I shouldn't have come. It wasn't worth it. All it's done is rekindle all the feelings I had managed to store away.'

Kit plucked a tissue from the box on the bedside cabinet and gently dabbed the tears escaping from her eyes. 'Tell me, Neve. Talk to me. Let me in to your world.'

'It's a pretty shit world to be in,' she said. 'You wouldn't like it there.'

'I'll be the judge of that.' He mopped more tears.

'I just ... I don't know ... coming here has made me feel so guilty.'

'Guilty for what?'

'It was my fault,' she said before a sob escaped. 'I should have listened to Megan. I shouldn't have gone deeper into the water. And when she came in after me, I should have stayed in the water. Rescued her. Swam out of the riptide with her. Or at least tried to but I didn't. I scrambled out onto the rocks. I saved myself.'

Kit reached out and took Neve's hand in his. 'Pearson told me you knew Lee Farnham when you were teenagers,' he paused, as he took in the look of shock on Neve's face.

'We all used to hang around together,' she said at last.

'Why you didn't tell me about Farnham.'

Neve cast her gaze down. 'I had spent so long distancing myself from the past, I was scared to even mention that I knew him. I hoped he would just disappear the same way he appeared.'

'Well, he's certainly done that,' said Kit.

'I'm so sorry, Kit. I should have told you. When Meg died, I didn't want to leave her behind. No one wanted to talk about her. It was like a taboo subject. I would see my mum looking at me and I was sure she was thinking things like, *why didn't you listen to your sister, it was your fault. Why wasn't it you? Why did it have to be Megan?* My dad just retreated further and further into himself.'

'It must have been difficult for everyone,' said Kit, remembering his own grief when he lost his wife. A time when his life should have been filled with such happiness at the birth of his daughter and was yet so tragic at the same time.

'Megan became a no-go conversation topic and Dad just pushed on with life. It was as if everyone wanted to forget about her. I used to go to the beach,' said Neve. 'I felt closer to Megan there. I don't know exactly when it happened but, after a while, I started thinking she was with me. I could actually feel her presence. It was like I had been able to conjure her up. If I had anything difficult to face or deal with, I imagined her by my side, willing me on. Somewhere along the line that changed too. I started to picture myself as Megan. It made me feel strong, brave and confident. I could do all the things I needed to do if I was Megan. I could be all the things Neve wasn't.'

Kit squeezed his wife's hand. He didn't know what to say. He hadn't been expecting this confessional outpouring. So many things about his wife that he didn't know. It wasn't just facts and history he didn't know, he was also totally oblivious to the emotional strain she was enduring. How had he missed that? Were there any tell-tale signs he should have seen?

Neve gave a sniff and wiped her nose with a tissue. 'Now can you see why they think I've lost it? Not only do I talk to my dead sister, I think I am her at times.'

'You were just trying to make sense of a tragic accident,' said Kit, softly. 'Such a traumatic event – it's no wonder you were looking for ways to process it.'

'Ah, you might feel sympathy for me now, but do you know where it all led to?'

Kit nodded. 'I know about the baby. I'm so sorry. I had no idea it was so late in the pregnancy. You never told me.'

'It was easier to tell you it was a miscarriage. It's what I've always told people. No one could cope with what happened. It made them feel uncomfortable. They didn't know what to say so, in the end, I stopped telling people the whole story.'

'I wish you'd told me,' said Kit, rubbing the top of her hand with his thumb.

'After what you'd been through? It didn't seem fair. Too much grief for one person, let alone two people who are trying to make a new start in life together.'

'I feel so selfish,' admitted Kit. 'I burdened you with my grief but never let you feel there was room for yours too.'

'You're too generous,' said Neve. 'You've no idea what sort of woman I am.'

'I do. If you're referring to Jasmine, I know.' He looked her firmly in the eye. Of all the things he had learnt about his wife, this was the hardest. The one that he found most difficult to associate with her. It also sent a nagging doubt at the back of his mind about the temporary disappearance of Poppy, but at the moment he couldn't deal with that thought. He needed time to face that demon. Christ, he so wanted it to be untrue and he needed this time with Neve to convince him.

'When I was pregnant, I knew we were having a little girl,'

said Neve. 'I thought I was forgiven for not saving Megan. She was going to be called Olivia Megan. I thought I could have a little bit of my sister in my own daughter. A memory to her. To show everyone that I hadn't ever forgotten Megan. So, when … when Olivia Megan … when I went for a scan and they discovered there wasn't a heartbeat, it was so hard to bear.' The tears came again, and Kit waited patiently for his wife to compose herself. He sensed that this was a cathartic moment for her, being able to tell him all the things she had kept locked away for so long. 'I didn't cope very well,' said Neve. 'It affected me deeply.'

'Is that what made you take Jasmine?'

'I was so confused. In so much pain,' replied Neve. 'The only way I could cope was channelling my sister. What would Megan do? It's been a question I've asked myself so many times. What would Megan do? Well, I suppose in my confused state, I somehow embraced Megan completely.'

'How do you mean?'

'Megan was the reckless, life-lover, go-getter of the family. She was impulsive, courageous, adventurous. When Gareth and Lisa asked me to look after Jasmine for the day, I was happy to do so. I think they felt they were helping me get over my loss. Everyone thought I was getting better.' She dabbed quotation marks in the air. 'They thought it would help me look to the future. Try for another baby. They meant well, but no one understood the pain I was experiencing.'

Kit stroked a strand of hair from Neve's eyes. 'People don't know what to say. They don't know how to deal with someone else's grief,' he said.

'I took Jasmine to the park and I don't really know what

happened, but it was like I was watching a film, starring Megan. She was in the park with Jasmine and somehow in my mind I could picture Olivia. And I was watching Megan, packing a bag and driving the car down to Devon. To our childhood haunts. To the beaches we played on as children during our family camping holidays. It was all so surreal. The doctor said afterwards that I had experienced some sort of disassociation from real life and from myself. I was at a point in my life where everything was black and I could see no light.'

'So, you took Jasmine away for the weekend.' Kit ignored the nagging voice of suspicion in his head. Neve had taken a child before, a member of her own family, driven by the loss of her own baby and a desire to have another, what was to say she hadn't done it again? She had been desperate then and he knew how desperate she was this time. She was under a tremendous amount of pressure, maybe it had stopped her thinking straight. She'd definitely been acting out of character lately and particularly so the last few days.

'I don't really remember much about taking Jasmine,' said Neve, breaking his thoughts. 'Gareth and Lisa were out of their minds with worry. Gareth phoned and phoned, texted me, pleaded with me to bring Jasmine home but I wouldn't listen. In the end they called the police and they came and found me. I was going to bring Jasmine home, I really was but everyone was scared of what I'd do. Gareth refused to press charges and only stopped Lisa from doing so by promising never to have anything to do with me again.'

'And that's when you left Wales and moved to West Sussex?'

'Not straight away. Me and Scott tried to make a go of things. I tried so hard to put what happened behind me, but I couldn't. Every time I went out, I thought people were staring at me, whispering behind my back, pointing me out to their friends ... I was the woman who stole the child. And not just any child, my own brother's child.'

'Didn't you get any help or support from your GP?' asked Kit.

'I did at first, there was a counselling programme, but I only went to a few sessions. I bumped into Ashley and he was the only person willing to talk about Megan. It was so comforting. I didn't want to go back to the counselling. By that point, I was disguising my grief with anger. I was angry at everyone and everything.'

'I get that, I really do,' said Kit. He remembered his own GP telling him it was one of the stages of grief he had to go through. Neve wouldn't look at him, her eyes were fixed on their hands. He was reminded of Gareth just now and how he seemed to want to say something but couldn't find the words. Neve had that same tormented look on her face. He wondered if it was connected with what Pearson had told him about her. Something that she had never shared with him and now that he knew, who could blame her. 'Neve,' he began. 'I know about the drugs.'

Her head flicked up. There was a look of shock on her face. 'You do?'

Kit nodded. 'Pearson told me.'

'And you still came?'

'I wanted to hear what you had to say about it. Your side of the story, if you like.'

It seemed like an age before she spoke and when she did, Kit had to lean in to hear her.

'I went off the rails after that thing with Jasmine. I was in a dark place.' Her finger was tapping Kit's hand at an ever-increasing rate. 'I did ... I looked for a release ... I started taking stuff to help me cope.'

'Stuff?'

The finger tapping upped its pace. 'Drugs,' she whispered. 'Class A. Coke.'

It sounded so different, hearing Neve say it to the way Pearson had delivered the information. Pearson had taken a stern, disapproving tone. One where he had no tolerance for the substance or its users. Whereas, hearing Neve tell him, it sounded close to heart-breaking and unbearably painful.

'Pearson said it was only because Scott hired a top solicitor that you got off without a custodial sentence. He said you would have just got a caution if you'd named your supplier.'

'It was my first offence. I had a tiny amount on me, so it was obviously just for my personal use. There was no intent to supply,' said Neve.

'Why didn't you name your supplier?'

Neve looked up to the ceiling and closed her eyes. 'The supplier was Ashley. I wasn't going to get him in trouble.'

'That wouldn't have been the first time you protected him, would it?'

'To be honest, it was easier than grassing on him,' said Neve. 'No guilt. No repercussions.'

Kit inhaled deeply as he took a moment to gather his thoughts. 'And Scott stood by you?' he said eventually.

'For a while. He tried, he really did, but it was awful. No

one would talk to us. We lost our friends. I was known as the junkie wife,' said Neve with a sigh. 'We even tried moving areas, but it turned out it wasn't just our community who turned on us, we turned on ourselves. It was bad. We argued all the time. I had become almost reclusive and Scott couldn't deal with that. He thought I was a total fruitcake when I said I wanted to try for another baby. He said he couldn't trust me with children. He would always be scared what I would do, even to my own children.' Neve's grip tightened on Kit's hand.

'Wow, I don't know what to say to all this,' said Kit. He felt exhausted just listening to his wife's confession, or rather confessions. Just when he thought there was no more to learn, she threw in another curveball.

'I would never do anything to harm a child,' Neve said with force. 'Never. Scott was wrong. I wouldn't hurt my own child. Or anyone else's for that matter.' She sat up straighter, looking intently at Kit. 'Have you ever had the slightest doubt about me and Poppy before now? Answer me – have you ever thought I'd hurt Poppy?'

'No. Not before all this,' admitted Kit.

'And now?'

'I don't think you would hurt her,' said Kit. He sat back in his chair, he suddenly felt exhausted both mentally and emotionally.

They sat in silence as they both digested what Neve had said. Kit felt a tremendous amount of sympathy for his wife. She had been broken, not once but twice and each time she hadn't really ever been fixed. And as much as he loved Neve and realised he could forgive her for all these things, there was still one question he hadn't asked. He could barely contemplate it, let alone voice it – had Neve been involved in Poppy's disappearance and was Farnham's appearance on the scene really just a coincidence? He couldn't yet bring himself to consider this further, it was too horrific to deal with right now.

Chapter 35

It wasn't until the following morning that the doctor agreed to let Neve go home with Kit. He'd be sending his report to her GP and strongly suggested she seek further counselling. Both Neve and Kit had assured him they would, although Neve suspected Kit did so with rather more conviction than herself. She wasn't sure if she could face talking about this with someone again. She was sure they'd confine her to a mental institution. Seeing dead people wasn't something a sane and competent person did.

'I'll get someone to bring your car back in the week,' Kit said, as they drove out of the hospital grounds. 'I know a couple of drivers who deliver for the firm, they'll do it for a bit of cash.'

'Thank you,' said Neve. She reached her hand out and covered Kit's. 'Thank you for being here. I don't know what I'd do without you.'

Kit took his eyes off the road for a moment, just enough to give her a reassuring smile. Her heart swelled as she felt a surge of love for him.

'Gareth is going to keep an eye on it anyway. I've left the

keys with him,' said Kit, as he returned his attention to the road ahead.

'He's been very kind in all this,' said Neve.

'He's your brother,' said Kit.

'I don't know if Lisa is quite so ready to call a truce.'

'I think she'll thaw eventually,' said Kit. 'I suspect she's never really had closure, as they say. That's why she sent the notes. She was still so angry about it, probably fuelled by the fact that you left all those years ago and she never got a chance to confront you in the cold light of the aftermath.'

Neve gave a small snort. 'You've been reading too many psychiatry books.'

Kit smiled. 'I had a long chat with Gareth last night. The fact that Lisa was OK with me staying the night can only be seen as a good sign. She said herself that after having a go at you yesterday, she went to bed thinking she'd feel satisfied, but she actually felt it was an anti-climax.'

'What are you getting at?'

'She harboured all this anger for all those years and now she's vented it all, she's nothing left in the tank. Sometimes the thought of something is enough to keep a person going and then the act doesn't live up to expectations,' said Kit. 'I definitely got the impression that she was genuinely sad about it all.'

'I did use to get on with Lisa really well,' admitted Neve, thinking back to the evenings out they had shared before Lisa had become pregnant. Shopping days spent together, keep fit classes and trips to the cinema. 'I would like to again, but I just never thought it was a possibility.'

'Give her time.'

Neve rested her head back against the soft leather upholstery and allowed herself to drift off to sleep. It was a safe place to be right now.

The journey from Wales back to West Sussex was uneventful and Neve was glad when she opened her eyes and the familiar sight of the South Downs came into view. Not long after that, they were crossing the bridge into the village and pulling onto their driveway.

Kit stopped the engine and checked his phone. 'Message from Mum. Poppy was fine. Went into school without any problems. Do you need me to pick her up?'

Neve noted that Cheryl hadn't enquired about her and although it hurt a little, she knew she didn't really deserve Cheryl's sympathy right now.

'We can get her,' said Neve.

As she said that, the sound of another car pulling onto the gravel driveway interrupted them. Kit looked in his rearview mirror. 'For fuck's sake,' he muttered.

Neve turned in her seat to look over her shoulder. 'What do they want?' she said with a deep sigh. 'I don't know if I can face them right now.'

'Wait there.' Kit got out of the car and with his hands in his pockets, Neve watched him wait for Pearson to come to a stop and wind down his window. She couldn't hear what was being said, but from Kit's expression she gathered her husband wasn't impressed with the response from Pearson. Kit trudged back to the car, coming around to her side. 'Sorry. They are insisting they need to come in and talk to us now.'

'Did they say what about?' asked Neve, unbuckling her

seat belt and accepting Kit's hand to climb out of the Mercedes. She looked over to the car, where Pearson and Sally remained. Pearson gave a nod of acknowledgement but there was no smile.

'Nope. I've told them to give us five minutes to get in and make a cup of tea.'

'Do they know I've been to Wales?' asked Neve.

'I just said you'd been to see your brother and had been taken ill,' said Kit, ushering her into the house. As he closed the door, his mobile rang. 'Kit Masters speaking. Oh, hello Edward. Yes, we're home now. She's not too bad. Tired but otherwise well, thanks.' There was a long pause as Kit listened before he spoke again. 'Right. That changes things. Yep.' Another pause, longer this time. 'The police are actually sitting on my driveway as we speak. Yes. They're waiting to come in and talk to us. No, I don't think that will be necessary. I'll call you afterwards. Thanks, Edward.'

'What did Edward want?'

'Just letting me know the police wanted to speak to us.'

'Oh, how does he know that?'

'I think he said that someone from the station had been on the phone to him. He asked if I wanted him to come over, but I said no for now.'

'Do you think that's wise? I mean, I'm still under caution.'

'We've nothing to hide.' He gave her that look which she couldn't quite read. 'He'll be there if they want us down the station for formal questioning. Now, don't be worrying, it's all under control.'

Neve replayed Kit's side of the conversation with Edward over in her mind. 'Is there something you're not telling me?'

Kit walked over to her and cupped her face with his hands. 'Everything is going to be just fine. Trust me.' He planted a small kiss on her forehead. 'Now, go and sit down, I'll bring in a cup of tea.'

Neve settled herself in the living room. Both her body and mind exhausted from the last twenty-four hours. She had a flock of emotions wheeling around like screeching seagulls when someone has tossed breadcrumbs onto the beach. She was finding it hard to think straight through all the noise in her head. If she could just harness one thought and focus on that, maybe she could get through the meeting with Pearson.

Kit had barely put the cup of tea down in front of her when the doorbell sounded out, followed by a firm knock.

'Just keep calm,' said Kit, as Neve jumped at the noise. 'Let me do most of the talking. You're not really in a fit state and I'll point that out to him if necessary.'

'Thank you.' She seemed to be thanking Kit an awful lot. She was so glad he was here fighting her corner.

Kit answered the door and showed Pearson and Sally into the living room, indicating for them to sit on the sofa, while he perched on the arm of Neve's chair, giving him an elevated position over the unexpected visitors.

'So, what can we do for you?' asked Kit. 'You only came around yesterday. I wasn't expecting to see you so soon.'

'Need to ask some more questions,' said Pearson. He looked over at Neve. 'How are you, Neve? I understand you were taken ill.'

'I'm fine now, thank you,' said Neve.

'You went to Wales to see your brother,' said Pearson.

'That's right,' replied Neve.

'May I ask why?'

Neve resisted the urge to glance up at Kit and instead maintained eye contact with Pearson. 'It's personal but seeing as you ask—'

Before she could continue, Kit spoke. 'After everything that's happened, it made Neve realise that life is too short to waste time not speaking to people you actually care about. She always assumed she had time on her side and that one day she probably would speak to her brother again. But these past couple of weeks have been a wake-up call. Neve realised she needed to make peace with her family before it was too late.'

Neve was impressed with Kit's little speech. It was fairly accurate too.

Pearson nodded. 'And was your brother of like mind?' He made sure he addressed Neve with the question.

'As a matter of fact, he was,' said Neve. 'Granted it took a bit of negotiating but we're good now.'

'Neve's been under a lot of pressure lately, we both have. I personally think after clearing the air with her brother, she was emotionally and physically spent. It all caught up on her at once and the relief of resolving a family rift, well, it all has to come out somehow,' finished Kit, making it sound all very simplistic.

'I'm glad to hear it,' said Pearson. 'Now, as you know, we've been trying to track down Lee Farnham. We had a report of him being seen down by the river at the beginning of the week, Monday to be precise. He was seen talking to a woman walking her dog.' He looked pointedly at Neve. 'Where were you Monday afternoon at around five pm?'

Neve knew she had to hold her nerve. She gave an embarrassed glance towards Kit. 'I was at home, with Kit,' she said.

'All afternoon?'

'Yes, that's right,' interjected Kit.

'You didn't take your dog for a walk?'

'Well, probably. We take her out every day.'

'And Monday you would have taken her for a walk?'

'Yes,' said Neve. 'And if you ask did I go down by the river, I did but I don't remember seeing anyone else and certainly not Lee Farnham. I think I would have told you if I had.'

'Would you?' asked Pearson. 'Would you have shopped an old friend of yours?'

'Inspector,' said Kit. 'What exactly is the purpose of your visit? My wife has told you she didn't see Lee Farnham. If that's all you wanted to know, then I'd like you to leave, please. Any further questioning, I'd like to have my solicitor present.'

'We're just trying to put all the pieces of this puzzle together,' said Pearson. 'You do want us to find out who kidnapped your daughter, don't you?'

'Of course I do,' said Kit. 'What sort of question is that?'

'We are trying to clarify your relationship with Lee Farnham,' said Sally, looking towards Neve.

'There isn't one,' replied Neve resolutely.

'My wife is innocent in all this,' said Kit. 'You're looking at the wrong person. You should be looking at Jake Rees more closely.'

'How do you work that one out?' asked Sally, barely disguising a snort of contempt.

'Jake Rees was pretty much obsessed with Neve,' said Kit, clearly agitated. 'He wanted to run off into the sunset with her. When she made it clear she wasn't interested, he wasn't happy at all. He said to Neve, he'd do anything to make her leave with him.'

Neve managed to rein in a look of surprise at this statement. Jake had never said such a thing to her and she certainly hadn't said anything remotely like that to Kit. She had no idea where Kit was getting this idea from.

'And what do you think he meant by that?' asked Pearson.

'I don't know,' said Kit.

'How far do you think he'd go?' said Sally, shuffling to the edge of her seat, suddenly not so dismissive.

'Who knows. Look, this is just me thinking out loud, I've absolutely no proof about it and it's a bit left field ...' Kit squeezed Neve's hand.

'Go on,' coaxed Sally.

'I think Jake thought he could be the one to rescue Poppy and then be a hero in Neve's eyes.'

'But that doesn't make sense,' said Sally. 'Why would he kidnap Poppy? Surely that would turn Neve against him.'

'Most definitely,' said Neve. She looked expectantly at Kit. She was just as interested as the detectives to see where this hypothesis was going.

'Neve was never supposed to find out. I've been thinking about this a lot,' continued Kit. 'He took Poppy to put our marriage under strain, more strain that it already was. And then when it came to finding Poppy, he was the one who would go with Neve and be the knight in shining armour.'

'And the notes?' asked Pearson.

'Ah, the notes,' said Kit. 'The first two were from Neve's sister-in-law. They had fallen out a long time ago and when she saw the appeal go out and Neve on TV, she decided to send some poison pen letters just to torment Neve.'

'OK. You said that was the first two. What about the ransom note?'

'Yes, that was hand delivered so we knew it hadn't come from Newport like the other two. The only other person besides us who knew about the notes was Jake,' explained Kit. 'Neve had told him about the letters. They were a Godsend for him, he could send his ransom note with instructions of where to find Poppy, go along with Neve, and be the hero.'

'But the key was found in Neve's pocket,' said Sally.

'Yes, because he put it there,' said Kit. 'When he realised the police were there, he shoved it in her pocket so she would get the blame.'

Pearson exchanged a look with Sally, who gave a shrug in response. Pearson drummed his fingers on his knee for a moment, before speaking. 'Is it possible Jake could have put the key in your pocket, Neve?'

Kit's explanation sounded plausible but in some mixed-up, sick sort of way. Would Pearson really believe that Jake would go to such lengths just so she would leave Kit? Neve wasn't convinced and from the look on Pearson's face, he wasn't either.

'I suppose he could have done,' she said at last. 'It all happened so quickly, I can't remember exactly.'

'Let's just say that was a possibility,' said Pearson. 'How did Poppy get to the windmill? There were no signs that she had been sleeping rough up there.'

'Perhaps Jake got someone to help him,' said Kit. 'It couldn't have been that hard for him to find someone shady enough.'

'What makes you say that?' asked Sally.

'All those oddballs he has at the studio,' said Kit. 'He had those kids from The Forum up there a lot. In fact, I wouldn't be at all surprised if it was that Lee Farnham.'

'That's quite an accusation you're making.' There was a cautionary tone in the detective's voice.

'But not beyond the realms of possibility,' said Kit. 'Why don't you ask Jake himself? See what he's got to say about it.'

Pearson looked at Kit and then at Neve. 'I wish I could,' he said. 'The thing is, and I'm sorry to be the bearer of bad news, but Jake Rees passed away in the early hours of the morning.'

Neve let out an involuntary gasp and covered her mouth with her hand.

'Shit,' said Kit. 'He's died? But I thought he … I mean, I thought he was going to pull through.'

'Internal bleed on the brain,' said Pearson.

'Oh, God,' Neve heard herself say. 'Oh, poor Jake.' What an understatement that was. Her heart was trying to punch its way through her breastbone and her stomach was flinging triple salchows.

'I'm sorry. I know it must be a shock,' said Pearson. 'But we now have a murder investigation on our hands.'

Chapter 36

'Murder?' said Kit, standing up. 'I think it's at this point I'll have to insist that neither myself nor my wife answer any more questions. Not unless it's during a formal interview down at the police station with our solicitor present.'

The DCI remained sitting. 'You sound very defensive,' he said.

'I'm entitled to be,' came Kit's response. He felt Neve slip her hand into his own. 'Murder is a serious matter.'

'Indeed,' said Pearson. He leaned forward, resting his forearms on his knees, and put his hands together. He looked at Neve. 'Did Jake ever say anything that would lead you to believe, in hindsight, that he might have kidnapped your daughter?'

Neve shook her head. 'No. I don't think so. I'm sure I'd remember if he had.'

'He didn't ask you any strange sorts of questions about your movements? What you were doing and where you were going? Did you tell him about the boat trip?'

Kit managed to stop himself from tutting. Pearson was irritating him now. 'As I said, formal interview from now on.'

Pearson stood. 'Of course. Maybe you could both come down to the station tomorrow morning. I'll need to speak to you separately.'

Sally rose from her seat on the sofa too and followed her boss out of the room.

Kit forced himself to show them out and remain polite. Really, he wanted to tell Pearson and his sidekick to fuck right off. They were playing games, he was sure. Trying to get a rise out of him or Neve. And they had nearly succeeded. He watched the car reverse out of the drive and head back towards the main road.

'I don't know how I kept my temper,' said Kit, going back into the living room. 'I swear he was trying to wind us up on purpose.'

'Well, he's done a good job,' said Neve.

Her face looked the shade of putty and her eyes were still red rimmed from the crying of yesterday.

'You can't let him get to you,' said Kit, pacing the living room. 'Now can you tell me the whole story of Lee Farnham?'

'There's not much more to tell,' said Neve. 'Lee was into his drugs and he used to get stuff for us. Usually just a bit of weed. Sometimes, if we could afford it, some tablets. We were all young and bored living in a small Welsh town with absolutely nothing to do.'

'He was your drug supplier.'

'You make it sound like the Bronx,' muttered Neve. 'When they carried out a post-mortem on Megan, they found traces of cocaine in her bloodstream. They said she must have taken it just before her death and they attributed that to her drowning. She was too high on drugs to save herself.' Neve wiped tears from her eyes. 'Lee supplied it. He was there that day on the beach. It's what we argued about and why I wouldn't come out of the sea. I didn't want to be around them. Megan was coming in the water after me and I just kept going further and further out. The next thing I knew, I was caught in the riptide.'

'Oh, Neve.' Kit dropped to his knees in front of her. 'How awful for you. What about Lee, didn't he help?'

'Lee had disappeared by the time I got out of the water and managed to get help. No one other than the three of us knew he was there. I didn't tell a soul. I didn't want to get him into trouble.'

'You covered for him?'

'He was my friend. I was only eighteen. I thought it was the right thing to do. He would have gone to prison if they knew he had supplied Class A drugs. He might even have been done for manslaughter.'

Kit screwed up his eyes as he processed all the information. 'He was your supplier. The one you wouldn't give up when your sister died. I'm guessing he probably supplied you with coke after what happened with Jasmine. And despite getting you caught, you wouldn't give him up then either?'

'I couldn't. It felt disloyal to Megan. He was her boyfriend. She really loved him.'

'And you kept all this from me.'

'I couldn't tell you. I was so ashamed. I didn't want you to know what I was like back then.'

'And when he turned up, your long-lost friend, it was a coincidence?'

'Yes. Totally. But he's not my long-lost friend,' said Neve. 'We fell out.'

'How come?'

She bit down on her lip and brushed a tear away from her cheek. 'After the court hearing, I told him I didn't want anything to do with him again. I was getting myself straight. He came round to the house one night when Scott was out. He thought he could persuade me to change my mind.'

'Persuade you?'

'He was high. He didn't know what he was doing or saying.'

'Still making excuses for him, covering for him,' said Kit, agitated by the remark.

'He thought I could be to him what Megan had been. He tried it on, but I managed to fight him off. I threatened to go to the police, name him as the supplier and have him arrested for attempted rape if he didn't leave me alone.'

She wiped more tears from her face, but Kit could see a steely determination in her eyes as she recalled the events.

'And did he leave you alone?'

'Yeah. Soon after that Scott and I separated and I came to West Sussex,' said Neve. 'When he turned up in Ambleton, it was like revisiting an old nightmare.'

Any anger Kit had felt towards his wife for the latest disclosure evaporated as a wave of empathy washed over him. Christ, she'd been through so much and he'd had no idea. 'You poor thing,' said Kit, holding her. 'I wish you'd told me all this.'

'It was too painful. It still is.'

He held her in his arms for several minutes, as his mind

churned over the information and the implications. Gradually, it came to him what he needed to do.

'Why don't you go and have a nice long soak,' he said. 'Get into bed for a while. Mum's going to pick Poppy up again and bring her home.'

'We could get her ourselves,' said Neve, composing herself once more.

'Let Mum get her,' said Kit. 'Mum can stop for a bit of tea. I know things have been a bit tense between you two, but I think we've all been under exceptional strain. Things are bound to get a bit tetchy.'

'I really don't want to fall out with your mum,' said Neve. 'Like you say, it's not exactly been easy around here lately.'

'Right, you go and have a soak. I've got a few things to do. I'm going to speak to Edward and put him in the picture. Don't be worrying now, I promise you everything is going to be OK. I'll go run your bath for you.'

'Kit,' said Neve, as he reached the door. 'What did Edward phone you about just now?'

'He was letting me know that Jake had died,' said Kit. 'He didn't want me on the back foot. I didn't tell you because there wasn't really time and I needed your reaction to be natural, not forced. I knew you'd be upset.' Kit left the room. If he thought about Neve feeling upset about Jake too much, he'd end up saying something he'd regret.

Once Neve was submerged in a froth of bubbles, with the gentle tones of classical music playing in the background, Kit went downstairs. He scanned the living room and spotted what he was looking for down the side of the chair – Neve's handbag.

He took out her mobile phone and checked the contact list but couldn't see what he was looking for. Undeterred, he rifled through Neve's bag until he found the small black pay-as-you-go mobile hidden in the inside pocket. He was pretty certain it was the one they'd first bought for Poppy before his mum had bought the smart phone for her. He looked at the contacts list. Only one number was listed. Kit made a note of it and replaced the phone in the bag.

Then going into the kitchen, from under the sink, Kit retrieved a Stanley knife. Making sure there was a blade in place, he slipped it into his pocket.

Lastly, he went into the living room and took a photo album from the shelf, where he selected a picture of Poppy taken earlier in the year. He slid it out from the place holder and put it in his pocket, along with the knife.

Taking his keys and jacket, he left the house, calling out to Neve that he was just taking Willow for a walk.

It had been a long time since Kit had used a telephone box to make a phone call but the one at the end of the village was still in use and hadn't yet been turned into a book library or transplanted into someone's garden. Although judging by the smell, some of the locals had used it as public convenience. He supposed he ought to be grateful no one had thrown up in it recently. Using the cuff of his sleeve he picked up the receiver and tapped in the number with the end of his pen.

It took two attempts before the call was answered.

'It's Kit Masters,' he said.

'Who?'

'You know who I am.'

'What do you want?'

'I want to talk to you ... before the police do,' said Kit.

'Why would I want to do that?'

'Because it will be in your interest. Financial interest.' Kit waited while his words were considered.

'I'm not local.'

'Tell me where you are and I'll drive to you.' Kit cast the details to memory. He didn't want to write anything down. 'See you in an hour,' he said before hanging up.

It took less than an hour to drive to Brighton. As agreed, Lee was sitting on the shingle beach directly under the i360, the two hundred and forty foot high glass observation attraction situated on Brighton seafront.

'What's so important that you wanted to see me?' said Lee, chucking stones at a discarded beer can ahead of him on the beach. 'I got the distinct impression last time I saw you that you wanted to kill me.'

Kit remained standing, looking out at the grey-blue sea and the white crashing waves. The wind was blowing hard this afternoon and the tide was on its way in. 'I may still want to,' he said.

Lee got to his feet and stood next to Kit. 'Nah, you don't look like the killing type.'

'Never judge a book by its cover.' Kit checked his watch. He didn't want to get caught in the traffic heading home. From his pocket, he took out the glass vial he'd found on the boat and held it out in the palm of his hand. 'Recognise this?' He studied Lee's face for a reaction. There was the faintest glimmer of recognition, so fast that if Kit hadn't been looking out for it, he may have missed it completely.

Lee gave a shrug. 'No. What is it?'

'Know anything about GHB?' said Kit, putting the vial back in his pocket.

'There's GBH and there's ABH. I don't know the difference between the two. But I'm not sure I'm familiar with GHB.'

'Don't piss me about,' said Kit, his voice dropping a level.

'You seem to know more about it than me,' said Lee, bending to pick up his rucksack.

Kit grabbed the sleeve of the man's coat. 'This came from you,' he hissed into Lee's ear. 'You gave this to Neve, didn't you?' It was a bit of a punt. Kit didn't know for definite it had come from Lee, but in light of Neve's confession earlier, he was inclined to take a chance on being right.

Lee tried to free his arm, but Kit held fast and spoke again. 'All it will take is one phone call from me, and the police will be on your arse. Do you want that?' He gave Lee's jacket a shake. 'They're very interested in you, looking for you in connection with Poppy's disappearance and Jake's murder. Oh, sorry, didn't you know about that? Shame. He died last night in hospital.'

It did the trick. The look of alarm on Lee's face told Kit he now had him where he wanted.

'Jake's dead?' Lee stopped fighting, his body slumping. And then he looked wildly at Kit. 'I had nothing to do with his death. Nothing. You can't make out it was me.'

'I don't have to. That's the police's job.' Kit let go of Lee's jacket. 'Shall we start again? Did you or did you not give this to Neve?'

'She asked me for it,' said Lee. 'Neve asked me if I could get her some.'

'What did she want it for?' Kit felt his world shifting under his feet. Every suspicion and fear was being realised. Neve was mixed up in Poppy' disappearance. He somehow managed to quell the explosion of outrage inside him. He looked to Lee for a response.

'She didn't say and I didn't want to know.'

'Where did you get it from?'

'I know people who know people. You can get anything you want at The Forum. You just have to ask the right person.'

'I'm asking this man to man,' he said, looking Lee straight in the eye. He paused, taking a moment to steady the adrenalin which was already surging through him at the prospect of what the answer might be. 'Did you take my daughter from the boat?'

'Me? No—'

Kit interrupted. 'Think very carefully before you answer.'

'Fucking hell,' muttered Lee, rubbing the top of his head with his hand.

'I'm not going to do anything. I just need to know.' Kit took out his wallet and opened it, flashing a wad of twenty-pound notes he'd withdrawn from the cash point on his way over.

Lee gulped, his Adam's apple bobbed in his throat. He looked up at Kit and then back to the money. He drew his hand across his beard and gave a low whistle. His eyes met Kit's.

'No. I didn't. Why would I get involved with something like child kidnap?'

Kit didn't believe him for a second. Lee was a lying scumbag. Kit maintained a poker face as he took out two hundred pounds and held it out to the Welshman, who went to snatch at it eagerly. Kit held onto the notes.

'Not so fast,' he said, taking a step closer to Lee so that his face was only inches away. 'I suggest you fuck off away from here. Far, far away.' He paused. 'In fact, I think it would be in your interest if you disappeared altogether.'

Chapter 37

Her body slipped and water sloshed over her face, racing up her nostrils and filling her ears. For a split second, Neve had visions of Kit's boat overturning and a scene not dissimilar to the movie *Titanic* flashed in front of her. The remainder of the second had her sitting up and spluttering as she spat bath water out of her mouth.

She must have nodded off. She had no idea how long she'd been lying in the bath, but the water temperature was several degrees lower now. She shivered not just from the chill but from the thought of Kit's boat.

She padded through to the bedroom and sat down on the edge of the bed and once again unbidden thoughts of *Blue Horizon* were thrown to the fore of her mind like a ship being tossed by stormy weather towards jagged and dangerous rocks. Neve wasn't sure who the rocks represented – Pearson or someone closer to home?

Snatches of memories breached the crested waves. Scenes that she would have once watched from her vantage point of being able to remove herself from her actions as her braver and bolder sister played them out.

Neve slipped down below deck, leaving Kit and Poppy sitting at the rear of the boat on the cushioned seats which lined the sides of Blue Horizon. *She was going to make them all supper. A simple meal of cheese and crackers, some smoked salmon, and because Poppy didn't like to deviate from her regular food groups, she had a tuna sandwich on granary bread for the fourteen-year-old.*

Neve could hear Poppy and her father talking. They were watching the sun set and discussing the various shades of orange, yellow and pink which spread across the sky like a pastel colour palette, sloshed with water.

Neve's hand shook a little as she dipped into her bag and retrieved a small vial with a cork stopper. It was an audacious plan, but the stakes were high and she was prepared to take the risk. It was her last chance to make Kit change his mind about a baby. If this failed then she would have to resort to plan b and plan b was in the form of Jake.

'How's that glass of wine coming along?' Kit called down to her.

'Just opening the bottle now.'

Neve poured two glasses of wine. She would wait until later before lacing the drink with the GHB. Lee assured Neve that she only needed a couple of drops to make Kit compliant and all she had to do was to get him into bed within a few minutes of taking it.

Neve took two glasses of wine and a lemonade up to Kit and Poppy. She sat beside Kit and they chinked their glasses together.

'To happy days spent on the water,' said Kit.

Neve echoed the toast and Poppy pulled a face but they both knew Poppy was in her element here on the boat.

Neve fetched the supper and watched as Kit tucked into the food and drank his wine. He was happy and relaxed. His guard was down, exactly how Neve needed it to be.

Neve closed her eyes at the memory. It had been such a risk but one she had been willing to take. A means to an end. Make or break. It had to be done.

Neve dried herself and picking up her watch she checked the time. She went to the top of the stairs and called out to Kit but was met by silence. He'd been gone a long time just to take Willow for a walk. Mulling over the various reasons Kit could be gone so long, Neve dressed and went downstairs to make herself a drink.

She tried watching the television for a few minutes, but channel hopped her way through every single station, not finding anything of any interest and ended up switching it off again. It was then she noticed her handbag at the side of the sofa where she had left it the night before. That in itself wasn't unusual but what did surprise her was the fact that the zip was undone. She never left her bag open.

Absentmindedly she drummed her fingers on the arm of the chair as a small flutter of nerves gave rise in her stomach. Someone, i.e. Kit, had been in her bag. There was no other explanation.

The phone!

Neve sprang across the space between the armchair and sofa, snatching up her bag. Her hand dived between the opened zip and sought out the side pocket. Relief extinguished the nerves. Her phone was still there. She plucked it from its hiding space and checked for any missed calls or messages. There were none. She wasn't expecting any. It was only Lee who had this number and they had agreed not to contact each other again unless it was an emergency. Neve replaced the phone, but still felt uneasy about her bag being open. It was bothering her and as much as she tried to reason or convince herself that she could possibly have left it open, the doubts just wouldn't abate.

It was like a self-perpetuating emotion. The more she tried to ignore it, the more anxious she became. The anxiety sending her straight back to the chain of events. She closed her eyes and shook her head. She didn't want to revisit those thoughts. She was frightened if she went back there too often, her carefully constructed compartments of thought might start to bleed out into each other.

She tried to think of other things but the image of the boat that evening, just kept on coming back.

'It's getting a bit chilly now,' said Kit. 'Shall we go below?'

He stood and began folding his blanket without waiting to see what anyone else wanted to do.

Neve looked across at Poppy. 'Want to go down into the cabin?'

'No.'

Neve gave an inward sigh. Her mistake. She should know by now, never to ask Poppy a closed question when trying to cajole her into something. 'Well, it's getting cold and we should think about settling down for the night soon.'

'Come on, Poppy,' said Kit, lifting the blanket from his daughter's legs. 'Look, Willow is waiting by the door already. Even she thinks we should go below.' Right on cue, Willow gave a whine and wagged her tail.

'I'll make you a hot chocolate,' said Neve, knowing that would probably do the trick. She had never known Poppy to refuse a hot chocolate.

'With marshmallows?' asked Poppy.

'Yep and whipped cream,' tempted Neve. It was the deciding factor and with the possibility of an argument averted, they all went below deck to the saloon.

Willow immediately made herself comfortable in the sheepskin-lined dog basket while Poppy hovered behind Neve, observing the hot chocolate preparations taking place.

'Sit down and I'll bring it over,' said Neve, looking directly at Poppy. She didn't want an audience for what she was about to do.

With a sulk and a scuff of her feet, Poppy did as Neve asked and positioned herself on the edge of the bench.

Neve turned so her back was to the rest of the saloon. Kit was sitting on a two-seater bench, his feet on the little footstool and the newspaper open on his lap. From her pocket Neve discreetly took out the vial. She paused. There was still time to back out. She lined the notion up with her motive. No. She needed to do this. She needed to put Kit through this. He had to feel the pain that she felt. He had to feel the utter hopelessness that she did. She had to make him change his mind.

Careful to put only half the amount Lee recommended

378

for an adult, into Poppy's drink, Neve gave the hot chocolate a stir and squirted liberal amounts of cream in a swirly pattern so it rose like a Mr Whippy ice-cream. She dropped a couple of mini marshmallows on top and scattered a few more on the saucer around the glass mug.

'Tah-dah!' said Neve, triumphantly as, with great care, she took the creation over to Poppy and placed it on the side. 'Be careful, it's quite hot. You may want to let it cool down.'

'Wow! Look at that,' said Kit. 'Almost makes me want to have one myself. Almost. How about another glass of wine?'

'Coming right up,' said Neve, forming a wide smile. She poured Kit's glass first, anxious not to get the two muddled up. Making sure Kit and Poppy were preoccupied with the hot chocolate, Neve tipped several drops of the clear, odourless liquid into the glass of wine. She picked up the glass and gave it a swill round, before taking it over to Kit.

'You not having one?' he asked.

'Just going to pour one now,' she said, hoping Kit missed the wobble in her voice. She poured a large glass and sat down with Kit. 'Cheers,' she said, holding the glass up towards him.

'Cheers,' said Kit, touching his glass against Neve's. He took a big gulp, while Neve sipped at hers and then he leant over and gave her a kiss on the cheek. 'Thank you,' he said.

'What for?'

'Coming today. I know the boat isn't your favourite pastime, but I appreciate the gesture.'

Neve's heart gave such a heavy beat at her betrayal, she thought Kit might hear it. 'I wanted to,' she said. At least that much was true.

'Does this wine taste all right to you?' Kit asked, swilling the glass round and lifting it to his nose to smell the aroma.

Neve hesitated for a moment. Lee told her that there may be a slightly salty taste but taken in alcohol Kit shouldn't be able to notice it. Neve took a sip of her drink. 'Mine tastes fine. Maybe it's the crackers and salmon that's made it taste funny.'

'Yeah, maybe,' said Kit, taking another gulp and then making clicking noises as his tongue sucked the roof of his mouth. He shrugged. 'Can't taste it now.'

'Maybe something was on the glass. Do you want me to pour you a fresh one?'

'No. It's fine.' Kit reached forwards and took another cracker. 'This is really nice,' he said. 'I love being here with my two favourite people in the whole world.'

'Me too,' said Neve.

Kit gave her a sideways look. 'You mean that?'

'Absolutely.'

He caressed her face with the back of his fingers and looked like he was going to say something, but he appeared to change his mind. He smiled and returned to his salmon and crackers.

The minutes crept by and Neve kept a careful yet, clandestine, eye on Kit. He was letting the newspaper slip from his lap and resting his head back.

'I feel quite tired,' he said, rubbing his eyes with the

finger and thumb of one hand. He took his hand away and was visibly trying to focus on his surroundings.

'Are you OK?' asked Neve.

Kit rolled his head in her direction. His pupils had dilated and filled more space than the blue irises. 'I'm ... I'm great,' he said, slurring his words.

Neve knew she didn't have much time before the full effect of the drug kicked in. She took the glass from him and placed it on the side along with her own. She glanced over at Poppy who was taking her first sip of hot chocolate.

'You're drunk,' Poppy said to her father.

'I am not,' slurred Kit, as Neve managed to get him to his feet.

'That's it, put your arm around my shoulder,' she said, wedging herself underneath his armpit. She managed to get him to stagger towards the fore of the boat where their cabin was located. As they reached the doorway, Kit lurched to one side and on his second attempt grabbed the door frame.

Poppy let out a howl of laughter. 'You are drunk!' she said, covering her mouth with the back of her hand. 'I've never seen you like this before.'

Kit swayed from one side to the other, his eyes unfocused, his mouth opened but no words came out. Neve thought he was going to collapse there and then on the floor. With a Herculean effort, she dragged Kit forwards. His feet responded, and he stumbled in to the cabin just in time before he collapsed on to the bed, taking Neve with him.

'Kit! You're on my arm,' she groaned. Somehow, she

managed to push him onto his side and pull her arm free. She got to her knees and, leaning over his shoulder, Neve lifted one of his eyelids. Kit's eyes were rolled back and he was fast asleep. Or, more precisely, heavily sedated.

Neve felt a deep sense of shame wash over her. She had really done that. For the first time, she felt an association with her actions. She couldn't pass it off as something Megan would have thought, said and/or done. No, she, Neve Masters, had to take full responsibility.

If Kit were ever to find out, he would never forgive her. He mustn't ever find out. She looked back at her bag and for the second time, she took the mobile phone from her bag. This time she sent a text message.

I need to see you. Just one last time. Meet me at the usual place. Tomorrow. Ten o'clock. It's important.

She studied the message for a moment and, deciding it wasn't strong enough, amended the last sentence before pressing send.

There's something I need to tell you face to face – it's really important and I don't want to say it over the phone.

She didn't know if Lee would come or even respond for that matter. They had, after all, agreed to only get in touch in an emergency and, in Neve's mind, this was an emergency.

After putting the mobile back in her bag, Neve tried once

more to settle, but her nerves felt like they were going through a paper shredder and her mind just couldn't stop thinking about what had happened on the boat. It was as if she was seeing it for the first time and the realisation was dawning on her. She tried to comfort herself with the thought that the end result would be worth it. Kit had agreed to them starting a family of their own. A baby to love and to care for was all she had ever wanted.

Her thoughts took a natural turn to her daughter who she'd so very nearly had before fate had taken her away. So precious. So beautiful. So tragic. It was a loss like no other. It was in a different league altogether. She felt a moment of guilt for not grieving for Jake how she probably should, but pushed it away into its metaphorical box and closed the lid. Another compartment she didn't want to revisit. Another compartment marked 'Pain'.

And as she did so, she remembered the bloody shirt she'd found in Kit's office. She hardly dared to think the next thought – the one that had lurked in the darkest recess of her mind. If only that was as easy to pop in a box. That box however would be marked 'Danger'.

It was all getting to her. She wished Kit would come home soon. How long did it take to walk the dog? Neve prowled around the house, unable to settle in any room.

Inevitably, her thoughts turned to Jake. She was still in shock about his death. How could it be that she was talking to him at the hospital one day and then a few days later he was dead? It seemed impossible and yet she knew it was real.

She knew she couldn't let the day end without having said

a personal goodbye to him. She looked out of the living room window. It was a beautiful sunny morning, one which Jake would have enthused about and, had it been an art day, he would have encouraged the students to paint outdoors.

Taking a pair of scissors from the kitchen drawer, Neve stepped out into the garden. The lavender which ran along the rear fencing was beautiful with its deep violet shades. She thought Jake would approve of that. She remembered a painting he had shown her when she had first started going to art therapy. It was of a sheaf of violets, laying in a wicker basket. He said it was given to him by his first art therapy student who had gone on to art college at the ripe old age of sixty-three having suffered in silence for years after being abused as a child. Up until that point, the student had rebelled against any kind of education because of the memories associated with it. Jake said it was one of his proudest moments as an art therapist.

Neve walked to the back of the garden and began cutting the lavender. Once she had a respectful number of stems, she cut some garden string and tied the stems together in a simple bouquet. As an afterthought, she took three of her paintbrushes from her bag and slipped them in behind the string. It seemed a fitting gesture which tugged at her heart.

'Oh, Jake,' she whispered. 'I wish it could have ended differently. You didn't deserve to die like that.'

She folded up the cloth roll in which she kept her paintbrushes and placed them into the main bag, before going back out to the garage to store them away. She wasn't sure if she would ever want to paint again. The thought was just too painful right now.

Collecting the flowers from the worktop, Neve climbed into her car and drove off to Jake's art studio. She was relieved that no one was about as she pulled up on the grass. Several bunches of flowers had already been placed against the gate-post.

Kneeling down, Neve carefully laid the flowers next to the others. She took a few minutes to read the messages that had been left.

May you rest in peace, Jake.
You will be missed by us all.
From all your colleagues at the college

Heaven has another star tonight.
Your light will always shine bright.
From all the staff at St Joseph's

Such a gentle man.
Taken too soon.
Julie, Mike, Dan and Kelly—Ann xxx

Always in our hearts.
RIP Jake.
Maggy and the gang.

You taught me how to live again
and I will always be thankful.
God Bless. Arthur.

Aware of another car making its way up the lane, Neve went back to her own. She didn't want to have to talk to anyone who might have known Jake and been coming to lay flowers.

Chapter 38

Kit didn't give himself time to think about what he was doing. If he was going to save Neve, save his marriage, and by default save his daughter the pain of losing another mother, then he had to act fast.

His heart was thumping hard in his chest. He swore he could hear it. Ba-dump. Ba-dump. Ba-dump. It filled the interior of the car, bouncing and echoing around the confined space. His hands were shaking and he gripped the steering wheel to try to steady his nerves. Breathing in through his nose, holding for the count of three and then releasing slow and controlled, Kit began to regain his composure.

He looked in the rear-view mirror. Not at the space behind him, but at the man looking back. He looked deep into the blue eyes. It was as if he could see right into his own soul and did he like what he saw? No, he didn't.

Kit shook his head to rid himself of the dark thoughts crashing around in his mind.

Putting the car into gear, he headed back towards Ambleton. The roads were clear and within fifty minutes he was driving over Bury Hill and turning off the roundabout towards the village. About one hundred metres along Kit pulled into a lay-by which overlooked the valley in which the village was nestled. All he had to do now was to cross the field and take the public footpath down towards the river. No one really walked this side of the bridge and once he was there, he could cut down through the meadow and into Copperthorne Lane without being seen. Even if he did bump into someone, with Willow tagging along, they would just assume he was dog walking.

'Come on, girl,' said Kit, opening the tailgate and letting the yellow Labrador jump out. He hooked up the lead and trotted across the road with her, following the edge of the farmer's field down towards the bridge.

As it happened, luck was on his side and he made it to Copperthorne Lane without meeting anyone. Kit let Willow off the lead. She ran along, her tail wagging and her nose to the ground, luxuriating in the smells all around, making snorting noises every so often.

Several bouquets of flowers had been laid at the gate to Jake's studio. Kit paused to read some of the cards. Jake had certainly been a popular guy with the locals and Kit couldn't help feeling a small surge of jealousy run through him. Yeah, Jake might have been a stand-up guy where the art therapy classes were concerned, but he certainly didn't embrace that ethos with other men's wives.

Something made Kit look at the card on the last bunch of flowers – lavender. Maybe it was the handwriting that had attracted him. He looked closer and read the message his wife had left.

Heaven is a much more colourful place now.
RIP.N. x

Neve must have been down here today while Kit was off in Brighton.

Kit's hand curled around the card, scrunching it up. He looked down at the crumpled message. He hadn't even realised what he was doing.

Shit. That would look bad now to anyone coming along. He plucked the card from the neck of the wrapping paper and tore it into four pieces and then pushed it into the pocket of his jeans. He'd get rid of that later.

He called Willow over and attaching the lead once more, he took her round to the back of the studio where she'd be out of sight and tied her to the fence.

He hoped Jake hadn't got around to fixing the rear window. Preparing for his break-in, Kit wriggled his hands into his black leather driving gloves and if what he was about to do wasn't so serious, then he would have laughed at the clichéd burglar's attire. He took the penknife from his pocket and jemmied it between the window and the frame, then slid it along until he felt the resistance of the sticky tape. The blade cut through the tape with ease and the window swung open.

Kit hoisted himself up and after a bit of effort, managed to climb in through the window, knocking a couple of paint pots and brushes onto the floor as he did so. He collected them up and placed them back on to the work surface.

The silence in the studio was stifling. It was hard to tell if the police had already carried out a search of the premises as everywhere looked untidy. The office housed a small desk butted up to the side wall, on which there was an open hardback A4 diary sitting next to a laptop, while an array of pens, pencils, chalks and charcoals scattered the desk. Several black A4 books were stacked on one of the corners, which Kit assumed were sketch books. Next to them were an assortment of reference books and on the left-hand side of the desk was a cordless telephone, sitting in its base unit and a small spiral notebook.

Kit looked at the jottings in the notebook. Names and numbers, paint colours and doodles.

Kit tried the drawers. They were unlocked and contained more or less a replica of what was on top of the desk, notebooks, sketchbooks, brushes, pens, all jumbled up in no particular order

Kit took a moment to look at the desk, deciding where would be the best place to leave the items he'd brought with him. It was then he noticed a thin drawer which ran under the desk top. Not a hidden drawer but one that ordinarily might be for pens and pencils. He pulled the drawer open and indeed there were a couple of pencils, a rubber and a few coins.

Perfect.

From his pocket, Kit withdrew the photograph of his daughter and laid it inside the drawer.

This was all going to be over soon. And then they could get back to some sort of normal life. A life where he still had his wife, he still had his daughter and his daughter still had a mother. He'd come close to losing both and he knew he couldn't let that happen again. Nothing else mattered to Kit and he was going to protect his family by any means he could.

Chapter 39

S till not wanting to go home to an empty house, Neve
drove back into the village, stopping outside the café.

'Well, hello,' said Lucie as Neve bustled in through the
door. 'I was just thinking about closing up.'

'Hi,' said Neve, glancing round the empty coffee shop.
'Sorry, I was just passing, and I thought … No, that's a lie.'
She looked at her friend. 'I was at home feeling shit and
needed a friendly face.'

'Aha, I see,' said Lucie, with a smile. 'You sit yourself down
there and I'll make us both a coffee but first …' She trailed
over to the door, switched the sign to 'CLOSED' and drew
the lock across. 'There, that's better.'

Neve sat in silence as Lucie made the coffees and came to
sit beside her friend.

'Thanks,' said Neve. 'Sorry, busting in here, I expect you're
dying to put your feet up.'

'Not at all,' said Lucie. 'Anyway, I am putting my feet up.'
She pulled out the chair beside her and swung her feet onto
the seat. 'So, what's up? Kit?'

'No, nothing like that,' said Neve. 'I went to see my brother.'

'Your brother? The one in Wales?'

'Yep, that one. It's the only one I've got,' said Neve, twiddling the spoon around in her cappuccino.

'Oh, right, how did that come about?'

'I guess all this business with Poppy and Jake made me realise that life is too short to hold a grudge.'

'Good for you,' said Lucie. 'How did it go. Was your brother of the same persuasion?'

'In the end,' said Neve. 'It was his wife, my sister-in-law, who took some convincing, but I think it's all good.'

'Excellent. So why the worry?'

'I don't know, just feels odd, I suppose. Fear of the unknown and all that.'

Lucie placed her hand on Neve's forearm. 'I'm sure it will be OK. Be brave.'

'Thanks,' said Neve, genuinely grateful for her friend's kindness.

'Where's Kit, then?' asked Lucie. 'Shouldn't he be giving you the pep talk, not that I mind you coming here at all but, you know what I mean.'

'He's out at the moment. I think I just felt a bit emotional,' confessed Neve. 'Poppy's at her nan's. I think I suddenly felt alone – lonely.'

Lucie hopped up from her seat and leaning over, gave Neve a hug. 'Hey, it's OK,' she said. 'You're bound to feel emotional after everything.'

Neve returned the hug. 'Thanks, Lucie. I don't deserve a friend like you.'

Lucie laughed. 'Oh, don't be so silly. Of course, you do.'

Neve dried her eyes on a rough paper napkin Lucie had plucked from the counter. 'You're very sweet. Thank you.' She stood up. 'I don't want to keep you any longer. I'm sure you've better things to do.'

'I'm in no hurry,' said Lucie.

'I'd still better go, though. Kit will be home soon.'

'OK, sweetie. But you know where I am if you need me.'

A rap of knuckles on the glass of the door, made both women jump.

'Shit, what the hell?' said Lucie, standing up. 'Oh, it's Kit. OK, OK, I'm coming,' she said, going over to the door.

'Kit, what are you doing here?' said Neve as Lucie opened the door.

'I was just on my way home and I saw your car parked outside,' said Kit.

There was something about his manner which set Neve's senses on high alert. She couldn't put her finger on it, but although he was smiling, the rest of his face wasn't living up to the expression. He didn't look angry but there was a tension that sucked the air from the room.

'I'll catch you later,' said Neve to Lucie.

'Yeah, no worries,' replied her friend, although the tone of her voice suggested otherwise.

Neve gave Lucie a quick hug. 'I'll be fine,' she whispered.

Neve followed Kit home, parking next to him on the driveway. As Kit opened the boot, Willow bounded out, wagging her tail excitedly at the sight of her mistress.

'Hello, Willow,' said Neve, bending down to make a fuss of the dog.

'The dog gets a better welcome than I do,' said Kit, blipping the remote locking on his car, before opening the front door.

'Everything OK?' asked Neve, once they were inside the house. 'You seem a little tense.'

'I'm fine,' said Kit, sounding anything other than fine. He went through to the kitchen and put the kettle on. 'Have we got anything for supper or have you eaten?'

'I'm sure there's something in the fridge I can put together,' said Neve, aware they were going through the niceties. The tension from the coffee shop hadn't been left there, it was more like a takeaway which they had just brought home and unwrapped. 'Did you get everything done this afternoon that you wanted to?'

'Yes.'

Neve took some cheese and pickle from the fridge. 'Cheese sandwiches tonight. Is that OK?'

'Yes.'

She turned to look at him. He was leaning against the worktop, his arms folded, watching her.

Neve placed the cheese and butter tub on the kitchen island. 'What's wrong?'

'Nothing.'

'Give me some credit,' she said. 'I can tell there's something wrong. I know you.'

Kit pursed his lips. 'Rather ironic turn of phrase,' he said.

'How come?'

'You know me or at least you think you do. Much the same way that I know you, or I thought I did.'

His words reached across the centre island and curled icy finger tips around Neve's throat. 'What's that supposed to mean?'

'Each day, I'm discovering more and more about you,' he

said. His eyes fixed on hers and Neve felt compelled to hold his gaze. She wanted to turn away, to brush off his comment, but it was physically impossible.

'As the saying goes, you learn something new every day,' said Neve in an effort to lower the intensity. The laugh she attempted to tag on the end was strangled in her throat.

Kit shook his head. 'Don't,' he said in almost a whisper. He took a step closer to the centre island and with precision, placed something on the work surface, before standing back, his eyes monitoring her for a reaction. 'I know everything,' he said.

The words had the power to freeze Neve's blood; so cold her veins stung like tiny shards of ice were coursing through her. There on the work surface was the glass vial Lee had given her.

'I must admit,' said Kit after a few moments of silence elapsed. 'If I was a betting man, I would have bet my life that you didn't have the nerve to do something like this.'

Neve pressed her lips together and swallowed hard. She needed a clear head to talk her way through this. She had no idea how much Kit knew.

'What do you think I did?' said Neve, surprised at the casualness of her voice.

Kit sprang forward, slamming the palms of his hands down on the work surface. 'Don't play games with me.' The veins in his neck bulged through his skin and a muscle in his jaw throbbed. 'You drugged me. You drugged my daughter. Jesus, Neve, you had Poppy fucking kidnapped!' He thumped his fist down onto the work surface. 'Why? Tell me why!'

The game was up. Kit knew everything. Neve's right leg

began to shake involuntarily. She fumbled with her hands to grab onto the dresser to support herself. 'I ... I'm sorry,' she whispered.

'Sorry! You're sorry? Is that all you can say?' Kit swiped his hand across the work top, sending a side plate smashing to the floor. 'Oh, that's OK, is it? You're sorry so that makes everything all right?' This time he booted the unit with his foot. 'Have you any concept of what you've done? Any at all?'

Neve curled her body into herself as if she could shield herself from his fury. He, of course, had every right to be angry. What she had done was unforgiveable, she knew that now. 'I wasn't thinking clearly,' she offered.

'That's got to be the understatement of the century,' said Kit. He dragged his hands down his face. 'Tell me, Neve. How you did it? How did you get Poppy off that boat? And why?'

'Please, Kit, you have to realise I would never hurt Poppy or you. All the time, I knew she was safe.'

'Just TELL ME!'

Neve flinched at Kit's raised voice. 'OK. OK. Please don't shout.'

Kit backed off another step, his hands palms up.

Neve revisited the events that had been haunting her all day long and carefully explained to Kit what she had done.

Neve looked at Kit laying on the bed in an arrangement mildly resembling the recovery position. Now the GHB drug had thoroughly worked itself into his system, he was like a ragdoll. Totally oblivious to anything going on around him and totally incapable of any conscious movement.

In the saloon, Poppy was finishing the last of her hot chocolate. Neve sat beside her daughter who yawned and rested her head back against the side of the boat.

'Your dad is fast asleep now,' said Neve. She ventured an arm around Poppy's shoulders and when the fourteen-year-old didn't resist, Neve gently pulled her in. Poppy shifted her head to Neve's shoulder.

'I'm very … tired,' she murmured.

'I know,' said Neve, dropping a kiss on to Poppy's head. 'Close your eyes, sweetheart.'

Poppy's eyes fluttered open and shut several times as Neve looked down at her, monitoring Poppy's transition from conscious to semi-conscious. It was a fine line between the two, but after a few more minutes, Neve was satisfied Poppy was no longer aware of her surroundings. Neve manoeuvred herself around and gently rested Poppy's head on a cushion.

Willow gave a small whine as she sensed the change in atmosphere on the boat. She looked excited. The sort of excited look she had when she thought she was going for a walk. Neve ruffled the Labrador's head. 'Sorry, Willow. You've got to stay here.'

Neve had to act fast now. She climbed up the wooden step ladder, out onto the deck. It was dusk and the landscape had taken on a monotone colour. She took the untraceable pay-as-you-go phone from her pocket and called up the one number she had stored.

'Where are you?' she asked without preamble.

Down the road, replied her accomplice. 'Are you ready?'

'Yes.'

She heard the engine before she saw the headlights. There was no one else about, just as she had expected. The noise of the car grew louder and the headlights appeared from around the bend in the road. Seconds later, the car, Neve's own car, pulled up next to her.

Lee got out the driver's seat. The keys he'd found in the prearranged hiding place dangled in the ignition.

Without an exchange of words, he waited by the car while Neve went back and managed to get Poppy to her feet. Poppy mumbled but didn't manage to form any coherent sentence. It was difficult on her own, but Neve had insisted Lee stayed away from the boat, so he didn't leave any trace of DNA there. Lee held the car door open and Neve poured Poppy onto the rear seat.

A voice in her head told her there was still time to back out. She didn't have to carry out this plan. But Neve elbowed the thought away as she argued with herself. She did need to do this. It was the only way she'd be able to get Kit to change his mind. If this didn't change his mind, nothing would, and then there would be Jake. Neve would be forced to leave Kit and Poppy behind. It would be so painful, but it would be necessary if she was to have a baby of her own.

Neve closed the door and turned to Lee.

'You've got all the food and drinks you and Poppy are going to need for the next few days,' she said. 'I've stored them in the boot. As soon as you've got Poppy in the house, remember to take the car back to my house,' she said, going through her mental check-list. 'Make sure you leave the key in this magnetic box, stuck to the driver's side

wheel arch.' Neve handed him a small black key box. 'Got all that?'

'Yep.'

'And remember what I told you to tell Poppy?'

'Yes,' said Lee impatiently.

'Repeat it to me, what you're going to say.'

Lee gave an annoyed huff. 'I'm going to tell Poppy that I found her wandering around in the road and that I'm trying to find her father's phone number to call him. When she tells me the number, I'm going to say that I can't get any answer.'

'And don't let her see your face. Keep your hood up.'

He lit a cigarette. 'Stop worrying, I've got it all sorted. Anyway, she won't remember a thing.'

'You must look after her,' insisted Neve. 'Don't give her too much of that GHB. If anything happens to her, I'll hold you responsible. Don't make me regret any of this.'

'Fuck's sake. Don't worry about me. You just make sure you've got the money you promised,' said Lee. 'And don't try to mug me off, we're both in this shit up to our necks.'

They eyed each other in the dusk of the evening. Lee was right. They had to trust each other from now on.

'Right,' said Neve, to draw a line under that part of the conversation. 'Take Poppy to Halnaker Windmill by lunch-time on Thursday. Tell her she's to stay there and wait for her dad. He's coming and he will be cross if she goes anywhere else.'

'Like I told you, I know what to say.' Lee got into the car.

Neve yanked the passenger car door open. 'And don't

give her any more of that stuff after midnight on Wednesday. It needs time to disappear from her system.'

Neve hurried back to the boat as Lee drove off down the lane. There she washed up the mug Poppy had her hot chocolate in and the glass Kit used for his wine. Then she washed up her own glass and stood them all on the draining board. Next, she made a bed up for Poppy in the aft cabin, ruffling the covers as if she had slept in it. Lastly, she rinsed out the vial, but as she picked it up, her fingers slipped against the soapy bubbles and the vial dropped to the floor, rolling away out of sight.

'Where's the bloody thing gone now,' said Neve dropping to her hands and knees. She peered under the base unit. She couldn't see anything in the dark. Willow padded over to see if it was some sort of game she could join in.

'Back in your basket,' whispered Neve. 'Go and lay down.'

Using the light on her phone, Neve illuminated the small gap between the unit and the floor. She was just about to reach out for it when a groan came from the cabin. It was Kit.

Neve scrambled to her feet and rushed through to Kit. He had rolled onto his back. Perhaps the GHB wasn't as strong as Lee said it was. Bloody idiot. If he cocked things up for her now …

Neve shuffled into bed next to Kit. She'd get the vial in the morning when Kit was distracted. Even if the police did happen to find it, she could pass it off as having found it outside and brought it in so Willow didn't tread on it, but she had then dropped it and it had rolled under the counter. That would account for her finger-prints being on it.

'So, you just let that fuck-wit drive off with my daughter?' Kit's voice was one of incredulity.

'She was safe. I trusted Lee,' said Neve. 'No harm came to Poppy.'

'But you didn't know that was going to be the case. There was no way you could have been sure of that. You took a gamble – a gamble on my daughter's safety!'

'It's academic now,' said Neve, trying not to sound impatient. 'All Poppy thinks is that a man found her and looked after her until we found her. She can't remember any detail.'

'Un-fucking-believable,' said Kit, as he stalked back and forth across the kitchen.

'I'm sorry. It seemed so logical at the time,' said Neve. 'I wasn't well. It was like someone else was doing it all, not me.'

Kit stopped walking. 'Wait, are you telling me this was one of your *funny turns*?' He sneered the last two words.

'It felt as if Megan was doing it,' admitted Neve. She could feel the tears stinging her eyes, but she blinked hard to stop them from falling. 'I know now it wasn't. I know it was me. Please try to understand Kit, I was in a bad place.'

'And now?'

'No. It's strange. It's like since what happened at Gareth's, I suddenly feel free. Like I've been able to shrug all thoughts of Megan away. For the first time since she went, I don't feel as if she's with me anymore.'

'This is all so bizarre,' said Kit. 'Forgive me if I have trouble taking all this in and making sense of it.'

'I'm so sor—'

'Stop saying sorry!' snapped Kit. 'So, you and Lee had it all planned out in advance?'

Neve nodded, causing the tears to spill from her eyes. She wiped them away with her fingertips and fumbled for a piece of kitchen roll.

'Why?' he asked eventually. 'I don't understand why?'

Neve pulled at the soggy kitchen roll in her hands, tearing it into two pieces and then folding it over, before scrunching it into a ball and dropping it into the bin to buy herself a few moments.

'Because I was desperate,' she said finally. 'I wanted a baby so badly. I wanted to have a baby with you. I wanted you to want a baby too.' She sniffed and acquired a fresh piece of kitchen roll. 'In my messed-up head, I thought if you wanted something as badly as I wanted a baby, then you would understand how I felt. You would have empathy for my feelings, my needs as a woman. I can't even begin to tell you the pain I felt when I lost my first baby.'

'How did you think taking Poppy would make me change my mind? I don't get it.'

'If you wanted something so badly, so desperately but you couldn't have it, then you would understand how I felt. If you were desperate but everything was out of your control, then you would be like me. If you would give anything in the world to have that one thing, then you would be like me. I wanted you to feel that. Not just understand it or know it, I wanted you to actually feel that anguish. Taking Poppy from you, taking away your power, leaving you at the mercy of another person's decision was the only way I could think of to make that happen.'

She was crying now, her words tumbling out amongst the tears and gulps of air, the catches of breath in her throat and the pain in her heart.

'I asked Lee to help me.'

'And he did without question or thought for what it would do to me and Poppy?'

'He owed me from way back. I never grassed on him about the cocaine. Besides, everyone has their price,' said Neve. 'Even you.'

'Even me?'

'Yes. You wanted Poppy back so much, you would have agreed to anything. And you did.'

'If only you'd told me everything, told me exactly how you felt. It didn't have to come to this.' Kit resumed his pacing.

'I tried,' said Neve, as another sob escaped her lungs. 'But we'd stopped talking and stopped listening to each other.'

'And Jake?'

'He was my plan b.'

Kit stopped pacing and faced Neve. 'But you don't have a plan b anymore.'

'I don't need it. I never even really wanted a plan b. I just wanted you. You've always been my one and only plan. The only one who I've truly loved.'

It was a few moments before Kit spoke. 'Neve, I've always loved you too. You fixed my world when it had been shattered into tiny fragments. You picked up the pieces and put them back together. I can never thank you enough for that. Never love you enough.'

She could see the truth in his words, hear the emotion in his voice. How the hell had they got to this when they loved each other so much?

'We can work through this,' she said, her words eager to be heard. 'I understand myself now. I realise I've never really come to terms with what happened to Megan. I know I need help and I promise you, I'll get help. I'll have counselling. I'll make myself totally better. You don't ever have to worry about me again.'

'I want to believe you, but you've put me through every parent's worst nightmare.' He came to stand in front of her. 'I should phone Pearson and tell him everything.'

She felt a rush of alarm. 'You wouldn't do that?'

'Why wouldn't I?'

Neve couldn't tell if he truly meant what he was saying. She needed to be convinced. She had one last card up her sleeve. 'Because you'd be implicating yourself.'

He gave her a quizzical look. 'Really? How's that?'

'I know what you did to Jake. I know it was you who attacked him. You don't want me to tell the police that any more than I want you to tell them what I did.'

'You really think I attacked Jake? And I suppose you have proof?'

'Yes. I do actually. I have your shirt. I found it in your office under the utility sink. It's got blood spatters all over it. Forensics will link it to Jake.' She could hear her voice calm and collected, the tears now subsided and making way for survival.

Kit's mouth turned to a small smile, he cupped his hands around Neve's face and leaned in, kissing her on the mouth, pausing a moment, before breaking contact. 'Neve, my darling, do you really think it will be my DNA on that shirt?'

'You were there. I know you were.'

'I was. But so were you and I think you'll find it will be your DNA, not mine. You attacked Jake. It was you who killed him.'

Chapter 40

Neve recoiled from Kit, but he held her face firm in his hands. She grabbed them with her own, pulling them from her face, trying to twist away from him. 'No. No. I didn't,' she could hear herself saying over and over again.

Kit held her hands. 'Neve. Neve – listen to me,' he said with an authority that penetrated her panic-stricken thoughts. 'You need to listen very carefully. I know it's hard to take in but please, just calm down so I can explain.'

He guided her over to the bar stool and made her perch on the edge.

'I don't understand,' said Neve, replaying her version of events over in her mind. She couldn't find the moment Kit was talking about. How could she not remember something like that? She attacked Jake? No, it didn't make sense.

'Right, listen very carefully,' said Kit, tipping her chin towards him. 'I was jealous of Jake, as you know, I thought there was something going on between you two. I got a little paranoid and, I know it's not a nice thing to do, but I accessed your phone and put the app "find my phone" on. That way, I could always monitor where you were.'

'You did what? You spied on me?'

'I had to know, I just had to.'

'A bit like you had to know about Megan and you had to know about Jasmine,' said Neve, mortified at the lengths he was prepared to go to.

'Look, it's not really important in the scheme of things. That night, I thought you were at Lucie's and when I happened to look at the phone, I could see you were down by the harbour. I drove down there. You and Jake were standing by his car. You were arguing. I don't know what about because as soon as I pulled up, you both stopped.'

Neve shook her head. 'No. It wasn't like that. I went up the hill. I saw a car. It must have been yours. I wasn't by Jake's car. I wasn't there when you pulled up.'

'Shhh, hush now. Let me finish,' said Kit. 'I was furious, I'll admit that. All I wanted was to smash his face in, I really did. But I didn't. I made you go and sit in my car. You weren't happy, but you did what I said. I confronted Jake. Told him to leave you alone and all that stuff. Yes, I shoved him, but it was just a bit of pushing, you know, handbags at dawn. Do you remember any of this?'

Neve shuffled the thoughts around in her head but still couldn't line them up. 'No. I don't remember a thing.' She felt sick. How could she not remember what happened?

Kit rubbed the tops of her arms with his hands. 'Next thing, you're out of the car, putting on my overshirt. I saw you from the corner of my eye, coming from the boot of the car ...' he hesitated.

'Go on,' said Neve, her heart thumping fast.

'I didn't see it until it was too late ... you had the mallet in your hand. You must have got it from the tool kit.'

'I had the mallet? No, it can't true. You must be wrong, Kit. Why would I do that?' Neve allowed the panic to take hold, she wanted to run away from Kit. She wanted to block her ears to what he was saying.

'Before I knew it you had whacked Jake on the side of the head.' He spoke in a soft voice, but the usual calming quality had no effect.

'I didn't!' shouted Neve. She pulled away from Kit but had nowhere to go, so pounded him with her fists. 'It's not true. You've got it wrong.' The rest of her words were lost in his jumper as he pulled her towards him and held her tight.

'I'm sorry, Neve. I didn't want to have to tell you,' said Kit. 'I know you don't want to believe it, but it all fits in now, can't you see? You must have been having one of those disassociation episodes the doctor mentioned. There's something that trips in your head when you're under duress, it causes some sort of short circuit, you get a blank in your memory.'

'No, oh please no,' said Neve through her tears.

'I'm sorry. I wish I was wrong but that's what must have happened when you hit Jake. You must have been blanking out.'

Neve could barely bring herself to ask, but she had to know. 'What happened after that?'

'He went down straight away and almost simultaneously, I pulled you away. You had blood spatters all over my shirt. I bundled you into the car, took the overshirt off and told you to go to Lucie's. I told you not to say anything to Lucie about what had happened and that I would deal with it.'

'I honestly don't remember.' Neve sniffed and wiped her eyes.

'I made an anonymous call from the phone box,' explained

Kit. 'I didn't want either of us incriminated in any way. It was bad enough as it was with Pearson asking questions about you and Jake. If we were there, then he would be bound to suspect us.'

'You did all that to stop me from being arrested?'

'Yes. I love you, Neve. I nearly lost you once, I wasn't going to lose you again. Not after everything that we had gone through.'

Neve clung to his first words. 'You love me?' He nodded. 'You still love me after what I did?' He nodded again. 'After what I did to you and Poppy and what I did to Jake?'

'It's the things you've done that I don't love, but you as a person I love very deeply. I don't want to be without you. I'm prepared to forgive you. People do bad things, but it doesn't mean they are fundamentally a bad person.'

'I'm so messed up,' said Neve. 'I've no idea why you still love me.'

'Were. Were messed up. I don't think you are now. You've won half the battle by acknowledging your actions. You just need professional help to win the rest of the war.'

'Oh, Kit. I don't know what to think. I still can't believe I'd do that to another human being.' And she couldn't but she also knew Kit's theory wasn't as far off the mark as it might seem. She had seen herself as Megan before, but she had always been aware of it. Always known what she was doing so why was it different this time? Was it because what she'd done was so awful, her mind wasn't allowing herself to even acknowledge it through Megan? Or was there another, more frightening truth? Was Kit lying to her to cover his own actions?

Despite her fears, she allowed Kit to hold her once more and somehow, it felt safe. It felt right. Whatever life had thrown at them, and indeed whatever, Neve herself had thrown at them, it seemed they were destined to stay together. If Kit really meant he could forgive her, she could still have a chance at happiness. If it meant seeing a counsellor, then so be it. At the end of the day she was going to have a family of her own, just what she had always wanted.

Even so, as much as she tried to focus on the good that was to come out of it all, the little nagging doubt of what really happened at the harbour was still there, prodding her thoughts, not staying in the box but slithering out and winding itself around her, hissing poisonous words in her ear.

'We need to get a few things straight for when the police talk to us again,' said Kit, pulling away from Neve. 'Pearson thinks he knows what's happened, he's just trying to prove it. We mustn't give him anything that will help him.'

'How are we going to do that?'

'You've got to stick to the story you told him already. Forget everything I just told you. Do you think you can do that?'

'Well, yes. I don't remember what happened, which is probably a good thing. I can only tell him what I remember and that is hiding behind a tree and then going back to Lucie's flat.'

'That's good. Keep to the story,' said Kit. 'Now, what I suggest we do, is you stay here and I'll go over to get Poppy from Mum's. We've got to carry on as normal. And the sooner we get back into some sort of routine the better.'

As soon as Kit left to fetch Poppy, Neve rushed up to the shower. She felt dirty from the inside out. She still couldn't take in what Kit had told her. It couldn't be true. She couldn't have killed Jake, she just couldn't. And if it wasn't her, then it could be only one other person. Could she live with this knowledge? With this man? More to the point, could she let a man like this father a child? Neve slumped to the bottom of the shower, hugging her knees tightly, her tears being flushed from her face by the pounding shower.

The next morning, the Masters' household was awoken by banging on the door and the insistent ringing of the bell.

'Who on earth is that?' mumbled Neve, rolling over and swinging her feet onto the floor. As she did so, her conversation with Kit last night, came flooding back, accompanied by a deep sense of sadness and disbelief.

'I'll give you two guesses,' said Kit, looking out through the vertical blinds. 'I'll go. You take your time.'

'Is it Pearson?'

'Two guesses were obviously generous.'

'What does he want?' Fear engulfed her. Was Pearson going to arrest her for murdering Jake? Had he worked it out somehow?

Kit pulled on a T-shirt and a pair of jeans. 'I'll go see what he wants. You come down when you're ready.'

'Someone is at the door,' said Poppy, appearing in the bedroom doorway.

'Don't worry, it's just the policeman,' said Kit. 'You stay up here out of the way.'

'But I'm hungry. I want breakfast.'

'If you wait until the policeman's gone, I'll make you some breakfast,' said Kit, squeezing past his daughter.

'I'll bring you up some toast and jam,' said Neve, going through to the en suite to use the toilet and brush her teeth. She left the door slightly ajar, so she could hear Poppy's response.

'But I don't have breakfast in my room. I have it at the breakfast bar.'

'Just this once, as a special treat, you can have it in bed, watching TV,' Neve called back, aware she lacked her usual amount of patience today. She flushed the toilet and washed her hands. 'It's best if you let me and Dad speak to the policeman alone.'

'Why?'

'Because sometimes adults need to talk to each other about adult things that aren't appropriate for children to hear.'

'I'm not a child.'

'Technically you are. You're under eighteen.' Neve squirted toothpaste onto her brush. 'Please, Poppy, just wait in your room.'

'I'm a young adult. That's what my teacher says.'

'Not a full-grown adult so my argument still stands.' Neve didn't hear Poppy's answer, but when she walked past her room on the way downstairs, she could see Poppy sitting on her bed, watching the TV.

'Ah, Neve, good morning,' said Pearson, as Neve entered the living room.

'Morning,' said Neve. 'This is an early and unexpected visit.'

'Yes, I was just explaining to Kit that there has been a development overnight.'

Neve exchanged a look with her husband. 'We were

carrying out a more thorough inspection of Jake Rees's studio and we discovered this in the drawer of his desk.' He held out a plastic bag containing a photograph.

Neve gave a small gasp. 'It's Poppy,' she said, stating the obvious. She looked up at the DCI. 'I don't understand.'

Her mind was flying in all directions. What was a photograph of Poppy doing in Jake's desk? Had she left it there? Somehow taken it with her by accident, caught up in her artwork, her brushes? Had it dropped out at the studio?

'You didn't give it to Jake at any point, did you?' asked Pearson.

'No. I was just trying to think how it could possibly have got there.' She looked at Kit. 'I didn't take it there.'

'No, I'm sure you didn't,' said Kit.

'Let me see it again,' said Neve. She inspected the photograph closer and then rushed over to the bookshelf. Kneeling down, she took out a photo album and after flicking through several pages, stood up, holding the album open. 'It's from here,' she said, showing the blank space on the page where the photograph had been. 'He must have taken it from here.'

'Had Jake ever been to the house?' asked Pearson.

Neve closed the book, thinking hard. 'He came one day a few weeks ago to drop some paints off that I'd ordered.'

'Was he left alone at any time?'

'No. We were in the kitchen.'

'Before that – had he been before that?'

'He was here about two months ago,' said Kit, stepping forwards and taking the album from Neve. 'He called round when Neve wasn't here. I invited him in. He made some lame excuse about wanting to speak to Neve about an exhibition. The bastard must have taken it then when I went to make him a drink.'

Neve was pretty sure Kit had never mentioned Jake's visit before. And she was also certain Jake hadn't either. She went to say as much, but the look she caught from Kit stopped her.

'We also found this,' said Pearson. This time he held out another evidence bag with a scrap of paper inside. 'It's an address. We're checking it out now as I speak but we think it may be the address that Poppy was held at until she was moved to Halnaker windmill.'

Neve read the address. Her stomach flip-flopped. It was the house where Lee had taken Poppy.

'Does that address mean anything to either of you?'

'No, not at all,' said Kit, reading it over Neve's shoulder. 'Neve?'

'What? Oh ... no, I don't know where that is either.'

'And the writing. Do you recognise the writing?' Pearson looked intently at each of them.

'Nope. Sorry,' said Kit.

'It's got a distinctive number seven, with the line across the upright. Like they do in Europe,' pointed out Pearson. 'And the number one, that's not how we write the number here. It's got a longer lead stroke.'

Neve could feel sweat prick her top lip, her whole body was heating up, like it was about to self-combust. She recognised that writing. It was Lee's – he'd written like that for as long as she could remember. It was a typical Lee gesture, something to do differently to everyone else. She couldn't understand what it was doing in Jake's desk along with a photograph of Poppy.

'Are you OK, Neve?' asked Pearson.

'Yes, I'll be fine,' said Neve. 'Just finding this all so strange.'

'We have a theory about the author of the note,' said Pearson.

'Which is …?' asked Kit.

'That they supplied Jake with somewhere to keep Poppy.'

'You believe Jake was behind it?' said Kit.

'It's a line of enquiry …'

'Don't give me that bullshit, this is my daughter you're talking about,' said Kit. 'Was Jake responsible for her kidnap? Tell me straight.'

'As I said, it's something we're working on, but we think, given the evidence, it's highly likely.' Pearson put the plastic bag back inside his pocket. 'We just can't settle on a motive.'

'I told you,' said Kit. 'He wanted to win brownie points with Neve. He thought if he could be the conquering hero who found Poppy, then Neve would drop everything to be with him. Either that or … well, I don't like to think of the alternative reason.'

'Quite,' agreed the inspector.

'I hope this means that my wife is no longer under suspicion,' said Kit.

The DCI pursed his lips. 'We haven't ruled anything out just yet.' He looked at Neve and gave a small nod of the head. 'I'm sure you can appreciate that.'

'It's bloody ridiculous,' said Kit.

'If it turns out the address was connected with Poppy's disappearance, we would like to speak to her again. With a trained member of staff, of course.'

'I'd sooner you didn't,' said Kit. 'She's been through enough and, touch wood, she seems to have come out of it relatively unscathed. I don't want any questioning to kick it all off.'

'No, I understand, but it will be trained staff, like before. It would really help us build a case.'

'What's the point though, if Jake is dead?' said Kit.

'We still have to be just as thorough, especially as he's no longer here to defend himself.'

'And what's happening on that front? Catching the person who did that?' said Kit.

Neve wished Kit wouldn't ask so many questions. She was sure he was getting under the inspector's skin.

Before Pearson could answer, they were interrupted by his mobile ringing. He apologised and took the call. Neve sat down on the sofa. She was still trying to work out what really had happened. None of it was making any sense.

'Sorry about that,' said Pearson as he ended his call. 'That was my colleague down at the address we found. Turns out it's an empty house on the edge of town. Been used as a squat in the past but not recently. The owner is in an old people's home. It looks like there's been someone camping out there. They found a hair bobble. Blue and white with a 'P' badge on it.'

'Poppy,' gasped Neve. 'Poppy has a hair band like that.' Although she was certain Poppy hadn't been wearing her hair tied up that evening on the boat.

'And was she wearing that the night she disappeared?'

'I don't think so,' said Kit. 'But that's not to say she didn't have it in her pocket or anything.' He ran his hand through his hair. 'Christ, she was just across town. So close and yet we had no idea.'

'Unfortunately, there's no CCTV in the area but we're making door-to-door enquiries just in case someone saw something.' said Pearson.

Neve felt her head tip to one side as the room tilted. She reached out and grabbed the arm of the sofa.

'Neve? You OK?' asked Kit, sitting next to her and putting an arm around her.

'Sorry, just don't feel too well.'

'Can we leave it there for this morning?' said Kit, looking up at the police inspector.

'Of course. That was all I needed to let you know,' he said. 'We'll keep you informed of any updates. In light of all this, I don't need you to come down to the station today.'

Kit saw the DCI out and then came back into the living room.

'I don't understand,' said Neve. 'The picture and the address. What was Jake doing with them?' She paused as she looked at her husband. He had an expression on his face that she couldn't quite place. It was one of … pride? Maybe that was too strong a definition, but she knew him well enough to know that he was pleased about something. 'Tell me?'

He came over to her and put his arms around her. 'You don't need to know. Just trust me on this. The police aren't going to be looking at you anymore in connection with Poppy's disappearance.'

Slowly, it began to dawn on Neve. 'You …' she began but Kit put his finger to her lips and shook his head.

'We have to trust each other now, Neve. It's us against them. If we want to keep all that we've worked so hard for, fought so much for and to have what we want in the future, then we have to stick together. Do you understand what I'm saying?'

The enormity of what Kit had done to keep her from being charged with kidnap and murder, wasn't lost on her. It only served to prove how committed Kit was to making a success of their marriage. 'I understand, totally,' she said. 'But there is one thing, what about Lee?'

'No need to worry about Lee,' said Kit. 'He won't be bothering us again.'

Kit silenced any further questions she had with a kiss. 'We can concentrate on each other, on our family and hopefully our future family.'

As Neve nestled into Kit's arms, she forced herself to think of a life ahead of them where they had their own child, and it made her heart sing. She was going to have the family she so desired. But there was a definite off-beat in that song. A dark undertone which she would have to learn to live with and ignore like she had all the other dark things in her life. She knew it was the price she had to pay for what she wanted. But the trade-off was worth it, or at least it would be. She could and would learn to live with the knowledge that one of them in the marriage was a murderer, she just didn't know which of them it was.

Chapter 41

THE WEST SUSSEX ECHO

Police have today confirmed they are no longer looking for anyone else in connection with the death of two local men who they believe were involved in the abduction of local schoolgirl, Poppy Masters.

In July 2018, the body of Ashley Farnham was discovered at the foot of Beachy Head, after going missing from Ambleton, West Sussex where he had been working at a home for young adults.

Poppy Masters went missing for four days from her father's boat, whilst it was moored up overnight in Lower Bury. She was unharmed during her captivity, and although blood tests proved inconclusive, it is thought she had been drugged during that time.

Police confirmed that the date rape drug, commonly known as GHB, was found in the rucksack of Farnham, together with a large sum of money. It was believed that Farnham and local artist Jake Rees were behind the kidnapping of Poppy Masters. Prior to the discovery of Farnham's body, Rees was viciously attacked at

Ambleton harbour and subsequently died from his injuries. A source close to the investigation claims that Farnham and Rees got into an argument about the ransom money and this lead to the attack on Rees by Farnham.

Neve closed the newspaper, folded it in half and looked out across the River Amble. Willow was sniffing about in the bushes a little way ahead on the footpath, the previous night's frost now disappeared. Neve pulled the collar of her coat up and wriggled her hands back into her gloves.

So, it was official. The case was closed. They weren't looking for anyone else in relation to Poppy's disappearance or Lee's death. It was there in black and white.

'You've seen the paper, then?'

The voice startled Neve. She hadn't been aware of anyone approaching. She recognised the deep tones immediately.

'Hello,' she said, forcing a smile at DCI Pearson. 'This is a surprise. I thought you'd retired?'

Pearson sat himself down on the bench next to her.

'Retired last month.'

'Are you enjoying it?' said Neve, as she scrambled her brain to guess why the former DCI was here.

'I'm glad to be out, to be honest,' said Pearson.

'Really? Why's that?'

'Policing has changed. These days it's all about money, resources, time, statistics and reassuring the public. Of course, what went on here is all wrapped up neatly now. The powers that be can congratulate themselves that a murder has been solved and a death accounted for.'

'Isn't it always about funding?'

'That and hard evidence,' said Pearson. 'Proof that will stand up in court.'

'Yes, I believe that's what makes a fair trial,' said Neve.

'Do you want to know my theory on Poppy's disappearance?'

'Not really.' Although Neve had a feeling Pearson was going to share it with her regardless.

'Just humour me, eh?' said Pearson.

Neve shrugged. On reflection it would be interesting to learn Pearson's take on it.

'I think Jake was a fall-guy, a patsy, a scapegoat. He was used to take the blame for Poppy's disappearance. He was in love with you and you used that to your advantage.'

'That's some allegation,' said Neve, forcing the most level tone she could. 'Totally untrue but, please, do go on. I'm intrigued.'

'You don't sound particularly outraged or surprised by that,' said Pearson.

'It's too ridiculous to be outraged about,' replied Neve. 'Anyway, as you were saying ...'

'You're a tough cookie, Neve. I'll give you that,' said Pearson. 'As I see it, somehow you arranged to meet Jake down here by the river. I don't know if you asked him to come, or he asked you, but that's by the by. You showed him the ransom note and was probably banking on Jake doing the noble thing and insisting he came with you. Prior to meeting Jake, you phoned the police with a tip-off of where Poppy was. I suspect somewhere along the line you had a pay-as-you-go phone. How am I doing so far?'

'It's like an episode of *Columbo*,' said Neve. 'Minus the mac, dodgy eye and cigar.'

Pearson gave a small grunt. 'Now, that note, I don't know if you really received a third note and you switched it for the ransom note, or what, but I'm certain it was a plant. I mean, who would kidnap for the sake of ten thousand pounds? Which, incidentally, happened to be the daily withdrawal limit of your ISA.'

'And I suppose I did all this, while keeping Poppy hidden away?' She held her nerve as she waited for the DCI to respond.

'You had an accomplice. Not Jake. I'm certain that wasn't his MO. No, it would be someone you could trust, someone you'd been in cahoots with before. Like an old friend, who very conveniently threw himself off Beachy Head. It's quite convenient for you that both men ended up dead, they can't prove or disprove my theory.'

'All this is pure speculation,' said Neve, standing up. 'What possible motive would I have had to kidnap my own daughter?'

Pearson rose to his feet. 'I don't know. You've got me there and one of the reasons why we didn't press charges.'

Neve called Willow over and clipped on her lead. 'Well, thanks for the afternoon story. If you don't mind, I need to get on.' She ran her hand over her rounded stomach. 'Midwife appointment.'

Pearson eyed her baby bump. 'When's it due?'

'Yesterday, as a matter of fact,' said Neve. 'I'm going in tomorrow for a C-section.'

'Boy or girl?'

'Boy,' said Neve, her heart filling with warmth. She couldn't wait to hold Louis in her arms.

'Good luck,' said Pearson. 'I hope it's been worth it.'

Neve watched him turn the corner of the river path and take the steps up to the road. The end definitely justified the means. Of course, it had been worth it.

Acknowledgements

I owe a huge debt of gratitude, not just to my amazing editor, Charlotte Ledger, but to the whole team at HarperCollins who have been involved in putting this book together. Particular thanks to Emily Ruston and Laura Gerrard, who have worked both patiently and tirelessly with me to help mould my story into shape.

Thank you to Rebecca Bradley for advising me on the police procedure regarding missing persons. Any mistakes are, of course, mine.

As always, much love and thanks to my family who are unflinching in their support – love you all.

Writing can be an isolating experience at times but thanks to social media, it has meant I can chat to my fellow writing pals on a daily basis. In particular, I would like to give a big shout out to Laura E. James, Catherine Miller, Mandy Baggot and Nicky Wells who are superb sounding boards, agony aunts, partners in crime and all-round good eggs!

Biggest thanks must go to my readers. I'm so lucky to be able to do a job I love and to be able to share that love. I'm constantly cheered on by you all, whether it's buying, reading, tweeting, reviewing, sharing or messaging me. It's a privilege I'm humbled by.